Til Death

a Fractured Souls novel

Til Death

a Fractured Souls novel

KATE EVANGELISTA

Entangled Publishing, LLC
2614 South Timberline Road
Suite 109
Fort Collins, CO 80525

Visit our website at www.entangledpublishing.com.

Edited by Liz Pelletier
Cover design by Liz Pelletier

Print ISBN   978-1-62266-232-6
Ebook ISBN   978-1-62266-233-3

Manufactured in the United States of America

First Edition March 2014

To my dad.
For being the president of my fan club way before I had one.

CHAPTER ONE

Dillan

HOME SWEET HELL

Banshees. Nasty, yellow-eyed creatures with poisonous claws. Dillan damned them and the mothers who birthed them to hell as the G6 taxied on the tarmac. He rolled down his sweater sleeves to hide the healing evidence of their claws. Similar scratches riddled his body. Thankfully, the majority of his face remained untouched. Still, bitches, all of them.

He eyed the two burly guards sitting opposite him. They grunted. The disgust on their ugly faces seemed to imply that looking at his injuries meant he whined. He gave them the finger. They couldn't touch him, despite the hostility in their glares. Their orders were to escort the banished to his prison. At least they didn't shackle him.

Who would have thought demotion in the Illumenari meant prisoner status? Not like he could blame them. As a Guardian, he had one duty. And he failed at it. Trained all his life only to choke at the last second. Pathetic. He'd disgraced himself and his illustrious lineage. The fact they allowed him to live with his guilt was punishment enough.

"Well, it's been a scintillating flight, gentlemen," he said, his first words since leaving Turkey. Slapping the armrests of his seat, he pushed up just as the flight attendant broke the door's seal.

Baldy one and baldy two shared a grunt and then sneered at him. Their silence spoke volumes. They might as well have called him trash. He would have. He waited, but they didn't bother getting up. Apparently, their job was done.

Package delivered.

Giving the guys one last middle-finger wave, he picked up his duffle and shuffled toward the door. The flight attendant smiled at him. He gave her a quick nod. Just doing her job, she didn't deserve attitude. Not like she judged him.

One huge downside of demotion?

He felt almost…human.

Shudders rolled down his body as he stepped onto the G6's steps, duffle bag over his shoulder. His gaze flicked to the insignia of three concentric circles at the tail that represented their fight for the side of light. The symbol meant something, and he'd shit all over it. His pride for what he did was at an all-time low. Nothing could make him feel less of a loser as the plane's engines screamed. The pilot powered down after the long flight. Heaviness settled on his shoulders, hunching them forward. A headache the size of a baseball formed behind his right eye. He hadn't slept in God knew how long.

At the top step, he huffed. Running his fingers though his hair to scratch an itch, he couldn't remember the last time he'd showered, and the inside of his mouth tasted like ass.

So much for traveling in style in the Illumenari private jet.

His guards wouldn't let him out of their sight, even to use the plane's facilities. The bastards. As if he'd escape at thirty thousand feet. Then again, he could have, and they knew that. But he wouldn't. No matter how much he bitched and moaned about his situation, he'd do his time.

He frowned up at the midnight sky. A different set of constellations blinked back, mocking him for his mistakes. He shook his head. Definitely not in Budapest anymore. And why in the hell did the air smell like Pine Fresh?

In the distance, a shadowed figure stood still. He squinted. A banshee? Heart kicking into his throat, his fingers closed around the charm attached to a leather cuff on his wrist. One rub and he'd have his weapon ready to defend himself.

"Welcome to Wyoming, Dillan," someone said in a calm yet detached voice, drawing his attention.

Rainer leaned against a sweet, cherry red '66 Mustang. Not ready to acknowledge his uncle just yet, he flicked his gaze back to the spot where he'd noticed the shadow. It was gone. He rubbed his eyes and blamed it on the jetlag. Taking a deep breath of the bracing air, he looked down at his uncle from the top of the plane steps. The second his feet touched the tarmac, he'd give up any advantage the high ground provided. He knew the stories. Regular children had the boogeyman. The Illumenari had Rainer Sloan.

Then his uncle's greeting registered fully. "Wyoming?" The word tasted foul. And because he just couldn't help himself, "What? No parade? Confetti?"

"Nope." Rainer shook his head, a half-grin on his lips.

"Is it too late for Siberia? I can leave the pilot here and fly myself there."

He didn't break eye contact as his uncle studied him. All Sloan men possessed the same brow, the same blue eyes, and the same straight as a razor jawline. It was eerie. Like staring in a mirror twenty years from now.

"Just like your father," Rainer "the Boogeyman" Sloan finally said, his assessment completed. "Come on. We have a long ride ahead of us."

The words "This is your life" flashed in Dillan's head as he jogged down the steps. "You mean this isn't *it* yet?"

Rainer pushed off the side of his car, moved around to the trunk, and popped it. "Consider yourself lucky."

"Lucky? Bullshit." He dumped the sum of his things into the trunk that could fit a body and a half. Then slammed the lid and made his way to the passenger side.

"Hey! Easy." His jailer sauntered to the driver's side, hand gliding over the gleaming metal. "Dent anything, and I use your face to fix it. Where's Sebastian?"

"He's not here yet?" His brow furrowed. The hellhound left Turkey before he did. The fact that he couldn't sense his partner anymore pissed him off. The restrictions on his powers blew. He'd have to relearn how to live without most of his abilities. Back to square one, i.e. the kiddie table.

"Being an Arbiter again sucks, doesn't it?" Rainer teased as if reading Dillan's mind.

Arbiter. He snorted. The title connoted a place of power. Someone in authority. He might as well be called a grunt. In the Illumenari hierarchy, Arbiters were the peacekeepers. They were sent to mediate disputes between Supernaturals. Only when an agreement couldn't be reached between parties could force be used, hence the lack of any real power. Never in a million years did he ever see himself back at this level of his career.

Patience reaching its limit, he barked, "Can we just go?"

"I think you're forgetting who I am and why you're here. Do I need to teach you a lesson in respect?"

As soon as the threat reached Dillan's ears, invisible, serrated teeth latched onto every part of him. He dropped to his knees, hands splayed on the blacktop. Without moving from his spot at the driver's side, Rainer brought him down by his aura alone. As if banishment wasn't humiliating enough. He gritted his teeth, refusing to cry out. He focused on his breathing, distributing what little energy he had in his body to dull the attack. The veins on his neck stood out from the effort. Blood rushed to his face.

Just when Dillan thought he was about to pass out, Rainer said, "And to think I had a case for you."

Raising his chin, he met his uncle's cold glare and croaked out, "What case?"

Like the tide, the supercharged air surrounding him receded. The Boogeyman threw his head back and laughed.

• • •

Two hours later, Rainer hadn't shared a single detail of the case. It was like he dangled the carrot only to yank it away. No matter how much Dillan grilled him, his uncle remained tight-lipped. At least he no longer felt the killing urge coming from the driver side of the car. Dick move on his part, pissing Rainer off. He suspected the guy only remained obstinate to torture him.

When they pulled into a quiet street lined with townhouses in the middle of Nowhere, Wyoming, the subject of high school came up. From the street to the garage, words like records and enrollment were stringed together. Shopping for school supplies may also have been mentioned. He couldn't be sure, having tuned out the moment the engine died.

"School's a load of crap," he said, fishing out his duffle bag from the trunk. The wards used to protect the property from any attacks by Supernaturals prickled along his skin. Another reminder of his demotion. Arbiters couldn't put up wards. He only had the basics now: defense, surface wound healing, and some attack options. He hated himself a little more with every second that passed.

"I don't want to raise suspicion," Rainer replied, not breaking his even stride as he led the way into the house via the kitchen. "If you don't go, people will talk."

"I don't need school," he insisted, trailing his warden through the living room and up the stairs. "Come on, tell me about the case. And just so you know, I've had a rough couple of days. Don't leave me hanging."

Rainer stopped at the top of the stairs. On instinct, Dillan reached for his charm. Every muscle in his body tensed. It might be suicide, but he would defend himself against the Boogeyman.

"Look," his uncle sighed, "in these parts, you're a minor." Dillan rolled his eyes. He hadn't been a minor since his grandfather had given him the cuff he wore on his thirteenth birthday. Ignoring him, Rainer continued, "I can't have you skulking around or staying in the townhouse all day. We have to establish your cover. And I'm a teacher here, for Pete's sake. I have a reputation to maintain. First day of your junior year starts tomorrow."

"How convenient. The Council couldn't have timed it better."

"You're going to school, end of discussion."

Before he could open his mouth to rebut, Rainer disappeared into one of the rooms on the second floor. Stunned, he stared at the place where his uncle once stood. No one had ever spoken to him like a child since…well, since he actually was a child. Seething, he bounded up the rest of the way and entered what he assumed was his bedroom, ready to argue further about not going to school. When he spotted the double bed pushed up against a wall, he barely held in a groan. The blue sheets begged him to bury himself beneath them.

A leather steamer trunk rested at one end of the bed, while a stack of notebooks, a penholder full of sharpened pencils, and a lamp sat together on a desk facing a window. In a clever use of the space, the closet blended in with the ocher paint. Books dominated the rest of the wall. He immediately calculated the many ways he could defend himself in this space in case of an attack.

"You like it?" Rainer gestured at the space.

"It's still a cell." He dropped his duffel and skimmed the titles on the shelves.

"Compared to some of the prisons I've been in? This is freakin' Caesar's Palace."

It took him a second to get the Vegas reference. He hadn't been back to the States since he'd left with his parents. He approached the desk and tapped the empty spot where a computer should be. "You forgot the laptop."

Eyebrow cocked, Rainer flipped a switch underneath the lip of the desk, and the tabletop parted. A panel with a laptop rose from a secret compartment. "The specs are standard issue, but I've added a few upgrades. It's connected to the Illumenari server."

Eying the ultra-thin, chrome laptop, his first impulse was to call his parents. Update them. His chest tightened. The disappointment on his father's face was still fresh in his mind. They wouldn't be speaking to him any time soon. Not until he'd redeemed himself.

Caught up in his own pity party, he didn't notice his uncle reaching for him until a hand landed on his shoulder. On reflex, he executed a grab-and-twist maneuver. An inhale later, he found himself face down on his new desk, his arm bent at a bad angle behind him. If he moved, it would dislocate.

"I'm seeing a pattern of disrespect from you," came the whisper into his ear.

Chills rippled over Dillan's skin. If death had a voice…

"Maybe I really need to teach you some manners." The Boogeyman added more pressure on his arm, and a *pop* followed. Dillan's vision tunneled. He bit the inside of his cheek to keep from screaming like a girl. His fingers went limp. Counting to ten, he forced himself to relax. Only then did Rainer release him and back away.

"You'll find everything you need in this room. The bathroom's down the hall. And Dillan…" He stopped at the door, his expression calm as if nothing happened. "Go to bed. You start school tomorrow."

Grunting, he pushed off the desk with his good hand. His arm hung loose at his side. The throbbing pain spread all the way to his chest, constricting every breath he took in. Biting his lower lip, he grabbed his elbow, braced himself against the desk, and popped his arm back in. The room spun. He closed his eyes and stumbled his way to the bed. His life officially sucked. Then he passed out.

CHAPTER TWO

Selena

MEETING MR. ROCK-STAR-NATIONAL-GEOGRAPHIC

*V*isions. For as long as I could remember, I'd had them. Snippets of my immediate future to be exact. Like what I got on a test or that my hot history teacher was going to walk into today's algebra class unannounced. I kept telling my best friends there was no use asking me for lottery numbers. Not *that* kind of ability. They were the only ones other than my grandparents who knew, and I wanted to keep it that way.

Think of it like a lame superpower. I wished I had visions of the winning lottery combination! Then I wouldn't have to find a part-time job to start a college fund, Grams wouldn't have to work at the diner anymore, and Gramps wouldn't have to fix tractors and trucks for a living. Sometimes my visions were helpful, sometimes not. And right now I wished that a vision would have told me to avoid my locker on this lovely first day of junior year.

The cellphone I set inside the small space buzzed as I stuffed all the essentials I might need for the coming year. Spare clothes. A toiletry kit. A small mirror to check my lipgloss. When the metallic rumbling stopped, I peeked at the message.

Penny: *Run!*

The familiar scent of chlorine masked by musky, cool cologne filled my next breath. The skin on the back of my neck prickled. I looked down to see long legs in jeans and boots. My locker door hid the rest of him. I quickly typed in my reply.

Me: *2 L8*

He just stood there. Why was he just standing there?

I closed my eyes and silently counted to ten. I didn't need this kind of aggravation. How could I have deluded myself into thinking I could avoid him in a school this tiny, in a town so small?

A couple of girls passed by, giggling.

I shot them a sidelong glance. Connie Everton, my lab partner from last year, twirled her hair and said something to a blond I almost didn't recognize. Samantha Torrington. Blond? Really? It was amazing what dumping a bottle of hydrogen peroxide over your head did. I opened my mouth to call out to them, but they were already too far without me having to shout. The last thing I needed was to draw attention to myself and the guy who stood beyond the protection of my locker door.

Again I picked up my phone.

Me: *Save me.*

Penny: *Cant. 2 far.*

Me: *H8 U!!!*

Penny: *Coming!*

Not fast enough. She could have teleported to me and it would be too late. I slipped my phone into my back pocket, resigned to my fate.

"Hey, Selena," said a deep, familiar voice.

A month since the breakup, and still a shiver ran down my spine like cold fingers. I hated it. I slammed my locker shut. Bang! As much as I wanted him to disappear, I had to deal with him eventually. Might as well be now.

Bowen rested a shoulder on the locker beside mine. His tall, broad-shouldered frame screamed all-American. For the life of me, I couldn't remember why I fell for all that. Include bronzed skin and sun-kissed brown hair, and you had a combination lethal to the female population of all ages, if I based my info on my grandmother's opinion. His eyes—the color of black coffee—raked over my body with a familiar possessiveness I never liked. They started from my face, down to my respectably sized chest, all the way to my skinny jeans.

My foot tapped an uneasy beat. "What are you doing here, Bowen? Don't you have practice this morning?"

His biceps bulged from crossing his arms. "We did." He pointed at his wet hair. "We just finished."

"Right."

"Hey, Bowen!" Penny skidded to my side, her long, black braid bouncing over her shoulder. Today she chose a ruffled, pink shirt and jeans combo with cowboy boots, embracing her inner farm girl. I breathed an immediate sigh of relief. "What's a jerkwad like you doing harassing my best friend this early in the morning?"

I smirked. Score one for Penny. The frown on Bowen's face filled my chest with satisfaction. Lots of it.

He shifted his gaze from Penny to me. "We need to talk."

Before she could answer for me, I said, "No. We don't."

"Selena—"

The bell interrupted him.

"Let's not." I held up my hand to stall anything else he had to say.

"See ya!" Penny tugged at my arm, and I went with her willingly.

. . .

My encounter with Bowen put me in a mood. The rapid *tap, tap, tap* of my pencil hitting my desktop helped distract me from the invisible two-ton hands that settled on my shoulders. Rogue, copper curls tumbled down my forehead. I blew them away, but they kept bouncing back down. Officially annoyed, I ran my fingers through them. Still no go. Giving up, I slumped forward, pencil squeezed between my thumb and forefinger.

At least I had Mr. Sloan's entrance to look forward to. But even the thought of seeing him again didn't lighten the zombie apocalypse feel math always inspired.

"Is it me or does our textbook get thicker every year?" I sat up and pushed the book away with my pencil. The less contact the better as far as I was concerned.

"It's you." Kyle, equation sympathizer, leafed through the glossy pages. A lock of dirty blond hair hid the devious sparkle in his eyes, highlighted by his too innocent smile. With his striking looks, he charmed members of the estrogen club, too, but to me—the best kept freak in Newcastle—he'd always be a mix of protective and annoying. Like a Labradoodle—half fun, half uptight.

"I can't help being allergic to math." I pouted.

"Not a real thing."

I heard the eye roll in his comment. "Oh, yeah? I break out in hives every time I start solving a problem. Explain that, Mr. I Like Math." I crossed my arms and eyed the cover photo of a kid smiling down at a worksheet.

"You sure this is about math?" his drawl cut through my bitterness.

"Okay, no." His question hit the nail on the head, and I was the nail. "Seeing Bowen before first period—"

Mr. Sloan walked in, cutting off all negative thoughts inspired by the ex. Math just got way better. All the girls gaped in silent adoration, while the boys sat straighter in their seats in an attempt to look cool in front of the man who personified cool.

Rainer Sloan. Even his name was cool.

Last year, someone had organized a vote for hottest teacher at Newcastle High for the yearbook. Mr. Sloan got 346 votes even though the school only had about 300 students. His dark brown hair framed his perfect face: high cheekbones, a straight nose, full lips, and an adorable dimple on his chin. And those blue eyes legit smiled. Always.

He made our math teacher, Mr. Hilton, look featureless as they stood side by side, speaking in hushed tones. If I took out my phone and snapped a picture of them together, Mr. Hilton would be the lowly mortal beside a Greek god.

Everyone leaned forward in a too obvious attempt to listen in. I couldn't blame them. After handing Mr. Hilton a white piece of paper, Mr. Sloan gestured for someone to come in. A second period latecomer.

"This is where my vision stopped," I said to Kyle through the side of my mouth, my eyes narrowing at the door.

"You mean…" his chair squeaked.

"Yeah."

The teachers ignored the collective gasp when a tall boy walked in, the strap of a messenger bag slung across his chest. He stood at the head of the class with a slight, downward curve to his lips and the ghost of a knot on his brow. The too-cool-for-school type, huh? The way he wore his clothes from the navy blue sweater to the dark jeans and well-worn boots screamed rock star. His hair, the color of rich chocolate…was that a faux-hawk? My eyebrow twitched. So five years ago. But on him, it seemed to work. And those eyes…like the clear, blue skies stretching up to forever all over Wyoming. If I imagined Mr. Sloan years younger, he would be the guy that just walked in, complete with slight chin dimple.

Great, just what we needed.

At Newcastle High, a new student was as rare as a fire rainbow streaking across the sky. It happened, but not often enough. The jury was still out on whether I liked this rare occurrence. But it seemed like I was in the minority.

As if a switch had been flipped, all the girls in the room turned their full attention from Mr. Sloan to the new guy. Lust at first sight. My ears rang from the chorus of sighs. Some girls fluttered, batting fake lashes and smiling outrageously. The newcomer acted like they weren't even there. Even Sheila Easton's infamous hair flip didn't change his sour expression. He just stood there and waited for Mr. Sloan to finish talking with Mr. Hilton like the last place he wanted to be was in a classroom.

"You didn't see *that* walk in?" Kyle raised an eyebrow at me.

"It doesn't work that way, remember? I only see what I see." I spoke through my teeth. He would so get me in trouble if he spoke any louder.

"Class, settle down," Mr. Hilton drawled.

On cue, a hush dropped over the room.

"I'd like to introduce Dillan Sloan." Mr. Hilton gestured lazily at our new classmate. "And yes, he's Mr. Sloan's nephew, so no need to gossip about their relation. Will you tell us a little something about yourself?"

New guy ignored him and took the empty seat next to mine. Of course he was his nephew. Mr. Sloan looked way too young to have a son Dillan's age. I wouldn't accept it.

"Hi," he said like he didn't mean it.

I did a double take. "You mean me?"

"Why not?"

I snorted. "Selena Fallon."

Just to be polite, I extended my hand. He reached out to take it. The second we touched, a spark zinged up my arm.

"Ye-aw!" I jumped out of my seat. All eyes in the room immediately focused on me.

"Miss Fallon?" Mr. Hilton harrumphed from the blackboard.

Dillan's expression swiftly went from indifferent to slightly pained, ending with confused anger. I stared. He stared. Hard. First at his hand, and then at me. Like he couldn't believe what just happened. Hell, even I didn't know. I looked at my hand, too. My palm sort of tingled. What the hell?

Chapter Three

Dillan

Anywhere But Here

*L*unch break couldn't come fast enough. With every subject he sat in, Dillan kept darting his eyes to the clock, mentally counting down the seconds. When finally the bell rang for lunch, he rushed out of the room and stood out in the hallway, trying to make sense of the map attached to his schedule. Why he needed one for a school so small annoyed him. Did they think he couldn't find his way around? From the haphazard representation of the school floor plan, it seemed like a six-year-old drew it. He'd seen ancient scrolls with clearer images.

In the chaos of the hallway, he stewed over the start of his day. Not since basic training had he been treated so horribly. Guardian status made him complacent, almost cocky. A demotion later, he had to force himself to adjust. Still, a bucket of water in the face wasn't usually how he liked to wake up. His fault, really. When his uncle said, "better get up or I'm pouring cold water on you," he should've listened. The stories were true. Rainer wasn't someone who spoke idle threats.

What he wasn't prepared for, and what all the training in the world never taught him, was how to deal with high school. Being homeschooled all his life, he only interacted with children from other Illumenari families. All of them disciplined. Each one hungry to begin their climb up the hierarchy. They trained together, competed in the yearly games. Even the blood-thirstiest Illumenari spawn he understood better than a normal teenager. At least in the Illumenari there was order. The chaos that was Newcastle High put a knot in his brow.

The stream of students filling the hallway moved in every which direction. No one cared who they bumped into. Some walked around obsessed by whatever was on their phones. A jock threw a football. A gaggle of girls stood in the middle of the way, blocking the flow. Cloying perfume mixed with unwashed bodies. Locker doors opened and slammed, wreaking havoc on his sensitive hearing—what little he had left of it. Day one and he already felt weaker than a pixie.

Just when things began to make sense, a girl in one of his classes zapped him. One handshake and she almost lit him up like a Christmas tree. She felt the electricity, too, judging from her reaction. He grunted. If he'd had his Guardian powers, he would have been able to sniff out what she was. Since he no longer had that luxury, he relied on instinct. She seemed human enough, but his gut told him to stay the hell away from her. Touching her seemed to have flipped a switch, because thinking about her made him seek her out. Even now, in this crowd, he scanned every face in the hopes of spotting her. How hard was it to find copper curls? She should stick out. It pissed him off.

Lesson of the morning?

School. Sucked. Ass.

He would rather have his balls in a vise than spend another

minute here. Yet, staring down at his schedule, he wondered how many more classes he shared with…what the hell? Again with the thoughts of *her* and that unmistakable pull.

"Focus, man," he mumbled to himself, his hand itching to crumple the confusing map and schedule. The idea of catching a bus out of this hick town tempted him. How many hours would it take before Rainer caught up with him if he bolted?

Nah.

No matter how much he wanted to run, the Council had frozen all his accounts. And working odd jobs sucked worse than school— even with the freak show encounter in class. He'd do his time. Didn't mean he couldn't fantasize about escape.

Looking left and then right, he noticed the students gave him a wide berth. Maybe they felt his slowly darkening aura and stayed away. This didn't seem so bad. He could tough it out. He didn't used to be the fastest rising star in the Illumenari for nothing.

How hard could school be?

Maybe less so if he found his locker before lunch ended. Taking his time in the shower forced him to skip breakfast. Stomach grumbling, he spotted a girl in a white dress no one else seemed to see at the end of the hall. She stood barefoot, and her long, brown hair framed a haughty heart-shaped face. His blood froze. The hand holding his schedule shook as her white, almond-shaped eyes stared at him. Her full yet blue lips pursed then spread into a smile. Hunger forgotten, he forced himself to blink. Apparitions usually disappeared when the eyes opened. And as expected, once his eyelids lifted, she was gone.

He counted his breaths, focusing on the in an out motion of his chest filling with stale, sweaty air. No relief came. Not when his mistakes haunted him.

"Need help?"

He jerked and turned toward a girl in a black and orange

cheerleading uniform. How long had she been there? He cursed himself for not paying more attention to his surroundings while she devoured him with her eyes.

Scowling at her blatant objectification, he said through gritted teeth, "I'm looking for locker 2-2-5."

A corner of her shiny lips pulled up. She gave him one more assessing glance then pointed down the hall. He twisted toward the direction her black fingernail indicated and walked away.

"You're Mr. Sloan's nephew, right?" She sashayed to his side, her voice as bubbly as her step.

"That's right," he said. His molars threatened to crack at his stupidity. He should have known the lockers were arranged in ascending order. Finally reaching his, he punched in the code written at the top of his semi-crumpled schedule.

The cheerleader flitted from behind the open door to his other side. "You just transferred in, right? Where you from?"

He stuffed books he didn't need inside the tiny space. "Budapest." Could she just go away?

"Where's that? Idaho?"

Slamming the locker shut, he stared wide-eyed at her. She had got to be kidding, right? Please let her be kidding. From the seriousness of her expression, she really expected an answer from him. But before he could respond with a zinger, a chill of dread ran down his spine. So much for avoiding the Boogeyman. Bad enough they'd be spending first period together for the rest of the year. Someone? Anyone? Save him.

"Ah, Ms. Easton, I see you've met my nephew," Rainer said from behind them, pulling said nephew to his side and mussing his hair.

"Jesus, don't you have a faculty lounge?" Dillan shoved at him. No go. Rainer clamped on tighter than a succubus on a sleeping human.

"Hall monitor." He wiggled his eyebrows at them.

Right. Playing the innocent—still a little creepy—uncle card. All an illusion based on the predatory glint in Rainer's eyes. His training kicked in. When faced with predators, stay still. Keep calm. They smelled fear.

Again. Anyone? Help?

The cheerleader laughed. "I was just about to introduce myself to him, Mr. Sloan. Hi, I'm Sheila." She eyed him like she couldn't wait to take a bite.

As if sensing his flight response kicking in, Rainer yanked him closer and whispered, "You better blend in."

He spoke without really moving his lips to keep the succubus... uh, the cheerleader, from noticing their conversation. She waved at a passing group, letting them know about a meet up at the mall. "And if I don't?"

In response, the Boogeyman squeezed the shoulder he had dislocated last night, causing Dillan's knees to buckle. Only his uncle's hold kept him standing. "Play nice, Dillan, or I won't let you investigate the disappearances."

From the corner of his eye, he saw Rainer speak while maintaining a perfect smile on his face. His gaze never left the cheerleader, his grip on Dillan's shoulder never slackening. One more squeeze and he'd pass out. He prayed to anyone who would listen that Rainer wouldn't humiliate him that way in front of so many strangers.

"Fine," he hissed, painted into a dark, dreary corner. Something had to give. If he wanted the case, he needed to play by Rainer's rules.

"I was just about to ask Dillan if he wanted to have lunch with us," the cheerleader finally chimed in, returning her full attention to them.

"I'd rather—" He coughed out the rest of his sentence as Rainer's elbow slammed into his side. *Dammit.* Even his love taps hurt. He righted himself as if nothing had happened. "Is there a child abuse hotline I can call? Minor, remember?"

"You two seem so close." The cheerleader blinked, completely missing the violence.

In the distance, he spotted copper curls pass a set of doors with Cafeteria spelled above them. That invisible pull he'd been feeling tugged him in that direction. Ducking out of Rainer's grasp, he hooked his arm over the cheerleader's shoulders and smiled.

"Forget him," he said, hiking his thumb at his tormentor. "I'm suddenly really hungry."

CHAPTER FOUR

Selena

DISTURBING THE HIVE

An annoying buzzing filled the cafeteria as everyone discussed the new kid's arrival. Or maybe my freaky reaction to the new kid's arrival. Who knew? I certainly hoped it was more the former.

Normally, the town gossips knew pretty much everything going on in our community, sometimes before it happened. But given the amount of chatter floating around the room, this piece of information must have slipped through the cracks. Uncle and nephew were entitled to their privacy. Except, I also knew that in Newcastle, where everyone knew everyone, secrets never stayed hidden for long. The biddies down at the diner missed this one. Not even Grams, the leader of the town gossips, mentioned anything about a newcomer when she got home from her shift at the diner last night.

With a frown, I dumped a brown paper bag on the table's glossy surface and plopped into my seat. "Look at them, talking about Mr. Sloan's nephew like he's so awesome. People need to get a life." I raised my voice for the last bit, not caring who heard me. A crumpled napkin sailed my way, which I dodged.

Kyle set his tray down to my left. "It shouldn't surprise you. He's new." He took a bite of his sandwich as his jeans made contact with a chair. "And he's cute. Can anyone smell Prom King?"

I latched on to the word "cute" and didn't even think of the consequences when I asked, "You mean he's your type?"

He snorted into his drink. "God no! I hate you for even mentioning it."

I lifted both my hands. "Okay! Jeez. You don't have to give me the stink eye. You said 'cute' — "

"And that gives you the right to ask me if he's my type?" he interrupted.

"You never talk about your type."

"Damn right I don't. I was just stating a fact. And if you repeat what I said here, I quit as your best friend."

I sat there, speechless. I didn't think he'd bite my head off for a simple question. I should have known better. Kyle came out in middle school after Penny had asked him to the Sadie Hawkins Dance. He'd been about to turn her down when she told him she'd known all along and only asked him to save him from having to turn down other girls. "The humanitarian thing," she'd said. Their relationship had been like that ever since — going to every dance together. I, of course, stood there in super shock when he eventually told me he liked guys. But after a long talk, and making me pinky swear I wouldn't tell anyone else, I understood why he kept it quiet. As someone with my own stuff to hide from a busybody town, I accepted why he wanted things on the down low and moved on.

His grumpiness pulled me back to the buzzing cafeteria when he said, "I don't go for arrogant types."

Since he seemed chatty today, and we were already on the topic…

"Well, if you did *go* for someone, who'd it be?"

He leaned back and folded his arms. I held my breath. His pose had SHUT DOWN written all over it. He scanned the crowd. My lungs burned from the waiting. Then he shrugged, breaking the tension.

"My type," he finally said, "isn't here."

I exhaled slowly, letting my brain catch up with what he didn't say. "You mean *he's* not here."

"Something like that."

I wanted more, but his tone—all final and flat like that—stopped me. Sometimes, Kyle clammed up. To avoid further awkwardness, I changed the topic. Well, technically, I returned it to the original one.

"Anyway, the school is treating Dillan like a shiny toy on display." I paused from unwrapping my lunch as I spotted the third member of our triumvirate heading our way.

With each step, Penny's long, black braid bounced against her ruffled, pink shirt. Her almond-shaped eyes, the same color as her hair, stored a good amount of mischief. I loved Penny to death, especially after saving me from Bowen this morning, but on days like these, being her friend could be hard. Compared to her polished appearance, I was gangly and awkward—coppery curls that broke brushes, a complexion like I'd never heard of the sun, and long limbs meant for banging into things.

"Hey, bitches!" Her volume barely made a dent over the *buzz, buzz, buzz.*

"Sit down before you fall over." Kyle pointed at a chair.

"I have news!" Penny's eyes sparkled as she took the seat to my right. Sandwiched between my two best friends, all was right in my world.

"Let me guess…" He shook his head.

She nodded like a bobble-head doll.

"What do you know about Dillan Sloan?" I asked to keep her

from exploding.

The doll deflated. "You already know his name?"

"We have algebra together." Kyle reached behind me and patted her shoulder.

"Oh. Well...that doesn't change a thing!" She brightened. "Anyway, Dillan Sloan, as you already know, is the nephew of Mr. Sloan, our wonderful and impossibly attractive history teacher."

I gave Penny my best *duh* face, tearing a piece of my egg sandwich and popping the morsel into my mouth. Yum. Grams added grated cheese today.

"I'm just getting started." She wiggled her perfectly plucked eyebrows at me. "Dillan's also the son of *the* legendary duo of archeologists: Dr. Jarvis Sloan and Dr. Lillian Sloan."

At the mention of Dillan's parents, Kyle-nerd emerged. "You mean the two who proved Atlantis is really in South America and not in Spain? *Those* Sloans?"

"You make them sound like superheroes out of a graphic novel." I poked him.

"Yep, those Sloans." Penny ignored me. "Dillan's *National Geographic* royalty. But that's not all." Her hand rose to stall any further questions. "It seems young Dillan has also been part of several, and I mean *several*, ad campaigns for designers like Calvin Klein and Armani, to name two, and was once approached to star in a movie. He's even rumored to have dated every young Hollywood starlet and immerging singer you can name. You know that Taylor Swift song—"

"The one about the guy who dumped her?" Kyle asked.

"Aren't they all about guys who dumped her?" I asked back.

"Anyway," Penny said exasperatedly, "here's the best part."

"There's a best part?" I scoffed. Her lower lip jutted out at me. "Okay, okay. Shutting up now."

"As I was saying," she continued. "Rumor has it Dillan was

responsible for unearthing a lost civilization in the Amazon."

"That can't be true!" My palm tingled from slapping the table, reminding me of the electric handshake.

Offended, she asked, "Which part?"

"Starting anything with 'rumor has it' only means it's a *ru-mor*. Where'd you get your info so fast from anyway?"

"Google." Her patented eye roll showed off her latest Cover Girl mascara.

"And when did you have time to *Google* him?"

Penny fished out a tablet and handed it to me. "iPad," she said like I was supposed to know what she meant, which I did, but I resented the insinuation anyway.

"Is that the latest one?" Kyle grabbed the device and tinkered with the touch screen. "It shouldn't even be out yet."

"Connections." Penny shrugged. "Daddy got it for me so I can stay connected during my internship in New York."

My forehead met tabletop. "You *Googled* him," I groaned.

"I'm sorry, it's just—"

Seeing the guilt on her face, I headed her off with: "That's why I keep you around. You supply all my TMZ needs." I sat up and squeezed her thigh. "Speaking of His Highness..." I tilted my chin toward the cafeteria entrance.

A gaggle of girls in the orange, black, and white of Newcastle High's cheerleaders stood around Dillan. That much pretty in one room should be considered against the rules. If I squinted hard enough, I knew I'd spot glitter and shine on the patina of popular coating their spotless skin. And too white teeth. And perfect hair. And...

I turned in disgust to see Penny gape before she said, "Our guy moves fast."

"Wipe the drool off your face. It's icky." I threw a wadded up tissue at her, which she swatted away.

Kyle looked up long enough to acknowledge Dillan's presence before going back to playing whatever new game Penny had downloaded from the App Store. When his inner gamer came out, nothing short of a natural disaster could distract him. I shook my head and couldn't resist returning my attention to the popular crowd swarming the guy of the moment.

While walking toward an empty table, he said something that caused the swarm to laugh. The buzzing that had ruled the room died down. Heads turned toward him like homing missiles recognizing a heat signature. Then, of all places, Dillan's gaze flicked toward me.

"What was that?" Penny glanced from me to him.

"What was what?" I asked back, acting nonchalant. I already knew what she'd meant. Not like I could escape it.

"Dillan just gave you a *look*."

I blew a stray curl off my face. "Oh, you mean the 'I'm-shocked-this-person-is-even-here' kind of look?"

"No, more like 'I-can't-believe-I'm-in-the-same-room-with-this-person' kind of look."

"Really? To me, it looked more like an 'I-can't-stand-this-person' kind of look." Kyle smirked at his own cleverness.

"That just sounds like you've put words and hyphens together." I nudged his shoulder, thankful for the comfort his addition to our conversation gave me.

Penny shook her head in dismay. "Go back to playing with your toy, Kyle."

He blushed and returned his attention to the tablet, the friend that truly understood him.

"Boys. What can you do?" She sighed.

I sighed along with her. "Dillan gave me that look in algebra, too. You know he actually *shocked* me?"

"Shocked?"

"As in electrocuted," I clarified. "I don't know what happened.

We shook hands, electricity zinged through me, then it's like I have leprosy."

"Maybe that's how he normally looks at people." Kyle reluctantly slid the tablet back to Penny. "Plus, it could just be static."

"Oh, believe me, that *look* was definitely directed at Selena." She slipped the device into the front pocket of her bag.

"Can we change the topic, please?" I begged.

"Are you ever gonna tell me why you broke up with Bowen?"

I gasped, completely forgetting that Kyle didn't know. "You just got back yesterday—"

"Now's as good a time as any," Penny interrupted.

"Penny knows?" His brow wrinkled.

"I got back a week early." She faced me again. "Come on. He deserves to know what that asswipe did."

My shoulders tensed. Telling Penny was a thousand times easier than telling Kyle. I knew how he would react. Even if he got back from science camp as early as Penny did from her summer internship, I still wouldn't have known how to break the news. I dropped my gaze, gathering my courage. He did deserve to know. Despite her matter-of-fact declaration, Penny slid closer. She hugged me and didn't let go.

"Selena?"

The worry in the way Kyle said my name ripped my eyes away from the remnants of my lunch to meet his gray gaze.

"A month ago…" I swallowed. "Bowen cheated on me."

He slapped the table and got up. Penny let me go so we could both grab an arm. We yanked him back down.

"That fucking asshole." He growled. Remember the Labradoodle?

I shook my head. "He's not worth it."

"Yeah," Penny backed me up. "Don't get suspended and ruin your perfect record for that pond scum."

"Just because he won State doesn't give him the right to put his dick in someone else."

"More like tongue." I blushed. I couldn't help it. "Just let it go, please? We're over."

Closing his eyes, Kyle puffed out a breath. Penny and I maintained our hold in him. When he opened his eyes and they were less stormy, we removed our hands from his arms. Penny returned to hugging me.

"You saw your break-up a week after you started dating freshman year." He tugged on the stubborn copper curl by my ear, telling me he let his anger go…for now anyway. "I don't understand why you keep thinking your visions won't happen. They've been proven time and time again."

"Call me stubborn." I gave him my Oscar-worthy, determined expression.

"*I*, of all people, should know your dreams come true. I learned that the hard way." He flexed his left hand self-consciously.

Of course he'd say that. In the fifth grade, I had a vision where Kyle broke his arm on the jungle gym. Even after I'd told him about it, he insisted on hanging from the metal bars. Five minutes later, he was rushed to the emergency room, a bone fragment sticking out of his wrist.

Guilt ate at me. Even now, years later, I still felt like I should have done more to stop him. I'd have reached for him if Penny's arms didn't pin mine down.

"Well, it wasn't really about the vision." My eyebrows pulled together. "I had to see where our relationship would go. He was my first *real* boyfriend."

"Yeah, I know where he went, straight down another girl's throat." Penny squeezed me tighter. "He doesn't deserve someone like you."

"It's been hardest on Grams. She's always been Team Bowen."

I felt my face crumple. "She found out through the town gossip line. I literally had to stop her from stabbing him. And forget about Gramps. He totally doesn't know, and we plan on keeping it that way."

"You know what they say about breakups…" Penny finally let me go. I didn't like the way she smiled when she added, "The best cure is a great rebound." She gave Dillan an oh-so-obvious glance.

"Not gonna happen." I wagged a finger at her, thankful the object of our conversation was looking in the other direction.

She took an exaggerated breath. "Oh, but smell the tension in the air. It has potential."

"Leave it alone." I did my own eye-rolling when she pursed her lips. "Anyway, Maggie's Diner after school?"

The bell rang. The buzzing morphed into chair scraping and shuffling.

"I have to get back to Hay Creek early today. Sorry, babe." Penny bounced away. "I'll text you tonight, promise."

"Kyle?" I brought out the puppy-dog eyes.

"Not today. Sorry." He placed his arm around my shoulders. My consolation prize.

"But we always go to Maggie's after school."

"I have an errand to run."

"You're not going to corner Bowen somewhere and beat the crap out of him, are you?"

He hugged me tighter. "You know I'd bury a body for you, right?"

The truth in his question warmed my insides. Yes, he would, and Penny would be the look out. My friends were the best, unlike some people. My attention drifted to Dillan just as he reached the exit. As if he felt my gaze, he returned my curiosity with a glare that held a combination of confusion and annoyance, like I disgusted him in some way. The guy really got on my nerves.

CHAPTER FIVE

Dillan

COGITO ERGO...SORT OF

*B*y the end of his first day in school, Dillan was ready to punch someone. That wide berth the students had given him didn't last long. Apparently, eating lunch with the popular kids opened a door he wanted kept tightly shut. Instead of flying under the radar, he was in everyone's sights. He couldn't walk down a stupid hallway or pass by an open classroom without being molested with questions. The guys, he chalked up to curiosity, sizing up the competition. But the girls. Jesus. An entire succubus population in one school? They made him feel like fresh meat ready for the taking.

He only went along with the popular hangout at lunch so he could keep an eye on the girl. She baffled the hell out of him. Selena Fallon. He couldn't stop thinking about her. About the electricity their contact created. Damn Rainer for even suggesting blending in, and he damned himself twice over for impulsively thinking she was more than ordinary. She spent the entire time with her friends. Touching them casually, no electric shocks passed from her to them.

Nothing suspicious at all. Still, he stayed until the end of lunch.

It soon reached him that someone had Googled him. All anyone asked him was if he had really dated Taylor Swift. He knew visiting the siren to settle a dispute between her and a current lover would one day bite him on the ass. He fucking hated the Internet and the lies it spread. But the Illumenari loved it that way. Create a lie here to keep the humans from figuring out the truth there. This allowed the Supernaturals to hide in plain sight. Convenient, but still annoying.

One thing he knew for sure, he'd rather get a root canal than spend another day in Newcastle High.

Feeling the hallways closing in on him, he ducked into the nearest bathroom and stumbled to the sink. He stared into the mirror, breathing in through his nose and out through his mouth. The girl from this morning—blue lips, pale cheeks, wavy hair— reflected back at him. A cold sweat dotted his brow from the effort to stay calm. Shit. He closed his eyes for a count of ten then opened them again.

She was gone.

Great. Just great. To top off his stint in the circle of hell Dante left out of Inferno, a ghost from his past haunted him. Guilt for what had happened already ate at his insides every second he thought of her. He didn't need to see her, too!

He flicked the tap up, cupped his hands under the stream, and watched them fill up. That was when his stomach twisted violently. He let the water fall back into the sink and ran for the nearest stall.

After losing what little lunch he'd managed swallow, he stumbled his way back to the sink. First he washed out the bitter stomach acid coating his mouth then splashed cold water on his face in a lame attempt to wash away his failure. Suddenly more tired than he'd initially thought, he lifted his shirt and dried himself. With shaking hands, he leaned against the sink. The water swirled clockwise. Ice settled in his chest with every inhale, numbing his insides. He pushed the tap down and punched the wall.

Tile clattered to the floor. The pain was quick, enough to remind him where he was and what he'd done to deserve this. He studied the back of his hand. No blood. No broken knuckles. For a second, he wished he'd broken the skin.

As his hand tingled from the beginnings of bruised knuckles, he turned on his heel and walked out of the bathroom. He needed a distraction, and only one person could give it to him. Down the hall to the right, he strode into Rainer's classroom, not bothering to knock. Screw manners.

His uncle hunched over his desk, hiding behind paper towers. Dillan stopped and stared, his eyebrow shooting up. Rainer reached for a sheet at the top of one stack, not acknowledging his presence. In the process, he elbowed the column to his right.

He smirked while his uncle scramble to grab at the pile before the whole thing came crashing down, only missing one. It wedged itself between the floor and his boot. How could Rainer leave the Illumenari for a soul-sucking job like teaching?

"I don't understand why you insist on wearing your hair like that," he finally said without looking up, busily rearranging his towers. "You look like a reject from the Village People."

Dillan tilted his head. "The what?"

The pen flew across each page again, making the paper bleed mercilessly. "Figures you wouldn't know who they are."

"Figures you *would*, Granpa. And don't insult the hair. It's the only way I know how to keep it out of my face without getting a buzz cut."

"Do you mind?" His uncle pointed at his boot with the pen.

He bent down and snatched the quiz. A groan left his lips. Think of the devil, and she appears. Couldn't he get away from her for more than a few minutes?

"You have to tell me who Selena Fallon is," he said, handing over the sheet.

"Why the sudden interest in her? Finally making friends?"

"Uh, maybe because she shocked me when we shook hands this morning and now there's this invisible string that's tying me to her? And hell no to the friends part."

"That's stupid." Rainer tapped the stack he'd finished grading. "You're imagining things."

"Don't go all Area 51 on me." He stared at his open hand. "I know what I felt. It's like touching a security fence. Then I started feeling strange shit."

"Like what kind of strange shit?"

"I don't know." He crossed his arms. "At first, I wanted to push her away, like she disgusted me. Then when she looked down at me with those aquamarine...who the hell has aqua eyes anyway? It's like I need to be where she is, like what's repelling me from her is pulling me in, too. When she's not there, thinking of her makes me want to find her. That's just jacked up!"

"That's called being a teenager. Hormones. Maybe you just have a crush on her."

Oh, now he wanted to punch his uncle's lights out even if it would mean his death afterwards. The satisfaction of giving him a shiner... "This is not love at first sight or some stupid crap like that. I'm telling you, it has something to do with that electric shock contact with her produced."

"Did you test this out? Touch her again?"

"No." His face fell. Why hadn't he thought of that?

"It's possible this is just a side effect of your demotion. You're jonesing for your powers, and it's making you loopy."

"This damn school is making me loopy." He tore his fingers through his hair. "Come on, Rainer, if you insist on making me stay here, you have to give me something to do."

In a quick move, Rainer pushed his chair back and stood up. He stuffed the graded papers into his satchel along with others he hadn't checked yet. "You want something to do?"

Dillan stepped back and let his uncle out of the room before following. "Are you finally going to tell me about the case?"

Whirling around, Rainer squinted at him. "What makes you ask that?"

Before he could lose his balance, he took a step back. "I clearly need a distraction, and you said you're going to give me something to do…"

The responding laugh reverberated down the mostly empty hallway. Some stragglers who lingered before going home glanced at them before returning to whatever they were going.

"So you automatically assume this is about the case?" Rainer asked between chuckles. "Oh, that is precious!"

His head dropped. "Don't tell me we're going home, and you're going to make me do homework. That's just lame."

His torturer hooked an arm over his shoulders. Dillan did his best not to Judo flip him. The retaliation would be swift, and it would be merciless. As if sensing his discomfort, Rainer pulled him even closer.

"We need food," he said.

"Seriously? We're going shopping. That's what you want me to focus on?"

"Why not? It's better than your silly theories about Selena Fallon."

Without thinking about the consequences, he flipped his uncle off. A second later, his middle finger was dislocated.

CHAPTER SIX

Selena

THE COLD SHOULDER GAME

I loved spending my afternoons at Maggie's Diner. I practically grew up amidst its red vinyl booths and home-style cooking courtesy of my grandmother. The owner, Nancy, bought the place from the Mendelsons two years back when their son, chasing dreams in bigger cities, thought owning a diner was boring. Blond and buxom Nancy was like a long lost aunt to me. But no matter how much I begged, Maggie's just didn't have any openings. I needed a part-time job like yesterday.

Sighing into my milkshake, I scanned the Want Ads in the *Newcastle Daily*. Dog walker didn't appeal to me. The movie theater only had day shifts. I needed something right after school and just until Grams got out of her shift at the diner. And preferably nearby. Gramps used the truck most of the day, and Grams took me to school in her car. Maybe the dog-walking job wasn't so bad.

Guys laughing pulled my attention from the newspaper. My heart twisted then beat faster the second I spotted Bowen walk in with his swimming buddies. Usually, they had practice in the mornings and afternoons. My forehead wrinkled. The only reason I felt comfortable going to Maggie's sans the best friends was because I was confident I wouldn't run into the ex.

Annoyed, I fished out my cellphone. I took a picture of him joking around with his buddies and sent it to both Kyle and Penny with the word deserter. We learned what it meant in history class. They should have been here to act as my buffers.

But, just as soon as it started, I stopped my feeling-sorry-for-myself moment. I shouldn't be hiding behind my friends. I survived three weeks of summer without them after finding Bowen feeling up Sally Thompson at the Stop and Pump when Gramps asked me to fill up the truck. I could definitely take care of myself.

Two seconds later, their replies came one after the other. Both sent me wink-y faces like they were in on some joke. So much for friendship. Why I continued to love them, I had no idea.

Lamenting my half-eaten burger and fries, I stuffed all my books inside my pack, including the daily paper, and slid out of the booth. My phone went into my back pocket. No time like the present to make the walk to Miller's grocery and take care of the list Grams had given me.

"Leavin' already, dear?" Nancy asked from the counter.

My shoulders hitched up as I froze mid-step. Of course it was too much to ask that I leave without getting noticed. Plastering a cordial smile on my face, I said, "Yeah. I'm heading off to Miller's."

Before she could say anything else, and especially before Bowen noticed me from the corner booth, I rushed out of the diner. Thankfully, Grams was busy in the kitchen, or she would have called after me as well.

Just as I crossed the street and relief filled my chest, heavy footsteps trailed my sneakered ones. I didn't stop, adjusting my pack on my shoulders. *Please don't let it be him.*

"Selena!"

Crap!

I kept moving. Maybe if I ignored him enough he would lose interest and leave me alone.

A large hand wrapped around my arm, yanking me around.

Apparently, not.

"Hey!" I yanked my arm out of his grip. "What's the matter with you?"

Bowen raised his hands in surrender and backed up a step. "You weren't stopping."

"Yeah? Maybe that's because I didn't want to stop and talk to you. Ever think of that?"

His eyebrows came together. "Look, Nancy said you were headed for Miller's."

I silently cursed my supposedly long-lost aunt and her unassuming kindness. She knew what Bowen did. The whole freakin' town did, and yet, she was polite enough to answer him when he asked where I was going. Kindness hurt sometimes.

"And that's your business because?" I left the heat in my tone. I couldn't let myself think about the two years of my life that I wasted on him because I'd begin to cry. I did enough of that weeks ago. My annoyance sparked into anger. Unadulterated anger.

"Come on." He hiked a thumb over his shoulder. "I'll give you a ride."

My eyes flashed. "And why would I get into a truck with you?"

"Because Miller's is a mile away, and hefting grocery bags back to your house isn't an easy thing." He raised a hand to stall my next tirade. "Look, I get it. I'm an asshole. Hate me. In fact, you have the right to. But don't deny me a good act when I'm clearly offering."

Damn. He was right about the groceries. Walking home with my pack filled with books plus however many grocery bags would suck. I hated myself for accepting the offer.

Muttering, I trudged toward his car. Bowen ran to my side and opened my door. I slipped in without thanking him. Dropping my pack at my feet and buckling in, I focused on the road. He started the truck and pulled into traffic.

In my periphery, I noticed him opened his mouth a couple times then shut it just as fast. He'd never been someone at a loss for words. I knew him as the confident athlete with an easy smile. Not this guy who awkwardly tried and failed to fill the silence between us.

. . .

The second Bowen killed the engine, I muttered a quick thanks and slipped out, slinging my pack over my shoulder. The opening and closing of his door almost made me groan. I didn't look back, shuffling as fast as I could into the store. The automatic doors slid aside when I neared them, and a blast of air ruffled my curls. I headed straight for the carts, but the second my hand closed around the bar of one, Bowen's larger hand closed around it beside mine. The sides of our fists touched, and I let go immediately.

"Bowen," I barked. It seemed he wasn't leaving me alone any time soon.

"Can I push?" he asked.

"Will you leave me alone if I let you?"

He nodded.

Rolling my shoulders to ease some of the tension there, I walked away. He clearly followed based on the squeaking wheels that trailed me into the canned goods section. I figured I might as well make use of him while we were here. Memories of going grocery shopping with him hit me hard. We used to do it all the time until…

"Grab a can of SPAM, will you?" I flicked my hand to the top of the shelf, but really I was flicking away the stupid, useless memory. Bowen complied like a soldier, efficient and without question. I dug out the list from my pack and checked it. "Okay, now we need milk."

He nodded as if he would milk a cow to get it if necessary.

I gave him a sidelong glance. "Why are you doing this? What? Sally already dump you?"

Never letting go of the cart handle, he said, "There's nothing between Sally and me."

Grabbing two cartons of milk, I did my best to avoid his expectant gaze. "That didn't stop your tongue from playing tonsil hockey with hers."

"Come on, Selena. I made a mistake. I get that. Please, let me make it up to you."

"There's no going back for us. Don't you get it?" I didn't want to get into this now, but since he started it... "You cheated on me. That's not something I can get over."

"Everyone makes mistakes." He pushed the cart faster to keep up with my quickening stride. The faster we finished, the sooner we could say good-bye. Excuses swirled in my head. I had to figure out how to get out of riding home with him.

"Yes, but it doesn't mean I'd let you off the hook because of it." I looked into his eyes, making sure he saw the hurt I wasn't trying to hide anymore.

"I'm not saying you should." He met me stare for stare. "I'm just asking for a second chance."

"But..." I bit my lip, considering his words. Damn. I shouldn't be considering his words. Penny's voice bounced around in my head, telling me I was being too nice.

He put one of his strong hands on my shoulder and turned me to face him. I reluctantly met his gaze.

"But what?"

"But I don't miss you." It was the truth, yet instant remorse closed my throat. When I broke up with him, I cried. I felt betrayed. But when I pulled myself back together, I realized I didn't miss him. At all. Yes, I enjoyed the two years we'd spent together. But now that I was free of him, I didn't regret it one bit. A part of me even felt relieved that he cheated. I was pissed more at the fact that his cheating on me made it seem like those two years didn't matter to him at all.

Bowen's lips disappeared into a hard line. A muscle along his jaw jumped. He let go of my shoulder and white-knuckled the pushcart's bar. His eyes blazed with barely controlled anger. The lines of his face seemed harsher. His shoulders twitched upward. A ripple went through his body, like he was trying hard to remain calm.

"Something wrong here?"

Oh, great. Just what I needed. My head whipped to my left. Dillan Sloan clutched a jumbo bag of chips with both hands. His expression unreadable. My gaze went beyond his shoulder to the end of the aisle where Mr. Sloan stood reading the back of a cereal box.

"Just walk away, Dillan," I said, glancing at Bowen. "Nothing to see here."

Bowen breathed in deep. His fiery gaze never left my face.

"Hello, Ms. Fallon. Bowen." Mr. Sloan joined us and parked his cart behind Dillan.

"Oh, hi, Mr. Sloan." I forced a smile on my face.

"Mr. Sloan." Bowen nodded at our teacher.

"Have you met my nephew?" Mr. Sloan inclined his head toward Dillan.

"Dillan Sloan."

"Bowen Gage." They clasped hands. "Heard a lot about you."

"Small school."

"Small town." Bowen released Dillan's hand.

I wanted to get out of there. All of them acting so cordial made me sick. If Dillan hadn't butted in, I could have finished what I started and hopefully ended this thing. Bowen was clearly pissed by what I said. Maybe if he held on to that emotion long enough, he'd forget about wanting that second chance.

Dillan glanced my way while Bowen and Mr. Sloan started a conversation about the team stats this season. I didn't meet his gaze.

Let him think what he wanted. This morning, he practically treated me like a leper he couldn't stand to touch. Now, his eyes darted from my face to Bowen's like he expected something to happen. I wasn't going to explain myself to someone who gave me death stares.

"By the way," Bowen's eerily calm voice tore my attention away from stewing over Dillan, "I just remembered something I need to do." His blank eyes landed on me. "Do you mind finding your own way home?"

"Yeah." I swallowed my relief. "Sure. I'll figure something out."

"Good." A flat smile. "Nice meeting you, Dillan."

Without waiting for a response, and only giving Mr. Sloan a nod, Bowen made his way out of the store. I exhaled the long awaited sigh I'd been holding in.

"Do you want us to give your grandmother a call?" Mr. Sloan suggested.

I shook my head. "Her shift doesn't end until later." Plus, I didn't need my grandmother knowing I was at the store with Bowen. Although, something told me it wouldn't be long until she found out. Then my gaze returned to Dillan. My brain refused to understand why he scowled at me like I'd just finished kicking a puppy. *What's his deal?*

"Are you—"

"She's fine, Rainer," he interrupted.

Mr. Sloan frowned. "What did I tell you about calling me by my first name in public?"

Dillan dropped his gaze.

"We'll talk about it later." He tsked at his nephew before asking me, "Do you want a ride home?"

I thought about it. Endure a ride with Dillan or walk home? Four miles was no joke with groceries plus my backpack. I steeled myself and said, "Thanks. That would be great."

Dillan's scowl turned murderous.

CHAPTER SEVEN

Dillan

CAN ANYBODY SAY AWKWARD?

In the front seat of his uncle's car, Dillan stewed. Just when he thought he'd gotten her out of his head, she crawled back in. The shopping trip actually helped get his mind off her, but the Fates were cruel bitches. The second he and Rainer turned into the cereal aisle, there she was, standing with a troll of a guy.

That invisible string he'd been talking about pulled taut. He sensed the hostility in the guy's attitude toward her. Without thinking twice, he found himself butting in on the lover's quarrel. From the way she scowled at him, she hadn't appreciated the interference.

Looking at Bowen, minus the rancid stench, his instincts had been right. The guy reminded him so much of a troll. Quick to anger, all brawn, no brains. Clearly, Selena was handling it. If he hadn't stepped in—and what could he have done anyway?—he wouldn't be in this situation. Sitting in a car with her strawberry shampoo filling his lungs.

Forced to listen to the constant, yap, yap, yapping, hurt his ears.

Rainer and Selena discussed school, of all things, and some stupid field trip he'd rather die than join. The beginnings of a headache pulsed between his eyes.

Arms folded close to his chest, he leaned back, trying in vain to relax. He called on some of the meditative technics taught to him by one of his instructors. He focused on his breathing, inhaling deeply then exhaling slowly. Yet, no matter how hard he tried to clear his mind, Selena's face kept flashing back in. Having her sitting so close to him...he bit his tongue to keep from asking her outright what she was.

Outside of town, the Mustang turned onto a dirt road. His still sore shoulder didn't appreciate the bumpy ride. Healing himself meant using energy he might need later. So he balled his hands into fists and sat through the pain.

In the distance, an old farmhouse of peeling, blue paint came into view. To the left stood what looked like a shed, only bigger. A garage, maybe? No fence. No protection whatsoever from any kind of attack. He searched for points where he'd place wards if he still had his Guardian powers. Then he remembered he was at a human's home. Well, human until he proved her otherwise. And he sure as hell wouldn't stop until he got answers.

Rainer shifted the '66 into neutral and said, "Dillan, why don't you help Selena with the bags?"

He cocked an eyebrow at him.

"No need. I can bring them in myself," Selena said from the backset.

His uncle's lips disappeared as he stared daggers at him. "Selena, let Dillan help you."

Hearing the finality in the "request," he unfolded himself out of the car, pushed down the passenger seat, and let Selena out. She slung her backpack over her shoulder and followed him to the trunk. Both his throbbing finger and shoulder stood as witnesses to what his uncle was capable of. After a loud pop, he lifted the lid and grabbed her grocery bags. He didn't look at her. Yet he was pretty sure her eyes were on him when he led the way to the front door.

Maybe a casual touch? He thought about it. A fingertip grazing her arm and he could prove he wasn't going crazy. That this girl did shock him.

"I can bring them in myself." She grabbed one of the bags, barely missing his hand with hers. Dillan yanked back until she was forced to let go. So much for casually touching her.

"Sure you can." He made his way up the gravel path to the front porch. "Just trying to avoid the long lecture I'd get if I didn't help." Among other more painful consequences. Maybe knowing about his uncle's violent streak was the reason behind the Council sending him to Newcastle. Rainer made the perfect warden. Sadistic.

"I don't want to owe you any favors."

The same stubborn fire he saw at the grocery store flared. He almost grinned. Almost. Instead, he stood by the door and waited for her to join him. "Trust me. You don't need to pay me back."

Selena matched his scowl with one of her own. "Why are you staring at me like I kicked a puppy? I'm not a bad person."

A cute knot formed on her brow. He cursed himself. He *did not* find her cute. "Why do you care how I look at you?"

They stared at each other. Her aqua eyes sliced through him. He didn't like the churning his stomach did because of it. Just when he thought he couldn't stand it any longer, she broke eye contact, pretending to adjust her bag. Huh. That was unexpected.

"Did you really date Taylor Swift?" she asked.

"What?" Her words didn't sink in fast enough. He was too distracted by the way the setting sun brought out golden highlights in her copper curls.

"Penny said she read somewhere that you dated Taylor Swift." She sneaked a peek at him through long lashes. "That she wrote a song about you?"

He watched her lips move, forcing himself to concentrate.

"It was one dinner." He should have been annoyed, having been asked the same question at least ten times already today. But he wasn't. Her already big, bright eyes got bigger. He imagined himself reaching out and touching the smattering of freckles across her nose. She flinched like she'd read his mind.

"What do you keep staring at?" She rubbed the bridge of her nose. The exact same spot he wanted to run his thumb over. "Is it my freckles?"

Without meaning to, he leaned in. "Now that you mention them..."

"What!" A blush spread across her cheeks. Jesus H. Christ, she was gorgeous. How hadn't he noticed before? Maybe because they'd only met that day? The thought of Rainer being right about hormones killed him. "Are they that obvious? Kyle says I'm being paranoid and that I don't really have freckles. I told him it was my face, and I know they're there."

"Kyle?"

"My best friend."

Why that statement relieved him, he didn't want to know. First the nutty Taylor Swift question, and then the freckles. His face hurt from trying to suppress the grin, but it was no use. He laughed out loud. For the first time since stepping off the plane, he truly relaxed. When she glared at him like he was an idiot, he quickly sobered. She'd caught him off guard, and it didn't sit well.

"Are you opening the damn door or do I have to kick it in?" he barked.

Selena scrambled for her house keys. Her hands shook so badly she missed the hole twice before finally inserting the key. A nervous laugh escaped her. His fingers tightened around the plastic bags. Eventually, she got the key into the lock. A click later, she twisted the knob and let the door opened.

"Kitchen. Hall. Back," was her barely coherent response.

He walked past her into the house. Framed photos littered the walls. Lots of smiling faces, some of them Selena's at different ages. The carpet beneath his boots was simple and clean. Not what he expected from a farmhouse with peeling paint. He suddenly missed his parents.

Heart heavy with the reminder of disappointing them, he deposited the bags on the kitchen table and turned on his heel. In his distraction, Selena collided with his chest and on reflex, his hands went up to steady her. She gasped, probably feeling the same jolt he did. Dammit. He wasn't imagining the electricity. Their eyes met.

"What are you?" he asked, shaking her slightly.

She blinked those big, clear eyes. "What do you mean, what am I?"

Catching himself, he lifted her and set her aside. He realized the price of getting answers might be too steep. If she didn't know what he was talking about then she was human, and humans couldn't find out about the Illumenari and the Supernaturals that walked among them. It would mean chaos.

Avoiding saying anything else incriminating, he left her in the kitchen. He closed the front door behind him and kept his steps measured, even. He wasn't running away. But in Rainer's car—after he'd strapped in—his self-control argued with his common sense. The shocks had to do with his diminishing powers. Nothing else explained the current. He shoved his fingers through his hair, further disheveling the meticulously styled strands. She was just some girl. Human. Completely human.

"What's wrong?" Rainer asked from the driver's seat.

"Maybe you're right," he answered, trembling. "Maybe I'm just being paranoid about Selena." Copper curls did nothing for him, he convinced himself. But those eyes. And not to mention that body. He didn't notice until now, but she filled out those jeans. Damn.

"But you're really pale."

"I..." He rotated his shoulders to ease the tightness between them. "I asked her what she was." Rainer sucked in a breath, which prompted him to quickly add, "But I stopped and got the hell out of there. She doesn't know anything. You were right. Can we just go?"

Without arguing, Rainer started the car and pulled out of the Fallon driveway. Dillan didn't want to think anymore. There was no point. He let the crunch of tires on dirt road anchor him to the present. The fatigue he'd been battling since leaving the school finally won. He tuned out the classic rock on the radio and lowered his eyelids.

Almost immediately, his mind moved from one girl to another. The ghost he tried his hardest to forget floated toward him. His heart twisted.

This time, he didn't close his eyes as she came closer. She wrapped her fingers around his neck. He didn't move, giving her every right to choke the life out of him. When she started applying pressure, someone called his name. She looked over his shoulder, easing her grip on his throat. For a reckless moment, he wanted to catch her wrists and keep her there. Beg her to finish the job. But it was too late. She faded into nothing.

He sucked in a breath and opened his eyes, reaching up to rub the sleep from them. It took him a second to regain his bearings. They had moved from gravel to asphalt, and an endless supply of grass stretched out on each side of the road. He cursed under his breath. Between being haunted and Selena acting like a human socket, he just wanted to pack up and leave.

But where would he go? A sobering thought. No matter where he ran, the Illumenari would find him and drag him back here. He'd have to deal if he wanted to survive staying with his sanity intact.

"You dozed off on me." Rainer ruffled his hair in an uncharacteristic show of affection.

He shoved his uncle's hand away. "How long was I out?"

"A few minutes, give or take. You were calling her name."

Any jetlag he had vanished. He sat up straighter. "No, I wasn't."

"Dillan, I'm not deaf."

"I wasn't."

"It wasn't—"

He punched the dashboard.

"Don't take it out on my car."

A part of him wished Rainer had yelled. He wanted a fight. Anything to numb the hurt and hate. Instead, his stupid uncle decided he'd be the bigger person, leaving him feeling hollowed out.

CHAPTER EIGHT

Selena

AMONG THE STACKS

I lay in bed that night confused about Dillan. He'd asked me what I was. What did he mean by that? And the zap happened again. If he hadn't held on, I would have fallen flat on my face. I couldn't understand what was going on between us. When I collided with his chest, there wasn't an ounce of flabby flesh there, just hard, unyielding muscle.

I rolled onto my side at the same time my phone buzzed. I reached for it on my bedside table and cued up the message.

Penny: *Heard about Miller's.*

Me: *Which version?*

Flopping onto my back again, I swung my arm across my eyes, leaving my phone by my side. Grams came home in a snit, having heard about what Bowen did. Well—I should be clear—she heard a version of the story. News traveled weirdly in Newcastle. You only get bits and pieces of it based on eyewitness accounts. Most people filled in the blanks. Of course, that was what Grams did. She'd heard Bowen followed me into Miller's, which was true. The part where he threw a fit and almost hit me wasn't. I had to remind Grams that I would never let a guy raise a hand against me, let alone actually hit me. This calmed her down. Thank God Gramps hadn't come home because we wouldn't have been able to keep the news from him with Grams threatening to spit in Bowen's food the next time he was at the diner.

My phone blinked this time, the sheets muffling the vibration.

Penny: *He drove U 2 Miller's. Argument. Then he left.*

Me: *Where do U get UR 411? Best version yet.*

Penny: *Secret.*

I giggled. Penny had always been good at getting all the right information. For as long as I'd been friends with her, she hadn't gotten anything wrong yet.

Before I could reply, my phone buzzed again.

Penny: *True or False. U rode home with hot teach.*

Of course she knew about that, too, so no use lying.

Me: *True. :)*

Penny: *U lucky b*tch.*

I rolled onto my stomach and kicked my feet in the air. Yeah, I was one lucky bitch. To get a ride from Mr. Sloan was definitely the highlight of my week. Then my stupid brain went back to Dillan.

Me: *Have 411 on Dillan.*

Penny: *WHAT!?!*

Me: *2morrow. Lunch. ;)*

Penny: *Tease.*

Penny: *411 on PT job.*

Me: *REALLY!!!*

Penny: *2morrow. ;P*

Me: *H8 U!*

Penny: *<3*

• • •

After school the next day, I stood in front of a brick building with a window display featuring recommended books and bestsellers. The store was conveniently only a couple of blocks from Maggie's Diner. I stared up at the Gothic-lettered sign proudly announcing ORMAND BOOKS in gold. Two black lions with snakes for tails bookended the store's name.

When I fell asleep after my texting marathon with Penny, I'd dreamt ofcters, beautiful scenery descriptions. in check sista!!at he'ust ignores her squivering in the exact same sign and of standing in this very spot. With Kyle off helping the yearbook committee, I had Penny to myself at lunch. As promised, she filled me in on the details of the job, and I told her about Dillan and what he'd asked me. She said it might have been a slip of the tongue. Maybe. I really didn't know. What if he knew about my visions? Penny quickly called bullshit. She was right, how could Dillan know anything about that?

Finding no answers, we promised to meet in front of the bookstore since Penny had a couple of things to take care of after school. Now that I waited, staring at the sign, I felt funny. Off in some way that I couldn't put my finger on.

Below the OPEN sign, a white bond paper was taped. It read: 'Help Wanted. Inquire Inside.' Of coursc the newly opened bookstore would need some sort of help. How Penny knew this place needed help was like magic. But with her network of "sources" I shouldn't have been surprised.

I took a second to decide if I wanted to enter the store or to continue to wait for Penny outside. The unease that simmered at a corner of my mind grew. A small voice in my head urged me to run away. I took a step back before I stopped myself, breathing in deep. I needed the job.

But it didn't feel right.

"Hey, bitch!" Penny bounced to my side and threw her arms around my neck in an impromptu hug, knocking me off balance.

I screeched as I took the full impact of her enthusiasm. My jeans kissed pavement, and it hurt.

"Oops." Her eyes sparkled as she helped me up. I rubbed my bruised backside. "*Soooorry.* Why were you zoned out anyway?"

Dusting off my shirt, I stared back at the sign above the door. "I don't know."

"Are you still thinking about Dillan?"

"No!"

"My, that gets you all riled up, doesn't it? To be honest, I really don't think it's anything. Plus, those electrical surges? I'll check it out if you want. There's got to be something on the Net about it."

"You don't have to do that." I watched clouds glide by before looking back at Penny. "You're right. I don't even know why I'm letting him get to me. Besides sharing two classes, I don't know anything about him."

"That's the spirit!"

"You're not gonna slap me in the ass are you?" I grinned.

As if I'd dared her, Penny's palm made contact with my still smarting butt. I yelped and danced away. She pulled me back to her and gave me a comforting hug. I loved her tons. I honestly wouldn't know what to do with myself without her.

"So what's got you zoning out?"

"This doesn't feel right." I gestured toward the bookstore. "The place gives me the creepy crawlies, you know?"

"Oh, don't be such a baby!" She patted the center of my back a little too hard. I felt it all the way through to my chest. "Unless Nancy fires one of the waitresses at the diner, you don't have anywhere else that's walking distance from school and the diner." She turned me around and pushed me toward the store. Digging in my heels didn't help.

A soft *you'll regret this* from somewhere in my head and a couple of deep breaths later, I pushed through the entrance. The bell attached to the top of the door tinkled its welcome as I stumbled in with Penny right on my heels.

An unusually cold blast of air greeted us.

The chill bumps on my arms made me long for the hoodie I'd left in my backpack with Grams at the diner. "Don't you think it's a little cold in here?"

"Not at all." My best friend hopped closer to my side. "Why are we whispering?"

"Shut up." I stuffed my hands inside my pockets. The AC didn't help the creep factor much, no matter how normal everything looked.

The counter had a cash register at one end and a pyramid of books for the featured author of the month on the other. A glass-doored bookcase filled with leather and cloth-bound books stood behind the counter. Each title was a different color with gold lettering along the spine.

"Isn't this great? Well, not as great as the stores in NYC, but it certainly has its charm." Penny shrugged.

"Sure." I nodded absentmindedly. "Don't you feel like this place is…I don't know?"

"Like?"

"Spooky."

"You're wigging me out." She poked my arm.

The place had two built-in shelves on each wall while three shelves divided the rest of the floor space in between, stretching from the front to the rear. My sneakers squeaked on the gleaming hardwood floors as I stepped forward. The sconces that decorated the walls reflected the gothic theme of the sign outside, spaced evenly between shelves. A lemony wax smell permeated the air.

"I'm sorry for the frigid conditions. I'm still struggling with the air conditioner controls."

I jumped as Mr. Glasses, partially hidden behind the book pyramid, poked his head out. He had shaggy hair the same color as the hardwood floors. I couldn't quite see his eyes from behind the grayish tint of his glasses.

"Did I startle you? By the looks of it, I did, didn't I?" He spread both hands on the counter.

How did he get there without us noticing? Was he there the whole time? My first instinct was to bolt, but the way he asked a question then answered it by asking another question made me smile, lifting some of my initial unease. Just the jitters. Maybe.

Penny skipped to the counter. "Mr. Ormand...I hope you remember me." She reached out and they shook hands. "Penny Collins. I was in here the other day telling you about my friend."

"This must be Selena." Ormand smiled. "Marcell Ormand, I'm pleased to meet you."

I took his offered hand in a light grip. His touch was gentle, albeit clammy. Not surprising considering the arctic freeze. "It's nice to meet you."

"I hear from Miss Collins here that you might be in need of a job."

Penny answered before I could inhale. "Yup, she really does."

"If it's still available, sir." I elbowed my overenthusiastic friend.

"Please, call me Ormand." His smile showed a set of uneven front teeth.

"I think my job here is done." Penny spun with a flourish to face me. "I'll text you tonight." She winked and sashayed out of the store.

I stared after my retreating friend. "I'm sorry about that, Ormand."

"Miss Collins is always like that, isn't she?"

"Pretty much." I shrugged. An uncertain pause then, "Uh… about the job…do I need a resume?"

"Not at all. I just need someone to mind the counter in the afternoons, help with inventory, dust the shelves, and arrange the books. You think you're up to it?"

The job seemed easy enough. We agreed on my wage and hours and decided that I could start the next day. Paranoia wouldn't pay for college. Ormand seemed nice enough despite the warning bells.

"Is that all I can do for you? Are you sure you aren't interested in a book? Employees get a twenty percent discount."

A tempting offer. "Do you have books on dreams?"

"Dream interpretation, I see. Fascinating. I have some in the Divination section. Feel free to look around." He pointed at the third row of shelves to the left.

With time to spare before Grams's shift ended, I followed his directions and made my way between the shelves. Rounding a corner, I spotted a lone figure sitting on a cushioned seat by the wall, reading with shoulders squared.

Crap. Dillan.

Everything in me screamed, "Turn and run!" But if I left, I might as well stamp CHICKEN across my forehead. If I stayed, I had no idea what would happen.

He wore a dark, long-sleeved shirt and jeans. I bit my lip, frowning at him. Memories of the ride home from Miller's and what happened afterward had my face roasting despite the cold the store.

My body still remembered what slamming against his chest felt like. And how did he lift me out of the way? I had some weight on me. He didn't have bulging muscles the way Bowen did, but hell, Dillan was strong. And those zingers his touch caused? Might not be static. At least, I thought so. Maybe I should have agreed to Penny researching it.

Dillan balanced a book in his hands with his elbows on the chair's armrests, seeming not to notice my arrival. Just as I started to retreat, my phone dinged. Crap! I'd forgotten I'd removed it from vibrate at the diner. I fished it out.

Kyle: *How's the job-hunting going?*

The book snapped closed. I flinched, almost dropping my phone. Ignoring Kyle's text, I met Dillan's gaze head-on.

"You stalking me?" he asked, his voice full of his usual annoyance.

"Well good afternoon to you, too." My shoulders slumped when he snorted. His stare was like bullets straight to my chest. "I'm just looking for a book."

"Oh, so you mean this isn't the supermarket?" He glanced around with mock wonder. "That explains the lack of canned goods and the abundance of paperbacks."

I pretended to laugh. Stupid jerk. He repaid my efforts to keep cool with an obnoxious, raised eyebrow. I paid no attention to the urge to grab tweezers and pluck until said eyebrow was completely gone.

"And you're laughing because?"

"Oh my gawd! You mean that wasn't a joke? That was you being a jerk?" I crossed my arms and cocked a hip. "Sorry, I didn't catch it sooner."

He smiled at me for the first time since we'd met. I didn't count the magical laugh after asking him about dating Taylor Swift. Loser move, by the way. I panicked, so sue me.

Just when I had him pegged, he did something completely opposite. Gah! And they said girls were complicated. I squirmed at the warmth of his smile. Why was he smiling?

"I like it when you bite back," he said.

A scowl pulled my eyebrows together. "That's just rude. You don't know me."

"I don't think I should get to know you."

The ice in his tone took me by surprise again. A complete one-eighty from his earlier smile. "Excuse me?"

"You're trouble, and I don't do trouble." He opened the book again and continued reading like I'd been dismissed. Well, his highness had another thing coming.

"Hey!" I snapped. "We're not finished here."

Like a lion eyeing its prey, he glanced up at me. My heart somersaulted.

"Well? I'm waiting with bated breath." He managed to sound bored and sexy at the same time.

"W-what…uh…" I tried to gather thoughts that slipped out of my head like paper falling from a binder. I blinked. "Why do you think I'm trouble?"

He suppressed a laugh by bowing his head. As if that helped hide his shaking shoulders.

"What's so funny?"

"You're a people pleaser, aren't you? You're the type that can't stand someone not liking you and showing it." Raising his head, he laughed openly now.

"That's just…" I wanted to take a book from the shelf beside me and throw it at him. "I don't even have a word—"

"Then I suggest you read a little more so you can find the word you're looking for." He hid his chuckle behind a fist.

Anger and defeat tasted bitter in my mouth. I wished I could stop the heat creeping up from my neck to my face. Before I could blow a gasket and ruin books I couldn't afford by throwing them at someone with a concrete head, I turned on my heel and walked stiffly out of the bookstore.

With my phone still in my hand, I quickly replied to Kyle.

Me: *Dillan, 1. Me, 0.*

Kyle: *Huh?*

Me: *TKO.*

Kyle: *Lost me.*

Me: *411 L8r.*

CHAPTER NINE

Dillan

HUNTER INSIDE OUT

After an awkward dinner where his uncle tried and failed to engage him in a conversation, Dillan stretched out on the living room's white couch. ESPN highlights lit up the huge flat-screen in front of him. Out on the road, he had no time for TV; although, he did get score alerts on his phone. He couldn't bring himself to focus on which team won what. His mind kept wondering back to his sparring match with Selena at the bookstore. With what happened at her house—his almost slipup about his identity—he'd vowed to leave her alone. They only shared two subjects together, the first two periods in the morning. It didn't seem that hard to avoid her for the rest of the day.

And then she walked into the one place he thought of as a sanctuary during his travels. He loved bookstores. Everywhere he went, he'd always made sure to visit at least one. The second he heard her voice he contemplated running out the back. Instead, he stood his ground. This invisible force may be connecting them, but he wouldn't allow her to run him out of the one place he could relax. He choked on a laugh, remembering Selena's expression when he called her out. Her face turned such a deep shade of red he thought her head would explode. And he'd wanted to touch her again.

He stared at his hand, opening and closing his fingers. Then he sent his life force to his fingertips until blue sparks flew out. The same energy that created the biting aura Rainer used on him at the airport. Almost immediately, he felt the drain on his system.

As a child, the first thing he'd learned was how to harness his life force. Other cultures called it chi. Being born in the Illumenari allowed someone to connect his or her energy with that of nature's. Technically, they were all still human, but with better upgrades. At least that was how he'd like to think about it. As an Arbiter, he could only rely on his body's energy and the energy he could take in from within a ten-meter radius. Rainer, being Legacy—the second most powerful class—could absorb energy from anything within twenty miles.

He considered the charge touching Selena caused as his energy probably reacting to hers as a human. Illumenari were forbidden to drain humans. Maybe his demotion short-circuited his system somehow, and every time he touched her a reaction happened. She could be a livewire of some sort. It had been known to happen, at least from what he'd read during his training.

This reasoning calmed him. Maybe he didn't have to avoid her. He wanted to test the theory. Touching her again quickened his heartbeat. Staring beyond the large men tackling each other on the screen, he imagined Selena's flushed face. The way her eyebrows came together and the corners of her lips turned down. A light sweat rose on his fingertips. At the farmhouse, he'd only touched her arms when he lifted her away from him. The skin there was so soft. So smooth. He could just imagine how much softer her cheeks were. And her lips…

What the hell was going on?

He rubbed his face hard. Selena Fallon spelled trouble. And something told him no matter how hard he tried, he wouldn't be able to avoid her. The second thing they taught an Illumenari child was to accept the inevitable. Accept that Supernaturals were a part of the world. Accept that there were things they couldn't explain. Embrace the unknown. How could he go against years of training?

"That's more like it," Rainer said from somewhere.

He pushed up and glared at his uncle over the back of the couch. "Just because I'm watching TV doesn't mean you're off the hook. Quit dicking around, and tell me about the case already."

His warden approached. "For weeks, dogs have been disappearing around town."

"Dogs?" That was unexpected, almost as much as Rainer doing something he'd asked.

"It might not even mean anything."

"You wouldn't have mentioned it if it didn't." He pressed mute on the universal remote. "If you think something's up, then I'll look into it."

"I'm not so sure anymore. Letting you run around Newcastle might be a bad idea."

Closing a fist around a pillow, he chucked it at his uncle. "Don't be a tease."

Without blinking, Rainer caught the pillow and hit him with it. The air in his lungs exploded like he'd slammed into a brick wall. Fuck. The Boogeyman was back, and he'd fused his considerable energy with the pillow, actually transforming it into a weapon. One of the reasons why many Illumenari were content to reach Legacy level. That kind of power? The ability to turn anything into a weapon was enough for most. He curled into a tight ball to minimize the pain and muffle the groan. Each inhale burned. He should have known better than to attack Rainer. Even as a joke it was potentially fatal.

When he could speak again, he said, "I really should call Child Protective Services on you. My banishment didn't include summary beating, you know."

His uncle didn't even bat an eyelash.

A couple more pained breaths later, Dillan's lungs worked again. "As much as I like to bum around, let me start tracking." He sat up. No one in the Illumenari could stay idle for long. It was always on to the next mission. He had lived a hard life for far too long to relax now. "I'll even do it in my spare time, after school and homework."

Rainer considered him for the longest time. He kept his mouth shut. He'd already made up his mind. Even if his uncle said no, he'd go out tonight. Besides tracking, he had to find his partner. It worried him that he hadn't heard from Sebastian since arriving in Newcastle. It was unusual for the hellhound to be incommunicado.

The silence between them reached an uncomfortable level. Rainer did it on purpose. Upper hand shit and all that. Dillan stayed still, waiting for his uncle's next move. The first to flinch always lost.

"You sure you can handle this case?" he eventually asked, pulling out his cellphone from his back pocket.

"It's missing dogs, Rainer."

"Alright." He tapped the touchscreen and grinned. "Then I need to introduce you to a couple of people first."

Unsure what his uncle was up to, Dillan leaned forward and rested his forearms on his knees. "This is ridiculous. Why don't you just let me go?"

"Indulge me."

"Why would I do that?"

"You know...just so you don't get killed. Isn't that right, gentlemen?" He spoke the question into the phone.

At the murmurs of agreement, he sat up straight. Two voices jumped out at him. One a deep baritone, the other gruff.

"Seriously? You have them on speaker?" He scratched an eyebrow. "Is this a test? Does the Council know?"

"This one is off the books." Rainer folded his arms over his chest.

"In short, the Council doesn't know."

The gruff voice laughed. "You have quite a handful there, Rainer."

His uncle snorted. "Believe me...I've lost count of how many times I've wanted to stab him in his sleep."

Both men chortled. Dillan bit back the curse at his throat. If this little charade allowed him to actually work, then he'd play along. Not exactly a mission by Illumenari standards, looking for missing dogs, but he'd take what he could get.

"Can we move this along?" he asked, successfully keeping his sarcasm at a minimum.

"Right." Rainer got serious. The phone line went silent. "Gentlemen, it's my pleasure to introduce Dillan Sloan. I believe you have the files I've sent you."

"What files?" He glared.

His uncle kept talking. "He'll be helping with our disappearances."

"What files, Rainer?"

"Good to have you here," said baritone. Dillan assumed he'd meant him. "We'll get the word out that someone's investigating."

He frowned, still shocked his uncle had a dossier on him and was disseminating it to strangers. Were the men he spoke to Illumenari? He felt compelled to test the waters.

"Why the cloak and dagger shit?"

Rainer was about to respond when the owner of the gruff voice beat him to it, "It's better this way, son. We're very proud of the privacy we've achieved here at Newcastle. Let's not put a wrench in it, shall we?"

Okay, maybe not Illumenari, because they would have revealed themselves as such. But they sure knew about them if they were acquainted with Rainer. Weren't they worried he would recognize their voices if they ran into each other in town? Maybe they were confident their paths would never cross. Bottom line was Dillan didn't like the sound of things. But instead of worrying about something he had no proper intel on, he cut his losses. They gave him a bone with this case, and he'd run with it. If a mysterious introduction was the price, he considered himself paid in full.

"Okay," he stood up, "they've met me. Now can I go?"

"Let the boy sniff around, Rainer," continued gruff. "If the dogs keep disappearing, we'll have trouble. I can't keep the ranchers calm any longer. They want to hunt whatever it is down before it goes for cattle or horses...not to mention people."

He was out the door before Rainer could change his mind. The senior citizens could continue their little chat without him. He'd initiated missions on less clearance. He got his directive: find whatever was taking the dogs.

Rolling his head from side to side until vertebrae popped, he stretched his shoulder. The ache had subsided. Even without the aid of healing, his body mended faster than the average human by virtue of his bloodline. But he couldn't risk reinjuring it. To give himself more time to heal, he made his goal for the night locating all of Rainer's wards and determining what exactly they kept out. With a huge grin on his face, he jogged to the lake behind the house then veered left toward the tree line and disappeared into the night.

CHAPTER TEN

Selena

GOT THAT SINKING FEELING

I didn't want to go to school today.

As the warmth of sleep left my body, memories of yesterday came as sour as my morning breath. Mr. Rock-Star-National-Geographic insulting my intelligence ate at me. I hadn't expected to see him at the bookstore. Arguing with him had been irritating. The humiliation of losing said argument unsettled my stomach. It was good I left when I did. Before that afternoon, I'd never come so close to pummeling someone until he bled senseless on the floor.

Then when I got home, I spent most of the night on the Internet finding answers for the electricity zinging through our bodies every time we touched. The closest I got was this study that showed some people more predisposed to generating static. Why would Dillan hate me for that? Okay, maybe he didn't know about the study. I debated whether to risk telling him about it or just avoid him altogether.

Speaking of avoiding someone, my vision of running into Bowen at school today resurfaced. I sat up, wondering if I could skip.

I shook my head. Bad idea.

Grams would never allow it.

One time, I pretended to have a fever to get out of a math quiz. Grams came into my room with a foul-smelling soup and ordered me to finish the whole bowl. I remember it smelled like skunk spray. It inspired a miraculous recovery. Unfortunately, my room stank for a week after that.

Shuddering at the memory, I slapped my cheeks lightly to get the rest of my sleep-haze out of my system before scrambling to the bathroom.

At breakfast and in the car afterward, I focused on the radio. The Morning Show was a part of my daily routine for as long as I could remember. Today, Jeanette Morris interviewed Committee Chair, Betty Hillsgrove, about the Fall Festival preparations and what Newcastle could expect this year.

Bowen and I always went to the festival together, along with Penny and Kyle. He'd been MIA since the afternoon he'd left me at Miller's. I said a silent prayer of thanks for small miracles. But, according to my vision, my luck had run out.

No matter how hard I tried to think of other things, all roads led back to him. Through the years, I'd come to realize that my visions eventually came true. I could stay away from my locker, but eventually, I would forget and end up there anyway, and the vision would play out. Even Grams's excited chatter about the widow, Mrs. Nixon—spotted at the movie theater in the middle of the afternoon with a certain younger gentleman—couldn't keep my mind from what was about to happen. Thankfully, being late for her shift meant my furrowed brow went unnoticed. She gave me a kiss on the cheek and left me at the school's parking lot with only a "Have a nice day."

With apprehension, I stared at Newcastle High's double doors for a good five minutes. I had to face Bowen and make him understand we were over, and I'd moved on. Why Dillan's face chose that moment to pop into my head, I had no freakin' idea.

• • •

Outside American History, I hesitated. Dillan was in my first two classes. What a way to start the day. My heart pumped like I'd just finished a marathon, and my palms practically dripped sweat.

"What're you doing out here?"

"Kyle!" I whirled around, eyes wild. "Jeez, don't sneak up on me like that."

"Ease up on the caffeine in the mornings."

"You know I hate coffee."

"Then something tells me you don't want to go into class," he teased. "Does it have to do with a certain teacher's nephew who's been giving you hell since he set foot into Newcastle?"

His amusement irritated me. "Please, let's not get into that."

"Come on, he's harmless."

I gave him my best withering glare. "Weren't you on the receiving end of a million texts yesterday?"

"My phone's practically bursting. I get it. He's a jerk for insulting you at the bookstore like that. Don't let him get to you."

"Too late for that."

"Oh, this is good! You *are* letting him—" he finished with a grunt when I stuffed my fist into his side.

"I'd say you're right." *His* voice roasted my cheeks beet-red.

Ladies and gentlemen, the thorn on my side, the pebble in my shoe, the bane of my existence had arrived.

"Shut it before I cut you." I poked Kyle on the shoulder, and then turned to glare at Dillan, who stood by the door with a book in one hand and his schoolbag in the other. I narrowed my eyes at him and said, "Don't ruin my morning by being a jerk, please."

"Is that the way you greet people around here?"

"Why you—" I hissed, the rest of my words garbled by the first period bell. If Kyle's arm around my waist hadn't kept me in place, I would have jumped him.

"Oh, stop staring like you plan to go in for the kill," he said to Dillan. "It makes me think you actually *like* each other."

Dillan and I glared at him and denied his accusation simultaneously.

Unfazed, he gave us his most charming grin. "Class is about to start. Mr. Sloan just rounded the corner."

With a non-committal shrug, Dillan walked into the room. I took two more breaths and glanced at Mr. Sloan's smiling face as he walked toward us before I let Kyle nudge me past the door.

Minutes passed, and even in the radiant presence of Mr. Sloan, I couldn't concentrate. Every time I tried to focus, my eyes flicked toward Dillan, who sat a few desks in front of me. Desperate, I resorted to staring at Mr. Sloan, but my anger, confusion, and anxiety clung like a cotton shirt on a muggy day.

My distraction eventually turned into embarrassment when I totally missed the announcement that class was splitting into groups. Mr. Sloan had to remind me twice to pick a number out of the glass bowl he held. I couldn't look at him while I fished out a folded piece of paper.

I hadn't even finished unfolding it when Kyle pulled me to his group. He grabbed a brown-haired boy's paper and exchanged it with mine. "You don't mind, do you, Peter?"

Peter blinked twice.

I smiled in apology.

Since grade school, Kyle and I had been groupmates on anything and everything. Even when we got into a fight, he still insisted I be in his group. When teachers suggested we split up, he always charmed his way into getting them to look the other way. This time around, the group consisted of a blond named Constance and the boy I wanted to throw into a well.

Of all the rotten… I bit the tip of my tongue. *Why couldn't I get a vision of this?*

"Yes, you're in a group with him. Deal." Kyle interrupted my train of thought.

We brought our desks together so we could brainstorm. Dillan's lack of discomfort made my situation worse. He sat there talking with Constance about a part of the instructions he'd missed as if the world only consisted of white rabbits and pink flowers and happy thoughts. It grated on my nerves like squeaky sneakers.

"Selena! Pay attention." My best friend elbowed my arm.

Unfortunately, his dumb move caught Dillan's attention. He watched me with a mocktastic grin. My chest tightened then expanded in panicked breaths. I wanted to flick my pen his way and hope it poked an eye out. But with my luck, the pen would probably just bounce off his inflated ego.

"Is there a problem here?" Mr. Sloan stood right behind his nephew with a charismatic smile on his old-Hollywood-leading-man face. The kind Grams swooned over on movie nights when she got to pick the flick. Always something black and white.

"I have two third graders in my group, Mr. Sloan. Don't worry… I'm a pretty good babysitter." Kyle returned our teacher's smile.

Mr. Sloan gave Dillan an all-knowing glance. Suppressing a chuckle, he moved away to check on the progress of another group. Dillan muttered something about uncles under his breath. It didn't sound respectful at all.

"Ouch!" I rubbed the arm Kyle had pinched. "What was that for?"

"You," he pointed at Dillan, "stop annoying her."

"What'd I do?" His face said shocked while his eyes mocked.

"Don't you dare say anything, Selena." Kyle gave me his famous librarian stare. I shut my mouth and squirmed in silence. Then he turned back to Dillan. "I'm not sure what you have against her, but unlike the rest of the world, who thinks you're charming, I see through your attitude, Mr. I-think-I-know-everything. And before you interrupt me, I'd just like to remind you that you're not the only one being graded here. I don't know about you, but I have an A with my name on it for this project. I don't care if Mr. Sloan is your uncle. Grow a pair, and suck it up! You're stuck with her just as much as she's stuck with you."

Constance clapped. "Nice! Saying all that in one breath. My mom can't do better." Her admiration sparkled from her eyes to her pearly smile.

My cheeks burned. Kyle had never lectured me like a child before because he never had a reason to...*until now.* I scowled at Dillan. He seemed unaffected. It was gonna be a long forty minutes.

By the end of class, our group had agreed to construct a diorama of the Boston Tea Party over the weekend.

"Can we have a sleepover?" Constance gave everyone in the group an expectant look.

"I don't mind," Kyle said. "We can have it at my place."

"Umm...this is a mixed group, Constance," I reminded her. Someone had to be the voice of reason. Plus, the idea of spending the whole weekend with Dillan appealed less than a tetanus shot. "Won't your parents mind?"

"Oh, no. Not at all." Excitement had her bouncing in her seat. "My cousins are coming over this weekend, and I don't really want to share a room."

"What makes you think Kyle has room to spare?" Dillan asked.

Before Constance could think of a reply, Kyle said, "There's room."

"There you go!" She clapped again. "What about you, Dillan? Would Mr. Sloan mind?"

He glanced at his uncle, who'd been erasing the blackboard. "He could care less," he whispered. It seemed only I had heard him, and I didn't know how I felt about it. Dillan Sloan and family drama didn't fit my image of him.

"What?" Constance tilted toward him.

He shrugged. "I said he won't mind."

"It's settled then." Kyle gathered his things.

My jaw dropped. Settled? Didn't I have a say? Apparently, the conversation was over when everyone stood up. Kyle's pointed stare spoke volumes about not changing his mind.

• • •

Head still spinning because of the upcoming American History project weekend from hell, I almost didn't spot the familiar back that walked ahead of me in the hallway before the next period. The project distracted me enough that I moved toward my locker without really thinking. My stomach tumbled. There really wasn't a point in avoiding the inevitable. If we had to settle this then there was no better time than the present.

"Bowen?"

He turned. "Hey, you."

His words flew above my head. The warm pools of black coffee eyes and that carefree smile confused me. Shouldn't he still be pissed?

Faster than lightning, he grabbed my hand. His long fingers wrapped around my shorter ones. He pulled me the last couple of yards to my locker. I yanked my hand back when my brain caught up with what was happening.

"What was that about?" I asked.

He leaned his shoulder on the locker beside mine as usual and stuffed his hands in his pockets. "I just wanted to remember how it felt. We always used to walk to your locker holding hands after class."

"Bowen—"

"The location's different from last year's, but the feeling's the same."

"That's not fair." I punched in my combination and pulled open the door, using it as a shield against having to look at him. "Look, about what happened at Miller's—"

"Did you get home alright?"

"Mr. Sloan gave me a ride." I unzipped my bag, snatched a heavy textbook, and shoved it in with the rest I didn't need for the day.

"With the new guy?"

The book I held remained suspended for a second before I stuffed it into my bag. This was gonna be harder than I had thought. "He was there. It's his uncle's car." I tugged the zipper shut and slammed the door.

Bowen went stilled. His massive hands clenched into tight fists. Good, the anger was back. I could work with that.

"Bowen…" I cleared my throat and sifted through my options. "It's really over."

As if I snapped my fingers, the heat in his eyes dissipated. His face fell, and his shoulders slumped. In the years I'd known him, I'd never seen him less than confident. This destroyed imaged was beyond me. My heart squeezed. Penny's voice echoed in my head, warning me not to be nice.

But before I could over think, I said, "Fine."

The hope that blossomed on his face killed me. "What?"

"Friends." I raised a finger to stop him from saying anything more. "Just friends."

The force of his joy came in the form of a bear hug and booming whoop. I barely had time to process being lifted off the ground. His laugh filled the hallway, startling the few loitering students. I stifled a groan.

• • •

"I think I just made a *huge* mistake." I dropped my head on top of my folded arms on the table. The cafeteria conversation swallowed the rest of my regret. Bowen sat with his teammates. Thank God! I couldn't take any more of him today.

"What did I tell you about being too nice?" Despite her disapproval, Penny rubbed circles between my tight shoulders.

"I don't know what happened. I really did tell him we were over. Now, I just want to disappear." I slumped lower into the cradle of my arms. "Kill me now. End it before I make a bigger fool of myself."

"Nope. You put yourself in this mess, and you have to get yourself out."

My shoulders dropped, my limp arms hung down my sides like spaghetti. "How was I supposed to know Bowen's sad face was my kryptonite?"

"Him cheating on you is a dick move." She closed her eyes for a moment and sighed. "But you have to admit that in the two years you were together, there weren't any sparks. Wait!" She held up a hand just as I opened my mouth. "I think you like his company more than anything else. The sad part is..."

Her lips pursed.

I waited.

She sighed.

"Spit it out, Penny."

"He fell in love with you."

Shocker. "Bowen never said he loved me! He cheated, remember?"

"He was a love sick puppy with nothing but you on his mind. It was sickening to hear him talk about you all the time. Just ask any of his teammates. Don't you think that maybe he cheated because he wanted you to get jealous? The Stop and Pump is like the worst place to hide a make out session. Even if you didn't see him, the news would have eventually gotten back to you. Unfortunately, his plan backfired."

I slapped the table. "Don't put that crap in my head."

"It was you and swimming." A pause. "My point is…the fact that you didn't see how Bowen was with you shows you didn't feel the same way. When he held your hand today, what did you feel?"

I considered it, opening and closing my hand. "Like the old days."

"No giddiness? No butterflies? No blush?"

"I'm a horrible person!" My forehead hit the table.

She patted my arm. "You're not. You just don't love him the way he loves you."

"I shouldn't have let his reaction affect me like that." My voice picked up a notch. "You're right, I'm too nice."

"Something tells me this won't the last time you mess up a relationship. Chalk it up as experience points." She inched closer and wrapped her arms around me. "Now, tell me about this weekend project at Kyle's."

I actually felt tears well up at that.

CHAPTER ELEVEN

Dillan

S'UP

*D*illan embraced the night, letting its shadows hide him. An excited, almost manic smile spread across his face. He reveled in the feeling of doing something useful again—a kind of euphoria that came with the job. After a painful day playing nice at school, focusing on the case was just what he needed. They insulted his intelligence. All of them. He still couldn't believe he had to spend an entire weekend making a crappy diorama. Who still did those anyway? If he were an idiot, he would have questioned Rainer's teaching methods, but the possible after effects of said line of questioning might not be conducive to maintaining his health.

Focused on finding canine tracks or signs of a struggle, he drew power from the darkness. The Illumenari didn't know about this aspect of his abilities. He'd discovered it when he spent a week in solitary for punching his cousin too hard during a sparring session. He'd dislocated Devin's jaw. Enveloped by inky blackness, with nothing else distracting him, he enhanced his senses by combining his life force with that of the shadows surrounding him. His pupils dilated, covering all the blue, allowing him to see farther. His nostrils flared, taking in the minute scents in the air beyond the pines, moss, and dirt around him. He grimaced at the pungent smell of raccoon. A side effect of his enhanced senses. Smell them all, or smell nothing. The coolest thing the darkness did for him was crawl onto his body, camouflaging him from prying eyes. That was why he preferred night missions and insisted he track after dinner. He'd looked over the list of addresses of families who'd reported their dog or dogs missing his uncle had given him to establish a grid. So far, no patterns emerged.

The forest behind the townhouse grew thick, forcing him to pick the cleanest path. He slipped between trees, studying the bark and branches for breaks and scratches. His feet barely touched the pine-needle-littered ground. He was finally in his element. No school. No annoying uncles. And no copper-haired girls or ghosts from his past.

Stopping by a rock formation, he checked the cuff on his wrist. His father forbade him to release his weapon during the banishment. If he were to read the fine print, no missions allowed. At all. If the case stayed as simple as Rainer made it out to be, he wouldn't have to defend himself. His grandfather—a member of the Council and the one responsible for his sentence—would flip if he found out.

Maybe he was dealing with some wild animal killing off the dogs. But no carcasses had been reported. That troubled him. Surely there had to be bodies or at least some sign that someone was stealing the dogs. According to Rainer, the authorities knew nothing. Humans, even the smart ones, tended to be sloppy. The dog-nappers would eventually leave some kind of trace. A Supernatural on the other hand...his grin turned wicked. He hoped it was a Supernatural.

The familiar excitement of the chase spread in his chest. It filled him with renewed determination. So he pushed off the ground and continued his trek through the dense forest.

He hadn't been out long when a shadow bounded a yard parallel from where he ran. He flicked his gaze toward the movement and nodded once. It responded with a warbled growl. He picked up the pace. An owl glided overhead. Predators hunted. *He* hunted tonight.

A breeze brought the scent of damp wood mixed with Rainer's aftershave. Faint. A few days old. Crouching down, he picked up a fistful of dirt. He brought it up to his nose. When he'd asked his uncle if he did his own investigation, he said he'd been too busy. The lying bastard. He'd been out here, too. He let the soil fall through his fingers.

A symbol had been carved into the tree's trunk he knelt closest to. He traced the ward, a triangle with a line down the middle. The Triumvirate. Protection against evil intent. One of the most powerful wards in the Illumenari arsenal. Rainer's energy jumped out and stung his hand. Even in ward form, his uncle's dislike for him showed. Chuckling, he pushed up, dusted his hands off before he ran full tilt in the direction his partner disappeared to. The dumb mutt surely took his lovely time.

At a circular clearing, he stopped. The Triumvirate marked the edge of Rainer's perimeter. The air beyond this point no longer bit into his skin. Letting relief from the discomfort wash over him, he took in his surroundings. Hands relaxed at his sides, he used his fingertips to feel out the energy around him. No immediate threats jumped out. The nocturnal predators stalked their prey, nothing more. He tilted his head back and glanced up at the sky. He still had several hours left before dawn.

He dusted off his knowledge of Arbiter protocols. Been a while. Council sanctioned or not, he had to follow procedure. If a Supernatural was responsible for the disappearance, he may need to mediate, see if a solution could be reached between the parties involved. In this case, the accused may have to be sent to a desensitizing facility. There specialists would help the Supernatural reintegrate into society. If the Supernatural was too far gone, then he might have to terminate it. As much as possible, as an Arbiter, he had to avoid the latter. If the culprit was human, he would leave the rest to the authorities. Human crimes were beyond Illumenari jurisdiction.

You have that look again. The shadow's rumbling voice pinged in Dillan's head. He rested yards away, bending into the darkness. Only his red eyes were visible. English folklore told of black dogs with red eyes. To see one meant death.

"Where've you been? You left before I did." He shoved his hands into his back pockets. He kept his expression as blank as possible, but since Sebastian could read his mind, the concern he buried would soon be exposed. "How'd I get here before you?"

Cheerful as ever, I see.

"Have you seen where we are?"

You prefer Siberia?

"The Yeti population always needs thinning." He kicked a pebble. "Stop dodging. And quit messing around. Where the hell were you?"

I had matters to attend to.

"If necessary, I will leash you if you don't tell me where you've been."

The shadow shifted slightly.

"Figures you'd come when we finally have something to do."

Missed me?

"You should have checked in, Sebastian. You know better."

The shadow harrumphed—his version of a human snort. *I am here now.*

Dillan grimaced. "Who saved your ass from rotting in that cave?"

You never let me forget.

"Seriously," he widened his stance, "where've you been?"

I must commend your uncle for his courage to defy the will of the Council by letting you investigate this case.

"Again with the dodge? I get enough of that crap from Rainer."

A chuckle, which sounded more like little barks, reached Dillan's ears. *Surely you would rather start working than continue grilling me about what I have been doing.*

He shrugged, a grin tugging at his lips. "Don't tell Rainer, but I'm just happy I have something to do in this place."

Not so bad here if you ask me.

"Not asking."

Sebastian panted, his tongue lolling out of his mouth.

"I still think the Council members don't know their faces from their asses by sending me here."

Leaves rustled. *You would rather talk about that?*

He hesitated. Sebastian knew him too well. "You hate it as much as I do."

You should have waited.

"It's done." He ran my fingers through his windblown hair. "I can't take it back."

The case then?

"According to Rainer, dogs are disappearing. He believes it's no coincidence. We need to find evidence of the animals or whoever took them."

If they are still alive.

The grim reality settled on his shoulders. "I don't think they are."

Something about Newcastle unsettles me.

"You feel it, too?" He cracked his knuckles. "I thought it was just me, but there's a strange static in the air. If I had my usual powers, I'd get to the bottom of what's going on here. The demotion is the only reason Rainer can hide stuff from me."

I feel nothing threatening. But you are right about it being strange. The sooner we get the lay of the land, the faster we find out what it means.

Sebastian had a point, so he nodded. "You take the south side, moving west, and I'll take the north, moving east."

Then double back here?

He allowed another grin. "You still owe me an explanation."

When did I ever ask you to explain the things you do no matter how idiotic they are?

"There is that."

CHAPTER TWELVE

Selena

WHAT DREAMS MAY COME

*M*ilky blindness. Too much light. Squinting, I brought a hand up for shade. Dim outlines took shape. I blinked a few times to focus. A white haze coated my eyes. I rubbed them with the heels of my hands. The light receded.

The clearing stretched out, bathed in silvery moonlight. A flat sea of ivory grass. Gray-green pines swayed. The air had teeth, latching onto the skin exposed by my white dress.

Rustling to my right put me on guard. I didn't know what to expect in the middle of a clearing in God knew where without a way to defend myself.

An all-black German Shepherd bigger than a cow padded out of a group of pines. The moonlight gave its midnight fur shining highlights that rippled with every move it made. Piercing, ruby eyes studied me intensely. Its breath came out in puffs of smoky mist.

Another rustling. This time to my left. A figure in a black-as-onyx cloak glided to the side of the large animal. The cloak's heavy cowl covered its face. But something told me I wouldn't want to see it anyway.

I suddenly wanted to be somewhere else. A haunted house. A graveyard. A dark forest. It felt like invisible shackles held my legs in place. I couldn't turn around. Couldn't run.

The figure raised its arm and pointed at me with a boney index finger.

I tried to understand what the action meant. It didn't make sense. What could the cloaked figure want?

Someone called my name. A faint sound, but I definitely heard it.

I searched for the voice in vain. No matter where I looked only pine trees, the dog, and the cloaked figure were visible. I ran my fingers through the wild halo of my hair.

I looked down.

A dark stain slowly spread from the center of my chest outward. I touched it. My fingers came away black and sticky. Pain rippled underneath my skin like a timer going off. My knees gave way. Sobs wracked my body. I crumpled to the ground. Being stabbed by a thousand needles couldn't come close to the pain rushing through me. It seemed to fill every cell. The wetness on my chest spilled out, pooling on the silver grass. It didn't take me long to figure out what it was.

Blood.

Every beat of my heart hastened the gush out of the wound. I raised both hands and applied pressure like I'd been taught in First Aid. The blood kept seeping between my trembling fingers. I tried to call out for help, but my throat closed. Each breath came in hicks and hitches as more blood spurted out. My lungs refused to cooperate, then like a popped balloon, they deflated.

In my panic, I only had one thought: *I didn't want to die.*

My fingers went numb. My hands and arms became deadweights.

My legs didn't feel part of the whole anymore. The ground drank every drop of life that left me.

The cloaked figure laughed. At me. At my struggle to stay alive. At my life slowly slipping away.

The black dog looked on, unmoving. Its red eyes glittered.

My heart sputtered. Its beats grew fainter.

The moonlight intensified, swallowing the black dog and the cloaked figure in milky whiteness.

Death didn't come as darkness but as blinding light.

• • •

I opened my eyes and sucked in the largest breath I'd ever pulled into my lungs. Exhaling in one slow compression, I gradually became aware of my surroundings. Bright sunlight blanketed every surface of my room. The warmth of my body between the sheets pushed the rest of my grogginess away.

Lying on my back, I stared up at the star stickers on the ceiling. Gramps had put them up for me years ago so I wouldn't be afraid of the dark. I had peeled off the stickers from their pad and handed them up to him while he stood on a step ladder creating a small cluster of constellations around my ceiling light.

"If you're ever afraid," he said at the time, "look up and the starry sky will greet you."

Before I could take comfort from the faded stars, the vision hit me. I died.

Icy dread sent shivers from my toes up to my head and back down again. My teeth chattered as I gripped fistfuls of my bed sheet. My visions had never been about anything so intense before.

Maybe it had been a regular nightmare and not a vision of my future? Really, where would I encounter a dog *that* big? And the cloaked figure…I'd seen Halloween costumes more creative.

Someday I'd die, sure, but not now. Not so soon. Only a nightmare. An ordinary nightmare that common, everyday people had. Nothing to worry about. Nothing.

I sat up. My hair tumbled over my forehead. I swiped the strands away only to have them bounce back.

"Selena! We'll be late, dearie." Grams called from downstairs.

Her cheery voice slapped me out of my gloom.

"Coming!" I pulled the light comforter off my legs.

• • •

A hot shower later, I came into the kitchen in jeans and a shirt with RECYCLE in bold letters across my chest. Streams of golden sunlight made the kitchen look comfortable and lived in. The smell of pancakes and ham helped banish any thoughts of black dogs and hooded figures.

The radio on the counter blared the Morning Show on KASL. The weather report was winding down when I dropped my school bag on the floor, pulled out a chair, and sat down. The day would be sunny without a chance of rain, beautifully clear—all blue skies and puffy white clouds.

No milky moonlight. No silvery clearing. No images of death.

I watched my grandmother—a small woman with a big heart—fill a plate with a stack of pancakes, slices of ham, and a mound of scrambled eggs. She had her white hair in a simple twist. When she turned around, her freshly glossed lips held a sweet smile that warmed me from the inside out. Grams moved like a storm in the kitchen, but instead of devastation in her wake, she left great food and shiny countertops.

"Morning." She beamed at me.

"Are we feeding a party of five?" I stared wide-eyed at the plate Grams set in front of me. Eat-a-horse hungry portions stared back.

"Nothing like a good breakfast to get the day started," she said as she glanced over her shoulder while squeezing juice from a couple of oranges. "You have a big weekend ahead of you."

"Ugh! Don't remind me. Where's Gramps?"

"In the garage." Grams placed a glass filled with OJ beside my plate. "He's getting his tools ready. It's another long day at Hay Creek Ranch."

"Their tractors acting up again?"

"I think it's just a check-up this time. Now, eat up, child! We'll be out of here in two shakes of a chicken's bottom."

I smiled, my right cheek bulging with pancakes.

About halfway through my breakfast, Gramps's towering height and massive frame filled the kitchen. His salt-and-pepper hair looked wind-blown, like he'd been running out in the prairie all day. I liked the laugh lines on his face best.

His gruff voice boomed. "Good morning, little lady!"

"Not so little anymore, hon." Grams playfully tapped his bicep.

"Well. She'll always be little to me!"

Having had enough of breakfast, I teased Gramps while I brought my plate and glass to the sink, "Everyone's little compared to you."

"Right about that." He kissed Grams on the cheek before staring at my half-eaten plate. "Not hungry?"

"Just late." I shrugged, trying not to connect my lack of appetite to the knots in my stomach.

"Did I happen to see the trashcans open this morning?" Grams raised an eyebrow at him. "I don't want those raccoons coming by again."

Like a delinquent caught shoplifting, he winced and quickly made his way out the door. "Well, ladies, I'm off to Hay Creek. You two take care now."

"You're one to talk! Don't come home with cuts or bruises."

Grams put her hands on her hips, a kitchen towel hanging from her apron.

"Yes, ma'am." He winked at her.

Suppressing a giggle, I slung my bag over my shoulder. Normal. Absolutely nothing but normal. I beamed, grounding myself in the moment. My grandparents' love acted as my safety net, catching me when I needed it most. I had nothing to worry about.

• • •

Unfortunately, my glow from basking in my grandparents' love didn't last long. Kyle kept bugging me about why I flinched every time he touched me. I'd been so keyed up that it felt like I had extra shots of Redbull in my veins. Surviving a day of school didn't used to be so hard. Thank god Bowen left me alone. Who knew granting him the friendship card would keep him away? I should have thought of it sooner.

As if my day couldn't get any worse, somehow Dillan's death stares grew more intense as the day wore on. I wasn't happy about the weekend, but I'd accepted it. If Dillan wanted to act immature by staring at me like I threatened his very existence, then fine. I had other things to worry about.

After making a pit stop at the arts and craft store for supplies, I sat in the back of Kyle's Prius trying to ignore the guy sitting shotgun. But Dillan's tapping kept drawing my attention. His fingers played a rhythm on the door panel.

"I think we should use tea to stain the water," Constance said, bouncing in her seat. "What do you guys think?"

"I like it." Kyle peered at her through the rearview mirror. "It ties in to the Boston Tea Party."

"What about glitter? It always makes a project pop," she added.

"I don't know. I think we should stick to traditional colors,"

Kyle said.

Again, my gaze landed on the one person I tried so hard to ignore. My fingers started their own drumbeat on the door panel at my side. A metallic object peeking out of his sweater sleeve caught my eye. A watch?

He stretched, and I realized it was a thin, leather cuff with a silver cross that had its four points connected by a circle. An opaque gem I didn't recognize sat on the intersection of the cross. Being interested in anything concerning Mr. Rock-Star-National-Geographic stamped down the temptation to ask why he chose to wear such a curious accessory.

"I can't believe you listen to Newcastle Afternoon," Constance teased, referring to the radio.

Kyle tsked. "Is there a law banning sixteen-year-olds from listening to a radio show?"

"I think what she means is: can we listen to something else?" Dillan turned to Kyle.

"Hey, I like listening to the news." He let go of the steering wheel for a second and shrugged.

Constance giggled. "That makes it even worse, Kyle. You sound like my Grandpa."

"What do you think?"

It took me a second to notice that Kyle spoke to me. "I'm sort of immune to Newcastle Afternoon since it's on at the diner after school, so I'm not the best person to ask."

"Two against one and an abstained. For the sake of maintaining peace, I fold." He stretched out his leg, eased out his phone from his jeans pocket, and handed it to Dillan after unlocking the screen.

Dillan scanned through the playlist. "The Beegees, Chicago, Duran Duran, *Air Supply*?"

"Who are they?" Constance leaned forward and looked over Dillan's shoulder. "Never heard of them. Are they new?"

"Total opposite." Dillan's voice said he grimaced. "You're worse than Rainer."

Kyle went on the defensive, "I happen to think Air Supply has some of the most poignant ballads."

"They're *old* bands?" Constance sounded like a six-year-old who just found out reindeers couldn't fly.

"Classics!" Kyle said indignantly.

"Yes, *classics*." Dillan's tone dripped sarcasm. "Oh, and I just found Abba. If I find Karen Carpenter in here, I will officially rule you pathetic."

"Don't you have any Taylor Swift songs?" Constance leaned back on her seat.

"I'm not a big fan." Kyle's expression turned blank.

Constance looked aghast. "Why not? She's probably the most successful country singer out there right now! I'm a proud Swifty."

He scratched his head.

Feeling bad for my friend, I bailed him out. "Constance, Kyle doesn't really keep up with all that stuff."

"Really?" She pouted. "That's…well, weird."

"It's not like I don't have a TV or the Internet." He rubbed his cheek. "I'm just picky with the information I put into my brain."

"Like what kind of information?" She perked up a little.

"National Geographic." He turned to Dillan for a moment. "I just saw that special your parents did on Plato and Atlantis. Brilliant work!"

"Your parents were on TV?" she asked.

Dillan stiffened at Constance's excitement. Seeing my chance for some payback, I wiggled in my seat.

"Didn't you know, Constance?" I waited for the blonde to look at me. "We're sitting with National Geographic *royalty*."

"What!" She beamed. "Can I have your autograph?"

Bingo!

Dillan twisted around and glared at me. His steely-blue eyes promised revenge. For the first time, I didn't know whether to find him scary or funny.

"My parents are archeologists," he said, then faced forward again. "They dig up crap, and people pay them for it. That's their thing, not mine."

"What's it like to have parents on TV?" Adoration oozed from the girl beside me.

"Annoying."

"Really?"

In another stroke of mischief, I said, "You said you're a Swifty right, Constance?"

She nodded at me.

"Selena," Dillan growled.

My smile stretched across my face. "Did you know she wrote a song about Dillan?"

"You *dated* Taylor Swift?" She squealed.

From my vantage point, I saw Dillan shake his head, wiping one side of it with his hand. The one with the leather cuff.

"Leave him alone, Constance," Kyle said like a parent scolding a child.

"But—"

"I want to listen to music." He glanced at Dillan.

"Since your playlist is for geriatrics, I'm taking over," he said. I heard his relief. Huh. His highness could get embarrassed like the rest of us mortals. He handed the phone back to Kyle and took out his own.

"Wait a sec." Kyle signaled for silence.

We all listened to the DJ announce that six more dogs had gone missing. He quickly followed up the announcement with the advice that families should keep a close watch on their beloved pooches. That a predator was on the loose. When the news ended, Kyle let Dillan sync his phone with the car's radio via Bluetooth. In seconds, the tribal-sounding drum sequence and chanting of Bastille's Pompeii filled the car. A corner of my eyebrow twitched. I never pegged him for someone who liked alternative rock, and a British band at that. I only recognized the song because it was the current theme of a show Penny was obsessed with. Huh. Just learned something new about him.

"Why are you interested in missing dogs?" Constance looked out the window.

"I'm more concerned about the predator," Kyle said neutrally.

The news brought to mind a conversation I had with Penny over text last night. "You know? Mr. Collins lost one of his herd dogs."

The car jerked to a stop. "What?"

Constance and I called out Kyle's name at the same time. Dillan's hands spread over the dashboard, irritation on his face when he turned to Kyle for an explanation.

"Sorry, I didn't notice the light change." He pointed at the stoplight ahead of us.

My stomach gave a nauseated lurch. "Concentrate! You know I can get carsick."

"What did you say about Penny?" He made a right, headed out of town when the light turned green.

"Not Penny." I settled back into my seat. "Her dad."

"How'd it happen?"

"Not sure. According to Penny, they usually don't wander off, so it's kind of weird, but when he rounded up the dogs, one just wasn't there." I noticed Dillan fidget with his cuff.

Kyle followed up with: "Did they look for the dog?"

"Of course they did." My phone vibrated in my pocket. I whipped it out.

Penny: *Good luck this weekend!*

Me: *:(*

I sent up a silent prayer for patience.

Chapter Thirteen

Dillan

Hide and Seek Isn't for Kids

Kyle turned onto a dirt road with a sign that read Valley View Acreage as Charlie Boy by the Lumineers played. The soothing guitar plucking wasn't enough to mask the sting of passing through wards. Dillan sat up and scanned the area. Tall pines and cedars lined both sides of the path, creating a green tunnel. His gaze darted to the car's driver. He tried to recall the guy's last name but drew a blank. If Selena and Constance weren't in the car, questions could be asked. Because of the witnesses, he resorted to a different tactic. He cued up Rainer's number on his phone and sent him a message.

Dillan: *What's Kyle's last name again?*

Boogeyman: *Hilliard. Why?*

He didn't respond, caught in trying to recall if there was a Hilliard name listed in the Illumenari database. Without access to his laptop, he couldn't log on to the restricted server. The wards were there. Powerful ones, too. They raised the hairs at the back of his neck.

Sunlight streamed through the green in soft orange rays. Making a point to explore the property and get to the bottom of why wards surrounded Valley View Acreage, he returned his thoughts to the missing dogs. Six more gone according to the news on the radio. He'd been up all night and still found no sign of the animals. Sebastian said they'd expand their search when he got back. The weekend being a complete waste of his tracking time bugged him. He'd rather be out there, helping his partner.

At the end of the tunnel, a stone monster came into view. It had huge pillars for bones and arched windows for eyes. Ivy crawled up most of the outer walls as if nature wanted to take back its territory from the invader.

Kyle eased into the driveway and parked his car outside a detached garage. Dillan slid out of his seat and headed straight for the trunk. He eyed Selena, who hovered next to him, as he and Kyle unloaded the bags and supplies. He half expected her to grab some of the bags out of his hands. She could try, but his grip would never let her. His mother taught him better. A few more seconds passed before she shrugged and closed the trunk. He caught a glimpse of her electric blue nail polish. Nice. She really got him with the National Geographic royalty and Taylor Swift dig. He half-respected her for it.

Grinning to himself, he followed the rest of their group toward a fire-engine-red door. It stretched wider than any two of them standing shoulder-to-shoulder. It reminded him of a bull's-eye in the middle of an all-white background.

"Constance," Kyle called, and she flitted toward him, "see that gold knocker? Will you reach in and ring the bell?"

"Why can't we just walk in?" She eyed the lion suspiciously.

"It's you're house right?"

"Because it's more fun this way." He winked at her.

Dillan rolled his eyes as Constance mastered her fear of being bitten by an inanimate object by shaking her hand before reaching in. Just as she pressed the button, Kyle poked her on the side, eliciting a girlish squeal. As a pleasant chorus of chimes echoed inside the house, Constance playfully slapped Kyle in the arm for scaring her.

In less than a minute, a woman in a navy-blue velvet dress with long, strawberry blond hair opened the door. She greeted them with a glamorous smile. Her cobalt eyes stood out from pale skin. He froze, almost dropping the bags, recognizing her immediately. Sometimes some Illumenari families used mercenaries as bodyguards. Her presence meant Kyle was an Illumenari son. He reached out with his energy toward his classmate. It was faint, but the telltale life force was there. Holy shit! Why did it take him so long to figure it out? Damn the restrictions to his powers and senses.

Beside him, Selena suppressed a chuckle. His teeth snapped when he closed his mouth. He hadn't noticed it had opened until then. She was taking things out of context. God only knew what she was thinking.

"Hello, everyone! Welcome to Valley View Acreage," the mercenary said in a singsong voice. "Kyle! Did you use the ring-the-doorbell-inside-the-lion-head bit again?"

"Everyone except Selena," Kyle said, not acknowledging the question.

"Gee, thanks."

He winked at her. "You know what I mean."

She smiled.

Kyle cleared his throat and tried again. "I'd like to introduce Riona Hearth, one of my legal guardians."

Legal guardian? He studied Kyle covertly. Well, that was convenient. Calling one of the most fearsome mercenaries a legal guardian? Many in the Illumenari knew of Riona's prowess, especially in harnessing nature's energy. Some referred to it as magic. Technically, it was called Channeling.

If Riona was in Valley View that would mean…

"Hey, Riona." Selena gave her a rueful smile accompanied by a tiny wave. Like she was braced for something. He didn't have to wait long to find out what it was.

Riona cupped her face with both hands. "How are you, my sweet?"

She wrinkled her nose. "The freckles are still there."

"No, no, no, no! They're a feature that brings out the sea in your eyes! You're beautiful." She kissed the tops of Selena's cheekbones. When she finally let the clearly embarrassed girl go, she said, "And who is this handsome young man?"

The slight widening of her eyes told him she already knew. But they were playing Lets Blend In after all. "Dillan Sloan, ma'am."

The boom of a deep voice from behind the door startled everyone but him. He'd been waiting for the other half of the fearsome duo to show up since recognizing her.

"What are you doing? Let Kyle's guests in, woman!" A massive arm snaked around Riona's waist and lifted her away. She laughed.

A bear of a man in his late thirties stood in her place. He wore his black hair clean-cut and short. He'd broken his nose enough times to give it a crook. A silver hoop glinted on his ear. He looked like a linebacker in an expensive suit. Garret Hearth. If the Illumenari had trading cards, Garret would be a collector's item. Dillan did his best to hide his awe by keeping his expression passive.

"I apologize for my wife," he said. "She gets excited when we have guests over. Come in, come in." Garret stepped aside and let them through.

A circular table dominated the foyer with a centerpiece made up of flowers. The combination stung his still sensitive—by human standards—sense of smell. At times like these, his training literally hurt. He flicked his gaze up. A circular skylight sent afternoon sun streaming into the space. Ahead of them, a grand staircase curled upward.

"Garret," Kyle said, "this is Dillan and Constance."

Like a fan meeting an idol for the first time, he quickly lowered the bags he carried and reached out his hand a little too enthusiastically. Then he stammered out, "Dillan Sloan, sir."

"Sloan?" A glint entered Garret's gaze.

"Rainer Sloan's nephew," Kyle clarified. As if he didn't already know.

"Ah! I see the resemblance. You have a strong grip, boy. Perfect for holding a sword, aye?"

He got the distinct feeling they were all bullshitting each other, especially now that he recognized Garret's voice as the second speaker during Rainer's "anonymous" introductions. He pulled his hand away and kept his annoyance in check. Despite the grin and wink, the bastard's joke was loaded. He might as well have introduced himself as a mercenary instead of Kyle's other legal guardian. In front of two humans, no less.

"I must apologize for my husband," Riona said sympathetically. "Besides cars, he's enamored with medieval weaponry."

"I'm not that bad, am I?" Garret grumbled.

Riona smiled sweetly at him.

The situation got stranger when the big guy wrapped Selena in a bear hug. This kind of affection confused him. The familiarity seemed off. He got familial closeness…and something else. It frustrated him not to know. He really had to corner Kyle somewhere and get him to explain this charade. He calculated how long the god-awful task of beginning the diorama would take. The sooner they finished for the night, the faster he could get to the bottom of what they were hiding in Valley View.

CHAPTER FOURTEEN

Selena

TAKING UP CROSS COUNTRY RUNNING

Kyle borrowed a whiteboard on wheels and multicolored markers from Garret's office and mapped out a plan of attack for the group and outlined a schedule. He deftly assigned tasks like a general commanding his troops. According to his calculations, and this was in his words, if we all stuck to his timetable, we'd be finished with the foundation before dinner, and done with the whole thing by late afternoon the next day. OCD much? From experience, only someone with a death wish messed with Kyle and his schedules.

Unfortunately, that evening, I must have had one, because everything went according to plan until the ticking time bomb that was me and Dillan in a room together exploded. This was one of those times I wished I had a vision. Not that I could avoid the argument, but it would have been nice to be prepared.

"We should use Popsicle sticks for the dock," I said, heat already entering my tone.

"Toothpicks are easier to manipulate," Dillan bit back. The sight of him glaring at me as if in challenge put my panties in a bunch.

"Popsicle sticks will make the dock look more authentic."

"No way. Their width would look too big for the clay people we'll add."

"You're just against this because I suggested it." My voice climbed a notch. I threw down a Popsicle stick. It bounced once then rattled.

"Don't flatter yourself." He leaned forward and placed his hands on the table. "Your freckles are clouding your judgment."

Blood rose up my head so fast I thought it would explode. I was shaking now, my vision tunneling toward my dark-haired target.

"Guys, guys," Kyle held up his hands, "where's this going?"

Constance continued mixing Plaster of Paris in a tub as she said, "Calm down, you two."

"I'm calm!" Dillan and I yelled in unison. If I went by the heat on my cheeks, my face was as red as his.

"Constance, come with me behind the whiteboard, please." Kyle grabbed her arm. "This is about to get ugly."

"Can't you just do what I say?" I narrowed my gaze at Dillan.

He smirked. "What happened to compromise? You know the meaning of that word, don't you? Or should I get a dictionary?"

I let out a keening growl and threw the tub of glue at him without thinking twice about it. The jerk had it coming. Too bad he sidestepped just in time. The tub sailed past his head, bouncing off the whiteboard and twirling to a stop on the floor. It scattered gooey white glop everywhere. I scowled in disappointment. The *thud* made Kyle and Constance peek out from either side of the board like prairie dogs.

After what seemed like the stare down of the century, Dillan left the living room through the way we'd come in. Not wanting to follow him, I escaped through the terrace doors, slamming them behind me.

My fingers clenched into fists while my lips disappeared into a tight line. Dillan brought out the worst in me. And I hated him for it. The jerk. I didn't deserve his attitude problem. I ran until the stone banister stopped me. I spread my hands on the rough stone and breathed in. Standing on tiptoe, I let the crisp night air clear my head of the urge to commit murder and plead temporary insanity.

Nothing bothered me the way Dillan did. I couldn't stand being emotional over something so petty. But right then, being petty was all I felt. I'd thrown glue at his head like a second grader. I closed my eyes and groaned.

"I can ask him to leave if you want."

The statement startled me more than the voice that said it. I didn't turn around. Kyle came forward until he reached the terrace's long, thick banister. He placed his hands on the rough stone. Our pinkies touched. Such a small gesture, but it brought a crashing wave of comfort. I hardly remembered my life before Kyle became one of my best friends. He helped hold my world together. Just like he did tonight.

"I don't know what's wrong with me." I kneaded my forehead. "It's stupid."

"It's called puberty."

"This is different. I'm not being hormonal."

"Of course not." He looked up at the sky already filled with stars.

I wanted to smack him, but I let my hands fall to my sides instead. I'd had too many violent tendencies for one day. I distracted myself by staring at my ratty sneakers. I needed to buy new ones soon.

"You like him."

My heart leapt into my throat and beat there for several seconds before it tumbled into my belly. Suddenly, I couldn't breathe. Kyle sounded like he believed what he'd said. Me? Like Dillan? The idea was certifiable.

"You didn't just say that." I stared at him, shocked.

"Oh, c'mon. Just admit it." He reached for my shoulder.

"Don't touch me!" I backed away slowly. "You can't just come out here and suggest I like that overbearingly arrogant guy and think I'd agree with you." My voice turned shrill. "That jerk's done nothing but annoy the hell out of me." My breathing came in and out hard. Without hesitation, and before I did something I'd surely regret, I turned sharply and walked away.

"Hey! Where are you going?" he asked, concern in his voice, but I didn't turn around.

"I'm taking the path to the river. And this time, I want to be alone." About halfway down the stone steps connecting the terrace to the garden, I whirled around and pointed a finger at him. "Kyle Hilliard, if you follow me, I swear to God, I'm taking this violent streak Dillan brings out in me and punching you in the face with it."

"You're overreacting!"

With quick, determined strides, I left the sweet scents of the garden and walked into the freshness of the forest, using the gravel path on the east side. The white stones caught the slivers of moonlight. It looked like a winding albino snake through the trees. It would lead to a bridge over a small river. I knew the path by heart and could walk it blindfolded.

An owl screeched in the distance, making me want to screech, too. I settled for a mumbled curse. I didn't think it was possible, but I was even angrier now than before we got to Valley View. Stupid Kyle! I kicked at the gravel, sending pebbles flying.

A soft *thump* came from my right.

I froze and waited, breathing heavily.

Another *thump*.

This would be the point where the audience would scream at me to run back to the house. But, like in horror movies, the heroine — i.e. me — moved to investigate. My foot nudged a stick as thick as a bat. I picked it up and copied a batter's pose, waiting for the pitch. I imagined the ball as Dillan's head and took a swing. Homerun!

Another soft *thump* came from behind a cedar. I swallowed. My breathing sped up. The cold air chilled my lungs.

Away from the glowing path, the shadows grew darker. I squinted as I neared the tree. Rustling noises followed another *thump*. I sidestepped and raised the stick above my head, yelling "Yah." The creature gave a startled squeak and dropped the rock it held.

A moonbeam punched through the thick canopy, revealing a raccoon. Its face, hidden behind a black burglar mask of fur, looked startled, hands in the air. It sniffed nervously. Its bushy tail—ringed black and white—twitched.

"Oh, hey there, little guy." I still had the stick ready for a swing. The raccoon eyed me, and I glanced up. "Sorry, I didn't mean to startle you." I threw the stick away.

It watched me for another second before scampering back to the cedar tree.

"Enjoy your dinner." I returned to the path.

My stomach grumbled. If I hadn't let my annoyance with Dillan get out of control, I wouldn't have stormed out before dinner. Now, I was really hungry.

"Jerk."

A soft breeze rustled the pines and cedars. I didn't need a mirror to see what thinking of Dillan did to my face. The blush horrified me. I so didn't like him.

I picked up several pebbles and stepped onto the bridge. The running water reflected the stars and the moon. Soft waves dispersed the light, turning the river into liquid mercury. The woods stretch on along the bank until darkness swallowed the rest of the faint moonlight.

My heart sank like the small pebbles I flicked into the river.

Soon, I threw pebbles further and further away, using all my strength. When the last pebble joined the others at the bottom of the river, I tried pacing away my pent up irritation. Muttering under my breath about not liking him, I brought myself to a boil that resulted in me kicking the railing of the bridge as hard as I could. The brilliant idea shot pain up from my toes to my thigh.

"Shit, shitty, shit, shit!"

The night air suddenly grew colder. I momentarily forgot the pain in my leg and regretted not wearing something warmer than a T-shirt and jeans.

A twig snapped.

"I thought I told you not to follow me." I stared at the dark outline of someone standing in the shadows at the other side of the bridge.

"Are you that hungry for a black eye, Kyle?" Not really meaning what I'd said, I took a step toward him. "Look, I'm not angry anymore, but we need to talk about this. You have to explain why you think I like—"

A groan escaped the shadow, stopping me mid-step.

"Kyle?" I craned my neck, trying to get a better look. "Kyle, you hurt?"

The groan came again, ending in a gurgle.

Another twig snapped.

I stayed in place. Something about the way the shadow moved didn't seem right. A lurch or a drag instead of a regular step forward.

"Kyle?" A shiver crawled up my spine like a long centipede with a hundred freezing feet.

The shadow groaned and stretched out its arms, lumbering out of the gloom in stages. Torn and cracked nails came at me first, attached to bone-thin fingers with pruned skin. The flesh had a sickly gray tint. What used to be a man wore a tattered blue suit. Only clumps of hair remained, and half its face sagged. The other half shredded. Several teeth were missing inside a gapping mouth. A maggot wriggled at the side of its lips. My eyes reached its feet—only one foot rested in a black leather shoe. The other a stump. The smell of dirt and rotted flesh overwhelmed the freshness of the pines. My hands shook. Where was that stick? A scream slowly built its way up my throat, but I swallowed it down. I couldn't risk drawing Kyle or anyone else to me.

My vision from last night came to mind. Was this it?

The corpse limped closer, groaning as if in terrible pain. Before I could fully make the connection between my vision and the situation, I noticed four more shadows behind the creature edged toward the bridge.

If I had to die tonight, then I'd do it protecting my friends. In a sudden burst of adrenaline, I turned around and ran. The harsh thumping, rattling, and scraping spurred me forward. My breath came out in misty puffs. The cold air froze my lungs.

Drawing them away from the house, I strayed from the path and weaved through the forest. Wild grunts and pained groans trailed behind me. I could almost feel the rancid breath of the corpses on my neck.

Don't look back! Don't look back!

I regretted not listening to the voice in my head. The five creatures ate up ground like cross-country runners with hands stretched out, groping at the space in front of them. Not paying attention to where I was going, I tripped and fell hard on my left knee. Pain sent dark spots popping in front of my eyes. I cried out and rolled onto my back. My self-preservation instincts kicked in, and I used my hands to push myself up into a sitting position, sending renewed pain into my joints.

My new position gave me a perfect view of the corpses—all five of them. The group stood a few feet away, watching and groaning, hands at their sides. Jaw tight, I nudged myself backward.

For every pull I made, the corpses took a step forward, as if invisible strings attached them to me. I backed away until the rough bark of a tree scraped against my arms. The corpses stopped and tilted their heads again.

Beside the man in the suit, a woman with long hair and a maggot-eaten, pale pink dress swayed. She didn't have cheeks anymore. To the left of the man, a teenage boy groaned, all baby-faced and fresh, until my eyes wandered to the gaping hole of his stomach—collapsed from rotting inside out.

My own stomach clenched. Dry heaves shook my body. Bitterness coated my tongue.

The three in front obscured a couple more behind them. The man's face had melted off at some point, leaving a slimy skull. The old woman had flaking skin and stumps for arms. Her hips bent at an odd angle. Like her spine had snapped.

They all watched me with cloudy eyes.

The head corpse, the one in the tattered, blue suit, groaned and raised its arms again.

Dropping my hands to my sides, I patted around for a weapon. There had to be one somewhere. Just as I lost hope, my hand closed around the roughness of another stick. Not as thick as the one I'd thrown away, but it would have to do.

"Yes!" I pointed it at the corpses. "Oh, it's on!"

CHAPTER FIFTEEN

Dillan

LIGHTNING IN THE BRAIN

*D*illan stepped out of the house to get some air before he forgot what his mother taught him and actually punched a girl. What was it about Selena that affected him so much? But not five minutes into his cooling off break, a powerful electric jolt sliced down his body. To say it hurt would have been funny. Because Jesus H. Christ it hurt. He only started thinking straight again when his feet carried him toward the woods.

That invisible line he'd first felt at the bookstore pulled taut. It reeled him in. His heart banged in his chest. He had no idea where the overwhelming sense of worry and urgency came from. All he knew was he had to be somewhere fast.

He blinked to adjust his sight to the evening gloom. The trees obscured much of the moonlight, better for him rush through the forest unscathed. Unthinking, his thumb rubbed against the charm on his leather cuff. He channeled his energy toward the stone, and the charm grew into a sword. Blue sparks from its blade showered the forest floor, setting it ablaze before snuffing out.

The telltale groans of the undead reached his ears. The wretched, rotting smell only served to confirm his suspicions. A feminine yell spurred him faster.

At a stand of pines, he caught sight of Selena swinging a stick at five corpses. She yelled something incoherent at them. They groaned back. He almost stopped to stare if it weren't for the prickly balls of panic bouncing around in his chest. What could be going on in that brain of hers to challenge a group of undead with a stick?

The corpse in a shredded, blue suit hobbled forward, its hands groping for Selena. Reaching her side, Dillan brought his sword down in a clean slash across the undead's chest. When the corpse turned into black goo, he reevaluated what they faced. The undead didn't turn into goo. They merely fell to the ground until their heads were chopped off. His gut twisted at the alternative. He'd rather face the undead.

As if they noticed their companion melt, the other corpses paused. He moved to dispatch the rest when Selena's questions distracted him.

"Dillan? What the hell are you doing here?" She stood at his side like some warrior ready for battle. "Is that a sword?"

Everything she asked entered one ear and out the other. "I should ask you the same thing. What the hell are you doing facing down these puppets?" There, he'd named them, and yet the knot in his gut didn't ease. Shit!

"I'm keeping these things from reaching the house," she answered simply.

Shaking his head, he elbowed her aside and buried his sword into the man with a skull for a face. Unfortunately, his move to save Selena from having to fight angered her more. She brought her stick down over the head of the corpse in the pink dress. The action brought the puppet into a frothing frenzy, grabbing at her with boney fingers.

"You need to cut them to dispose of them," he said through his teeth. He whirled in a tight circle and severed the head of the corpse Selena annoyed with her stick.

"You can't just expect me to sit here and let you take over. I can fight," she insisted.

"Are you hearing me?" He slammed an elbow into the puppet with a hollowed out stomach. It stumbled backwards with a gurgling grunt. "You need to *cut* them."

Blowing a curl away from her face, Selena reached out for him. "Then lend me your sword."

"Not gonna happen. Now shut up, and let me take care of this." But before he could move, Selena was on him. She made a grab for his sword. Shocked like a deer in headlights, he let go of its hilt. She closed her hands around the handle and swung it at the corpse that used to be an old woman attempting to bite him. The blade hit the puppet clumsily. The only reason it cut the puppet's arm off was because Dillan kept it sharp with his life force. The weapon was an extension of his body, and it pissed him off to have someone else touching it. Especially if that someone was Selena.

Using his annoyance to regain his wits, he yanked the weapon away from her grasp. "Give me that before you hurt yourself." He scanned the forest. "I count four down. Weren't there—"

"Behind you!"

Without looking, he closed both hands on the hilt and stabbed backwards. A sickening squelch followed the blade entering the puppet he'd elbowed earlier. Shifting, he faced the surprised corpse. In seconds, it joined its friends as goo on the forest floor. He flicked the rest of the residue off before pin-wheeling the blade with a twist of his wrist forward twice then backward once. His weapon returned to its inert state at his cuff. Using his dark enhanced senses, he scanned the area. Nothing else moved. The regular sounds of the night resumed. What happened to the wards of the property? How did the puppets get in?

"What the hell were those things?" Selena asked, breathing ragged.

"Puppets." He grimaced.

"Is that a new word for zombies?"

He rolled his eyes at that. Humans and their fixation with Hollywood monsters. "There's no such thing as zombies." He stopped himself from saying anything more. Then reality hit him. Shit. A human encountered puppets. How the hell was he going to explain this? So much for keeping his identity a secret. He mentally counted the number of rules he'd broken by telling her about the puppets until Selena staggered against the nearest tree and used its trunk for support.

"What's wrong?" The invisible string pulled him toward her.

She gave him a wobbly grin. Sweat coated her forehead. "I fell and hit my knee."

"And you still fought against them?" He didn't know how to feel about that. A part of him found it stupidly reckless. Another part found it incredibly sexy. He closed his eyes and banished the combination of Selena and sexy from his mind. "You know how many kinds of stupid that is?"

"Didn't you hear me?" She struggled to stay upright. "I was trying to keep them from getting to the house."

The same hammering in his chest returned. Stupid, stupid girl, and yet he couldn't stop himself from taking her into his arms. The familiar electric shock zoomed through him. Her answering gasp told him she felt it, too. The second their bodies touched, a loud popping followed, like the shorting of a circuit. Apparently, if they held onto each other, they blew a fuse. Good to know.

"What are you?" he whispered into her strawberry-scented curls. Damn. He breathed in deeply. He could inhale that smell all night. His body reacted to it like cats to catnip.

She reached behind him until her hands anchored onto his shoulders. "I read on the Internet that some people are predisposed to generating more static shock than others."

He chuckled at that, all the panic and worry draining out of him. "I hate the fucking internet."

Touching her felt unreal. She wasn't human. She couldn't be after tonight. He knew this in his gut. He'd known since the first time they'd met. Maybe he wasn't breaking any rules after all by telling her about the puppets. But why were they in Valley View?

He held her closer, unable to let go.

CHAPTER SIXTEEN

Selena

NO MATTER HOW HEAVY, FEELINGS STILL FLOAT

The adrenaline from all the action still had my blood ringing in my ears, my heart racing. I couldn't stop looking at the ooze stains on the ground. Questions flew through my brain too fast to focus on one, but I pushed them aside for now. I had to concentrate.

I couldn't wrap my mind around being in Dillan's arms. The crisp, clean scent of soap filled my senses. Considering the rotting corpse smell still in the air, inhaling eau du Dillan was a welcome change. My face fit in the hollow of his neck and collarbone. It was an all access pass to the yummy. I couldn't help myself. I closed my eyes and breathed in.

When my brain decided to work properly again, the warmth spreading through me turned icy. Dillan Sloan. Me. Hugging? No vision could have predicted it. Murder, maybe. But hugging? I must have hit my head and woken up in an alternate universe, one where Dillan was actually a nice guy.

I felt his erratic heartbeat against my chest as he crushed me to him. The urge to push away became overwhelming, no matter how good being in his arms felt. I needed to get away. Not far. Just enough to make sense of what just happened.

I tried taking a step back. "Dillan—"

"No," he said, his voice muffled by my hair.

Maybe I misheard him. "Huh?"

His arms tightened around me. I sighed at his body heat against mine. It felt like a blanket on a rainy day—comforting and safe. Nothing like the arrogant Dillan I knew.

"No." A hint of pleading crept into his tone. "Not yet. Don't move yet."

Some part of me wished I could erase what I'd just heard. But another part of me—the crazy part—was really happy for some reason. His stance tense and muscles rigid.

"It's okay." I pressed my cheek into the hollow I fit into. "Everything's okay now."

How'd I go from ready to die to comforting the guy who helped save everyone else? Shouldn't I be the one freaking out here? I knew, when those things came at me, I would do everything possible to keep them from the house. A small voice inside my head I'd never heard before told me to fight. And fight I did. Then I grabbed Dillan's sword and actually cut one of them. I actually got to hold a freakin' badass sword, and it felt oh so right. In what universe did that happen? Not in mine. And yet…

I pushed aside my confusion. Maybe I was in shock. It seemed I wasn't dying today, so I had time to figure stuff out. Dillan buried his face into my hair and inhaled. His arms loosened their death grip, and his tense muscles eased. He let go of me in stages. First, he lifted his head. Then he took a small step back until his hands on my shoulders were our only physical connection. From the way he looked at me, his eyes seemed to memorize each line, plane, and angle of my face. The moonlight made his blue eyes shine. I shivered. I had no idea what to make of his intensity.

"What?" His brow wrinkled.

"Just…" I wanted to ask him why he looked at me that way, but it wasn't a safe topic. "Those things…I can't wrap my head around what happened." And then some.

He let go of my shoulders, leaving me cold. "You're in shock. It's not every day you're defending yourself against puppets. It's a rush."

The hardening of his face irritated me. "You sound like you know more than you're telling me."

His gaze fell. "I don't get what they're doing here."

"Oh, yeah? What do you think they were after?"

Dillan performed a dramatic shrug. "I honestly don't know."

My stomach curdled. "Do you think they wanted to eat us?"

The corners of his lips twitched. "No, that's the undead. Puppets don't eat anything because they're already D-E-A-D. Weren't you listening?"

"Of course I was!"

"There's a difference between hearing and *understanding*."

I wanted to stomp my foot in frustration. Only my iffy balance and throbbing knee stopped the impulse. This Dillan split personality thing gave me a headache. One second he wouldn't let me go, like his life depended on me being there for him, and now he went back to being Mr. Rock Star National Geographic. Arguing with him… when was I going to learn it was useless? I was a masochist, because I kept coming back for more. To prove I'd been listening…

"What's the difference—" I cut myself off. Asking meant I believed in what he'd said, or what had happened.

His gaze returned to the black slime. "Puppets are usually under the control of someone called a Maestro."

"A what?"

"A dark channeler," he said like I should know this stuff. "The technical term is Conjurer."

Shock over how normal he sounded hit me. "You actually believe what you're saying, don't you?"

"After being attacked, I'd think you'd be the believer."

"We're not talking about denial here. Even *I* know what I saw. It's just my brain's having a hard time accepting it." A lie. A part of my brain—a deep part I never thought I had—understood. That voice that told me to fight. Dillan asked me what I was. At first I thought he might know about my visions. Now I wasn't too sure. "Your cuff turns into a sword. If that isn't something out of *Lord of the Rings*, I don't know what is."

"Doubt Tolkien had swords like mine in his books. Come on. We should head back. They're probably worried by now."

He didn't have to clarify who "they" were. The thought of Kyle, Riona, or Garret wondering where I'd disappeared to, and the possibility of them looking for me, worried me.

"You don't think there are more of those things out here, do you?" My stomach tumbled. I didn't want Valley View to turn into a bad version of *The Walking Dead*. "We have to warn everyone."

"No!" He whirled back so fast I almost fell.

"What do you mean *no*?"

"I mean," his hands clenched into tight fists, "there aren't any more. They'd have attacked by now. Plus, they won't believe you."

My brow puckered. He had a point, but still, I trusted Kyle. "They'll believe me. All I have to do is say I—"

The sudden interest in his expression stopped me from completing the sentence. Shit! I almost told him I had visions. This guy I hardly knew and who lived to torture me almost found out about the freak in me. Over my dead...my eyes returned to the black goo. I swallowed. Too soon.

"Finish what you were about to say." He stepped closer, eyes never leaving mine, watching my every move.

"You're probably right," I said. Now that the adrenaline was wearing off, the fear of how stupid I'd been, thinking I could fight the puppets, was slowly sinking in. "Even *I* don't believe me. But we should at least warn them about *something*."

The predatory look in his eyes disappeared when he mulled over my words. "We can say feral dogs chased you. That's why you hurt your knee. I was taking a walk, saw you, and helped scare them off."

"I'm pretty dense sometimes, but even *I* know that's not gonna fly."

"Any better ideas?" That obnoxious eyebrow lifted.

"Fine. We'll go with that." I pointed at him. "You better not suck at lying."

"You don't know me well enough."

He was right. The part of me that conveniently forgot how mean he could be actually wanted to get to know him better. This was probably the crazy part, because no sane girl should want to get to know Dillan Sloan better. It had DANGER written all over it.

"Can you walk?" He hovered close.

"Of course I—"

He swept me into his arms, carrying me like we were newlyweds about to cross the threshold. I yelped at the renewed electric charge sprinting beneath my skin. I'd never been so embarrassed in my life. That included watching Grams and Gramps sing an off key duet at the Spring Fling.

"Put me down!"

"Stop squirming, or I'll knock you out."

Insulted, I said, "You wouldn't."

He grinned like the devil. "If it means I can carry you in peace, then *I will*. Bad enough that you're the human socket."

"I so am not. Maybe you're the one who's been electrocuting me this whole time."

"That's not the issue right now. All I'm saying is it helps sell the lie better if you're unconscious. So if you don't shut up…"

He didn't have to finish for me to know what he'd meant. I crossed my arms and glared. "I hate you."

"You're welcome."

Thank God it didn't take us long to run into a charging Garret. His suit jacket was gone, along with his silk tie, and he had his sleeves rolled up to his elbows. His hulking figure was difficult to ignore even in the purple darkness of the forest.

Dillan—without consulting me, BTW—decided not to use the path. I groaned, too humiliated by being carried like a princess. Now that Garret saw us, I wanted to shrink away. Never to be seen or heard from again. They'd put my picture in milk boxes. That kind of disappearing act.

"We were just about to look for you." He sounded like a general reprimanding a lower-ranking officer. But before Dillan could explain, Garret interrupted him. "Selena! Are you hurt?" When I didn't answer fast enough, he hurled the question at my knight in not-so-shining armor. "Is she hurt?"

The utter menace in Garret's expression made him look like a man who knew people who specialized in making annoyances disappear, no questions asked. I almost volunteered Dillan.

Speaking of guys I wanted to disappear, he said, "She's fine."

"If she's fine, why are you carrying her?" Garret had his hands on his hips.

"I fell and hit my knee a little. That's why Dillan's carrying me," I finally said, sucking up what was left of my pride.

"Do you need a doctor?" Garret's words still came out as barks mixed with worry.

"I think I just need some ice and a good night's sleep." I flicked my gaze at Dillan. "You can put me down now."

He glared at Garret a second longer before he glanced down

at me, his grip tightened. "What changed from me finding you and now? Did your knee miraculously heal or something?"

"I think I'll take it from here." Garret reached out.

In a dizzying whirl, I found myself exchanged from one set of arms to another. I wanted to scream, but when my head rested on Garret's shoulder, the last of my adrenaline buzz faded. A strange, warm sensation seeped into me. Suddenly, I was sleepy. Like I didn't want to think about what had happened between me, the puppets, and Dillan—not specifically in that order.

I wrinkled my nose at Garret's expensive, woodsy cologne, and longed for Dillan's soapy, clean scent. A pang of unexpected loneliness hit me. Irrationally, an urge to reach out for him and crawl back into his arms came over me. Just an argument ago, murdering him in his sleep seemed possible. Now, I melted into a whimpering heap. This wasn't me.

"That's right, sweet, rest. We'll get you inside," Garret whispered.

I was vaguely aware of his words. A new wave of warmth caused my eyelids to droop, as if forcing me to sleep.

"And you!" He snapped his chin toward Dillan. "You have some explaining to do."

The last thing I saw was Dillan stuffing his hands into his pockets. "Can't wait."

Chapter Seventeen

Dillan

Under Arrested Development

After dinner, Garret led the way to Kyle's study. Dillan trailed behind, putting all his ducks in a row. If he wasn't sure about Valley View before, the way Garret infused energy into Selena to knock her out blew away any and all doubt. The puppets roaming their property didn't inspire confidence in their security. The mercenaries should have known. Then a chill went down his spine. Maybe they did know and didn't do anything about it. Garret sure did reach them fast enough when the fighting was over. He shook his head against concocting conspiracy theories. Too early in the game for those.

Once he had pieced enough of the puzzle together, he got a clearer view of what was going on. If he chose to leave Valley View to confront his uncle about it, no one could stop him. But he couldn't ignore what happened. Kyle and those who protected him deserved a debriefing of some sort. Illumenari code of ethics above ego—now and forever. T-shirts should be made.

Hands in his pockets, Dillan studied Garret. He snorted. Mercenaries.

"Whose side of the family are you from?" he asked when they turned into a long hallway.

Garret grinned at him from over his shoulder. "Kyle's grandfather."

He nodded. Made sense. Kids born from a union between an Illumenari and a human usually produced human children, too. Except if the Illumenari was male. Sometimes the humans knew what their spouses did for a living while others didn't. It was like being in the CIA. Only essential personnel were read in. "When did your life force manifest?"

The mercenary shrugged. "Pretty early."

Dillan winced in sympathy. The earlier the manifestation, the sooner the training began. And for mercenaries, it was particularly grueling. He didn't know if the organization made the training intentionally brutal to thin out the herd or discourage them from ever using their powers. So few survived the process. And those who did never gained much respect within the community. They were always seen as a level below an Arbiter even if some of them, like Garret and Riona, had reached Legacy status where their powers were concerned. "I'm sorry."

He wondered if Selena was mercenary born. It explained the thunderbolts of energy. Maybe she didn't know about her powers, and every time she touched Dillan, a spark happened—her latent life force reacting to his. It also gave credence to how she was able to snatch his sword away from him. Only those with Illumenari blood could touch Illumenari weapons.

They reached a large, black door at the end of the empty hallway. The bare walls were odd. Usually, portraits were hung or some kind of art, even light fixtures at least. Keeping the hallway bare dared those new to the house to explore what was behind the door at the end. Kyle might as well have an arrow that pointed to his lair. Dumbass.

Garret knocked once then opened the door. He moved out of the way pretty fast considering his size. Dillan reminded himself not to underestimate the man. He kept his expression passive when he sauntered into the room and stopped at the center of an expensive rug.

Kyle sat behind a desk that was too large for his frame. He no longer sported the boy-next-door attitude. His eyes were an icy gray, tipping toward glacial. They watched his every move. The lines on guy's face looked too harsh, even in the soft light. Like he'd aged ten years since dinner. He reminded Dillan of Rainer. Well, maybe a little less bloodthirsty.

The study seemed too dark from the wood on the floor and the furniture. If he had to work in a place like this, he'd be depressed within a week. His gaze landed on the confirmation of his earlier suspicions. At a far wall was a large, framed family tree. Every family in the Illumenari had one. His family's held a place of honor at their ancestral manor, and it tracked the Sloan line from the very first Sloan, who was part of the ten families that created the Illumenari. The one in Rainer's study was of his late wife's family. His eyebrows rose. From the looks of Kyle's family tree, his line was one of the oldest, too. Not a first family, but pretty close.

"Leave us," Kyle said.

Garret grunted. "Are you sure that's wise?"

He settled a level stare Dillan's way. "Are you planning on stabbing me any time soon?"

"Call off your guard dog, Hilliard." He tilted his chin at Garret. "We need to talk."

Behind his smile hid something cruel when he returned his attention to the mercenary. "I can handle him."

"Call if you need me." Garret stabbed a pointed glare at Dillan before he left the room.

He shrugged off the mercenary's machismo. He may admire the man's talents, but even he had limits. "Does Selena know about you?"

"Sit." Kyle indicated one of the chairs across from him.

"I'm not a dog, you asshat. Why don't I recognize the Hilliard name?" Dillan moved to the family tree and traced its branches with his eyes. Many of the names were crossed out, much like his own family tree.

"My family left before I was born," he said like an aside. "I make it a point not to talk to anyone in the Council if I don't have to."

"I'm president of the club."

"Don't. It makes me itch to think we have something in common."

"That explains the mercenaries."

"Garret is my grandfather's bastard. Riona is born of a line that died out before she turned ten." He tapped his chin. "You're smarter than I thought."

"I have my moments." Dillan took a seat, crossing his legs. "You didn't answer my question."

Kyle leaned back and tented his fingers. "She doesn't know. And it's going to stay that way."

"What is she?"

"Excuse me?"

"Don't pretend you didn't hear me." Dillan folded his arms over his chest. "She's not human."

A knot formed on Kyle's brow. "Leave it alone, Sloan."

"Is she a mercenary?"

"I said *leave* it."

Kyle should have left out the silent threat. Now he had to push. It was his prerogative. "What's an Illumenari son like you doing with a couple of mercenaries hanging around a town in the middle of nowhere? What? Is Newcastle the destination for wayward Illumenari now?"

As if he brushed off Dillan's questions, Kyle reached for the iPad beside him. "It says here you've been banished by the Council for failing to fulfill your duty."

Dillan froze. The hairs along his arms stood on end.

Kyle slid his finger across the touch screen. "Because of your failure, you've been demoted. The first one in our history. Interesting."

Ignoring the bait, he forced his muscles to relax. He called on his breathing exercises, even if all he wanted was to reach across the table and slam the iPad into Kyle's face.

"The wards along your perimeter suck," he challenged. "You should look into that."

That got his attention. He set aside the iPad, his sharp eyes returned to match Dillan's insubordinate stare. "Garret's checking them now. What happened?"

"Five reanimated corpses made it through your wards."

"Undead?"

"No. Puppets. They turned to ooze when I cut through them."

Kyle's lips pursed. "Which means they returned to their graves."

"At least you know your stuff." He leaned forward, resting his forearms on his knees. "I don't have time to give you a lesson in Necromancy 101."

"I can forgive you for teasing Selena, but I don't appreciate you mocking my intelligence."

"You should show this side of yourself more. It's fuckin' adorable."

"Rainer warned me you had a mouth. Could you be any more childish?"

He hadn't seen childish yet, but Dillan stayed on track. After tonight, the sleepy town of Newcastle stopped being boring. "Best I can tell? We might have a Maestro in the area."

"First the missing dogs, now this." Kyle closed his eyes and leaned his head back. He looked more like himself again. At least, the self he chose to show the public. "What can you tell me about what you've found so far? I assume you've started your investigation?"

Dillan debated how much to tell him. He decided to leave Sebastian out of it. "You should assume the dogs are dead."

He opened his eyes and straightened in his seat. "Tracks?"

"Nothing yet." Because he hadn't actually seen any carcasses yet. But he'd rather die than admit that to the asshole sitting across from him.

"The ground's been pretty hard. And considering the grass on the prairies, tracks would be hard to find."

"I didn't say I didn't find any." He sat up. "I'm going back to my search after this godforsaken weekend is over."

"Dioramas too juvenile for you?"

"If we're done here…" He stood up.

"Correct me if I'm wrong, but why would the fastest rising Illumenari son fail his duty?"

The wood creaked when his hand closed around the back of the chair. He met Kyle's mocking stare and flipped him off before walking out.

• • •

Not five minutes after closing his eyes, something straddled Dillan's waist. His hands grabbed soft skin, forcing him to open his eyes. Wavy hair rained down around his head as a pale face hovered above him. He stared into her sightless eyes. She frowned. He breathed in the cinnamon scent of her.

"You failed me," she whispered.

She was right. He said her name in response. He ran his hands down her arms and closed them around her tiny wrists. Without asking for permission, he lifted her limp hands to his neck.

"Go on." He swallowed, sliding his hands to her waist. "Do it."

Understanding softened her expression. She nodded before her cold fingers circled his neck. She didn't need any encouragement from him. The pressure pinched his throat closed. She squeezed harder. His lungs burned, struggling for air. His heart hammered inside his chest as he grew lightheaded. Soon, his survival instincts kicked in, but he fought against throwing her off the bed.

When his eyes rolled back into his head, he gasped awake and sat up. He let his sight adjust before he scanned the room they'd given him at Valley View. Nothing. He reached for the bedside lamp. Yellow light pushed away the dark. Still nothing. He fought against breathing too hard too fast. His throat hurt when he swallowed.

Adrenaline-laced blood pushed him off the bed. He dropped to the floor and counted out fifty push-ups. Then he jumped to his feet and manifested his weapon. He lunged and slashed at the air, repeating several other maneuvers against invisible targets. He needed to anchor himself to the present. Shit. That dream was too real. He pulled out of a lunge and stood straight. Sweat rolled down his back by the time he returned the sword to its alternate form. Reaching behind him, he pulled off his shirt and tossed it aside.

The invisible tugging forced him out of his room without a second thought. He roamed the halls of Valley View, not really sure where he was going. His legs led him somewhere, and like at the forest, he let them take him where they will. He shoved fingers through his sweat-damp hair. When he finally realized where he'd stopped, he thumped his forehead against the wall. A sad laugh escaped his throat. An hour of roaming and where'd he end up? At *her* damn door. How'd he even know where she slept?

The tugging continued. He pushed off the wall and opened her door. The last person that left her didn't think to lock it. What kind of a household did Kyle run? They were sloppy.

Disappointed at the crappy security, he poked his head in, and his eyes focused on the sleeping mound at the center of the bed. In seconds, he was closing the door behind him.

The floor creaked when he took a step forward. *Dammit!* He froze, holding his breath when Selena murmured. She shifted. He swallowed his heart back down and waited until her breathing turned rhythmic before daring to move again.

He picked his way to her bedside, avoiding any more creaking floorboards. Maybe the lack of air to his head after his near strangling dulled his common sense. Shit. He slowly realized when it came to this copper-curled girl, he had no common sense. He should have been in bed. But no. Instead, he found himself standing like an idiot beside her bed. Shirtless.

Dillan never thought of himself as a creeper until this moment. And yet, he couldn't help himself. His gaze traveled to her leg. It was the only part besides her head not covered by the comforter. Someone had pushed up the pant leg of her pajama bottoms. Her white skin stood out in the darkness. His tongue stuck to the roof of his mouth. The icepack had fallen off her knee, exposing the beginnings of an ugly bruise.

The invisible force spurred him onward, rubbing the charm on his wrist. The blue sparks of his sword lit up the room. Small flames of his energy danced on top of Selena's comforter without burning the fabric. Mesmerized by her sleeping face, he closed both hands around the hilt and positioned the tip of the blade over her body.

CHAPTER EIGHTEEN

Selena

IT'S A MIRACLE—OR NOT

*M*orning light made my eyelids warm and heavy. I didn't want to open them for the rest of the day, but the chirping birds outside said "Wake up! Wake up!" The smell of peonies filled the deep breath I exhaled into a yawn. I stretched sleepy arms, coaxing them awake instead of giving in to the temptation of rolling over and sleeping some more. My skin tingled when deliciously soft fabric rubbed against my body.

Several lazy blinks later, I remembered the project and the sleepover. I groaned into a pillow. Did I have to wake up? Did I have to face another day involving his highness, National Geographic? I couldn't take another minute of him. And that electric hug? Wow. My skin tingled just thinking about it. And he kept asking what I was like I wasn't human or something. Definitely weird. Then he gets all cold and serious on me before he becomes all hot and sexy again carrying me back to the manor. He confused the hell out of me.

My gaze landed on the nightstand. The clock had its short hand on the nine and its long hand just before the twelve. A melted ice pack lay beside it. The fog of sleep lifted. I pulled away the covers and rolled out of bed without thinking. The instant my weight settled on both legs, I looked down.

No pain.

I tugged at the pant leg of my pajama bottoms. The swelling and bruising I vaguely remembered Riona treating last night wasn't there anymore. I experimentally shifted all my weight to my supposedly injured leg. Still no pain. It didn't make sense. I touched the ice pack, sliding it to the edge of the dresser. Sure, an ice pack could ease swelling, but a bruised knee healing overnight? Not possible. Or was it?

· · ·

After getting dressed, walking down the hallway to the grand staircase without a limp became a surreal experience. Just like being chased by corpses—or whatever Dillan had called them. I half-expected the pain to come back when I least expected. It forced me to hold onto the railing just in case. Tumbling and breaking my neck wasn't allowed.

The clink of utensils hitting plates and pleasant conversation stopped me just outside the archway entrance of the dining room. I stared at my jeans. I was sure what happened last night did happen. The pain had been real.

"Is there something the matter, Selena?" My head whipped up, and Riona's eyebrows rose.

All previous conversation and eating stopped.

I straightened so fast I momentarily lost my balance.

Everyone sat—plates in front of them—with different expressions on their faces. Riona looked curious. Garret, who sat at the other end of the table in a dove gray suit, glanced at me once then went back to reading his morning paper. Kyle looked panicked for a second before putting on his usual calm. Dillan looked disinterested, while Constance got up and rushed to my side.

"I heard you fell last night. Does the knee still hurt?" she asked with genuine sympathy. "Do you need help getting to the table?"

I stared at Constance, unsure of what Dillan told them about last night. Deciding to play it cool, I said, "Actually, it doesn't hurt anymore. The swelling's gone. That was some ice pack you gave me, Riona."

Kyle exchanged an odd glance with Riona before going back to eating his stack of pancakes. Riona's beautiful face showed concern, but she said nothing. She pushed back from the table and walked over on dancer's feet.

"I'm glad you're feeling better, sweet." She held my face between her hands and kissed my cheekbones.

I endured her kisses and wondered why no one seemed concerned over my sudden recovery.

Riona led me to a buffet at one side of the dining room. It was filled with platters of pancakes, bacon, several cuts of cheese, toast, an assortment of cereal, sausages, eggs, and the usual breakfast beverages: orange juice, milk, coffee, and tea. The amount of food on that table could feed all the customers at Maggie's at full capacity and still have leftovers. She went overboard. Usually—having only me and Penny over—she'd let us make our own breakfast.

"Come, Constance, let's let Selena get her breakfast." She pulled the smiling girl back to where she sat beside Kyle.

Confused, I surveyed the room.

Everyone resumed eating their breakfast like normal, regular people. But after what happened last night, the normal didn't seem...well, normal. The scene reminded me of an obscure movie Kyle took me to a couple years ago about a girl that discovered the people in her hometown had been changed by aliens into mindless puppets. There was this part where the girl was telling her family at breakfast about the aliens. She didn't know they had been changed, too. They turned on her, trying to kill her with forks and butter knives.

I grabbed a plate from the stack at the beginning of the buffet when my fears of being attacked went away. Once I picked out scrambled eggs and bacon, I carried my meal over to the dining room table. The only seat available was next to Dillan.

A table that could sit twelve comfortably only had six chairs. And—except for Garret—we were all seated near the head. Of all the freakin' luck. Eating on the floor seemed like the better choice, but I doubted Riona would let me. I stifled the urge to move the chair closer to Garret's end and sat down beside Mr. Rock-Star-National-Geographic.

"Feeling better?"

I flinched at his question. The temperature in the room went up a few more degrees. My body remembered how his arms felt wrapped around me. I sneaked a peek at his hand—holding his mug of coffee firmly—and my back tingled. My body turned traitor against my head. For some reason, I wanted to feel the electricity again.

"I'm fine," I answered before stuffing my mouth with eggs to avoid saying anything else. It led to swallowing wrong and a coughing fit.

Dillan, with a neutral expression, handed me his glass of OJ.

I took the glass and gulped down the pulpy juice, causing more coughs.

"Easy." He patted my back. Tiny zings coincided with each one. I guess, be careful what you wish for, huh?

Everyone watched us in silence at first. Then, like a bomb about to blow, a mass retreat followed. Kyle stood up, muttering something about getting the living room ready. Constance took a last sip of her hot chocolate before running after him. Riona commented about going into the garden, and Garret chuckled his way out, folded newspaper tucked under his arm.

"What just happened?" I covered my mouth, smothering the last of my coughs.

"Way to clear a room." Dillan whistled. "Slow down. Don't make me have to use the Heimlich on you."

I wanted to tell him what he could do with his Heimlich. The smugness in his voice brought back the reasons why I hated him. But, by some miracle, I let the steam in me die down in favor of a more diplomatic approach.

"Why did they all leave?" I asked.

"Hell if I know. Just finish your breakfast." He shrugged—a slight movement of his shoulders. "I'll stay with you until you do. Chew this time." He winked.

Normally, I would have been flustered by that devastating wink. However, the confusion provided far more discomfort. I had to know I wasn't crazy. "Last night really happened…right?"

"If by 'last night' you mean your overdramatic exit from the living room after throwing a tub of glue at my head, then yes. It did happen." He stabbed a piece of sausage hard. The fork tines clicked when they reached porcelain.

I moved chunks of egg around. He wasn't going to let that go. I wanted to reply, but guilt choked it back. Fortunately for me, he was chatty this morning.

"If you mean the time after that when you were chased by five reanimated corpses, hurt your knee, and were saved by a dashing, sword-wielding guy, then yeah, it did happen, too." He grinned before he took a bite of the sausage he'd skewered.

"*Excuse me?*" I dropped my fork with a clang. "If I recall, I was holding my own out there."

"*Eat your damn breakfast.* We have a diorama to finish."

Picking up my fork, I said, "You're just pissed because I had to hold you afterward."

His cheeks flushed. Score one for me then.

• • •

We separated once the diorama was completed. Just a report to put together tomorrow and we were all done. Riona asked Kyle to run an errand while Constance followed her to the garden. Dillan left the living room without telling anyone where he was going. I personally could care less where he went. Having nothing else to do, I went back to my room and packed my stuff. I wanted to be ready to leave as soon as possible. I'd had just about enough of this freaky weekend from hell. My phone buzzed on the side table.

Penny: *Killed him yet?*

Me: *:(*

Penny: *Deets pls.*

Not having the heart to reply, I left my phone on the table and went back down stairs to check if Kyle got back yet. I wanted to talk to him about what happened last night and my knee. I didn't want lies between us, no matter how unbelievable the truth seemed. If there was someone who would understand, it would be my best friend. At the foot of the staircase, snippets of someone speaking floated toward me like soulful musical notes.

"As just as fair…"

My heartbeat quickened. As if with a mind of their own, my feet steered me toward the voice.

"…had worn them really about the same."

A beam of light streamed through the library door left ajar.

The large space had three walls dedicated exclusively to floor-to-ceiling shelves. A rolling ladder taller than me rested near the door, used for the hard-to-reach books. I'd only been into this room once before. Years ago, Kyle showed me his favorite reading chair—his father's chair. But he never spoke of him anymore. The death of his parents stayed a taboo subject, and no one who knew him brought it up.

"Oh, I kept the first for another day!"

I slipped in quietly, not wanting to disrupt Dillan. I was mesmerized by the cadence of his voice and wanted to keep listening. He sat by the large fireplace, drawing all my attention as he kept reading.

"I shall be telling this with a sigh."

He leaned back, shoulders squared and comfortable, with his legs apart. He held a small book in one hand. With the other, he lazily stroked a Russian Blue cat, its eyes heavy-lidded while the end of its tail flicked in contentment. The lower half of the cat's body lounged between his legs while the upper half draped over his thigh.

Unexpected warmth gathered in my belly. I stuffed my hands into my pockets, feeling like a spy, like I shouldn't see this. But I listened anyway, in awe of the way his voice pulled me to him.

"Two roads diverged in a wood, and I—I took the one less traveled by, and that has made all the difference." He sighed like he tasted the meaning behind the words. The cat on his lap purred. "You like Frost, huh?" He glanced at the contented feline. "I know. The man can rhyme."

I wanted to stand there forever, watching him read poetry to a cat with such a peaceful expression. If it could tolerate him, then maybe—a big *maybe*—he wasn't so bad. The guy could be human after all.

"Stalking me again?"

The question startled me. I jerked and lost my balance. My shoulder collided with the rolling ladder. I winced, pain shooting down my arm. Nice. My smile wobbled when I steadied myself by grabbing the rail.

"Uh...um...why would I do that? I have a life. I was looking for Kyle." A flaming blush spread across my cheeks. Lord, I was making a mess of myself.

The cat turned its head and stared at me with its stunning lime-green eyes. I quivered. Those eyes were almost too intelligent, as if to say: "Idiot."

Dillan set the book aside, but continued stroking the cat's steel-gray fur from head to tail.

"You made friends with Constantinople." I pointed at the half-asleep cat. I swallowed, trying to stay cool in the presence of the heavy stares of a serious feline and a boy who made me feel hot and cold all at the same time. "He's never good with strangers."

Constantinople turned its head away from me and closed its eyes again, purring like a small generator. Remember that crazy part of me? Well, it wished, just a little, that I could take the its place. Even worse, I wondered how my skin would feel if his fingers decided to glide over it. Would I feel those tiny electric shocks again? Goose bumps rose on my arms and legs. I had to stop thinking dangerous things before I made a fool of myself.

"That's your name." He reached for one of the cat's front paws. "It's nice to meet you, Constantinople. Dillan Sloan, at your service." He held the paw, and Constantinople gave him a warbling meow, which turned into a yawn. Mischief glittered in his eyes as he gave me a smile. "Never thought Robert Frost would send a cat snoozing."

Who knew being in the presence of a playful Dillan Sloan was wickeder than being with the arrogant and annoying Dillan Sloan? One guy, two different people. It was enough to give me whiplash.

My heart sputtered. Damn, he looked good. I fought hard to stay focused. "I think it's your voice."

He shrugged nonchalantly. "I was there before I came here, but it's not called Constantinople anymore."

"What?" I reached for one of the rungs of the rolling ladder.

"Istanbul…I was just there."

The change in his expression made me ache. He went from mischievous to lonely. He got so quiet, like he retreated into himself.

I let go of the ladder and stepped forward. "Why were you there? That's in Turkey right?"

"Yes." The gray cloud that settled above him lifted a little.

Without his usual, biting tone, he came off as vulnerable. I fought to concentrate on his next words in an effort to ignore the need to comfort him. Images of him in my arms while I whispered nonsense things into his ear woke flutters in my stomach.

"My parents are there on a yearlong dig just outside the city. They're collaborating with Istanbul University and the Topkapi Palace."

"And your parents took you with them?"

"My parents always take me with them when they're on a dig."

"But…what about school?" I took another tentative step forward and skimmed my fingers over the giant globe at the center of the room.

He gave me an are-you-learning-impaired look. A face I knew all too well. This was good. I could handle myself when on familiar territory.

"I usually stay in the city with my tutors. I was homeschooled until recently."

"So why are you here?" I pretended to search for Turkey on the globe.

"It doesn't matter. I'm here, you're here, Constantinople is here."

The cat settled its head on its front paws, murmuring as if in response to Dillan's careless words.

"But it does matter!" I covered my mouth with both hands. Where the hell did that come from?

As if reading my mind, his eyebrows shot up. A hint of a grin formed on his lips. Constantinople gave me a withering stare, silently reprimanding me for disturbing his nap.

"Really? Why?" Mischief returned to those startling blue eyes, and something else…something unfamiliar that caused heat to flow under my skin.

Feeling weak against that stare, I hedged, "What matters? What did I say?"

That mocking eyebrow went up a notch, forcing my head to work on overtime. The smile accompanying it made me dizzy. Did the air in here just get lighter?

"Don't play dumb." He picked up a slightly disgruntled Constantinople as he stood and deposited the feline on the seat with deliberate yet graceful movements. I couldn't take my eyes off him. The voice in me that told me to fight the corpses screamed for me to run now. But I couldn't move. After giving Constantinople one last head-to-tail stroke, Dillan faced me. He dusted cat hair off his hands and jeans without breaking eye contact.

When did the library get so hot? I resisted the urge to pull on my sweater collar. My palms sweated. I forced myself to move. For every forward step he made, I answered with a step back. Our little dance continued until the far wall bookshelves pushed against me.

A glimmer of pleasure surfaced in his eyes.

My skin practically sizzled.

"Come on." He rested his hands on the shelves, boxing me in with his body. "Tell me why it matters that I'm here."

"Well…" I faltered. His clean scent scattered my thoughts.

"Well?"

I bit my lip. My worst idea yet. His eyes left mine to focus on my mouth. I shivered. Oh, Lord Almighty. Slowly, he bent his head toward me. The tip of my tongue darted across my lower lip. This couldn't be happening. What was he thinking?

Willingly suffering the shock, I placed my hands on his chest and pushed him back gently. He pinned me with a questioning glance. When I didn't respond fast enough, he added an eyebrow arch.

I shook my head, feeling light-headed. "Whatever you think you're doing, don't."

"And what's to stop me?"

What was to stop him? If he wanted, all he had to do was move faster next time. But I couldn't let that happen. I steeled my expression against his challenging grin.

"I'm just not ready for this. Whatever it is," I said.

All expression left his handsome features. My chest clenched in response. He opened his mouth to say something, but shut it. And just as quickly, he dropped his hands from the shelves, turned on his heel, and sauntered back to the reading chair.

I sagged against the bookshelf. My knees trembled. An annoying part of me wondered if I did the right thing by asking him to stop.

CHAPTER NINETEEN

Dillan

BACK TO THE REAL WORLD NEWCASTLE

*H*appy to finally be rid of this disastrous weekend, Dillan climbed out of Kyle's car Sunday afternoon. He took the steps to the townhouse two at a time without looking back. He didn't need keys since the doors stayed unlocked. Any locks wouldn't stop what they normally went up against. The wards discouraged Supernaturals from entering the home. And any human would be stupid to break into an Illumenari protected household. Well, maybe not so much the Hilliard household. Chuckling, he pushed in and dropped his duffle by the door. The stillness inside deceived the casual onlooker. Rainer was around. He felt his menace. Just as his uncle felt him the second he came in.

"Rainer," he called, keeping his excitement in check. He didn't want to give his uncle the wrong impression. Banishment just got better. Newcastle wasn't the sleepy town he initially thought it to be. "Rainer!" He moved further into the house, not having the patience for his uncle's mind games. "You dick, I know you're home."

"Quit squawking." His warden stepped out of his study. He snapped the book in his hand shut. "I didn't think I'd miss the quiet until I had the weekend all to myself."

"It's back to babysitting the prisoner, Granpa."

"I did laundry while you were gone. For someone who moves around a lot, you have a crap load of clothes."

"There's a Maestro in town."

That caught the Boogeyman off guard. His brow furrowed, and his gaze turned murderous. Executing a precise about-face, he motioned for Dillan to follow him into his study.

Rainer sat down behind his desk and asked, "How do you know?"

Taking one of the seats across from his uncle, Dillan used the least amount of words to recount what had happened. "Saturday, at Valley View, five puppets broke through the barriers."

"Puppets?" Steel entered Rainer's gaze. His mounting anger charged the energy in the room until it bit into skin.

The killing urge reached across the table and washed over Dillan. Unable to avoid it, all he could do was nod, keeping his hands flat on the arm rests. Mentally, he calculated the distance between the chair and door. He considered his options. Maybe he could make it out of there before his uncle pounced. The power in the Boogeyman's aura pinched his arms, forcing him to abandon any escape plan. Predators always ran after prey. The less he moved, the better. If the chair hadn't been holding him up, he'd be on his hands and knees already.

"What were they doing there? Valley View has the strongest wards. I helped put them up."

"Your wards had holes. I caught them with Selena—"

"Fallon?" His interruption came with stillness. The pulse on Dillan's neck quickened, and sweat drenched his palms. The oppressive air in the room made his pinky twitch.

He swallowed against the tightness in his throat. "It could have been anyone. She was there because..."

"Because?"

From the way Rainer looked at him, lying to save himself wasn't a good idea. Backed into a corner, he went with the truth. "Because..." He swallowed again. "I was being an idiot. We argued. She stormed out."

When his uncle relaxed, he breathed again. Shit. He hated it when his jailer got all killer instinct on him.

"How are you so sure they—"

"Five reanimated corpses that turned to black ooze at a single sword strike." He left out the fact that one of them turned to ooze because of Selena. Rainer would never let him hear the end of it. Losing his sword to a girl. Not good for an Illumenari.

"I'm sure you already know who Kyle Hilliard is?"

He pushed back on his uncle's stare. "What are you hiding here, Rainer?"

"Nothing that concerns you."

"Damn it doesn't. I'm investigating dog disappearances and saving a girl I don't even think is human from puppets. I'm a part of this, whether you like it or not. If you want me to do my job, I need to know everything."

"This isn't official, remember?" Rainer leaned back. His chair tilted until it creaked. He rubbed his face with one hand then he sighed. "You're not cleared for what we have going on here."

"What's that supposed to mean?"

"Besides the dogs, I need you to expand your search to include the Maestro. He needs to be found and eliminated."

"Eliminated?"

After some throat clearing, Rainer clarified. "He threatened a resident of the town, which in turn may expose who we are. That's grounds for execution."

Dillan couldn't argue with that. He was thankful his uncle didn't grill him on how much Selena knew. "And here I thought you'd want to take this one yourself."

"I can't." He shook his head before rubbing circles on his temple. "I may not be able to brief you on everything, but this I can say. There's a delicate balance that needs to be maintained here. The reason why I gave you this case—"

"Only after I begged you for it," he interrupted.

"Be that as it may, I needed someone impartial. Since you're not from this town, you'd handle things without any bias."

"So you're saying there's politics involved." Rainer's lips slashed into a rigid line. Dillan took that as an affirmative. "Newcastle isn't just a small, sleepy town is it?"

"Not by a long shot."

· · ·

Dillan paced the entire length of his room, unable to sleep. He should have been fine with not knowing what Rainer and Hilliard kept from him. The Illumenari lived on a need to know basis. Yet something didn't sit right. The energy swirling around Newcastle unsettled him. Missing dogs. A girl who seemed human but who wasn't. A Maestro and puppets. These three things didn't seem connected no matter how much he tried to mash them together.

Dillan.

Sebastian's voice broke through his brooding, causing him to bump into his desk chair. Its corner caught him right in the shin, sending piercing pain up his leg. Concentrating his life force, he dulled the pain, unable to completely heal it if he wanted to conserve his strength. Cursing, he went to the window and opened it. Bracing his hands on each side, he propelled himself to the ground. Once he landed, he lifted his fingers to his lips and whistled.

A rustling ahead of him forced focus into his brain. "How's the search going?"

Finally stumbled on a body. Sebastian shifted, his massive bulk still covered by shadow. Like Dillan, the hellhound used the night to his advantage. *Carcass is a better term. I have never seen mangling that bad.*

"Do you suppose it's another animal?"

Humans do not have a set of teeth that could do what was done to that dog.

Finding the body gave him hope. Unfortunate for the dog, sure, but it meant it didn't die in vain. The carcass—right word choice—would yield more clues. And maybe finally give him some answers.

He let out a slow exhale. "Where's is it?"

Approximately ten miles northwest of here.

"Northwest? That's outside our search grid." He scowled at his partner. "What were you doing outside the grid?"

Easy there. Sebastian pawed at the ground. *I did not mean to stray.*

"God dammit! We have a system, you mutt!"

If you keep it in your pants long enough to let me explain, you will understand.

Biting back a string of nasty curses in several languages, he gestured for the hellhound to continue.

I felt an energy anomaly.

"Anomaly?" This meant many things, but the most important of them was it involved a Supernatural. Half his mouth pulled up.

See? Knew you would understand. Sebastian dipped his massive head in his version of a nod. *I followed the anomaly, and it led me to the body.*

"Good."

What?

"I don't have to kill you for breaking the system."

Anyone ever tell you how anal retentive you get when on a case?

"We're heading out," he said, ignoring Sebastian's quip.

And why is that exactly?

"Because I want to see the body." He took off full tilt, not waiting for his partner to follow. Having something to do distracted him for running around in circles in his head. Too much thinking led to things he didn't want to confront. Not right now. Not anything involving Rainer, Kyle, and especially not Selena Fallon.

CHAPTER TWENTY

Selena

SHOOT ME NOW

*M*onday morning, I found myself staring at the jumble of books, papers, and stuff inside my locker. I had to pull something out, I knew that much, but my brain shorted the second I opened the door. I woke up in a cold sweat in the middle of the night. My vision again. If it really was my future, then I had to do something about it. All the my-fate-is-in-my-hands new age crap had to count for something, right?

The rest of the night, I tortured myself trying to think of a solution, of some way to prevent the vision from coming true. Unfortunately, my vision track record left me hopeless. Now I was reduced to staring inside my locker without knowing what I needed. I sighed and shut the door. When the lock clicked into place, a finger tapped my shoulder.

I jerked and twisted around.

"Hey, easy there, jumpy. It's just me."

I looked up at Kyle and relaxed immediately. "Hey, you. What's up?"

He dropped his gaze, massaging the back of his neck. Okay, not a good sign.

"I know you wanted to talk before you dropped me off at the diner yesterday, but I really wasn't feeling it," I said apologetically.

"Yeah, about that." He sighed. "I asked Penny to come with us today, but she said she needed to get home early. So it's just you and me."

My brain didn't connect the dots right away. "Where are we going?"

The hurt in his eyes when his gaze finally met mine broke my heart. "You forgot."

I rummaged through the trashcan that was my brain and came up empty. Worrying my lip, I squeezed his arm. "It's been a crazy weekend, I haven't recovered yet. So where are we going?"

"Greenwood."

The name of the town cemetery automatically flooded the information my muddled head needed. "Oh, god! Is that today?" I gathered him into my arms. "I'm so sorry I completely spaced out. I'm like the worse best friend ever."

Despite what a rotten friend I'd been, he willingly stepped into the hug and returned it. "So, pick you up after your shift at Ormand's?"

I held him at arms-length and stared into his eyes so he could be sure I meant what I said. "I'll be there. I promise."

He nodded, dropping his gaze again. "Come on. Don't want to be late."

•••

Kyle, to my surprise, was his usual calm-and-cheery self when class started, considering what we had planned for this afternoon. Visiting his parents' grave couldn't be easy, but he stood in front of everyone with the rest of our group. Our diorama presentation for American History went straight to an A+.

If he could handle the anniversary of his parents' death like a pro, I certainly could chill over my vision. Maybe if I didn't worry about it too much, the answers would come. So by lunch, I'd let go of my worries and let the hum of conversation wrap around me like a security blanket. My normal.

Kyle and I ate at our table when an unusually subdued Penny came and sat down. She took a bite off the apple she held with an audible crunch.

"I'm pissed at the both of you," she said and pouted after taking another bite. "Just so you know."

"What'd we do?" Kyle pulled the tab off his soda can.

"Why aren't any of you responding to my texts, huh?" She raised a perfectly plucked eyebrow, a smirk forming on her pale, yet well-glossed, lips.

My brow crumpled. Yet another thing I had to apologize for. "I'm really sorry. The weekend took it out of me. Plus, you know the reception at Valley View is spotty."

"That's two nights worth of dish you've yet to fill me in on, Selena Fallon." She glanced around. "Or should I say Selena Sloan?"

Kyle choked on his soda.

"Has a nice ring to it, if you ask me."

"*What?*" I gaped. Images of what almost happened in the Valley View library decided to haunt me then, sending a full on blush to my cheeks. "Where'd that come from?"

"Constance is talking about all sorts of things, and no one can rely on what she has to say. Remember the fingernail in the cola incident last year?"

I shuddered. Constance insisted she'd found a fingernail in her drink. No one believed her since she couldn't show any evidence.

Maybe there was hope for me yet.

"It's obvious she has more of a crush on Kyle than Mr. Rock-Star-National-Geographic. So that leaves you." She gestured with her apple at me.

"How come I don't get a special name?" Kyle mocked.

Penny rolled her eyes at him. "As long as you come home to me, Mr. Two-Timer, we're square."

"You'll always be my beard," he said with satisfaction.

"So, what do you have to say for yourself Mrs. Dillan Sloan?"

"Stop saying that!" I hissed through my teeth.

"Yes, what *do* you have to say for yourself?" Dillan gave everyone at the table a cheeky grin before he sat down beside Penny.

Kyle laughed at the look of horror that must have been evident on my face. My heart had a mind of its own whenever Dillan was around. It pumped like there was no tomorrow. In my case—death vision excluded—maybe there wasn't where he was concerned. I didn't need any more aggravation from him. He still owed me answers for what happened at Valley View.

I took out my annoyance on Kyle by pushing him off his seat.

"Ow!" He picked himself up off the floor.

Dillan's expression turned conceited as he took out a sandwich from a paper bag.

"You plan to eat *here*?" I shrieked.

"Keep your panties on, Selena. It's a cafeteria. Eating *is* expected." He took an exaggerated bite from his sandwich and smiled as he chewed. "And I think I'm adding to your cred by being here."

"I know a few things you can do with—"

"Selena." Penny nudged me with an elbow. She leaned across the table toward me and turned to where the swimming team usually gathered. "Bowen's looking this way."

I followed her gaze, and sure enough, Bowen gave our table a curious glance. Before I could make out his expression, a push on his shoulder by one of his teammates quickly distracted him. They all laughed at something. Then my eyes landed on the table beside theirs where the cheerleaders congregated.

"Great!" I sagged into my seat. "The cheerleaders look like they're going to eat me! If Sheila Easton had a knife, she'd be sharpening it right now."

"Oh, don't worry about it." Penny sounded as if the world continued to revolve around her. "You know cheerleaders hardly eat."

"Well, I think they'll make an exception." I winced when the gaggle of girls whispered to each other.

Penny glanced at the primly pony-tailed group in white and orange with black trim uniforms and whistled. "I think you're right."

I wanted to say something else, but Dillan's all-knowing grin distracted me.

"I think I just got my answer." Penny winked at him.

He shamelessly returned her wink as she stood up.

"Penny!" I grabbed her arm. "What answer?"

"Oh, if you don't know by now…" The traitor kept her sentence unfinished and yanked away her arm, leaving the cafeteria with an extra bounce in her step.

Ugh! *Shoot me.*

No.

Shoot Dillan.

Chapter Twenty-One

Dillan

Dazed and Confused in Italian

Dillan walked into the bookstore hoping to decompress from another day at Newcastle High. He rubbed his arm through his sweater sleeve when the cold air from the overkill AC hit him. Two women stood by the romance section. But other than that, the place seemed empty. Did no one read in this hick town?

His gaze eventually landed on the girl he loved to hate but couldn't seem to anymore. Her expression when he sat down at their table for lunch was priceless. Thoughts of teasing her into agitation pulled his lips up mischievously. Nothing like seeing Selena pissed to make his afternoon better.

She stood behind the counter with her back to the door, feather duster in hand. The words *Divine Comedy* in gold script stretched over the spine of the book she held in the other. He smirked, approaching the counter.

"*Lasciate ogne speranza, voi ch'intrate,*" he said.

"I'm sorry?" She whipped around then froze when she

recognized him. Her beautiful eyes squinted. He would have paid a million dollars to know what she was thinking right then.

He gestured at the book, "It's from Divine Comedy. 'Abandon all hope, ye who enter here.'"

It took three seconds for her to digest. Ah, he loved the wrinkles on her brow when he annoyed her.

"So, does quoting Dante in…" She flicked the feather duster at him.

"Italian," he supplied.

"In *Italian* get you the girls?"

"Nope. I go to Shakespeare for pick-up lines." He raised his eyebrow a notch, knowing the action coaxed out his favorite expression of all from her. "When I'm facing the gates of hell, I quote Dante."

She scowled. He liked it when she scowled. Maybe a little too much, because her nose scrunched up and the tops of her cheeks tinted pink. She clutched the handle of the feather duster so hard its feathers quivered. Her lips contorted. Whatever promises he'd made himself about avoiding her went unfulfilled. Something about her always pulled him in. Why fight it? If getting to know Selena better cracked the nut of Newcastle's mystery, then who was he to say no?

"Okay, you've moved from mildly annoyed to eye-gouging angry." He raised both hands, stifling a chuckle by pressing his lips together. "This is a public place, Selena. I like reading, remember?"

She gingerly slid Dante's *Inferno* back into its place then pointed at the door. "The supermarket's that way."

"Good one." It always warmed him every time she bit back. He placed both hands flat on the counter and leaned in. He wondered more than ever what those petulant lips tasted like. "You're getting better at this."

Just when he had her on the run, one of the women came to

pay. Selena hid the feather duster under the counter and plastered a strained smile on her face.

"Excuse me," the woman said. She flicked an interested gaze his way, which turned the warmth in his chest into icicles of dread.

"Be my guest." He moved aside.

"Don't you have other things to do?" Selena hissed while she fumbled with the cash register. She was too cute when pissed.

"I beg your pardon?" the woman asked.

"Oh, no. I'm sorry, ma'am." Her face burned stoplight red. "I meant *him*."

"I'm here to read." He nodded once then sauntered toward the shelves. "*Ciao*."

"I'd like a piece of him," he heard the woman say. He tried not to cringe. Or run. Cougars were known to give chase.

"Thank you very much for your purchase," Selena replied cheerfully through her teeth. "We hope to see you again soon."

"If he's here every day, then you definitely will."

The woman let out a hum of appreciation. Dillan's stomach dropped. Jesus. Did all women in Newcastle hunt? He didn't want to go there, instead focusing on which book he'd read for the afternoon. Just as he slipped between shelves and got about six steps in, a thump stopped him in his tracks. He turned in time to see Selena limping behind the counter, muttering under her breath. He bit the inside of his cheek to keep from busting at the seams. Oh, this was so good. He moved to tease her when the bell at the door rang.

"Ouch! That must hurt," Bowen said when he entered the bookstore.

He moved toward the counter before he spotted the lounge chair opposite where he stood. It was near enough for him to hear their conversation. Without looking at the shelf, he pulled out a book and positioned himself on the chair. He pretended to read *The*

History of Root Vegetables while he reached out with his hearing toward the counter. Once in a while, he flicked his gaze Selena's way. If he kept still they wouldn't notice him. At least, he hoped so. Why the hell was he spying on them? It wasn't like anything they had to say to each other interested him, yet he couldn't move from where he sat.

"Haven't you ever stubbed a toe before?" Selena continued pacing.

"Not in such a hilarious way, no." Bowen covered his laughter with a fist. Okay, Dillan knew all too well he would have laughed, too, but he realized he couldn't take anyone else laughing at Selena besides him. The jerk snorted when he placed his hands on the countertop exactly where Dillan's hands were earlier. For some reason, his hackles went up at that. "What's gotten you so riled up today?"

She didn't meet his gaze. "Dealing with Dillan being a jerk can mess up any saint on a good day. And you know I'm no saint."

One side of his mouth twitched up. She had sported the exact same scowl all throughout lunch today. Definitely his favorite expression of hers. It brought out the blue in her aqua eyes.

"The new guy? The one at your table?"

"Uh…" She cleared her throat. "Yeah."

Bowen grunted. "I don't like him."

"Well, I don't, either."

He did his best to ignore the pinch her words caused. So what if she didn't like him? *Yeah, keep telling yourself that*, a voice in his head said. Stupid conscience!

The tightness of the troll's jaw eased. He reached out to touch her cheek, but stopped midway. Dillan's fingers curled tight around the book. The guy didn't smell right. He couldn't put his thumb on it exactly. The chlorine and cologne he wore muddled his true scent. Thankfully, his hand returned to the counter.

"So, what are you doing here, Bowen?" Selena shifted her weight.

"Is that what you'll ask me every time I see you from now on?"

She didn't say anything. The hesitation in her expression was almost enough to pull Dillan to her side. It took all the strength he had to stay put. If the guy so much as twitched the wrong way at her, he was losing a hand.

Bowen sighed when it became clear Selena wasn't going to break the silence that was quickly becoming awkward. "Anyway, the Fall Festival's this weekend." He took her hand. Dillan saw red.

"Already?" She sounded nervous.

His nostrils flared from the deep breaths he inhaled to stay calm. Well, relatively calm. He pushed up from the chair then froze. He checked himself. He'd been about to start a fight. For what? He slumped back into his seat. The leather creaked, so he pretended to cross his legs, but neither Selena nor the troll glanced his way.

"And I thought *I* was busy," Bowen continued. "How could you miss it? The radio announcements? The posters everywhere? Surely Grams told you about it."

"She might have mentioned something," she replied. "And yeah, I heard about it on the radio."

"So...go with me?"

For the several seconds it took her to respond, Dillan stopped breathing. Was she actually considering going with him?

Finally, she said, "I don't think that's a good idea."

Using the book to muffle the sound, he puffed out the breath he'd been holding. For a second there, he really thought she would say yes.

"Come on, Selena," Bowen urged. "Just as friends. Kyle and Penny will be there."

Her brow furrowed. "They're okay with this?"

He shrugged one shoulder. "It's for old time's sake."

"Bowen."

"Look, I'm not leaving here until you say yes."

For a split second, he caught Selena give a quick glance in his direction. At first, he thought she'd seen him. But from her non-reaction, he'd been wrong. All she had to do was say the word, and he'd kick him out. He'd take great pleasure in it. Instead, she let out a long sigh and nodded.

"Pick you up?"

"Meet you there." She pulled her hand out of his grasp.

"Is Grams still banned from the pie competition?"

"Ever since the lovely people of Newcastle realized no one would win first prize if she entered."

They shared a laugh. Selena's sounded more strained than what he was used to. He eased his fingers, smoothing out the creases he'd made on the book. He may have to buy it now, but what would he do with the history of root crops? Maybe he could hide it among other books, and no one would notice.

"See you there," said the troll.

An awkward smile formed on Selena's lips when she nodded. Bowen turned to leave then stopped. He leaned over the counter and gave her a peck before walking out of the store. She put a shaking hand on the cheek he'd kissed and stared at the front door. The bell still rang from his exit. Anger overtook Dillan's common sense, launching him off the chair, the creased book forgotten on the cushion.

Not thinking of the consequences, he walked back to the counter and clapped slowly. "Very touching, Selena. Bravo."

She slapped the countertop. "Spying on me now?"

"You like that big football troll?"

"Swimming."

"Excuse me?"

"He's a swimmer, not a football player." She crossed her arms and widened her stance.

His eyebrow arched. "I never pegged you to fall for the big and dumb types."

"And just what type do you peg me for, Mr. Rock-Star-National-Geographic?"

"One thing's for sure, the guy you're supposed to be with shouldn't look at you like something he can possess," he murmured loud enough for her to hear. He marched out of the store before he said, or worse, did something stupid.

CHAPTER TWENTY-TWO

Selena

THROUGH A VALE OF TEARS

At the end of my shift, Ormand asked me to check on a new shipment of young adult novels that just came in. I hated going in the back. It was creepier and colder than the actual store. I made a mental note to ask Ormand if we could call a handyman to check the thermostat, because no matter how many times I upped the temperature the frigid conditions didn't cease.

Rubbing my arms, I said a little prayer and stepped into the backroom. I reached for the light switch. The single bulb sputtered to life. I swear I could see my breath. It was that cold. I checked the boxes one at a time. Nothing was labeled young adult, so I went deeper into the bowels of the storeroom.

The light from the bulb only stretched so far, so when I reached the middle of the room, it looked like twilight. I continued to scan the boxes. Where the hell did Ormand put the new arrivals? I always arranged new boxes closest to the door. He really needed a system.

Suddenly, the bulb died, blanketing the room in darkness. I

yelped, bumping into a stack of boxes. I reached out, steadying the column so it wouldn't tumble and trap me inside the room that just got a hundred times scarier.

"Hello?" I called out, hands still on the precariously leaning tower of boxes. "Can anybody hear me?"

A cold sweat rose across my forehead. I twisted the box I was holding to stabilize the stack. Once I was sure it wouldn't fall on me, I gingerly moved away. I couldn't see a thing. Not even my hands in front of my face. Shit!

I tried to remember just how far I was from the door. I couldn't have been a few yards into the back. The storeroom wasn't that big, but in the pitch black, it seemed like a huge cavern. Hands out in front of me, I inched my way to where I thought the door was. One painful step at a time. It seemed to take forever.

A hiss stopped me in my tracks. "Hello?"

This was right about the time in the slasher flick where the heroine encounters the bad guy. Oh, god! Oh, god! Oh, god! My heart tried to beat out of my chest. For all I knew, it wanted to run away as much as I did. My knees knocked together when whatever it was in the room with me hissed again.

The already arctic temperature dropped further. I could actually feel ice form on my skin. My whole body shook. When I inhaled, a putrid smell of rotten eggs made me cough. I pulled up my shirt's collar to cover my nose and mouth.

"Hello!" My voice rose in desperation. Regardless of the hissing that seemed to grow more insistent by the second, I kept moving. I wanted to run, but if I did I could collide with the badly stacked boxes, and that would be the end of me.

"Ormand!" I screamed now. "Ormand! Help!"

The hissing grew deafening, drowning out my screams for help. I covered my ears and sank to my hunches. I couldn't move anymore. Fear paralyzed me. The darkness all around seemed like a wide abyss I could no longer cross.

My heart beat so hard, my chest hurt.

The voice I heard in my head at Valley View commanded me to get up. I shook my head against it. Again and again it kept saying I should get up.

"I can't, I can't, I can't," I kept saying.

"Selena?"

Light flooded the room. I opened eyes I didn't think I'd shut and looked up. Ormand stood by the door, his hand on the light switch. I'd been a yard away. Just a couple more steps, and I would have been free.

Embarrassed, and still a little shaken, I stood up. "I couldn't find the box of new YA titles." I ran my still shaking fingers through my curls. "I'm sorry."

"You better come with me," Ormand said.

"What?" My heart thudded in my throat. "Why?"

He blinked, and what I thought was menace in his eyes disappeared, replaced by that crooked-toothed smile. "Your friend's outside waiting for you."

Kyle. Relief showered over me, followed closely by a new sense of dread when I remembered where we were going. I thanked Ormand for his help and hurried out of the backroom.

· · ·

The heavy atmosphere in Kyle's Prius welcomed me when I slid into the front seat. I was still preoccupied by the freakiness of the storeroom when the uncomfortable silence abruptly pulled me out of trying to make sense of it. He didn't greet me like he usually did. He didn't even spare me a glance. I had just snapped my seatbelt on when he drove off toward town limits.

I said nothing. His I'm-okay act in school had run out. Not

having to hide anymore with me, his anxiety and sadness were both on display in the wrinkle on his brow to the firm line of his lips. He gripped the steering wheel like a lifeline.

The sweet perfume of roses made me turn around and glance at the backseat. About two dozen yellow roses lay across the seat. His mother's favorite. I smiled sadly. He still thought about what she would have liked.

Facing forward again, I reached out and squeezed his right shoulder.

"Everything's gonna be okay," I whispered around the lump in my throat. I needed to pull it together for him.

He nodded once, keeping his eyes aimed forward. The sun dipped lower, casting heavy shadows across the road, giving the quiet in the car an edge. I thought about the time I first met my best friend. It was a very exciting day for my six-year-old self. Grams thought I was emotionally stable enough to go to Maggie's with her. When we entered the place, I spotted Kyle sitting at the counter with Garret. He'd been answering the puzzles on the kiddie paper placemat with crayons. It had been a year since my parents had abandoned me. I had been a complete wreck, crying myself to sleep every night, wanting them back.

Because of my fragile state of mind, my grandparents kept me secret from the town that entire year—no small feat. They didn't even enroll me in school. The town didn't even know about me until that day at the diner. Of course, my grandparents told everyone the truth: my parents died during a hurricane in New Orleans. Nobody asked questions after that explanation. Not even Kyle.

Grams plopped me on a stool beside him and slid a puzzle placemat in front of me. He smiled the charming smile I knew so well now and slid the plastic cup of crayons my way. Something about him put me at ease right away, especially when he helped me with the puzzles. We'd been attached at the hip ever since. And when I found out I had visions of the future, he had been one of the few people I had the courage to tell. He didn't believe me at first, but he kept my secret anyway.

I never got a chance to meet his parents. They were always away on some business trip together. Even then, Kyle was under the care of Riona, while Garret ran the family business. But he never resented his parents' constant absences. Apparently, they had video chats every night.

They died in a plane crash a few months after Kyle's tenth birthday, leaving him with two legal guardians and a multi-billion dollar web company. His devastation affected those around him, especially Penny and me—we didn't know what to do or say. And since no bodies were found, he refused to believe they were really gone. He said he'd keep searching until he saw evidence of their deaths for himself. Year after year, his hold on that hope grew weaker and weaker. Finally, two years ago, he allowed Garret to set up a grave marker for them. I didn't see him for a month after that. When he finally returned to school, he acted like nothing happened—all genuine warmth and sincere smiles. Penny and I didn't have the heart to question him about his disappearance.

Now, in his car, I felt the sadness growing around him as we drove down Highway 16. It was my turn to support him. It didn't matter what I was going through, I needed to be here for one of the most important people in my life.

I gave him discrete, sideways glances while he drove up the winding road that had tall pines flanking each side like pillars holding up the sky. About a mile away from our destination, Greenwood's low walls stretched out like uneven toy blocks piled together by a toddler. My thoughts mimicked the aged stone, stacked over each other and held together by mortar made of worry and anxiety.

After shutting off the engine of his hybrid at the entrance, he stared at the open wrought-iron gates. He sat and just looked at the bold, black letters spelling out GREENWOOD in an arch. Knowing to wait, I settled into a comfortable position in my seat and stared at the interlocking vines of the gate's design. He sighed heavily. I turned my head to face him until my cheek touched the headrest. To my surprise, he'd done the same thing. His slate-gray eyes never looked as tired as they did then.

Without breaking eye contact, I reached for his hand, which rested on the side of his seat. I squeezed his clammy fingers hard. I wanted my warmth to seep into him and tell him that I wasn't going anywhere. That I'd do this with him no matter what.

Then, like the first sunrise of autumn—golden-yellow brightness—he smiled. It formed in stages, beginning at the corners of his mouth. His lips pulled up, causing his cheekbones to become pronounced, ending with his eyes crinkling. A genuine smile, same as the one he'd given Penny and me the day he returned from his month-long absence.

"Ready?" I asked tentatively.

He returned my squeeze. "Ready."

Everything was going to be fine.

I repaid his smile. Then I let go of his hand and opened my door.

The moment I stepped out, imaginary cold hands touched my back, sending shivers all over my body. Creepy, much? The same unease I felt the first time I stood outside the bookstore, and most recently, in the stockroom, wrapped around me like a heavy blanket. I rubbed my arms to stop thinking of the eerie air surrounding us.

"Cold?" Kyle asked while he pulled out the yellow roses from the backseat.

"It's weird," I said, looking around. "It's just the end of September. Aren't you cold?"

He blinked a couple of times. "No. But if you are, I have a jacket in the trunk."

"I think it's being here."

"Then let's get this over with." He tilted his head toward the gates and walked on ahead.

I kept up with his long strides. I felt nervous being among the dead. The thought of corpses crawling out of their graves freaked me out. My *Night of the Living Dead* experience at Valley View picked that time to replay in my head. I rationalized my fear by thinking I didn't want to leave Kyle because he needed me for support. The croaking frogs and humming crickets didn't help ease the spooky quiet. Large pines loomed ominously in clumps on each side of the clearing, like silent guards watching over the gravestones.

"Did you know," Kyle said. "Gravestones were once believed to have been used to keep the living dead from rising from their resting places?"

I laughed nervously. Why'd he have to mention that particular factoid now? Gravestones didn't stop the puppets at Valley View. "Do you believe the dead can..." I swallowed. "You know..."

"What?" He stopped and looked at me, yellow roses in his hands.

I rubbed my arms. "Do you believe that the dead can rise again?"

He laughed, cutting the eeriness of being the only two people in Greenwood. "If I knew you'd be this freaked out, I would have come alone."

He meant it as a joke, but I still felt bad for showing any weakness. I blamed it on my stockroom experience. My nerves were still too raw. Despite that, I reminded myself of why I was here. I let go of my arms and stood up straight, jutting my chin out.

"I can do this," I said with a shaky grin.

"That's more like it." He returned my enthusiasm with a small smile.

I ran to his side and entwined my arm with his. "Let's go."

Even with his answering shoulder bump, we still hurried past rows of tombstones, marble statutes, and a variety of crosses. In the distance, a large, marble angel came into view. He slowed his pace. The lightness around him turned heavy again. The storm cloud above his head returned. I matched my steps with his while looking straight ahead.

The angel, once pristine, now showed the effects of weather and time. With its wings tucked behind it, the statue's arms and face reached for the heavens as if asking for blessings. Or deliverance. I couldn't be sure. Below the angel's feet, a gold-lettered granite slab stated: *Alexander and Tanya Hilliard, beloved parents. Never found. Never lost.*

Tears threatened to fall from my eyes. The inscription got me every time. I lifted my hands to cover my trembling lips. Kyle still believed his parents were alive somewhere. He fell to his knees and placed the bouquet of roses on the patch of grass beneath the angel. His shoulders shook as he covered his face with his hands.

Sobs filled the air around us.

The sun had set beyond the tall pines by the time Kyle wiped away the last of his tears and stood up. He stretched from his fingers all the way to his toes. I distinctly heard some joints popping.

The coming gloom brought with it a gray twilight. A soft mist gathered on the ground, covering the graves in a damp, smoky blanket. Kyle faced me again, and in the dim light, I could see the tip of his nose was red, and his usually light gray eyes copied a stormy sky.

"I'm really glad you came," he said softly.

I bridged the gap between us and threw my arms around his shoulders, giving him the biggest, warmest hug I could muster. He pulled me up until my toes barely touched the ground.

"I braved the scary cemetery for you," I said even if my eyes welled up.

"I owe you one." He barked a sad laugh. After a minute, he said,

"I still miss them."

My heart crumpled a little. "Every damn day," I replied.

"What?" A sniff escaped his nose.

"I miss my mom and dad every day," I clarified in a gentle tone. "The loneliness and the missing them never goes away."

Kyle buried his head deeper into my shoulder, and I felt the spreading dampness from his tears on my sweater. We shared the same sadness.

I understood that he was closer to his parents than I was to mine since they died when I was much younger than him. But grief was grief. I only had a few concrete memories of them. Actually, if Grams didn't have pictures of them hanging on the walls of the living room and up the stairs, I wouldn't have been able to recall the light in my mother's eyes or the laugh lines on my father's face. They were more like flickers of light at the back of my mind now, but it didn't mean I thought of them any less.

Forgetting all the craziness in my life, I lost myself in memories of my parents' scent and touch and Kyle's comforting embrace.

CHAPTER TWENTY-THREE

Dillan

NO TIME FOR SARCASM

*D*illan stood in the shadows of an outcropping of pines as Kyle and Selena walked hand in hand toward the cemetery's entrance. He didn't expect to encounter them on this detour Sebastian had him on. The hellhound was positive it felt the Maestro's energy signature within the grounds. He would have confirmed it if he had more of his powers, but right now all he had to corroborate Sebastian's instincts was the hint of sulfur in the air. Not enough for humans to pick up. Conjuring—the dark side of Channeling—always left an acrid scent behind.

But instead of concentrating on the case, his eyes never left Selena. It took all of his willpower to resist the urge to run after them. He'd been feeling insanely jealous of anyone in her company since the bookstore. It made no sense. Even he knew that. But when he saw them hugging, he almost charged them just to pull them apart.

What happened at Ormond's still pissed him off. That girl had no sense of self-preservation. The way Bowen looked at her…like something to eat. He should have separated them, too. She was a bundle of trouble. One he couldn't resist anymore—no matter how hard he tried, she dragged him back in like riptide. Only when the thought hit him did he notice his fingers had gone numb. He looked down and forced his hand to relax.

That the girl?

Sebastian smugness grated at his ego. "Shut up."

The black canine shook his massive head. *What about—*

"You don't have to bring her in to this." He scowled.

She visits you.

"Just stupid dreams."

But—

"You know why." He rolled his eyes toward the darkening sky. "She has the right to hate me. Wherever she is. If she's still—"

Stop blaming yourself.

"Get out of my head, you mutt. We don't have time to talk about that now. We can't get caught out here at night. I count more than two hundred graves in the new area alone."

A long minute passed without another word from the hellhound. Then he said, *You have no reason to be jealous.*

"Jealous?" A puff of laugher came out of him.

I feel no attraction coming from the Hilliard son toward the girl.

"Her name's Selena." And damn if that didn't make him feel better. Forehead like an accordion, he grumbled, "Let's get back to work."

Why do you think they were here? The Hilliard boy should have known better.

He took a minute to make sure no one else was in the cemetery before he approached the place where Kyle and Selena stood earlier. At least two dozen yellow roses lay below a weeping angel. The names on the granite confused him. "Why would Kyle's parents be buried here? When I got a look at his family tree, they were still indicated as alive."

Symbolic?

"Trust me. The prick wouldn't know what symbolic meant if it hit him in the face."

A grumble bark came from behind him. *I get it. You hate him.*

He raised an eyebrow over his shoulder at the large animal behind him. "You really gotta work on your sarcasm."

A coughing sound followed.

"Yeah, laugh it up, asshole."

He waited until Sebastian sobered. He didn't understand what had come over him. Why would Kyle's arms around Selena piss him off? They were best friends. They had the right to hug it out. They were in front of a grave. It seemed appropriate. But it didn't make sense. If Kyle's parents were dead, their names should have been crossed out. The mystery got more complicated. Just when he thought he'd figured things out, twenty more questions popped up.

"Do you get the feeling the mutilated dogs and Maestro have nothing to do with the rest of what's going on here?" he asked more to himself.

We cannot rule out any of the possibilities. The Maestro is here. I can feel its presence tainting the air.

A charge hung around them. It surprised him Kyle hadn't felt it. Or maybe he'd chosen to ignore it. He deliberately put Selena in danger. The prick mustn't have been listening when he told him about the puppets in Valley View. One concrete reason to really hate him.

Dillan cracked his knuckles. "Nothing makes sense to me anymore. And just so you know, I've never come up against a Maestro before, but I've read the texts. He's hiding himself well."

That is comforting.

"You should really quit with the sarcasm."

Now you know how I feel.

"Will you just investigate the north side while I take the south? I want to get out of here in under an hour. Got that?"

Since you asked so nicely.

Only after Dillan added an exaggerated "please" did they dash deeper into the cemetery.

CHAPTER TWENTY-FOUR

Selena

NEVER FALL AT A FESTIVAL

*E*very night for the rest of the week, my vision plagued me. I barely caught a wink of sleep. Sometimes it felt like my head just hit the pillow, and seconds later, Grams was already calling down for breakfast. I'd never had images persist this way, and it worried me. Made me jumpy. By the weekend, I was ready for some fun at the Fall Festival. No matter how exhausted I felt leaning against the window of my grandfather's truck.

For two years, the Fall Festival had been a shared experience. It was always me, Penny, and Kyle. Then when I started dating Bowen, we became a foursome. I shouldn't have said yes to going with him. But I did say I'd give the "friends" thing a try. I took a deep breath and exhaled slowly.

The Ferris wheel towered over everything when we pulled up to the fairgrounds—the most popular ride, allowing some *alone time* for couples. The Hi-Miler, the Skyride, the Zipper, the Water Log, and other scream-inducing attractions surrounded the monolith.

The shorter than you-must-be-this-tall crowd had the Merry-go-round, Spinning Teacups, and the Flying Dumbos alongside colorful food stands and game booths.

Gramps pulled into the make-shift parking lot, setting off a dust storm from the dried dirt field. Once the dust settled, I slid out of the truck. Hacking up a lung wasn't a pretty picture. Bowen stood by the fair's entrance in his letterman jacket over a white T-shirt and jeans, looking all-American and handsome. Go Tiger Sharks!

Grams barely hid the frown on her face when we reached him. She had always been a huge Bowen fan, in and out of the pool. But after his cheating hit the airwaves, she'd lost all love for him. If Grams kept a top ten kill list, he would be in it. Gramps, having no idea about the cheating incident, stayed protective of his ladies. He eyed Bowen suspiciously and straightened to his full height to look extra intimidating. I was pretty sure if he'd known, his fist would be meeting my ex's chin right about now.

"Young man," he said. Although, from the way he squinted, I could have sworn he knew a thing or two about what happened.

Unfazed by my grandfather's scrutiny, Bowen reached out for a handshake. "Good to see you again, Mr. Fallon."

Gramps grinned and took Bowen's offered hand while patting him hard on the shoulder. "How's that truck of yours?"

The "love pats" sounded harder than they were. Bowen had the grace not to cough. A lesser man would have bent forward. I guess that was one of the reasons why I liked him when we started dating. He stood up against Gramps without being impolite. Maybe that was why Gramps grudgingly liked him, too, and why he would murder Bowen if he ever found out about the truth.

"Tuned and sounding better than ever," Bowen replied.

Both men smiled that secret smile only guys who loved cars had for each other.

"That's m'boy!" Gramps patted his shoulder again.

Then the ex turned to Grams. "Looking more beautiful than ever, Mrs. Fallon." He treated her to a big hug. I shook my head then rolled my eyes.

Grams bristled, but her good manners didn't allow her to be rude, so she tapped his chest when he finally put her down. "Bowen, it's good to see you."

Gramps grunted. "What do you say we leave these two alone? You have a pie contest to judge." He pulled his frowning wife away before she could say anything else. To Bowen, he said with a pointed stare, "Take care of my girl."

"Yes, sir." He waved at their retreating backs before he asked me, "Grams is finally a judge?"

"This year's organizers realized the benefits of having her on the panel."

"Is it just me or was Grams about to punch me in the face?"

"Bowen," I sighed out. "You honestly didn't think what you did would only hurt me, did you? You're lucky Gramps still doesn't know." I turned away from him. "Maybe this isn't such a good idea."

His hand went to my shoulder, and I stopped. "I'm sorry." I heard the sincerity in his words, but I still doubted him. "I'll apologize as many times as you want me to. Please, give me a chance to make it up to you today. If you still think you can't forgive me, then I'll leave you alone."

"You'll leave me alone?"

"So long as you give this afternoon a chance."

I considered it while he bought tickets at the booth by the entrance. The festival was one of my favorite events of the year. I didn't promise him anything when he matched his pace with my lazy stroll.

"Where's Penny and Kyle?" I asked, searching the crowd for them.

A sad laugh reached my ears. "Penny fooled him into riding the

Ferris wheel."

My eyes bugged out. Kyle hated heights. I imagined him white knuckling the guardrail and taking deep breaths every two seconds. I laughed, too.

Bowen stopped and stared down at me.

"What?" I sobered. I lifted a hand to my nose and self-consciously rubbed. "Is there something on my face?"

"No." He nudged my hand away. "It's just been so long since you laughed like that around me. Nice."

I ignored the heat in his gaze and headed toward the game booths. "Come on. Let's see if you can still win me a bear."

We passed a clown handing a toddler a red balloon and took a right at a mascot of an elk wearing a sign that read: HUNTING SEASON. Fifteen minutes and several dollars later, I happily clutched an enormous, stuffed rabbit while eating cotton candy.

"I forgot how good you are at target shooting."

"I'm not *that* good. The booth owner just likes you." He shook his head and shoved his hands into his jacket pockets.

I offered him a fluffy, pink pinch. "Oh, come on, you held your own out there. I have Mr. Snuffles to prove it."

He chewed. "You already named the rabbit?"

"Of course I did, isn't that right, Mr. Snuffles?"

He pointed at Penny dragging a nauseated Kyle to another ride before the pair disappeared. I looked from the rabbit toward the direction of Bowen's finger. I initially thought I'd need the friend buffer Kyle and Penny would provide, but so far, being with him felt normal. Just what I needed.

"Poor Kyle." I sighed. "I wonder what Penny has on him."

"I don't want to know."

Before I could turn my attention somewhere else, I spotted a familiar faux-hawk of dark chocolate hair in the crush of people. He stood in line for the Ferris wheel, wearing his usual long-sleeved shirt and jeans, but since the weather had gotten cooler recently, he had a jacket vest on. With a relaxed stance, he casually slipped his fingers into his back pockets, leaving the thumbs out. He laughed. A girl affectionately touched his arm.

I moved forward.

"Going somewhere?" Bowen asked after he handed his payment to the vendor for the supersized soda.

"Sorry. Didn't notice you were buying something," I said absentmindedly while anxiously waiting for him to get his change.

"Where next, boss?" He took a sip and offered the giant cup to me.

I waved off his offering. "Can we go on the Ferris wheel?"

His lips pulling up into a slow smile, he willingly led me to the line. Right then I was too irrational to think of the consequences of that smile. If I hadn't seen Dillan with some girl, I wouldn't have even thought to ask Bowen to the Ferris wheel. When we reached the tail end of the queue, I finally recognized who he was with. The pair stood about three couples ahead.

"Constance." My voice had enough venom to poison everyone within a five mile radius. All thoughts of being friends with her went out the window.

"Who?" Bowen looked around.

"I can't believe Dillan has the nerve to bring Constance to the Fall Festival." I motioned with my chin toward the front of the line.

"The new guy?"

"Don't sound so confused. I thought Constance had more sense not to fall for his fake charm."

"I thought you didn't like the guy."

"I don't."

For the whole wait to get on the Ferris wheel, I whispered my disappointment at how Constance let herself fall into Dillan's trap. When Bowen and I finally got on the ride, I told him about how much of a jerk Dillan could be. I bitterly recounted every mean and nasty thing he'd put me through—omitting all the other heart pounding moments, of course. Bowen joked about the situation. His humor earned him another few minutes of how guys always ended up protecting their own. Bros over hoes and all that crap. By the time the ride ended, I'd worked myself up into such a coil that Bowen's temper snapped.

"I thought you just needed to vent, but now I think you're actually jealous." He towered over me.

Anxiety filled my stomach like a fizzy drink, but I stood my ground. "Jealous? Don't be dense. I just spent the whole ride telling you how much of a jerk Dillan is."

"My point exactly. You let him get under your skin so much that seeing him with another girl makes you angry for no reason." He gestured toward the direction Dillan and Constance went after getting off the Ferris wheel.

Our raised voices drew in a crowd.

Ignoring the people around us, I continued my rant. "I'm not jealous! Maybe you're the one who's jealous."

"Don't I have the right to be jealous when the girl I'm trying hard to win back is drooling over another guy?"

I paused, unable to speak for a couple seconds, trying to process his words. "You're trying to win me back?" I parroted.

He heaved a heavy breath. "Yeah."

"No one told you to do that."

"Free country."

"See, that's your problem." I poked his chest. "You don't listen to me."

"Don't make this about me!" He ran his fingers through his hair, disheveling the dark, sun-kissed strands. "You're the one with a problem."

Like something in me snapped, I calmed down. Ice froze my

insides. "Thinking that I have a problem is what got us here in the first place."

He held up his hands in apology. "I don't think—"

"Tell me this, *Bowen*. Did you cheat on me to make me jealous?"

He blinked at me, stunned. "I...I...Selena, you don't understand."

"I thought so." I pushed the rabbit into his arms and marched away without looking back.

• • •

Snaking my way through the throng into the flea market, it dawned on me that when it came to all things Dillan, I was certifiable and the people around me became collateral damage. Meeting him changed me somehow, and I didn't know if it was a good thing.

I ran a hand through my wild hair and had to tug several times to free my fingers. Frustration boiled in me. In search of a distraction with some retail therapy, I scanned the stalls.

A jewelry merchant caught my eye. The booth had multi-tiered displays with scarves scattered everywhere as accents. I studied rings modeled by ceramic hands. When nothing jumped out at me, I moved on to a row of small hooks where necklaces with assorted pendants dangled.

A squat man whose beer-belly plumped up his gypsy costume came over. He had an easy smile. "Find anything you want?"

"Not yet." I returned his smile and noticed a glass case with more necklaces. A thin, silver chain with a perfectly circular pendant called to me. I looked at the gemstone and saw a soft blue light glowing from within the white clouds.

"That's a moonstone."

"Oh." I kept staring, reminded of the pommel on Dillan's sword. And just like that, I thought of him again.

"It's not a very popular gem. Most girls go for amethysts or rose quartz."

"How much for the necklace?"

"I have an aquamarine necklace that would look good with your skin tone and eye color," he volunteered.

"How much for this one?" I pointed at the moonstone.

The man sputtered a price. I happily made the purchase and left the booth feeling better. Pocketing the small, paper envelope with the necklace in it, I froze. A feeling of unease struck me like an unexpected slap. Memories of the storeroom at the bookstore sent the hairs on the back of my neck standing on end. I forced myself to move. This was a public place, surely I'd be safe. A thick blanket of fear wrapped around me as I joined the crowd again. My heart pounded in my chest when the sensation of being watched hit me.

The crowd kept moving like a steady stream. No one seemed to notice anything wrong. A couple held hands and laughed. A little boy asked his mother to buy him a truck. A group of girls noisily tried on hats in front of a stall selling accessories.

The bazaar had no alleys for anyone to hide in. The booths stood too close together.

The anxiety buzzing through my veins turned into an alarm, like an ear-splitting bell. Unexplained panic climbed up my throat, threatening to choke me. My lungs fought for every breath. Cold sweat dotted my forehead. I turned in a tight circle, searching for the source of my fear. In my periphery, a black German Shepherd with red eyes bared its teeth at me. Oh, God. _I'm gonna die._ Underneath the fear, my heart twisted. _I'm gonna die._ I didn't have time to let the idea sink in. I took off as fast as I could. I elbowed my way through the crowd, ignoring the protests of whoever I bumped into. I had to get away.

"Selena?"

I stopped and looked over my shoulder, hand on my chest. "Mr.

Ormand?"

"Is something the matter?" He came closer.

The voice in my head said *run. Find the Guardian.* What did it mean?

The feeling of being watched persisted like a pair of hands slowly closing around my throat. I grabbed at my neck, trying to remove the invisible fingers. The intensity of my fear tasted like metallic bitterness on my tongue.

"I'm sorry," I choked out. "I really have to go."

I didn't wait for Ormand's reply. This time I wouldn't ignore the voice in my head. I turned around and bolted.

CHAPTER TWENTY-FIVE

Dillan

AROUND GOES THE FERRIS WHEEL

Since arriving at Newcastle, Dillan got good at spotting Selena in a crowd. For a whole week, he took it upon himself to avoid her. Still his eyes scanned the hallways. Only when he saw the bright mess of curls did he move. The crowd at the Fall Festival was no different. He'd seen her running through the mass of people. Every few steps, she'd look back over her shoulder. He sensed her panic from where he stood. The same jolt of electricity that went through him at Valley View zipped through his body now, prompting his feet to carry him toward her without hesitation.

She ran straight into his arms and yelped. He ignored the initial shock upon contact with her skin. It was easier now that he expected it. Not that it hurt less. Just like the last time, he heard a pop and the electricity was gone. Her second of surprise ended with fists pounding his chest. He braced himself against the blows. If she decided to start kicking, too, she'd have direct access to a spot he preferred to remain unmolested. Having no other choice, he let go of her for a split second so he could wrap his arms around her. This pinned her fists between them, holding her in place. She took a deep breath and looked up. Recognition formed in her eyes, followed closely by the flood.

Shit.

Like a band tightening around his chest, he found himself unable to breathe in the face of tears. Worse? They were *her* tears. A sudden urge to find what caused her distress and pound it to the ground washed over him. He bit the inside of his cheek. The resulting pain distracted him enough from his mounting anger to focus on her. If he wanted to find out what made her cry then subsequently kill it, he needed to calm her down enough to speak.

"Hey, hey," he whispered, stroking the back of her head. "Shhh. You're fine. It's fine."

She paused, holding her breath. A stray tear fell. Her bottom lip quivered. Then fatter tears rolled down her cheeks. He winced. Ah, shit. His attempt to comfort her only seemed to make things worse. He knew Selena to be stronger than this. She held her own against the puppets, so anything that got her this upset worried him. Without thinking, he pulled her closer until she buried her face in his chest. She grabbed onto his shirt and sobbed.

At a loss for words, he held on. The fabric of his shirt grew damp. She continued, alternating between keening cries and hiccupping sobs. Remembering the bandana in his back pocket, he reached behind him and pulled it out. He inched away only to have Selena pull him back. She shook her head against his chest.

"It's okay," he said.

Slowly, she let go of his shirt. He bent down and gently patted her face dry. She sniffed. Her aquamarine eyes grew big and round. He smiled. How could he not when she looked so adorable right then? She tried to return the smile, but ended up in a fit of hiccups. Thinking fast, he guided her to a secluded bench, away from the stream of people passing them. A few were already curiously staring. He kept close in case—God help him—she fainted. Girls did that. When a minute passed and nothing happened, he silently thanked his lucky stars she'd stayed conscious. She had some fight left in her.

"I'll get you something to drink," he suggested.

She grabbed his sleeve and shook her head, hiccups rolling through her.

"Okay." He sat back down. His mother had taught him a trick to stop hiccups. "Take a deep breath then hold it until I tell you."

Nodding frantically, she inhaled and waited. He counted in his head. When her neck turned red, he gave her the signal to exhale. The hiccups were gone. He grinned. Mission accomplished.

After Selena had taken two more deep breaths, he pushed a curl away from her damp forehead and asked, "Why were you running like a horde of undead was chasing you?"

"Not funny." She scowled. If she could get annoyed with him again then she'd be okay. "Didn't you see the dog chasing me?"

"What dog?"

"The big black one with red eyes. It was chasing me."

"Okay." He flicked his gaze from her face to the passing festival goers then back again. "When did this happen?"

"I just finished buying a necklace at the flea market when it felt like someone was watching me." She rubbed her forehead as if it helped her remember better. "I panicked, and when I saw this ginormous black dog snarling at me, I high-tailed it out of there. Crap. You saw me cry. I didn't want you to see me cry. If you dare tease me about it, I swear I'm never talking to you again."

When she mentioned the black dog, Dillan cursed Sebastian to the deepest pits of hell. What was his partner doing at the fair where anyone could see him? He slid closer to her side. "You sure it was after you?"

Her mouth opened to answer, but no words came out. Only

after swallowing hard was she able to say, "I heard it growl."

It couldn't be his partner. He and Sebastian had been out every night this week. More carcasses had turned up during their search for what could be mauling them. Slowly, he noticed each one they'd found got closer and closer to the Fallon farmhouse, which was outside of their original grid No wonder they hadn't found any evidence until recently. He couldn't understand why at first. But Selena being watched had to be connected somehow.

"You're gonna think this is crazy." He looked into her eyes so she wouldn't think he was kidding. "I think you're being targeted."

Her disbelief came in stages. First, her eyebrows rose. Then her mouth opened a fraction. He kept his mouth shut until the idea finally sunk in.

"Targeted?" she repeated.

"After what happened to you at Valley View, I don't think it's random anymore."

She stood up and walked away.

"Selena!" He pushed up and rushed after her. "Selena, wait."

He grabbed her arm and twisted her around. Her glare shocked him enough to let her go, moving his hand through his hair instead. This wasn't going the way he'd imagined it would. Then again, in what scenario would he ever think Selena would react normally to what he'd just said? To think she handled the puppet attack so well. In any case, he might as well have told her the world was ending.

"You just told me you felt someone watching you," he said, taking Sebastian out of the equation. They would have words later. Stupid mutt. He stifled the urge to stuff the hellhound into a cage for scaring the shit out of Selena.

"I did!" Fire burned in her eyes. She believed in what she'd felt, so she should believe in what he had to say.

"I don't think you should be alone right now."

"I panicked. That doesn't mean I'm suddenly some target. What does that even mean?"

"If you'd let me explain…" He looked away. Even if she wasn't human, it still wasn't easy to reveal who he really was. In the back of his mind, he watched all the rules that had been drilled into him for years shatter. This girl with her messy curls and determined eyes brought out his intense protective instincts. "I mean…shit!"

Her eyes narrowed. "You're doing that thing again where you know more than you're telling me."

"Rainer's gonna kill me." He kicked the bench they'd been sitting on. His brows knotted as he ran his fingers through his hair over and over again. He needed to think. Everything strange that had been happening in Newcastle seemed to revolve around Selena. It couldn't be a fluke anymore. She couldn't be that unfortunate. He paced. Walls of air closed in on him, making it hard to breathe.

He turned his back on her. "Ah, fuck it!"

"Are you having a stroke or something?" she asked.

"The puppets at Valley View are proof." He faced her again. If he was going to break the rules of the Illumenari, it might as well be in the service of keeping someone safe.

"I don't understand."

"It's complicated."

"Then un-complicate it."

"You need protection."

"I can protect myself." Her annoyance collided with his.

"I know that, but this is beyond what you can do. You have to let me handle this."

"So, what? You're suddenly Superman?"

"I'm…" He hesitated. He hated that he did. Unable to utter the truth in public, he grabbed her arm and pulled her behind one of the booths. She struggled, but he held tight. He looked around and made sure no one would hear them before he said anything more. Selena scowled at him the whole time. She folded her arms over her chest and waited.

He dropped his gaze to the ground and took the leap. "I'm an Arbiter of the Illumenari."

"I'm sorry?"

"I said—" His voice rose. Damn this girl and the things she made him do. He lowered his voice to barely a whisper. "I'm an *Ar-bi-ter*. Someone who can protect you from...that's not important right now. All my plans down the drain for someone like..." He turned his back on her again. She tried his patience. All the breathing exercises in the world wouldn't help calm the mix of anxiety and annoyance in him. He shook his head. He'd already jumped into the shit pit, might as well make it work. When he faced her he said, "Think about everything that's been happening to you, Selena. Think really hard. Tell me every unusual thing that has happened to you over the last few weeks."

"The forest at Valley View..." Her arms dropped to her sides before she pushed back curls from her forehead. "And the stockroom..."

"What about the stockroom?" His heartbeat sputtered.

"Ormand asked me to look for a box of books in the back when the light went out and something was hissing there inside with me." Her voice shook. "Are you saying all of this is happening because of me?"

He frowned. "I don't know that yet. I want to be wrong, but I seldom am."

She returned his frown.

"The puppets, the storeroom, and then you feeling someone was watching you. These can't all be coincidences. This was supposed to be a simple case of missing dogs. I wasn't even supposed to use this here." He pulled up his sleeve and showed her the cuff. "I just had to find out why the dogs were disappearing, and then you came along."

"Sure, like being chased by rotting corpses..." She stopped, then used her inside voice. "Like that's my fault. Where did you get this?" She closed the gap between them and touched the charm. "It's like it's alive."

"It's a family thing." He tugged his sleeve back down. "My grandfather gave it to me on my thirteenth birthday. Everyone in my family has something like it."

"An accessory that turns into a weapon? Does Mr. Sloan have one?"

"He has two."

"So, you're an *Arbiter* for the Ill…what?"

"Il-lu-me-na-ri. My family…we protect people."

"Like me?"

"As special as that sounds, no. When I say people, I mean *humans*. Mortals. All of mankind. Simply, we are what stand between you and chaos. Humans aren't the only race in this world. In fact, there was a time when you were bred purely for the purpose of food. Many of those we protect you from still consider you as food. In the Illumenari we call them Supernaturals. Basically everything that goes bump in the night."

She took a step back. "But your parents—"

"Are archeologists," he finished for her. "Long story short, their job is to find certain things the world would be better off not knowing about."

"And Mr. Sloan?"

His jealousy reared up at the awe mixed in with her confusion. "Him, too. He's retired."

"Is that why you're really here?"

"I was on assignment with my parents in Turkey when… something went wrong. They sent me here to clear my head." He barked a laugh. "I wonder what Granddad will think when he finds out I managed to land in another *situation*." He sandwiched the last word in air quotes.

"I feel like I should be insulted by that." She pursed her lips.

"You should. After what you've put me through—"

"I didn't ask for this. And I'm certainly not asking you to protect me." She glared.

He shrugged. "I have no choice anymore. Meeting you changed something. Now I'm in this mess whether I like it or not. Don't even get me started on the electric shocks when we touch."

"Yeah, what about those?"

"It's not static for sure." He didn't want to push his curiosity about what she really was. Maybe Selena didn't know and him repeatedly questioning her would only make things worse. She had enough to digest.

"So what now?" she asked through her teeth.

"We find out what's targeting you and why."

"Not happening." She backed away. But before she could run, he grabbed her wrist and towed her toward the Ferris wheel. He cut through the line and flipped off anyone who protested. While Selena struggled against his grip, he reached into his pocket and pulled out a bill. He shoved it at the stoned operator.

Selena gasped when he ushered her none too gently onto the seat. "Did you just give that guy a hundred dollars?"

"Shit! I thought it was a twenty." He slid in next to her, blocking all chance of escape.

"What are we doing here?"

"You need to process."

"And you think being high up in the air will help me do that?"

She stiffened when he stretched his arm over the back of the seat. He did his best to ignore the scowl on her face. She needed to think and he would be damned if he left her alone to deal with things by herself. For the first time in his life, he wanted to prove himself wrong about all this.

CHAPTER TWENTY-SIX

Selena

ROCK THE BOAT

Five turns on the Ferris wheel later, I still had no idea what to think. Dillan and I never left our seat, much to the annoyance of the couples waiting to take our place. He really must have slipped the ride operator a Benjamin because the guy didn't make us leave. He kept letting our car pass the unloading dock.

The second Dillan gave the signal to let us off I hurried away without actually running. What he told me freaked me out. What scared me even more was how all the information about Arbiters and the Illumenari and Supernaturals clicked in my head. Like a memory I'd forgotten until someone reminded me of it. That was just batshit loony. How could I feel comfortable with knowing all this? And I was a target? Of what? And what did that voice mean by finding the guardian. Who was that?

Again with the thousand and one questions with no clear answer in sight. Either I needed the guys in white coats to take me away now or my life just got super complicated and possibly dangerous.

One thing I knew, I needed to figure things out.

"Where are you going?"

His question startled me. I'd forgotten he was even there.

"Can you leave me alone?" I asked, weaving through the crowd as the sunlight around us turned orange and the sky blushed. It should have been beautiful. This afternoon should have been my chance to let loose. Instead it spiraled into a fun house version of hell. I just wanted it to end. All of it.

A hand caught my arm. I let my forward momentum swing me around, my right hand landing on Dillan's face. The *smack* caused those around us to stop and stare before continuing on their way. I gasped. My eyes widened.

"I don't know where that came from," I said. The smell of stale popcorn and bubblegum filled my lungs. Laughter mixing with excited squeals from the rides around us drowned out the loud beating of my heart. The festival looked far from slowing down as night fell.

"I think I deserved that, but I'm not sure what for." Each of Dillan's words sounded deadlier than the last. "I don't like taking a hit for no reason. Start talking."

I stood my ground. "I need to be alone."

"Dumping all this information on you is confusing. The unknown is always a scary thing. You've already been attacked twice, and most likely, the attacks will keep getting worse until they get what they want, which is probably you. So why not let me to protect you? What do you have to lose?"

He didn't get it. He just didn't get it. "This is all psycho. I want my old life back."

"Too late for that, babe."

"Don't call me *babe*!"

My lips trembled.

After a long pause, he closed his eyes for a second and breathed.

When he opened them again, they had less murder inside the blue. "Where do you need to be right now?"

I licked my lips, swallowing down some of my anxiety. "I need to meet my grandparents at the main tent. Judging must be over by now."

"I'll walk you there."

I heard the period at the end of his sentence. The determination in his eyes stopped any complaints I had. What was the point? I had a sneaking suspicion that if I blew him off, he'd still follow me at a distance. I gave up and went in the direction of the contest tent.

I took out my phone and punched in a message to Kyle.

Me: *Where R U?*

Kyle: *Took Penny home. She ate a bad batch of corndogs.*

That actually made me smile despite today's madness.

Me: *Meet me @ home? I need 2 talk.*

Kyle: *Got it.*

Without checking if Dillan followed, because I knew he did, I entered the massive white tent the organizers used for the contest. Long tables showcased pies, preserves, and cakes. You name it. If it could be judged, it was part of the Fall Festival competition. The sea of people parted, and in less than ten seconds, I spotted my grandparents conversing with a tall, buxom woman gesturing wildly with her hands. I plastered a smile on my face the moment I heard Nancy's booming voice. I needed a distraction, and I was standing in front of the people who would give it easily.

"There's my girl!" Nancy ran and pulled me into a bear hug.

"Nice to see you, too," I squeaked.

"I want my granddaughter back in one piece, Nancy," Gramps harrumphed.

"She's just showing her love." Grams patted Gramps's bulging bicep.

"You call that love?" Gramps pointed. "Looks more like a UFC choke hold to me."

"Hogwash," Grams exclaimed.

Nancy finally let go when she noticed Dillan. "Who's the handsome devil?"

He ran a hand through his already disheveled faux-hawk. His nervous habit. I didn't even think he realized it.

"Dillan Sloan, ma'am," he said.

"Rainer's nephew?" Grams moved forward to gawk at him. "My, my, my, you're just as good looking as your uncle. Hair needs trimming though."

"Leave the boy alone, Caroline," Gramps grumbled.

I stifled a much needed giggle as Dillan endured the attention of both women. He was doing well until I noticed the muscle on his jaw jump. From the way Nancy and Grams circled him, I wouldn't be surprised if they pinched his cheeks…among other parts of his anatomy. Those jeans fit him too well. And I shouldn't have been thinking about them on top of everything else.

I must have frowned, because Gramps wrapped an arm over my shoulders and drew me close. "Something bothering you, honey?" Of course he would notice. I was a good actress, but I wasn't good enough to fool him.

Before I could come up with a lie, he followed up his question with, "Where's Bowen?"

I almost exhaled in relief at the mention of his name. Right. The perfect excuse. Thank you, Bowen.

I shrugged. "I don't think we'll be seeing him for a while, Gramps."

He frowned at me. "You alright?"

I shifted my weight to my toes and kissed his chin, the only part of his face I could reach. "I'll be fine."

I really, really hoped it was true. My gaze landed on Dillan again.

. . .

Exhausted, but still wired from all that had happened at the festival, I rested my chin on a fist while looking out the window of Gramps's truck. The prairies zipped by, covered by a blanket of night. I sighed. My breath formed a small circle of fog on the glass. Grams filled the ride home with raves about Dillan Sloan—gracious, a total gentleman, good breeding, just some of the words she used. Words I would never have used. Within the first five minutes of meeting him, Grams was all for Team Ego.

"What's that, Grams?" I immediately said in response to a question I didn't hear.

"Where's your head been, dearie?" Grams turned to stare at me from the front seat. "I asked, is it true Dillan was homeschooled until now?"

Memories of the true identity of Dillan's parents still left me freaked, so I gave Grams the PG version. "His parents travel a lot and he goes with them. So, yeah, homeschooled."

"He sounds like such a smart boy." Grams swooned.

"Polite, too," Gramps added.

I had to smirk at the fact that they didn't know about the arrogant, know-it-all, Mr. Rock-Star-National-Geographic.

"Is that Kyle?"

Grams's question snapped me to attention. I craned my neck to try and get a better look at the shadowed figure sitting on the front steps of our farmhouse. I squinted. Another figure entered my mind. Cloaked. Faceless. Pointing at me. I shook my head until my curls covered my face. No time for that. Gramps parked his truck by the garage and we all slid out, making our way to the front porch.

"You off to take my granddaughter somewhere?" Gramps stood at his full height, puffing his chest out like a silverback gorilla.

"No, sir," Kyle said. "Just planning to sit outside."

"I asked him to meet me here," I added.

"Good! Wouldn't want her out late. That dog killer's still out there."

"Don't scare the children, David." Grams's voice sounded a little unsteady.

"I'm just telling the truth, dear."

"I know." Grams touched his cheek. "Now, let's leave these two alone. I'll bring you some iced tea in a while," she said to Kyle and me before she tugged Gramps up the steps.

"If you see anything, boy…" Gramps's forehead wrinkled.

"I'll be sure to holler." Kyle tipped his head in a brief nod.

I raised an eyebrow as Gramps and Grams disappeared into the house.

"What?"

"That look between you and Gramps."

Kyle shrugged. "What look?"

"Don't pretend it didn't happen."

"I'm not."

I sighed. If Kyle wanted to clam up, I'd need the Jaws of Life to get anything out of him. So I changed the topic. "Today was all kinds of weird."

The top step creaked when I sat down. I spread my legs in front of me and leaned back on my hands. He sat down beside me and rested his arms on his knees.

"Define weird."

A cold finger ran down my spine. I'd been keeping way too much from him. My dream. The puppets. And now, the black dog. Oh, and the fact that Dillan admitted to being an Illumenari and how all that made sense in my head. When did having visions of the future become the least weird thing I had to deal with?

I puffed out my cheeks. "I actually don't know how to answer that."

He let out a slow whistle. "Sounds serious."

"You have no idea."

"So, what are you thinking about?"

"Dillan." It was true.

"How did we suddenly go from your day being weird to him?" His expression shifted from confused to complete guy shutdown. "Is this a girl thing?"

"He…" I paused. What to confess? "He said some things to me this afternoon."

"Okay, officially lost me."

"That's pretty obvious."

"I thought you spent the day with Bowen? He asked Penny and me to stay away so he could have some 'alone time' with you. His words, not mine."

My heart stopped. "Yeah, about that…"

"Whoa! Is that why you and Bowen were fighting?"

A groan escaped. "You heard about that?"

"Penny and I were in the crowd. That was one nasty blow up. We knew better than to follow you while you were still pissed."

Lips pursed, I said, "Anyway, it's safe to say Bowen and I are officially done."

"He doesn't and will never deserve you, Selena."

"He cheated on me. I get it."

"It's not just that. You deserve so much better."

Crickets chirped around us. I studied Kyle's profile from where I leaned on the newel post. When did I start keeping things from my best friends? I used to tell Kyle and Penny everything. It was time for me to trust someone.

"Have you ever felt like someone was watching you?" I asked.

He winked at me. "When don't I? Particularly when I'm in the shower."

"Oh, shut it!" I shook my head in disbelief. Trust Kyle to make jokes when I needed total and complete seriousness from him. "Come on. I'm trying to tell you something here. No jokes."

"What's life without jokes?"

"Anyway," I continued with an eye roll, "this afternoon I came out of a booth at the flea market and the feeling hit me like a slap in the face. At first, I was just uneasy. Then the feeling got more intense. And then I thought I saw this huge black dog with red eyes. I ran."

His eyebrow twitched.

"That's when I ran into Dillan. He thinks I'm being targeted."

"Targeted? What the hell does that mean? By who?"

"I know you think this is crazy, but it gets worse."

"Worse than spouting weird stuff about you being a target?"

"Dillan told me he's an Arbiter for this group called the Illumenari. And the weirdest part is…" I paused. "I think I believe him."

All the color in his face drained like a bucket with a hole. His mouth opened, but nothing came out. He stood up and practically ran to his car.

"Where are you going?" I blurted out.

"It's getting late," he said.

"Kyle?"

"I need to take care of something."

Slack-jawed, I watched him go. He didn't even look back when I called his name again. He got into his Prius and drove away. When I'd thought my day couldn't get any stranger, it did.

Chapter Twenty-Seven

Dillan

Sucker-Punched and Grass-Stained

Dillan grimaced at what had once been a golden retriever. From the rigor and the dried blood, the carcass couldn't have been dead more than a day. He'd ruled out wild animal the second he saw the first dog. That many teeth marks didn't belong to anything the animal kingdom could come up with.

Tonight's find made twenty. His gut told him there were many more. The prairie was too big for him and Sebastian to cover every inch of it, but every day the number of missing dogs reported increased. He shook his head. How was this thing getting away with it without being seen? Surely a rancher would have noticed something by now.

He didn't see a pattern until they found more bodies. The one he stood beside now was a little over a couple of miles from Selena's house. Whatever killed the dogs seemed to leave the bodies for the Fallons to find. But why? What for?

Worry unsettled him. He stifled the urge to run the last few miles and stake out the farmhouse all night. That wouldn't be creepy at all. The worse part? He'd actually risk it, wincing at the truth of the thought. Christ. One second she twisted him up. The next she pulled him apart. He blamed those damn aqua eyes. They turned a clear shade of blue when she looked up at him through tears.

Sloan.

Pulled from dangerous thoughts, he lifted his head at Sebastian's call. His partner was close, but not enough to where he could see him. He didn't have to wait long for the hellhound to continue what he was about to say.

Tracks. A mile east of where you are.

"You sure?"

He growled.

Using the stars above to orient himself, Dillan shifted to his left and took off at a run in the direction Sebastian indicated. They finally had a lead. He believed Selena was the target of the Maestro and whatever was killing the dogs. His protocol mandated he go straight to eliminating the potential threat.

He jogged up a hill and stopped. Sebastian snorted, pointing his snout down. He crouched and studied the tracks that led away from their location. They looked like some kind of paw print.

"A lion?"

Insane, but yes, Sebastian confirmed.

He spread his hand over the print closest to him. His fingertips didn't even reach the edges. "It's a big cat, that's for sure."

A lion in Wyoming?

"It's not a lion." He pushed up to his feet. The print proved they were dealing with a Supernatural. A damn big one. "Not in the way we're thinking. The teeth marks are too different. No incisors."

"Sloan!"

Dillan didn't have time to brace himself against the fist that collided with his face. He twisted as he fell, landing on his hands and knees. Sebastian growled. He was just about to leap to his feet and repay his attacker in kind when he recognized who stood over him.

"Yeah," Kyle said, breathing hard. Even in the dim light, his eyes burned like hot mercury. "Stay down or someone is ending up in a pine box."

A metallic taste coated Dillan's tongue. He spit everything out and swiped at the wet trail running down his chin. "I'd watch it, Hilliard," he said then gestured with his chin toward Sebastian. "My friend over there won't be happy if you try anything. Consider the first punch free."

Kyle whipped his head toward the huge canine ready to pounce. "Only you would use a hellhound in a fight. Cheating bastard." He pointed at Sebastian. "You scared the hell out of Selena."

Dillan was about to say something when Kyle answered, "Stay out of it."

"Screw you, Hilliard."

"I'm not talking to you!" he barked back at him.

Shutting his mouth, he shrugged. He should have known Sebastian was communicating telepathically with the guy. The throb on his cheek distracted him from thinking straight. He pushed some of his energy toward it, but his effort wasn't enough to heal the damage. He'd have a hell of a time explaining the bruise away.

"I don't need a hellhound telling me what to do." Kyle paused. Probably listening. Then he spat out a string of curses, which was a ballsy thing to do against Sebastian, who could snap his head off. "Leave her alone."

Officially feeling left out, Dillan thumbed his bruised cheek. "I'm sure what you and my partner are talking about is fascinating, but shouldn't I be included in this conversation? I was the one who took the blow to the face after all." He added extra special mockery in his voice. "Normally, I'd angle for a fight against you, Hilliard. But before I start beating your ass, mind telling me what the shiner's for?"

Kyle waited a beat before he faced him again. "I knew Rainer was making a mistake by letting you come here. You should have been sent somewhere else, but no, your uncle insisted he could help you. Why his parental instincts had to kick in now—"

"Fuck you!"

"You're such a monumental ass."

"You really gotta work on your insults." He wrapped his legs around Kyle's. One twist and the other guy landed on his back. He straddled Kyle and lifted a fist.

"What we have here is something very important." He glared. "I won't let you undermine everything we've built here for Selena."

His breath caught mid-inhale, fist still in the air. "What about Selena?"

"If it's a normal life she wants then that's what I'm giving her. What *we're* giving her."

Stunned, Dillan let Kyle push him aside. What did he mean by "a normal life"? Kyle rolled to his feet, still speaking.

"And I don't care what I have to do to make her happy. She doesn't deserve being dragged into this the way you're so intent on doing."

"Hey—"

"What possessed you to tell her you're Illumenari, Sloan?"

Dropping his gaze, Dillan closed his fingers around grass and pulled until the roots snapped. The less he said the better.

"We were handling it. She doesn't need to know about this life."

What Kyle said brought up his suspicions. "Who is she, Hilliard?"

"You don't have the right to know."

"She's already in danger. If you don't see that then you're stupider than I thought." Dillan bared his teeth. "I don't know what you're hiding here, but she deserves to know. If only to protect herself."

"What's the use of her knowing about the Manticore and the Maestro?"

That stopped Dillan cold. "Manticore? Body of a lion, a human head, a scorpion's tail, and all that shit?"

All the blood drained from Kyle's face.

"What Manticore, Hilliard?" He pushed. "You know I'll get to the bottom of it. How 'bout we cut the bullshit and you start yapping?"

"For some time now I suspected a Manticore was behind the killings." He pointed at the deep depressions on the ground. "But I wasn't sure until those tracks."

"Who's the Manticore?"

He shook his head. "I don't know."

"You're shitting me right? How can you miss a Manticore?"

"You can't," he barked back. "There are several families living in Newcastle."

Now *that* drained all of Dillan's blood. He almost lost the ability to speak. For the first time, his being demoted to Arbiter became a disadvantage. "Newcastle's harboring Manticores? Does Rainer know?"

He knew the answer before the other guy's eyebrow shot up. Of course Rainer knew. Now what his uncle has told him about politics and being impartial made sense. No wonder he couldn't investigate the case himself and sent Dillan instead. This shit got real in the worst kind of way. His jaw hurt from biting down too hard. The secrets. The deception. Something bigger was happening in Newcastle beyond the threat of a Maestro and now a rogue Manticore.

"He sent you to investigate, didn't he?" Kyle sighed. "I should have known better than to confront you while I was too pissed to think straight. Rainer's going to kill me."

Dillan jumped to his feet and manifested his sword. In an

instant, the watch on Kyle's wrist morphed into a metal staff and blocked the oncoming blow. Their weapons grated against each other. Neither was willing to let up.

"You don't have to worry about Rainer," Dillan said. "Not telling me put Selena in danger. And I still owe you for bringing her to that fake grave you have for your parents knowing a Maestro is in town."

Kyle pushed back with surprising strength. "What do you know about my parents?"

"They're not dead."

"What?" He pulled back.

Dillan pitched forward. He hated the hope in the other guy's eyes. Anger and hate, he could handle. But hope? He tapped his fingers against the hilt of his sword. "You didn't know."

"They're dead," he insisted.

"You don't know what the family tree does, do you?" Dillan staggered back and laughed. "Oh this is precious."

Faster than a snake strike, Kyle leveled his staff against his throat. "Spit it out, Sloan!"

Unfazed, he flicked it. "The family tree automatically crosses out the names of the dead."

Understanding dawned. "They're alive?"

"Now who's dense?"

Kyle pointed at him. A fearless move. But a stupid one. With a flick of his wrist, he could chop the digit off. Feeling just a bit more generous tonight, he used the blade to push his finger aside instead, cutting the skin.

"Look, don't tell Selena anything more." Kyle dropped his hand, letting the finger bleed. "She doesn't need to know. Believe me...you'll cause her more pain than it's worth."

"I'll tell her anything she needs to know if I think it'll keep her safe."

"Now I get why Selena keeps having violent urges. Arguing with you is useless."

"And I thought you were the smarter one."

Kyle turned on his heel and walked back down the hill.

"See you at the field trip," he called out and Kyle flipped him off. He threw his head back and laughed.

Manticores? Not excited to go up against one of those.

Sebastian's comment washed over Dillan. He gripped the hilt of his sword, taking comfort from its solid weight. Forget interesting, Newcastle just got dangerous.

"What did you tell Kyle?"

That I knew what I was doing.

He heard the shrug in Sebastian's voice. "I still need to talk to you about that. Stupid move, mutt."

She needed my help.

"Did you get a look at what was after her?"

The hellhound shook his massive head.

"Then you really weren't helping. No point in worrying about that now." Returning his sword to its inert form, he faced Sebastian. "We need to find this thing before it moves from dogs to its favorite meal."

Humans.

He nodded once.

What about the Maestro?

"One life threatening Supernatural at a time." He stared into the distance. A little over a mile from where he was lay the closest mutilated carcass. Add a couple more miles to that stood the Fallon farmhouse.

Chapter Twenty-Eight

Selena

That Little Thing Called Drama

*T*he bright light.

The biting air.

The black dog.

The pointing hooded figure.

The blood.

All the blood from a hole in my chest. The taste of copper and rust on my tongue. It tasted like fear.

Screaming. Lots and lots of screaming.

Who could it be at this time of night? What could have happened? She sounded like she was in pain. So much pain. I couldn't take it.

The door to my room burst open, almost tearing from its hinges. A woman in a cotton robe rushed in. Her white hair hung down loosely over her delicate shoulders. A towering man in a shirt and sweat pants, holding a baseball bat, filled the doorway after her.

The screams continued. Hoarse now. The voice was running out of steam.

"Selena!" The woman sat on the edge of the bed and grabbed my arms. She shook me. "Selena! Wake up!"

I wanted to say "stop," but the cries drowned out the word in my head.

"Slap her, Caroline," the man said.

The crack of a hand against skin cut through the screams, silencing them.

The sting on my cheek spread, waking me in slow degrees. I blinked dry eyes, panting and swallowing. Over and over I panted and swallowed. My hands white-knuckled the comforter that pooled on my lap.

"Water," I begged hoarsely.

The man disappeared out my door.

Shivering, I focused on the woman. My brain told me I knew her. That I was supposed to know her. But I couldn't remember her name. Slowly, I let go of my comforter—one aching finger at a time.

"Selena." Her brow puckered. "Do you recognize me?"

I ransacked my brain for the right answer and came up with a whole lot of nothing.

The man came back with a glass of water, an equally worried expression on his handsome face. "Here, my dear, drink."

Taking the glass with shaking hands, I brought its rim to my lips. I reminded myself to take slow gulps, listening to what the man and woman were saying.

"…years since she's been this way," the man said.

"Not since they died. That look, that empty expression. Those screams. Oh, David." The woman covered her mouth with a trembling hand.

"Shhh." He gathered her in his arms. "She's strong. She'll come back to us. You'll see."

The screams came from me? I made those horrible sounds? Every sip of water confirmed the rawness of my throat. It hurt to swallow. Then the vision came back to me. I stared at the couple holding each other, finally recognizing them.

"Grams?" My voice was so small, not like what I was used to hearing from me.

Tears raced down her face. "Oh, Selena," she said. She gathered me into her arms and sobbed into my shoulder.

I looked up at the man. "Gramps?"

"Yes, dear?" He looked so fragile for such a big man.

I pushed away the disturbing images of my death. Closer now, more than ever. I felt it. "I'm sorry I woke you."

"Don't you dare apologize," Gramps scolded.

Grams broke the hug and dried the last of her tears with the sleeve of her robe. Her piercing eyes held mine.

"What did you see?" she demanded.

I scrambled for a lie. "A nightmare."

"Are you sure?"

Lying to Grams and Gramps shredded my insides, but I had to do it. I didn't want them to worry more than they already were. Even if I barely had clear memories of them, I pulled out the big guns: "Mom and Dad."

Grams's granite expression softened. She wrapped her arms around me again. Gramps joined in, taking the both of us into the wide expanse of his reach. We all rocked in silence for what seemed like hours.

The darkness outside gave way to pale morning light by the time Grams fussed about making breakfast. I watched them step out of my room like they didn't want to leave. I kept a smile on my face even though I was dying inside. I couldn't tell them. I couldn't tell anyone.

• • •

A few miles out of Newcastle, Mr. Sloan stood in the aisle of the school bus beside the driver and happily explained what the class could expect from our trip to Mount Rushmore. It seemed like I was seeing him for the first time, my American History teacher. I would have never suspected him of being anything other than the guy smiling and enthusiastically answering questions beside the driver. He was Illumenari. Speaking of which, my gaze landed on Constance and a brunette named Tina giggling. Their heads were close together, whispering and sneaking peeks at Dillan, who sat with a brown-haired boy named Tim two rows in front of them. He ignored Mr. Sloan by staring out the window. The boy who, in one afternoon, flipped my life on its head. I had a feeling he'd rather be doing something else than be stuck sitting on a bus full of teenagers. Maybe policing those he called Supernaturals? I was pretty sure he was about my age, maybe a year older, but sometimes, when he got really quiet like he did now, he seemed older. It still wigged me out how calm I was being about all this. Like the life I had before yesterday wasn't the one that was normal. I sent a silent prayer for strength to whoever would listen.

Our group rode in the first bus while the other half of the eleventh grade rode in bus number two. Penny grumbled about the fact that she couldn't ride with our class when we all gathered at Newcastle High's parking lot that morning. Mr. Sloan insisted she stay with her class in the second bus. I smiled at the memory of Penny's mock devastation. My phone was filled with frown-y faces—all from her.

My brow wrinkled at my seatmate after I deleted yet another message with a frown emoticon. "What did you say?"

"Are you sure you're okay?" Kyle asked, angling his head to get a better look at me. I shrank away from him, pushing my phone back into my pocket. "Your eyes look all puffy."

"Just didn't get a lot of sleep. Was super excited about today."

The lie, once it started coming out of my mouth, sounded like the truth. I twisted around and grabbed his hand, examining his bruised knuckles so he couldn't stare into my eyes. "What happened here?"

He shrugged. "Slammed into something, I guess."

"Like what? A wall?"

"Don't you just love field trips?" Kyle asked. His expression was unrepentant.

Whoa! Sudden topic change. Great. The amount of things we kept from each other seemed to pile up now. How long until we stopped sharing things with each other altogether?

I glanced out the window.

"What happened after you left me on the porch?" The question came out of me when I couldn't take the silence between us anymore. At least give me an A for effort. I *was* trying.

After a long, deep breath, he finally said, "I had an errand to run. Honest."

"Close to midnight?"

He rubbed the back of his neck. "I remembered Riona asking me to buy her some pasta."

For the first time in our years of friendship, Kyle lied to me point blank. It hurt more because he didn't even try to hide it. My chest ached. He was deliberately keeping things from me, and he wasn't even very good at it. But then my own secrets surfaced. I lived in a glass house and I was throwing stones. I saw no point in arguing when he clearly didn't want to tell the truth. I breathed away my rising temper and let the lie go.

· · ·

When we got to the memorial, the entire eleventh grade gathered around Mr. Sloan in the parking lot. He passed out brochures with a map and information about the monument while explaining that we had the day to explore. By two in the afternoon, everyone needed to meet back at the amphitheater to watch a program describing the construction of the site. After one last warning about staying on the Presidential Trail, Mr. Sloan allowed us to break into groups.

I called for Penny to join Kyle—the big fat liar—and me on the trail. This was right about the time Bowen—the lying, cheating ex—grabbed my arm and pulled me aside. I stumbled and glared up at him. Before I could call him out for being rough, he'd already asked his question.

"Can we talk?"

"Selena?" Kyle waited, worry in his eyes.

I debated making him stay or letting him go. Something about the earnest way Bowen looked made me want to find out what he wanted. If this got ugly, I didn't want any witnesses. This was my problem, and I'd handle it.

"Go ahead with Penny. I'll catch up." I waved Kyle away.

After some hesitation, Kyle shrugged and joined Penny at the entrance. When I was sure he was out of earshot, I folded my arms and glared at Bowen. "Ouch, by the way. Handle me like meat, why don't you?"

His brows came together as he shoved his hands into the pockets of his jacket. "Sorry. I just really wanted to talk to you."

"As far as I'm concerned, we have nothing to talk about."

Bowen's expression combined serious and something else— something that whispered of dark nights and scary things. I caught a malicious spark in his eyes I'd never seen before. My fingers twitched. I squeezed my arms tighter and reminded myself to keep calm.

He closed the gap between us and placed his hands on my shoulders. "I miss you. I miss the way we used to be together." He trembled as he spoke, a fire in his eyes that turned the black coffee color into pure inky midnight. "Cheating to make you jealous was a mistake." A frightening, obsessed stalker-like determination tinted his words. "I wish I'd shown you how I felt earlier, but I thought to take my time. That got me nowhere. Now, I'm showing you all my cards. I want you back in my life."

Self-preservation, the type that came from years of human evolution, snapped me out of my daze. I unfolded my arms and held on to his wrists. My fingers wouldn't even go all the way around them. I stepped out of his hold.

"Enough," I said. "We can't be together. Not anymore."

"Why not?" His expression clouded over, danger in the hard set of his jaw. This was worse than that afternoon at the supermarket.

"I just can't."

"You have to give me a reason why."

I scrambled for the one reason he might buy. If he thought I'd moved on then maybe he'd drop this ludicrous idea of us getting back together. I focused on his eyes and willed my rapidly beating heart to slow. I needed to sound convincing or he wouldn't believe me.

"I like someone else," I forced myself to say with conviction.

He cocked his head to the side. "Who?"

I scanned the last of our classmates heading for the Presidential Trail and found the guy I was searching for.

"Dillan!" I called and he turned to face me. I waved him over and he raised an eyebrow at me. Great. Now wasn't the time for him to be a jerk, especially after insisting he'd protect me. Some lame bodyguard he was.

"Him?" Bowen scowled at Dillan over his shoulder.

Finally taking the hint, Dillan trotted to my side. And in a move I hadn't expected, he wrapped his arm around my shoulders and pulled me close. I did my best not to step away despite the rush of warmth spreading over my cheeks.

"You ready to go?" he asked me without paying attention to the fuming Bowen in front of us.

"You'd better leave before I wipe that grin off your face." Bowen growled.

"Oh, you'd like that." Dillan grinned wider. "But this isn't the time or place to teach me some manners. Do you really want to get kicked off the swim team?"

His words hung in the air until Bowen said to me, "I hope you're happy."

A chill ran down my back as he turned around and stalked away. Not knowing what to think, I focused all my attention on the first thing I saw.

"Where'd you get that?" I reached for Dillan's bruise.

He tilted away, dropping his arm. "I ran into something."

"Huh. Kyle said the same thing on the bus." For some reason my shoulders felt empty without the weight of his arm there. "You two aren't fighting, are you?"

He gave me a half grin. He thumbed the bruise. "You know guys. We talk best with our fists."

"You're shitting me." I shifted my weight, unsure which to do first: be pissed at Dillan or worry about Kyle. I settled for worry. "What did you two fight about?"

"I'm kidding." He raised both his hands. "I don't know what happened with Hilliard. I really did run into something."

Something told me not to believe him, but the distraction worked to calm me down. "Thanks for the back up."

"Yeah, what was that about?"

"Hopefully showing Bowen I'd moved on."

"Huh." He smiled. "Moving on wouldn't happen to be in my direction is it?"

I rolled my eyes and walked away. "Don't kid yourself."

Without comment, Dillan let me lead us to the Presidential Trail. I flipped open the brochure Mr. Sloan gave out and followed the marked path. It didn't take long until we caught up with Penny and Kyle at the Grand View Terrace.

The grandeur of the site washed over me. My encounter with Bowen became a distant memory compared to seeing the magnificent granite carvings of four influential presidents in American history. I reminded myself not to let anything else spoil my day. Every little piece of normal I could get mattered. My vision left me no other choice. If I was supposed to die then I'd live every second of my life—not that I was giving up on finding a way around the vision. Just, right now, I wanted to live in the present.

Penny excitedly bounced to my side. "There you are!"

Her voice was so loud birds flew out of their perches. She winced and had the sense to look guilty. Pushing away the last of my morbid thoughts, I listened to her upbeat explanation of the history of the memorial. From Gutzon Borglum's planning of how the structure would look to the origins of the mountain's name, Penny didn't miss a thing. She even narrated the story of how Borglum's son took over after his father died in 1941, complete with dramatic pauses and grand hand gestures.

The amount of trivia she knew didn't surprise me. She was my information central after all. But after a while, I noticed something different about her. Penny's eyes seemed glazed and unfocused, like she stared past me instead of at me.

Kyle called out from a few yards away, "Let's go, ladies. We have to start the trail if we want to see the Sculptor's Studio and Borglum's Viewing Terrance before the amphitheater."

I waved at him, chalking up what I saw in Penny's eyes to paranoia. "Kyle the control freak. Never gets old."

"You got that right." She linked her arms with mine. The picture perfect friend. To the boys, she said, "We'll take it slow, guys. Go on ahead."

I added, "We'll be fine."

Dillan and Kyle shared a glance then shrugged at the same time. Penny and I giggled.

"Boys," she said.

"Boys." I sighed. This was good. Time outdoors. Some fresh air. The company of a good friend. Just what I needed.

I matched my pace with her ambling as Kyle's and Dillan's long legs ate up the trail. I said a silent prayer of thanks that Penny wanted to go slow. The beauty of the Presidential Trail would have been wasted if we went as fast as the boys did.

Nature upon nature. Snapdragons, sunflowers, and violets scattered everywhere, giving the abundance of green from the pines a much needed punch of color. The cool breeze spread the woodsy smell of the place. I breathed it in deep.

The guys had just disappeared around a bend when a prickly sense of anxiety beat with my heart. An invisible hand slowly closed its clammy fingers around my neck. My eyes darted to Penny. My friend's expression stayed content. But her silence was unusual. She should have been talking my ear off about the other things she'd learned about Mt. Rushmore. Or at least ask me about my talk with Bowen.

The feeling of something being really wrong twisted in my chest. Searching for the source, I didn't notice Penny had pulled away from me until I saw her walk up to a snapdragon at the side of the trail. The sense of being watched choked my every breath. The guys were too far away now to call out to without shouting. No one else walked the trail with us. Odd. The number of tourists who visited the site should've meant we were never alone.

When I returned my attention to my best friend, debating whether to tell her what I felt or not, she smiled at me. My small measure of relief shattered when she stepped into the forest. Gut twisting panic overrode the voice inside my head warning me not to go after her.

CHAPTER TWENTY-NINE

Dillan

FIELD TRIP PINES AND NEEDLES

*D*illan glanced back just in time to see Selena dart off the trail into the forest. His heart dropped. Shit. He grabbed at Kyle's shoulder too hard.

"What the hell, Sloan!" Kyle yanked back, adjusting his shirt.

"Selena just went off the trail."

"What?"

He pointed in the direction Selena disappeared from. The invisible line that connected him to her tugged, becoming tauter every second that passed. Soon the mind-numbing electric wave would come. His instincts told him so. "I don't see Penny anywhere…"

Kyle didn't wait for him to finish. He bolted toward where they'd last seen the girls. Dillan chased after him. Panic rushed through his body like a nasty case of chills. Just before Kyle left the trail, he grabbed his arm.

"Let me go, Sloan!"

He ignored the murder in the other guy's eyes. "I'll go after her.

You stay here."

"And do what?"

"If we're not back in ten minutes, get Rainer. Don't blow your cover now by going after her. She already knows what I am and what I can do."

Kyle let out a slow breath then nodded once.

Not waiting for verbal confirmation, he darted into the forest, his sword already manifested. Whatever forced Selena off the trail couldn't be good. The air around him sizzled with energy. He cursed leaving Sebastian in Newcastle. He'd insisted the hellhound continue searching for the Maestro's lair.

Fifty yards from the trail, he spotted Selena and raced to her. She tripped on a rock sticking out of the ground and stumbled forward. He caught her before she face-planted.

"Where's Penny?"

"Dillan!" She gulped in a lungful of air and said, "I don't know. We were on the path and then she ran off and left me."

He scanned the area, using his energy to feel everything out. Like a rubber band, it snapped back into his body. He cursed his limitations. They might as well be sitting ducks in these woods.

She panted and continued, "I called out to her, but she started running. Then I lost her."

"You're never walking behind me again." He rubbed her arms, using some of his warmth to ease her trembling.

"We have to find..." She stopped, her gaze darting from one spot to the next. "Something's here!"

Something whooshed past them. They ducked instinctively. A needle the length of a barbeque stick, three times as thick, stuck out of a tree directly above his shoulder. It reminded him of a porcupine quill.

Three more came after it.

Not willing to become a pincushion, he grabbed Selena's hand, winced at the shock then shouted, "Run!"

They ran side by side. Dillan used his body to block any of the needles that they might not dodge. He set a bruising pace, zigzagging between pines. Selena gripped his hand, keeping up with him.

"Where are they coming from?" she shouted over the blood roaring in his ears.

"I'm not sure," he answered through the noise. "Just keep running."

Something sped past him. He stumbled, hitting the ground hard. The barrage of needles suddenly stopped. A burst of pain emanated from his side. He clutched at the wound. Selena slid to a stop then scrambled back to where he landed. Like a trained soldier, she yanked him behind a large pine. Then she crouched at his side and squeezed his arm. He grunted from the electricity that came with the contact as he leaned heavily against a tree. He couldn't feel his legs anymore when she pushed aside his hands.

Her eyes widened a fraction. "You've been hit."

"It's just a scratch." Sweat drenched his face.

"Let me see." She bent down. He looked down with her. An angry cut bled out just above his hip. A purple haze surrounded the wound, spreading across his skin fast. His already rapidly beating heart sped up even more.

"It burns," he said. "Son of a bitch, it really burns!" He breathed through his teeth. "The needles must be poisoned."

Selena grabbed his sword and cut across the wound until blood gushed out. He bit down on another scream as pain spasmed through his body. Flaming pin pricks spread all over his torso. His blood felt like acid eating away at his insides.

As she began to bend over the wound, he stopped her. "What are you doing?"

"I need to suck out the poison."

He shook his head. "We don't know if it'll poison you, too, if you do that."

"It's spreading fast. If I don't get it out, who knows what will happen to you."

Ignoring his continued protests, she bent over him and sucked at the wound she'd created. Embarrassing heat flooded his face at the touch of her lips on his skin. He hardly felt the succeeding electric shock upon contact. His body shook so hard his teeth chattered. She spit out a mouthful of blood and returned to the wound a second time. Seconds later, his eyelids drooped, but he couldn't stop staring at Selena. She embodied some wild creature then, saving his life without concern for her own. By the third time she bent over him, the pain subsided.

"It hurts less," he wheezed out. "How are you feeling?"

She turned aside and spat before speaking. "Nothing. Maybe the poison only works when it's in the bloodstream." She studied the wound. The purple haze was smaller now. She bent over it two more times.

About to pass out, he upended his sword so the moonstone at its pommel hovered over the cut. He'd be really weak afterward, but if he didn't close the wound, he won't be able to stop the bleeding. "Where'd you learn to do that?"

"Gramps taught me basic First Aid. I figured a snake bite would be almost the same as being poisoned by a needle. What are you doing?"

A soft crackle followed by a small shock entered his body through the gash as he siphoned his energy and sent it back into his body. He channeled as much of the surrounding life force as he dared without sucking any from Selena. Tiny sparks flew out of the moonstone into his skin. She gaped. Her eyes darted from his face to the wound. The blood clotted and the cut closed. Energy zinged through him from his hip to his shoulder blades. When only a welt remained, he pulled his sword away.

"H-how…" She blinked several times.

Dillan's world spun. He closed his eyes and breathed through his mouth to avoid the coming nausea the power drain brought.

"How'd you know the needles were coming," he rasped out. His mouth had gone dry.

"I…I'm not sure." He heard the shrug in her voice. "I just felt like someone was watching me."

"Like at the festival."

"Yeah."

Not wanting to get caught helpless, he forced himself to open his eyes. The world spun a bit, but he managed to blink it away. He returned his sword back to a charm, refusing to show any more signs of weakness in front of the girl who just saved his life. She pulled his sweater down and jumped to her feet.

"I think it's over. Can you stand?"

"Yeah." He used the tree for leverage, pushing himself up. The simple move cost him dearly. Besides breathing heavily, the sweat on his face turned cold. "Give me a sec."

"Do you have a spare pair of jeans?"

"Do I look like the type who brings around spare jeans?"

She pointed at his legs. "That's a lot of blood."

"Just get me to a bathroom and I'll wash it off before it dries." Not dwelling on how bad the trek back to the amphitheater would be, he pulled out his bandana and handed it to Selena. She looked at him then at the bandana.

"Use that to yank out one of the needles," he said, still leaning against the tree. "And be careful."

"Yeah, yeah, it's poisonous." She pulled out one of the needles and wrapped it in the bandana then handed it back to him. He shoved it into his back pocket.

"What are you going to do with that?"

"I have to show this to Rainer."

"Now? We're in the middle of a field trip."

Still feeling the effects of the blood loss and the drain from healing himself, he didn't answer. The tree he leaned against was his friend. He swiped at the sweat rolling down the side of his face.

"We have to find Penny. If whatever those needles came from is still out there, we have to make sure she's safe. What if she got hit like you did?"

"Let's get back to safety, and then we'll put together a search party to find her." He didn't have the patience to argue. Selena was his priority. Pushing away from the tree, he hooked an arm over her shoulders and guided her back to the trail.

• • •

Fifteen minutes later, he stood in a bathroom in only his boxers washing off the blood from his jeans and drying it under the hand dryer. The aftereffects of the energy drain had waned, a small miracle considering he'd closed a wound. He studied the welt for a second. Maybe not all his original powers were gone. He didn't dare to hope. To keep Kyle's cover when he and Selena stumbled out of the forest, Dillan explained that he'd cut himself and needed to clean up before they went to the nurse. Selena and Kyle went with it for, what he suspected, were totally different reasons. This hiding shit thing was getting harder by the second.

Now the two friends stood watch outside while Dillan cleaned up. He still couldn't believe Selena had thrown caution in the wind and sucked out the poison from his body. She'd saved him. He couldn't decide whether it was sexy or reckless. The latter aimed at himself since he—the once rising star in the Illumenari—had fallen so far from grace that he'd let a girl save him.

Once the wet spot on his jeans was gone, he slipped his pants on and walked out of the bathroom. Kyle stood beside the door.

"Where's Selena?"

He pointed at the opposite door with a stick figure in a skirt. "What the hell happened out there?"

Not knowing how much time they had before Selena came back, he filled her best friend in with the least amount of explanation it took.

"You let her suck out the poison?" he hissed.

"I had no choice. She was already on the wound before I could push her away." He raised his hand to stop the coming tirade. "Look, I get it. I screwed up. But you're missing the point here. Selena ran into the woods after Penny, and we were attacked."

"How is that possible when I just saw Penny meet up with Tina and Constance?" Kyle tilted his head toward the group of girls. "I thought they'd gotten separated when you ran after Selena."

"This doesn't feel right."

Selena picked that time to walk out of the bathroom. She waved her wet hands and said, "Their dryer is busted."

The girls Penny stood with giggled, catching Selena's attention. She hurried to them. Dillan shared a look with Kyle before they trailed after her.

"Penny! Where've you been?" Selena grabbed the other girl's shoulders.

Dillan and Kyle flanked her. He eyed Penny closely. The look of shock on her face seemed genuine.

"I was with Constance and Tina most of the day," Penny answered. Her confusion sounded real to his ears. He needed his fingers on her pulse to determine if she was telling the truth, but based on the natural cadence of her voice, he didn't doubt her response. Unease writhed inside his gut.

"What's with the panic? Did something happen?" Penny continued, more subdued than usual. Her eyes looked glassy.

Selena's hands dropped to her sides. "Don't you remember

being on the Presidential Trail with us?"

"She's been with us most of the day," Constance said. The other girl—Tina—nodded in agreement. Something wasn't right here. And judging from the tension surrounding Kyle, he felt the same. Penny was with them. Unless she magically had a twin sister, this whole situation reeked of a Supernatural manipulation. Damn. The Maestro. He'd read the conjurer could control humans, too. How could he miss this? He should have anticipated the escalation. If it couldn't get corpses to nab Selena then the humans closest to her seemed the next viable choice. He and Kyle were safe since their Illumenari blood negated mind control via conjuring.

Thinking fast, he took out his phone and typed into the screen MAESTRO then PENNY and discretely showed it to Kyle. He flicked his gaze at the screen. Dillan erased the unsent message as Kyle's lips disappeared into a tight line.

"How…" Selena took a step back.

"Selena," Penny's voice softened, "is something wrong? You're really pale."

Dillan grabbed Selena by the arms from behind and said, "I think Selena got things mixed up." To Selena he said, "Maybe you're just tired. Right, Kyle?"

"Yeah, even I feel turned around," he said.

Penny tilted her head. "Are you sure?"

Selena nodded. Dillan supported her weight as she leaned against him, moving one of his hands to her hip.

"Everyone!" Rainer announced from the entrance. "Please start filing into the amphitheater. The program is about to start."

Students shuffled past their group. Dillan exchanged a glance with Kyle. He nodded at him once. An awkward silence passed before Constance and Tina said they'd save Penny a seat. The two girls headed for the theater, whispering to each other.

"Do you want to sit together?" Penny offered.

"I think," Selena cleared her throat, "I think I'll sit with Dillan and Kyle."

"You sure?"

She gave her a smile. "I'll text you later."

Penny shrugged and walked away.

"That's not Penny." Selena spoke to the floor.

"How can you be so sure?" Kyle asked.

"In the years we've known Penny, when did she ever act less than peppy?"

CHAPTER THIRTY

Selena

On the bus, I sat in the furthest corner of the last row. A dull ache thumped behind my eyes. The breeze from the open window ruffled my wild hair and cooled my flushed cheeks. It didn't bring the comfort I needed. I pressed my temple against the glass and half-listened to Dillan and Kyle discussing comic books, of all things.

What had happened today didn't make any sense. I was with Penny at the Presidential Trail. We'd locked arms. We'd walked together. When she darted into the forest, I went after her, but the deeper I got the farther she pulled away from me until she completely disappeared. Then Dillan and I were attacked by needles. I told him Gramps taught me to suck out the poison from his wound, but actually, the voice in my head instructed me on what to do. I acted before thinking. Then Dillan used his sword to heal his wound. I was more confused now than ever. What was happening with my life?

Kyle was no help when I asked him about Penny during the program. He kept telling me to shut up because he didn't want to miss anything from the documentary about the construction of Mt. Rushmore. Dillan had little to add. He and Kyle had gone on ahead when Penny suggested we'd take it slow. So really, I'd been the only one with her. My head reeled into a dead end.

I bit down hard and shut my eyes, listening to my breathing. Huffs. Puffs. And deep sighs. My foot tapped on the seat in front of me.

I didn't want to think anymore.

. . .

At Newcastle High's parking lot, our class listened to Mr. Sloan's final announcements before filing out of the bus. Each step I took felt like a ton—a pound for every question swirling inside me. Once we were all on the pavement, Kyle started for his Prius.

"Hitch a ride home?" he asked me over his shoulder.

His offer stopped my mindless progress so abruptly that Dillan rammed into me. I stumbled a step and mumbled a vague apology to him, which he didn't respond to.

"I'll take her," he said from behind me.

Kyle fished out his keys and unlocked his car. "With Mr. Sloan?"

I looked over my shoulder and caught Dillan's grin. "I have my own ride."

The casual exchange flew over my head. For the first time in my life, I was truly angry with Kyle. He was hiding things. Possibly things that could get me killed. What kind of a friend did that?

Not willing to take his crap anymore, I had two choices: walk to the diner and wait for Grams's shift to end or catch a ride with Dillan. I was exhausted, so there was only one choice.

"You have a car?" I raised an eyebrow at him.

"Just got it back yesterday actually."

My so-called best friend frowned before he said, "Fine, take her home. Call you later?"

I didn't answer him. The sadness in his eyes mirrored my own. His lips disappeared into a thin line, like he kept what he wanted to say prisoner. After today, I didn't have the strength to fix what was broken between us. I needed time. I turned away from him and let Dillan take my backpack. I followed him to the other end of the parking lot.

"What do you mean *just got it back*?" I asked, trying to keep up with Dillan's ground-eating strides.

"I left it in Budapest when I was…sent here. It takes a while to bring a car overseas."

I accepted his explanation with a slight shrug.

Taken unaware, my heart sputtered the second a dark gray Mustang with black racing stripes running from its hood to its rear came into view. *Now* I understood why he'd bring that car anywhere. Hell, I'd never let that car out of my sight if I owned it.

"That's a…" My voice broke.

Dillan stopped by the driver's side and took out his keys from his back pocket. "A '68 Shelby GT500," he said casually. In short, a very, very nice, classic muscle car. If a vehicle could be a person, the GT would be Dillan all the way—all hard lines and handsome finish.

He opened the door and threw his bag and mine into the back seat. "It's fine to come near the car, you know. It won't bite."

I shut my mouth and took tentative steps toward the car. I grew up with Gramps talking nonstop about this car. He'd dreamed about a '68 Shelby GT500 since before I was born. He said he just needed to get lucky at the junkyard and he'd devote everything to restore it. Gramps's fantasy car—in all its gleaming glory—sat patiently in a high school parking lot. It looked so out of place among the trucks.

But that was what Dillan was. He seemed out of place in this little town I called home.

He opened the door for me with an impassive expression. Oh, but he couldn't fool me. I knew very well that he gloated inside. He had the right to. I'd be gloating aloud if I were him. I slid into the plush black leather seat and ran my hands over every surface I could touch after buckling my seatbelt. Awe, like a slow burning fuse, spread all over my body. My fingertips sizzled. It was one thing to hear Gramps talk and completely another to actually sit inside the fantasy.

"Should I give you two some time alone?"

"What?"

His smile gave me unexpected quivers. "Stop molesting my car."

"I wasn't—"

The engine roared to life with a twist of his wrist.

Pummeling my annoyance into submission, I focused on the sweet ride. "Is this a GT500KR?"

"Yup." He nodded. "Under the hood is a 428 cubic-inch fully restored Cobra Jet V8." He shifted to third gear when we reached the edge of town.

"That's 335 horsepower," I purred. In garage speak it meant the car was a beast on the road. I sighed. "The universe is so cruel."

He took his eyes off the road for a second to look at me. "You know your cars."

"I really don't. This is the only one I know about because Gramps is a mechanic. *He* knows his cars. And we happen to be sitting in one he's been dreaming about since forever." I ran my hand over the dashboard. "How did you get a car like this?"

"Long story short, I had nothing else to do in Italy a couple of years ago—"

"What, no scary things to kill?"

"After seeing the sights, I found this baby in a scrapyard and started putting it together to pass the time."

"Everything on the Internet about you, is it true?"

"Nothing like a fake life to hide the real one." He snorted.

I shook my head in disbelief. "Yup, the universe is cruel."

"Stop saying that."

"What are you…sixteen?"

"*Seventeen*," he corrected.

"Right." I suppressed a grin. Knew he was older. "I'm turning seventeen in November. Only months apart and already you've experienced more than I have."

"You make experience sound dirty." He chuckled. "You're not going to mention that Taylor Swift thing again are you?"

"There's that." I ticked off points on my fingers. "You belong to a famous family. You look the way you do. You can handle a sword like nobody's business. You're smart. And you own an awesome car."

"If you continue, I'm going to think you like me."

A roaring blush exploded on my face. "I'm not finished."

"There's more?"

"I'm just glad you're a jerk and your arrogance is annoying." I faced him and smiled, my teeth showing. "Those are your only redeeming qualities."

He laughed so hard at my sarcasm he almost drove us off the road. My stomach flipped many times over. I still couldn't believe such a sexy sound came from a mouth that could say the meanest things. Despite what his laugh did, I stayed on topic.

"I'm sure half the people in Newcastle wish they had your life."

The laughter stopped.

I glanced back at him. "What's with the quiet?"

A muscle jumped on his jaw. "You don't know anything about my life," he said. Then he looked at me with piercing sapphire eyes. It almost hurt to stare into them. "You know what they say happens when you assume. You make an ass of you and me."

I swallowed the prickly lump in my throat. "Why so defensive?"

"I'm not defensive." He sighed, loosening his grip on the steering wheel. "I just don't wish my life on anyone else. I'm compassionate that way."

The corner of his mouth curled up as we pulled onto the road leading to the farmhouse. He shifted moods from zero to sixty in less than three seconds. I was beginning to see that he said mean and snarky things as a defense mechanism.

"Why didn't you want Kyle to drive you home?" he asked after another couple seconds of stiff silence between us. "I thought you were besties."

I wanted to kick him for being so perceptive. "Don't say 'besties.' It sounds weird coming from you."

He leveled a pointed stare at me.

"Kyle's been lying to me," I said plainly. "We've been best friends for so long, and this is the first time he's ever lied to me."

"That you know of."

"Excuse me?"

"Fun fact about life, Selena: everyone lies."

Anger wrapped my stomach in prickly brambles. "I don't know what kind of a life an Illumenari lives, but around here, friends don't lie to friends."

"Even if it means protecting each other?"

"Even then."

"Then you're naïve."

My mouth opened, but my anger blocked my comeback. He had a point, even if I refused to accept it. My friends didn't lie to me just like I didn't...my heart twisted. I'd kept my vision a secret. I didn't tell Kyle about the puppets or what happened today with the needles. I lied by omission. My righteous indignation crashed, landing as a pile of rocks in the pit of my stomach. Again with the stones in my glass house. Frustration blurred my vision. I had no right to judge.

"Shit. Are you seriously crying?" He pulled over onto the side of the road and turned off the engine. "I'm sorry, Selena. It was a jerk thing to say."

"You're always a jerk." I used the heel of my hand to wipe away the tears that refused to stay in my eyes.

"Shit. Don't cry. Please, don't cry."

"You're the weak-against-tears type, huh?" My voice hitched. Still, the tears came.

"Occupational hazard." He hauled me into a fierce hug, sending the now familiar electric current all over my body.

About fifteen minutes later, tears dry, I led the way to the front door of the farmhouse. It was dark inside. No one was home yet. Being alone didn't bother me as much as Dillan staring at me like I was a crystal swan about to shatter. After my mini breakdown, he kept asking how I felt. So un-Dillan like.

It was the truth. I really did feel better. After all that crying, my head cleared and I saw the Kyle situation in a new light. We needed to talk. The sooner the better. If I wanted him to be honest with me, I had to tell him everything.

The quiet of the prairies magnified our footsteps on the wooden porch. I turned to take my bag from Dillan, but he had already lowered it to the floor. I studied it like it was a UFO, with some curiosity mixed with a little fear. And then, I lifted my eyes to his face. A mistake. I'd been making a lot of those lately. The striking cerulean his eyes became took my breath away. Who knew blue eyes could have so many shades?

"Dillan?" I hated that my voice trembled when I said his name.

"Shhh," he said, and with a hand on my hip, pinned me against the screen door.

I stared at his gorgeously serious face. "Dillan, what are you doing?"

"What I should have done at Valley View," he said.

Slowly, like the moon rising, he bent his head and kissed me. First, a tentative touch, then a second, and when I thought he wouldn't fully commit to the kiss, his lips claimed mine possessively. Forget fireworks on the Fourth of July. The electricity that sparked every time we touched gathered on our lips and exploded. The second his tongue touched mine, the contact felt like Pop Rocks in my mouth. I couldn't get enough of it. Heat and energy flowed from his lips to mine. Just when I thought he'd pull away, he tilted his head and nibbled at the corner of my mouth until he reached the center of my bottom lip. He parted them with his tongue. But, when I let him in, he stopped, resting the tip between my upper lip and teeth. In one experienced move, he traced the sensitive valley. It curled my toes. Only at my gasp did he go all the way in again.

Dillan didn't just kiss. He slow danced. We moved in sync. I wanted to lose myself in him. In his touch. Right then the world seemed like such a perfect place. He had one strong arm around my waist while his other hand gripped the back of my neck. I slid my fingers up his chest and into his hair, linking them behind his neck. I couldn't get close enough. I wanted to drown in his fire. His clean scent enveloped me completely, replacing my worries with hunger. My only concerns became taste, smell, touch. But when I reeled my senses from the abyss, I pushed him back while leaning heavily against the screen door.

"What?"

I sighed, scrunching my nose. "We can't do this."

He tilted his head in confusion. "This?"

Gesturing between us, I said, "You and me and the kissing."

"You don't like the kissing?"

"Oh, no. I like the kissing. The kissing is good." I bit my lower lip. "I mean, I just got out of a relationship."

"Okay." He pulled back a little farther. "If you want me to stop, I'll stop."

Unable to take the cold caused by the growing distance between us, I grabbed his shirt front and pulled him back to me. He went willingly, a devilish grin on his face. "Maybe five more minutes."

CHAPTER THIRTY-ONE

Dillan

LITTLE GHOST OF MINE

It took everything Dillan had to leave Selena that afternoon. Kissing her...he couldn't compare it to anything he'd ever experienced in his life. Forget the shocks. If sitting on an electric chair had a mind-blowing counterpart, sign him up. He never knew a million volts felt so good. If it weren't for the case and her grandparents coming home, he would have stayed with her all night. Unfortunately, the second he left the farmhouse, everything quickly spiraled into a dark pit of frustration.

He stumbled into his room after investigating with Sebastian, bone-tired of all the dead ends. He was no closer in finding the Manticore than when his partner discovered the first carcass. The tracks they'd previously found hadn't helped at all besides identify what they were dealing with. The sheer expanse of the prairies was a clear disadvantage. It seemed like he and the hellhound were just running in circles.

Feeling useless for only the second time in his life, he toed off his boots and fell into bed face first. He groaned into his pillow. Screw a shower. He could do it tomorrow.

Sebastian had no leads on the Maestro either. The conjurer bastard hid himself well. After what happened at the field trip, he couldn't let his guard down for a second. He left investigating Penny to Kyle since he knew the girl better than he did. Without a shadow of a doubt Selena was the target. He hated to be right, especially after that kiss. A danger level this high usually meant a higher class of Illumenari took over. Hell if he'd let Rainer take over now. He'd protect Selena if it killed him.

His head hurt, most likely an aftereffect of nearly draining his powers to heal himself. He took a deep breath, deciding to let go of his current feelings of failure. He needed rest. With each exhalation, he let his body relax. No point in answering all the questions tonight. Like he'd been trained, he let himself slip into the darkness.

· · ·

When he opened his eyes, Dillan found himself on a chair in the middle of a dark room. He craned his neck every which way. A light came from somewhere because his chest, arms, and legs were visible. He tried to stand, but an unseen force tugged him back to the chair.

Keeping his breathing even, he focused on the footsteps coming from his right.

You have someone else now.

He froze. A cold sweat rolled down his spine. He knew that voice…too well. He couldn't mistake it for anyone else. Shit. He swallowed and forced himself to answer as calmly as his rapidly beating heart would allow.

"What do you care?"

She stepped out of the darkness in front of him, wearing a white dress to her knees. She stopped a couple of steps away and hid her hands behind her back. Anxiety churned the acid in his stomach at the sight of her. In the back of his mind, he knew she came to finish what she'd started. Haunting him wasn't enough for her anymore. But his feelings had changed. He no longer wanted to give her his life for his mistakes.

He pinched his thigh hard. Pain shot up his leg, but nothing happened. He didn't wake up like he expected. He shut his eyes then opened them again. She didn't disappear like before. Not a ghost. Something else. Something probably worse.

She shook her head. *You're not going anywhere.*

"What do you want?"

Is that how you treat me now? She frowned, flipping her hair over her shoulder. *Before, you couldn't wait for me to end it.* She disappeared then reappeared straddling his lap. Her freezing fingers wrapped around his neck. He hissed. His skin burned beneath her touch. She giggled.

"You're not real," he said, more for himself.

She froze. Tears flooded her eyes. He bit his tongue to stifle the urge to comfort her. She was gone, taken from him. From the Illumenari, he corrected himself. He couldn't help her anymore and suffered the consequences. He had someone else to protect now. Someone he promised himself not to fail.

Like she'd read his thoughts, she teleported to stand in front of him. She swiped at the fallen tears. She always acted younger than she was. It annoyed him half the time. She snapped her fingers and a screen he hadn't seen before played a movie in black and white behind her. At first, he didn't understand what was happening until he recognized Hero's Square. Its large column centerpiece stretched up to the night sky. Several statues flanked it on both sides.

His eyes widened. "Budapest."

She nodded. *You left me there.*

"No!" He struggled against the invisible ropes holding him down. "Dammit! Let me go."

You were supposed to stop them.

The truth of it hit him hard. Dejection wrapped around him like a straightjacket. He bowed his head. He didn't need to watch to know what happened next. In the movie, he ran into a small alley between two shops. She stood at the end of it surrounded by screeching banshees. He fought them off and pulled her to him, but they were trapped. There was too many of the horrid creatures. He'd been clawed badly, bleeding from so many wounds he could barely stand. She begged him to end it. To do what he must to keep them from capturing her. His training told him what he had to do, but he couldn't bring himself to move.

Yes, she said. *You were supposed to keep me away from them. But you didn't. You let them take me.*

The disappointment in her voice broke him. "I'm sorry."

You were supposed to keep me away from them.

She repeated the sentence over and over again. He bit his tongue until blood seeped out of the side of his lips and ran down his chin. The metallic taste made him gag. Despite the pain, he didn't wake up. She deliberately kept him there to watch his failure.

Someone, somewhere screamed his name. He wanted to call out, to reach for whoever summoned him, but his throat refused to work. He swallowed the blood flooding his mouth and tried again.

The voice asked him to wake up.

"I'm trying, dammit!" he said.

Her eyes darted from place to place, like she searched for the voice, too. Then she laughed. He'd never heard her sound like that. More a cackle than a laugh. She doubled over and hugged herself. When she straightened, her face froze in an ugly mask. He barely recognized her.

He didn't scare easily, but her next words made his blood run cold.

• • •

Finally, Dillan opened his eyes and gasped. He rolled to his side and coughed. Blood splattered on his pillow. More coughs shook his body. A pulse of pain emanated from his side.

"Dillan!"

He flopped flat on his back, clutching his side. Sweat dotting his brow, he closed his eyes and breathed away the pain. "Calm down, Rainer. I'm not deaf."

The side of his bed depressed. "You were screaming her name."

His uncle's words forced his eyes open. The light in his room seemed too bright, making him squint. His eyes burned, but he focused on his uncle sitting there in his gray T-shirt and pajama bottoms.

"It's nothing," he mumbled. He hated the worry in Rainer's eyes.

"It's not nothing." His uncle pointed at where he clutched his side.

He tried to sit up. Sadly, the pain wouldn't let him, so he settled on his elbows. He looked down as far as he could. A red stain spread across his shirt. Rainer pushed his hand away and examined the wound. It caused the blood to spill over to the blue sheets, staining it brown. He must have nicked something major.

"You stabbed yourself."

"Duh, Sherlock." He closed his hand around the hilt of his sword, unsure how he accomplished it. Everything he tried to wake himself up from the dream hadn't worked.

"Don't be cute with me." His uncle glared, flicking Dillan's ear.

"Ah, a little help—"

The Boogeyman spread his hand over the wound. It healed instantly in a rain of blue sparks. He fell back on the bed and drank air like water on a hot day then returned his sword to its inert form before it cut another body part.

"Why did you stab yourself?"

He bit back the real answer. "I don't know."

Rainer crossed his arms. "Tell me everything."

"It's nothing."

"Dillan!"

He didn't flinch at the bark. Staring at the ceiling, he said, "I rolled in at about three and went to sleep. The next thing I know, you're shaking me awake."

Out of the corner of his eye, he watched Rainer study the room. "The wards are holding and your window is shut. No sign of forced entry anywhere. And I don't feel anyone else but you in this house."

"I hate to disappoint you, but your safeguards don't always work." He realized his mistake the second the Boogeyman's eyes settled back on his. He closed his hand around Dillan's shirt and pulled him up. He didn't struggle, knowing it was futile against a Legacy. As an added safety precaution, he kept his hands at his sides.

"What aren't you telling me, boy?" Rainer asked in a deadly whisper.

"What? You're allowed your secrets and I'm not?"

He shook him. "Not when your life is clearly in danger."

To avoid answering his unasked question, he shifted the topic. "What about when Selena's life is in danger?"

Rainer opened his fist and let him fall back down on the bed. He stood up and moved to the bookshelf. He rubbed his forehead, his eyes closed.

"Besides the attack at Mt. Rushmore and the puppets at Valley View, has anything else happened?" he asked after dropping his hand.

Dillan sat up and swung his legs over the side of the bed. "What's going on here, Rainer? The attacks are clearly escalating. This isn't good. I need to know…hell, Selena needs to know."

They watched each other for the longest time. No one moved. They barely even breathed. Dillan knew Rainer couldn't hide things for much longer. The truth rose to the surface no matter how deep it was buried.

"Then bring her here," his uncle finally said.

Chapter Thirty-Two

Selena

Nuts, Bolts, and Catapults

*T*he next day, Dillan picked me up for school. He texted that he was worried about my safety and he would be hanging close until he found the threat against me.

The roar of the GT's engine had Gramps jerking away from the breakfast table.

"Is that what I think it is?" He turned toward the front of the house. If he'd magically transformed into a dog that second, his ears would have been perked up and his tail would be wagging uncontrollably.

I stifled a giggle into my orange juice. "Go see for yourself."

Gramps bolted like a kid on Christmas morning, ready to tear up wrapping paper to get to the toys inside.

"What's that all about?" Grams raised an eyebrow at Gramps's disappearing act.

"Dillan's taking me to school in a GT500." I shrugged and finished my juice. Grabbing my bag off the floor, my stomach quivering at the idea of seeing him again, I hurried after Gramps.

"Oh, Lord." Grams followed me to the front porch.

I burst out laughing the moment I got outside. Gramps had his hands all over the car, a goofy smile on his face. Love at first sight. Dillan looked on with an expression that seemed to be a cross between pride and concern.

"You better not leave me for that car, David." Grams called from the porch steps as I walked to Dillan's side.

"Hey, baby, where have you been all my life?" I heard Gramps say, awe in his words. His reaction to the car was worse than what I could have imagined.

"Should I be worried?" Dillan asked me when he took my bag, then he did something I didn't expect: he gave me a peck on the cheek.

I blushed. "I think so," I answered after clearing my throat, memories of our epic make out session resurfaced. I suddenly had a craving for Pop Rocks. What a change a kiss made. "Gramps, we'll be late for school."

He didn't seem to hear, circling the car like a tiger scenting a female in heat.

"David, I swear, if you don't leave that car alone this instant, I'm filing for divorce," Grams yelled from the porch.

From the longing on Gramps's face, I had a sinking feeling he actually considered it. He slowly backed away from the car. Dillan opened the door for me and I hopped in, telling him to hurry before Gramps changed his mind about letting us go.

At the school parking lot half an hour later, I spotted Kyle locking his Prius as I slid out of Dillan's car. I had held off on texting him last night. What we had to talk about couldn't be done over the phone.

"Kyle," I called out to him.

He walked away without even looking my way.

I frowned. Okay, if he wanted to act all childish about this whole thing, then two could play that game. To think, I'd just made up my mind about telling him everything. But, even after convincing myself I didn't care, it still hurt. No matter how angry Kyle and I ever got with each other, we never avoided each other. *First time for everything, I guess.*

"Maybe he didn't hear you," Dillan said when he reached my side.

"From ten feet away?" I let him take my hand. I didn't mind the shocks anymore. They didn't hurt at all. Holding hands. Huh. Another unexpected action from him, and from the looks of everyone in the parking lot, I wasn't the only one who noticed. Did holding hands just tell the world we were going out? I mentally shook my head and focused on my best friend's retreating back. I sighed and said, "I doubt that."

When Dillan and I entered American History, Kyle had already taken his usual seat, and was busily reading from the textbook.

"Did you hear me when I called your name in the parking lot?" I asked as I sat down beside him, deciding to give him another chance. I owed our friendship that much.

His eyebrows rose. "I didn't, honest."

I bit the inside of my cheek to keep from screaming at him. He did hear me because he never said "honest" at the end of any sentence.

"I have a busy week ahead of me. I won't be able to join you for lunch," he continued.

"You never have a busy week," I countered. "Not really anyway."

"Well, this time I do. I'm helping out with the yearbook committee. I have an article to submit for the paper. Ashley Emerson asked me to tutor her."

In my head, his steady stream of excuses became *blah, blah, blah*. No use. I leaned back on my seat as Mr. Sloan entered the classroom.

At lunch, Dillan and I expected to meet Penny at our usual table when I spotted her sitting with Tina and Constance. When did that happen? Penny didn't always stay long in the cafeteria, but when she did, she always hung out with Kyle and me. No exceptions. Now she laughed with Tina and Constance. I whipped out my phone and quickly tapped a message.

Me: *What's up?*

I waited. Penny fished out her phone, glanced at the message, then returned her phone into her pocket. What the hell was the about? I stifled the urge to walk over there. I was too pissed. Making a scene wouldn't help things between us.

"You okay?" Dillan asked.

"I don't know yet," I grumbled.

This happened every day for the rest of the week. Kyle had things to do, Penny hung out with other people. Dillan stayed with me the whole time, but I missed my friends. Although, I couldn't ignore the steely gazes Bowen shot our way at the cafeteria.

By Friday, I was officially lonely. The only balm to my gloom was when Gramps managed to convince Dillan to bring the GT around for a tune up and an oil change. Mr. Sloan didn't have enough equipment for him to maintain the GT at their townhouse. To be honest, when Gramps offered the use of the garage, I suspected he only wanted to have the car over.

They had the GT on four jack stands when Gramps got called away on an emergency at one of the ranches. "Tractors," he muttered to himself as he grabbed his spare tool kit. He gave the GT one last loving glance and left without even a good-bye to the both of us. Smitten. Totally smitten. Poor Grams.

Meanwhile, I didn't think Dillan could get any hotter. Seeing him in a white tank was just all kinds of illegal. I literally stopped and stared when he stripped off his jacket and sweater to work on his equally handsome car. Just an oil change, but dang!

I sat on a paint can while he slid under the Mustang. I couldn't believe I made out with *that* just a few days ago. The way I saw it, I was both blessed and cursed. I heaved a long sigh. From where I sat beside the tool box, I had the best view of his jeans and scuffed boots.

"Pass me the socket wrench, will you," he said from under the car and reached out his right hand.

I handed him the wrench. "Dillan?"

A series of clicks followed him taking the wrench. "Mmm?"

"Are there other Illumenari like you?"

"Knew this was coming," he grunted.

So he was expecting it, which might mean actual answers. Or more lies.

I shifted the paint can and continued, "Well, sorry I couldn't get around to asking you sooner. If you haven't noticed, I'm not having the best week. Kyle's been avoiding me. Penny's hanging out with Tina Conners—"

"Tina?" He scooted out from under the car and spread newspaper in the place he'd been.

"The girl she and Constance sat with in the amphitheater. Worse? They're not answering any of my messages."

"Don't do that."

"What?" I looked up to find him staring at me.

"Let them bring you down. You're better than this."

Twisting to my left, I grabbed a bucket and shoved it into his hands. Not in a million years would I give him the satisfaction of agreeing with him. But he had a point. So what if they wanted to avoid me? I had no time for this drama. Then a thought hit me. Maybe—considering the threats against me—my best friends avoiding me might not be so bad. If they weren't near me, the safer they'd be.

"Just answer my question," I pressed, feeling a ton better.

His brows lifted. "Many."

At first I didn't get his answer then I connected it to the question. Duh! I scrambled for my next question. "Like *how* many?"

"Excuse me while I take a census." He bent over to slide the bucket under the GT's oil pan. The move gave me an unobstructed view of his perfectly shaped...I shook my head to clear it. Holy shit, staying focused was harder than I thought.

"Very funny." I looked anywhere but at him. "Come on, I'm serious."

After removing the oil plug, he sank to his haunches and placed his hands on my knees. "I don't know the exact number. But, trust me when I say, enough of us are out there because the world hasn't gone to shit yet."

My heart fluttered. From his answer or his hands on my knees, I couldn't tell. "So, there are just the Arbiters?"

He turned thoughtful. "There's a hierarchy."

"Fancy."

"Now who's mocking?"

"Can't help it." Like metal attracted to a magnet, I touched my forehead to his and closed my eyes. I breathed in a mix of motor oil and his clean smell before pulling back. Having him close tempted me.

"I want to know more," I said after opening my eyes.

A grin filled with mischief played on his lips. "But then, I'd have to kill you."

"How unoriginal." I pushed on his shoulder, which should have been enough to topple anyone backward. It was a testament to his balance that he stayed seated. "So, this hierarchy..."

"There are four classes in the Illumenari. The Arbiters, the Guardians, the Legacy, and the Council." He switched the socket with an oil filter wrench and scooted under the car again. "The lowest are the Arbiters. They're sent to settle disputes between Supernaturals or investigate cases that involve maintaining the safety of humans. Think of it like gaining experience points in an RPG."

"Like right now? You're investigating what's been happening to me?" My eyebrows came together. Now that he was far away, I could think. I shuddered at the thought of what else could be out there, and Dillan coming into contact with it. Genuine concern ate at my nerves like termites. I disliked the idea of anyone hurt because of me.

"I'm on vacation."

"Illumenari go on vacation?"

"We have dental and medical, too, in case you're wondering."

I kicked his boot. "Jerk."

"Admit it. You like it when I get snarky."

The name of the second class sunk in. The voice in my head—which didn't bother me as much as it should—had said I needed to find the guardian. Could it mean the Illumenari? "Tell me about the Guardians."

Thankfully, he moved on. "They guard. We don't complicate the naming of things."

"Guard what exactly?"

A grunt then a pause. The plug seemed to be giving him problems. "Whatever's assigned to them?"

I thought about it. He said he'd protect me. "You're an Arbiter, right?"

"Yeah." He tsked like he'd bitten into something bitter. "Now, shut up and let me finish."

He waited. I bit the inside of my cheek to keep from talking.

Only then did he continue. "There's the Legacy. Almost like special ops. They get sent on the most difficult cases. And lastly, the Council. They control everything."

"Everything?"

"They assign the cases. Everyone answers to them. They're the judge, jury, and executioners." He slid out from under the car, went to the hood, and removed the oil filler cap.

I shuddered at the last part about the same time our American History teacher came to mind. "Is Mr. Sloan an Arbiter, too?"

"No, he's Legacy." He placed the cap beside the wrench and the drain plug.

A newfound awe for our history teacher blossomed in my chest. A special ops Illumenari? Could Mr. Sloan be any cooler? "You told me he's retired. Why? He's so young."

A taut silence followed.

Dillan leaned against the driver's side door and folded his arms. He focused on a point beyond where I sat. "There are many reasons for someone to retire, Selena. Sometimes people burn out. Others get really injured and they can't function well anymore. Then there are others who lose everything, even their minds."

"Where does Mr. Sloan fit into all that?"

"The losing their minds part."

A pinch of pain stopped me from asking more personal questions. I knew what it meant to lose everything. I spent a whole year of my life not really in the present, so I got the "losing their mind" part, too. I moved on to a different question.

"That time you were poisoned" —I shivered— "how'd you heal yourself?"

He rubbed the charm on his cuff until his sword materialized. Dillan, ribbed shirt, sword. I nearly fainted. Oblivious to my reaction, he clutched the grip with one hand and pointed at the opaque gem.

"This stone connects the natural abilities of an Illumenari to the outside world," he said. "Call it power, magic, chi, whatever. The point is…Illumenari can use the energy within their body to manifest anything needed by using the stone as a catalyst. That afternoon, I used it to heal."

"That explains the blue sparks."

"Correct. That was my energy. But at my current rank, I can only heal small wounds. If the scratch was any deeper than it was…"

Our gazes locked then. The steely blue of his eyes turned stormy. With sure movements of his wrist, his sword returned to its charm state. Then he pushed away from the GT and, in purpose-driven strides, stalked toward where I sat.

Not once did I break eye contact. The tip of my tongue darted across my bottom lip. My skin prickled at the raw strength of him barely tamed by the grace of his stride, the confidence of his stance, the arrogance in his stare. He'd hooked me. I saw it in his eyes. I understood then what made wild animals so beautiful. I never wanted to tame him.

I swallowed. Hard. The temperature in the garage rose. The smell of motor oil and metal and sweat bordered on intoxicating.

No smile. Not this time. He bent down until his hands rested on my legs. His fingers gripped my knees, but not hard enough to bruise. He distributed his weight, so I didn't bear the brunt of it. Tortuously slow, his face inched its way closer to mine. When I shifted to meet him half way, he pulled back and waited until I moved away again. It almost physically hurt to keep still. Whoever said patience was a virtue didn't have Dillan's lips so close. I wanted to scream.

His dark chuckle vibrated into me, gathering just below my navel like golden honey. He let the tip of his tongue travel the edges of my mouth, sending a crash of thrilling awareness to the pads of my feet. I gasped, and he charged in. Yes. Got my Pop Rocks fix. He playfully explored the underside of my tongue, finding ticklish corners that had me giggling then moaning into his mouth.

I threaded my fingers through his hair, delighting in the softness of each strand. No gel today. Maybe because he knew he'd get all yummy, sexy, sweaty this afternoon. I couldn't get enough of what he gave, needing more and more of the friction until I had to force myself to come up for air.

He had other ideas. Those sinful lips traveled down the column of my neck. He nibbled on my pounding pulse. It made my back arch. Pleasure and pain fused into one smooth sensation. He soothed the place he'd bitten with a small lick then traveled the length of my collarbone to the other side of my neck. I'd lost all coherent thought when he reached the delicate curve of my ear.

"Are you busy tomorrow?" he whispered.

"No." I tried to twist away to put some space between us, but he grabbed the back of my neck and held me prisoner. He wasn't done tormenting my ear apparently.

"Come with me tomorrow."

"Where?" More a gasp than anything else.

"Just say yes."

With my eyes still closed, I imagined the word YES. A quick nod came out instead.

"Close enough."

• • •

I sat alone on the porch, waiting for Dillan to arrive. At breakfast, Grams and Gramps went about their day as if I didn't wake up shrieking my lungs out again, like the night before the field trip. My throat still hurt from it.

The rumble of the GT's engine broke through my funk as it drove up the gravel path. I launched off the top step and ran toward the driver's side even before Dillan could get both legs out of the car. I leapt into his arms and buried my face in the hollow of his neck, breathing him in. I used the contact to keep me in the present, remind me I was still alive.

"Hey, someone seems happy to—" A pause. "Selena? You're

shaking. Fuck. What's going on?" His hands rubbed up and down my back, pressing me closer to him.

I shook my head.

"Babe, come on," his voice filled with concern, "you've got to talk to me."

Breathing in and out one more time, I moved back and plastered a smile on my lips. "Don't call me babe," I teased even if the endearment was enough to push all my fears away.

He tilted his head to the side. A glimmer of doubt entered those blue eyes. "Get in."

The sweet scent of leather had a strangely calming effect on me. "So," I said. "Are you going to tell me where we're going?"

"Are you going to tell me why you were scared shitless?"

I flinched. "Bad dream."

He gripped the steering wheel. "Bullshit."

"Don't you have bad dreams?"

"Don't answer my question with a question."

My stomach churned. I wanted to take the lie back. The urge to confess, to share, overwhelmed me so much that I had to choke down the truth. My throat ached with every gulp.

As if sensing I had no inclination to elaborate, Dillan exhaled. The tension in his shoulders melted. For the entire drive into town, we didn't speak. I thought he was mad at me until he reached out and traced a line from my temple to my chin as he pulled on to W. Main Street. I let the touch happen. Something told me he needed the contact more than I did.

"You know you can tell me anything, right?"

I blinked at him. "Yes…yes, I know."

"Good." He nodded once as if that was that. I was glad he didn't push. "Can you get out of your shift at the bookstore?"

"Where are you taking me?"

He eased the GT into a parking slot in front of Ormand's and killed the engine. Then he squeezed the back of my neck, pulling me closer. His lips touched mine while he spoke. "Just get out of your shift."

I zipped out of the car and into the bookstore in five seconds flat. The bell at the door announced my welcome while the rush of cold air hit me like a bulldozer. I almost stumbled out again. Jeez!

Ormand stood behind the counter, bagging a customer's purchase. "Selena," he greeted. "You're early."

"Not exactly." I waited with impatient energy as he thanked the customer. I stared at my sneakers. "I was wondering if…"

"Yes?" His smile revealed his crooked teeth.

I fiddled with the edge of my jacket. "Can I take the afternoon off?"

His smile wavered. "Hot date?"

My blush burned to the roots of my hair. "Yes."

A honk interrupted whatever Ormand was about to say. The goose bump-inducing feeling that came and went when I was in the store washed over me now. I backed away slowly.

"I'll make it up to you. I promise," I said when I reached the door.

Dillan kissed my cheek the second I slid into my seat.

"What was that for?" I touched the spot his lips just left, instantly forgetting Ormand and the bookstore.

"I'm a sucker for blushes." He grinned.

Heart thrumming, I buckled in. "So, spill. Where are we going?"

"My house."

CHAPTER THIRTY-THREE

Dillan

FUNCTIONALLY DYSFUNCTIONAL

Selena talked. And talked. She kept on talking for the whole drive up to the townhouse. Dillan chuckled. If he'd known she'd be this nervous, he'd have told her what to expect. She wouldn't let him get a word in. So, lips tight, he let her talk and talk. When the townhouse came into view, she described its brick and glass as if this was the first time he was seeing it, too. He nodded dutifully and just listened. It still bothered him to have her in his arms shaking the way she did when he'd picked her up. It made him feel helpless. Maybe the danger of the situation was finally catching up with her. He tightened his grip on the steering wheel as she mentioned the black mailbox and the happy gnome standing at the foot of it. He wouldn't let anything happen to her. He'd do whatever it took to keep her safe.

When he pulled into the two-car garage, right beside the scarlet '66 Mustang, Selena paused in her monologue. He found her adorable as she stared at his uncle's car like she was about to say something then sighed instead. He waited, watching her fiddle with a loose thread on her sweater sleeve. He wanted to reach out and tangled his fingers with hers. Touching her had become his newest addiction. The soft skin on her face, her un-callused hands…he could go on and on.

"Mr. Sloan's here?" she finally asked.

Rolling his eyes, he got out of the car and hurried to her side. "You look disappointed," he teased, opening her door.

She stepped out. "I just thought…"

"As much as I like that you're actually disappointed Rainer's here, I didn't bring you here to ravish me."

"Shut it!" She slapped his chest. The shocks didn't even bother him anymore, and from the calm expression on her face, she hardly felt it either. The need to have her touch him outweighed his want to do the touching.

"Dillan?" Rainer's voice came from somewhere inside the house.

Ignoring the call, he wrapped his arms around Selena's waist. He figured they had a couple of minutes before Rainer showed himself. Keeping his gaze locked with hers, he eased her closer until they stood hip to hip. It scared him how much he liked having her standing so close to him.

"You've got to stop blushing," he whispered, his lips touching her ear. He delighted in the shiver that ran through her, took pride in being the one to cause it.

She kept her hands on his chest and leaned back. "It's not like they're intentional. Stop seducing me and I'll try not to blush."

"Like you really want me to stop."

"Dillan, what's taking you so long?" Rainer stood by the door that led into the house from the garage.

"Don't get your panties in a bunch." He glared at the mood killer. "Just about to bring her in."

A hard glint entered Rainer's eyes before he blinked it away. "You have a phone call."

"Who?"

"Your grandfather."

His arms tightened around Selena. He didn't want to leave the bubble of comfort being around her created. For the first time, he had something beautiful in his life and he'd be damned if he let anything happen to her. Whatever she was didn't matter anymore. Human or not, all he knew was he was quickly falling for this girl with her smattering of freckles and crazy copper curls. Lips in a grim line, he held Rainer's intense gaze. A call from his grandfather could mean many things, and he didn't like any of them.

"You shouldn't keep him waiting," Rainer said. "We'll wait for you in my study."

Reluctantly, he released Selena. If he had to face his grandfather, now was as good a time as any. And Rainer was right about not keeping him waiting. He may joke about it, but pissing off the head of the Illumenari Council wasn't in his best interest. After placing a quick kiss on Selena's lips to give himself courage, he padded past his uncle. He muttered every step of the way. Before he reached the limits of his hearing range, he heard Selena ask, "Italian?" He hadn't even realized he'd slipped into a completely different language.

"Greek," Rainer said. "I'm sorry about that. He never likes talking to his grandfather. Come in."

The truth of it was he never liked talking to anyone in the Council. His grandfather just happened to be his least favorite of the bunch. He winced at his uncle's amused tone. If he didn't know any better, he'd say Rainer lived to torture him. What an honor. Shaking his head, he took the stairs to the second floor two at a time. When Rainer said phone call, he'd meant video chat. He booted up the laptop, punched in the password, and then logged on to the secure server reserved for the Illumenari. The handle G_Sloan topped the list of those online. One click and three rings later, an older version of his father and uncle came into view.

Not wanting to prolong the ordeal, he didn't sit down. Instead, he leaned down so the webcam caught his face.

"Not like you to give me a call," he said.

The old man sighed. He looked tired. "I'm not here as head of the Council, Dillan. I just wanted to check in on you."

His eyebrow lifted. The man who didn't think twice about banishing him wanted to "check on him"? Bullshit! "As you can see, I'm still breathing with all fingers and toes attached. Rainer's doing a bang up job taking care of me."

His grandfather frowned. He knew the expression all too well, had been on the receiving end of it numerous times. "Respect, Dillan. Learn it."

He breathed out slowly, keeping his temper in check. "Granddad, I have other things I need to do." Like keep Rainer from biting Selena's head off. Who knew what they could be talking about right now?

His grandfather's eyes closed. He reached up and pressed two fingers against his temple. When he opened his eyes again, hard steel replaced the softness. "You know what you've done despite your responsibilities to our family. You have a legacy to uphold, yet you seemed to have forgotten all that at the most important moment in your life. This," he gestured behind Dillan, "is your doing. If you did your job, you wouldn't have been banished."

Pushing away the hurt the reminder of his failure caused, he said, "I'm sorry I'm not the favorite anymore, Granddad. You can put all your focus on Devin now. If you're done telling me how much of a disappointment I am, I have to go. Tell Mom and Dad 'hi' for me."

He logged off before his grandfather could say anything else.

Chapter Thirty-Four

Selena

Broken Hearts, Broken Parts

I followed Mr. Sloan through a kitchen with gleaming marble counter tops, honey-colored cabinets, a large center island with copper pots and pans hanging above it, and a stainless steel fridge. Mr. Sloan wore a moss-colored sweater and dark jeans, looking oh-so-casual and doubly sexy. Genes like that shouldn't all go to one family. I could just imagine what Dillan's parents looked like to produce someone as hot as him. I made a mental note never to tell Mr. Ego that or all hell would break loose.

We passed a sunken living room dominated by a massive white couch. I let myself imagine Dillan lounging on it, reading a book with that same intense concentration he wore the first time I'd seen him at the bookstore.

At the end of the hall, Mr. Sloan motioned for me to enter a room with huge glass windows along one side. I blinked repeatedly because of the sudden brightness compared to the more muted lighting in the living room. When my vision cleared, I gasped. In the distance, a pond gleamed where a gathering of ducks bobbed over the water's surface. A group of geese flew by in a loose V.

"Wow," I said. "Amazing view, Mr. Sloan."

"Yes." A clipped answer, not at all like the warm and inviting Mr. Sloan I knew from school. Dillan's comment about losing his mind rang in my ears. What could have hurt this man?

In my periphery, I noticed a large frame spanning one wall. I turned to gape at a family tree with at least a hundred names. It pulled me closer, like I should know what it represented. My eyes searched the names and found Rainer Sloan and Aluara Sullivan. Most of the names carried the Sullivan last name. And Mr. Sloan's was the only name not crossed out.

"This was my wife's family tree."

"You were married?" I asked when he came to my side.

"A long time ago." A robotic answer. Cold.

"I'm sorry."

"So am I."

His words forced me to face him. I couldn't believe this was the same Mr. Sloan that taught American History at Newcastle High. I barely recognized the guy who stood beside me now. He looked so withdrawn. The warmth had disappeared. His eyes stayed on the family tree, but from the deep lines at the sides of his lips, I could tell he held something back.

"Did you retire because she died?"

Icy blue eyes settled on me. I almost flinched back. Almost.

"She was the last of her family," he said. "I keep the Sullivan family tree here to remind me betrayal can come from anyone. Even those you trust the most."

His words scared me. I didn't like this version of Mr. Sloan. Was that all an act? How much more lying could I take? The normal life I'd so carefully built around me seemed to crumble with each new piece of information I gathered.

"Intimidating her already, Rainer?" Dillan walked briskly into the study and moved to my side. He snaked an arm around my shoulders. "Witness the Jekyll and Hyde that is my uncle. Sunny outdoors, chilly indoors. Make sure not to swing at him or you lose an arm."

"What did your grandfather want with you?" Mr. Sloan regarded him with the same ice he used on me.

"Oh, he just wanted to make sure I'm still the failure he thinks I am."

The desire to defend, the need to protect, flowed through me when I heard Dillan's self-deprecating words. "You're not a failure."

He planted a soft kiss on my temple. "Thanks. But that doesn't erase the fact."

"Enough PDA." Mr. Sloan walked to his imposing lava stone desk opposite the framed family tree. On top, Dillan's bandana and the needle he asked me to pull out of a tree from Mt. Rushmore waited for us. "We have much to discuss."

I leaned closer to Dillan and whispered, "Why do I get the feeling I'm not going to like this?"

"Because you won't." He nudged me forward. "Remember what I told you about the things that go bump in the night? Well…"

"Don't over simplify this, Dillan," Mr. Sloan scolded. He sat down on the leather swivel chair behind his desk and tented his fingers. "You know better."

"You're right, *uncle*."

A quiver went through me. Something about the way Dillan said *uncle* spoke of moonless nights and menace. Beneath the surface of his charm and arrogance hid a deadly aura that reached out and grabbed my spine, causing it to straighten like a rod. There was still so much I didn't know about him. The playful guy who looked hot in a ribbed shirt was just one side of the whole. I couldn't let my guard down for a second.

I broke the awkward silence that settled in the room. "So, you know what's after me."

Mr. Sloan pointed at a chair. "Take a seat."

"I'll stand, thank you."

He wasted no time when he asked, "What do you know of Manticores, Selena?"

The word set off a chime of recognition in my brain. I should be familiar with it, but the light bulb moment seemed too far away for me to reach. My hands came together in a tight grip until my knuckles turned white.

Not waiting for my answer, he shifted his icy glare to Dillan. "Enlighten her, please."

"Manticore. A creature that has the body of a lion, the tail of a scorpion, and the head of a man with lots, and I mean *lots*, of sharp teeth. Its name means man-eater in Old Persian. In ancient times, it was known to lure men off the road with its melodious call and eat them."

My throat constricted, cutting off the air I so desperately needed. "What does it have to do with that needle?"

"Manticores shoot poisonous needles from their tail." Mr. Sloan indicated the spike with his finger. "That's certainly from a young one."

"How do you know it's young?" Dillan asked.

Mr. Sloan pinched the bridge of his nose. "You're alive. The older the creature is, the more potent its poison. The wound should have killed you instantly, but it didn't." My teacher studied me closely. "Are you aware of the kind of danger you're in, Selena?"

His question hit me square in the chest where fear gnawed away. "You tell me. Only a month ago, I thought my life was normal. Now, I've been attacked by corpses, I find out about the Illumenari, and you're telling me a creature that shoots poison darts—"

"Needles," Dillan corrected.

"Whatever." I glared at him. "I wish I could say I want my old life back, but it's not going to happen. So, you tell me, *Mr. Sloan*. Do you think I'm not aware of how dangerous my life suddenly is?" Dillan squeezed my shoulder in warning. I ignored it. I was on a roll. "Instead of telling me what I already know, why don't you share something useful, like how I can survive this?" I still held on to the hope that everything that had been happening had nothing to do with my certain death.

"I believe now is the time for you to speak to your grandparents." He tapped his desk.

My brain switched to overdrive. "What do they have to do with all this?"

"More than you might think." He nodded. "We've been monitoring the situation, but the creature continues to elude our efforts to capture it. Dillan can't seem to find proper tracks that could lead us to where it hides."

"It's probably a rogue." He rubbed his chin.

"Manticores are obsessive creatures. When they latch onto someone, in this case—"

"Me." One bleak syllable that distracted me enough from the big ball of anxiety growing in my gut. My grandparents? I wanted to run out of that study, go home, and grill them. Did everyone in my life lie to me?

"They tend to stick around until the object of their obsession is claimed. Since this creature is young, it is still inexperienced." Mr. Sloan's expression became thoughtful. "But, it certainly doesn't connect to the Maestro. They seem to be working separately but with the same goal."

A groan escaped before I could suppress it. This just kept getting worse and worse for me. "But I haven't been attacked by the puppets since that night at Valley View."

"Just because you haven't been attacked doesn't mean you're

safe. A Maestro is smart. What happened at Valley View could mean it tested our defenses."

"I don't think we should lump the two together," Dillan said. "Selena might be a common denominator or she might not. It's foolish to jump to conclusions."

Mr. Sloan smiled ruefully. "Spoken like a true Sloan."

Dillan grimaced at the compliment that sounded more like an insult.

• • •

After hours of listening to Dillan and Mr. Sloan bicker about why *two* seemingly unrelated supernatural creatures stalked me and how I should stay home for the next couple of days just to be safe, I called it a night. Well…late afternoon. I had other things on my mind, like how to broach the subject of all this to my grandparents. I got the feeling Mr. Sloan had Dillan bring me to their house to drive home the reality of my situation. My life was never normal to begin with. His words made so much sense now. Betrayal could come from anyone, especially those I trusted most.

With a heavy heart, I looked out the window of Dillan's car as he drove me home. The sun bathed the prairies with fading orange light. The sky looked a rosy shade of pink, the color of my favorite summer dress. I didn't care why mythical creatures wanted me. What I cared about had to do with staying alive. Considering the track record of my visions, I had an ice cube's chance on a radiator that I wouldn't die any time soon. But the vision involved a black dog and a cloaked figure, not some creature with a man's head, lion's body, and a scorpion's tail.

"I've never seen Mr. Sloan so…cold," I said, my chin on the palm of my hand.

"He just wants you to be safe." He took my other hand and

placed it on top of the gearshift.

"That doesn't sound reassuring."

He sighed. "Rainer has his faults, but he does have his not-so-psychotic moments."

"Dillan Sloan complimenting someone?"

"It's the closest you're gonna get."

I looked at my hand under his while he shifted from first to second gear. The intimacy of our connection curled my toes. I kept my hand as slack as possible, so he didn't have trouble shifting. The charm on his cuff bumped against my wrist. Its pulse reminded me of the power it contained. So did the electricity that ran through our bodies.

"I still can't believe this is happening to me."

"Me either. A few weeks ago, all you did was get on my nerves."

"Ugh! You're one to talk, Mr. Rock-Star-National-Geographic."

He flinched. "How'd you come up with that name anyway?"

My shoulders slumped forward. All teasing had left the building. Or in this case, car. "Penny put it together."

"What's with the tone?"

"Penny's being all weird. Kyle hasn't spoken to me properly since the fieldtrip. I miss my friends. And I have to have a 'conversation' with my grandparents I so don't want to have right now." Something in the distance caught my eye. "What was that?"

A flicker of movement then a shadow.

"What?"

I squinted and pointed. "There. Is that Kyle?"

"Where?"

"Stop the car!" I removed my seatbelt. "Stop the car!"

Dillan pulled over to the side of the road. I hopped out without waiting for him and ran in the direction Kyle went, about fifty yards away. My best friend held a long staff in his left hand. I lost him when he crested a hill. Barely aware of Dillan running alongside me, sword in hand, I ran as fast as my legs would let me. About halfway up the hill a growl similar to the whole trumpet section of an orchestra reverberated from the other side. I stopped and covered my ears. Kyle was running toward that sound. I couldn't see him, but I needed to get to where I assumed he was before whatever growled hurt him.

"What's that?" I shouted over the trumpeting wail.

Dillan grimaced. "The Manticore."

I stood still, shocked for a second, then took off. Dillan grabbed my arm and yanked me back.

"Urgh! Dillan? Kyle's running into that thing! Let me go!"

"In case you're forgetting, that *thing* is after you."

I twisted out of his grip and ran full tilt toward the sound on the other side of the hill. He cursed a blue streak behind me. I didn't check to see if he followed. I knew he would. My main focus currently involved how to get Kyle away from the man-eating thing.

Adrenaline-laced blood roared in my ears, muffling the voice that asked me to turn and run. It annoyed me to no end. At Valley View it asked me to fight; now it wanted me to run? I was no coward.

At the top of the hill, I had a clear view of nothing but grass. A solitary pine in the distance, then more grass. The growling had stopped.

I turned to the left. "Kyle!"

I scrambled down the hill toward him. I didn't care where the creature was. Kyle needed my help. He lay on this stomach, unconscious. I skidded to a stop beside him and knelt down. Breathing hard, I couldn't get my brain to work properly. All the First-Aid training I'd learned in school went out the window. My hands hovered over his back without really touching him.

Dillan knelt beside me, feeling for a pulse on Kyle's neck.

"Is he…" I couldn't say it. The word refused to come out of my mouth.

"He's alive," he said.

I didn't like the harshness in his tone. My heart in my throat, I asked, "But?"

"Help me turn him over." He grabbed Kyle by the shoulders while I held on to his legs. In one quick heave, we flipped him over.

"Oh, God." My hands covered my mouth so I wouldn't scream.

Four diagonal claw marks ran from his left shoulder to his right hip, like a large cat had swiped a paw at him. He bled, soaking his tattered shirt and jeans. His skin had turned ashen.

Dillan removed his jacket and bunched it into a rough pillow, then placed it under Kyle's head. "He needs healing."

I flashed him a quick glare for stating the obvious. To argue with him wouldn't help Kyle, so I tamped down the temper and worry twisting my insides and focused on the more important stuff.

"Can't you—"

"His wounds are too deep," he interrupted.

I worried my lip to keep from screaming my frustration. "You've got to do something."

"I will…but you have to promise not to freak out."

"Why would I—"

"*Selena?*" The voice, silky smooth, sent goose bumps through my body.

At the edge of my field of vision stood the one person I didn't expect to be in that prairie with us. I slowly turned my head, lips parting in amazement and mounting fear. It couldn't be.

"Bowen?" My tongue felt thick in my mouth.

He stood a few yards away. Completely naked. Oh. My. God. "You're here."

Dillan spoke before I could answer Bowen. "Selena, I need you to get out of here."

My heart felt like a fist knocking on my chest. Every beat hurt.

Every breath a struggle. My head groped for reasons to explain why Bowen was here of all places.

"Don't tell her what to do." Bowen cracked his knuckles. "Or you'll end up just like Hilliard over there."

The mention of Kyle's last name snapped me back. I focused on Bowen's face. "Why are you naked?"

He smirked. "Like what you see?"

I stifled the urge to shake my head. Built like a Greek god, nothing about Bowen's body was ugly. I'd seen him in the pool enough times to know. But I was beyond staring at him. I put the pieces together. I trembled to my core when I realized what Bowen being naked meant to Kyle's injuries.

I had to force the words out of my mouth. "Did you do this to Kyle?"

His coffee-colored eyes barely glanced at Kyle. A cruelty I'd never seen before crept into his face. "You're coming with me."

Dillan tensed at my side, a tiger ready to leap.

Cold sweat trickled down my back. Forcing myself to keep calm, I said, "I can't right now. I have to help Kyle."

"I don't care about Kyle. You're coming with me."

"No, she's not," Dillan said.

"Dillan. Don't." I touched his rigid forearm.

"Enough." Bowen grimaced. "If you don't want to give her to me, I'll just take her from you, *Illumenari*."

A gust of wind forced me to look away, but I glanced back after a series of *pop, pop, pop*.

Bowen's body contorted. He doubled over on his hands and knees. His arms and legs morphed into the front and hind legs of a large cat. Golden fur grew out of his skin. His sun-kissed hair formed a full mane around his head. A long tail lashed out from behind him, thudding on the ground. I couldn't blink even if I wanted to. My eyeballs were dry, but I continued to stare anyway. His head remained human except for his mouth where three rows of jagged teeth dripped saliva. The boy I'd known for years transformed into something that shouldn't even be real.

"Manticore." Kyle shuddered.

I tore my eyes away from Bowen to look at my best friend. "Hey, you," I whispered. "Stay with me, okay. Everything's gonna be fine." My smile broke before it could fully form.

He raised a trembling hand and I took it in both of mine. "I'm sorry," he whispered back.

"For what?"

"Not telling you." He coughed then fainted.

"Kyle?" I patted his cheek. "Kyle? Open your eyes. Please, please open your eyes. Don't you dare die."

"She's coming with me," Bowen said in a trumpet-like voice. I looked up from Kyle's increasingly pale face. His scorpion tail aimed threateningly at Dillan. Long needles stuck out from its tip, dripping with a sticky, purplish substance.

In my worry over Kyle, I hadn't noticed Dillan move. Now he was standing between Bowen and me. Sword in his right hand. Stance wide. Shoulders squared.

"Bowen." My voice shook more than I thought it would. "Why are you doing this?"

"The Maestro wants you." He licked drool off his lips.

"What about the dogs?" Dillan hissed out.

Bowen's face crumpled into a bizarre reproduction of a frown. "A diversion. To keep everyone in town occupied."

Dillan charged Bowen. The creature roared and jumped aside to avoid the incoming blow from his sword. Dillan took the momentum of his charge and used it to dodge the spiked tail coming at him. Then he sidestepped a swipe from massive paws with razor-sharp claws. They moved so fast, all I could do was watch. All this time Bowen worked for the Maestro. I couldn't believe it.

"You gonna wipe the grin off my face now?" Dillan taunted.

Three rows of jagged teeth snapped at his head. I gasped. He ducked and lunged forward, landing a blow on Bowen's left shoulder. Black blood oozed out of the wound, but Bowen stood as if he felt no pain.

"The last thing you'll feel is my teeth squeezing your head like a zit." He snapped his mouth. He brought his tail around and shot poison needles aimed at Dillan's chest.

Dillan tucked and rolled, only evading half of the volley. Six needles embedded themselves along his arm. He grimaced, and a small scream escaped my throat before I clamped my mouth shut. In the movies, bad things always happened to the guy when the girl couldn't keep her mouth shut or stay put. I reminded myself that as he struggled to his feet. With preternatural quickness, he circled Bowen and lopped off the tip of his tail. It bounced a few feet away. Bowen screeched and bounded over to Dillan. He stood on his hind legs while his front paws struck out like a lion ready to collide with another head on. Dillan took the opening Bowen provided and lunged forward. He plunged his blade deep into the creature's chest.

Bowen sank his teeth into Dillan's shoulder and ripped at both sides of his ribs with unforgiving claws. He cried out and twisted his sword. I gagged at the sickening squelch of something exploding. Bowen's body went limp and fell to the ground taking Dillan with him. He pried open the creature's jaw and pushed himself to his feet. His shoulder was torn badly enough that I saw bone. He pulled the weapon out of Bowen's chest with a grunt and flicked the blood off the blade with a twist of his wrist while watching the creature morph. In seconds, Bowen's naked body lay motionless on the grass.

Blood spread from his shoulder and sides. He staggered toward me, his face a pale expressionless mask. Sweat gleamed on his forehead, intermingling with the blood spatter on his face. I let go of Kyle's clammy hand and ran to him. I caught him just as he fell, his sword returning to its original form. I sank to my knees and cradled his limp body on my lap.

"Of all the stupid, moronic, idiotic—"

He coughed. Blood trickled from the corner of his lips to his chin. "Selena."

"What?"

"Remember…" He swallowed. "Remember the not freaking out part?"

"What? Now?" My voice rose a couple octaves at the absurdity of his request.

"I'm going…" He coughed again, a horrible hacking of air and blood. I clutched at a ragged piece of his shirt. He bled in too many places for me to put pressure on anything, but he managed to continue. "I need you to whistle as loud as you can."

"Whistle?"

He tried to nod and ended up wincing. "Like right now."

I couldn't react fast enough. Fear gripped me so hard. Even as my hands dripped with his blood, I lifted two fingers to the corners of my mouth, like Gramps taught me, and whistled, which resulted in a pathetic, breezy whimper. The metallic salty taste flooded my mouth. I spit to suppress the gag reflex.

"Selena." He touched my cheek with an even bloodier hand. "You have to calm down," he said as if he didn't just kill a mythical creature. Then his eyes rolled into his head.

"Dillan?" I slapped at his cheek repeatedly. "Dillan? Oh, God. God. Please. Don't do this to me." Wiping my fingers on my jeans, I lifted them to my mouth again. Still no go. Wracking sobs left my body. I bit down hard, the pain centering me, and tried for a third time.

"Come on!" I screamed out. I spat again, took another deep breath, and puckered my lips.

This time, a high note came. Literally music to my ears.

The silence seemed to eat up the sound. Nothing happened. As I prepared myself to whistle again, a black shape appeared in the distance. It bounded toward us, sleek and swift, cutting through the prairie like an arrow flying to a target.

Panic churned in me.

A dog.

A German Shepherd. Bigger than a cow.

And it came straight for us.

It stopped about a couple yards away, studying me with its ruby-red eyes.

I hugged Dillan's limp body closer and hissed. "Don't come near us."

You called me. I will not hurt you.

Another voice came from somewhere inside my head, stopping my heart for a second then causing the muscle to rev up again.

Please, you have to let me help him.

I looked around for the source of the second unfamiliar voice. "Where are you?"

Selena, please, Dillan is dying.

"Where are you?" Terror and confusion mixed with my question.

In front of you.

My eyes locked with ruby-reds. "You?"

The dog dipped its head. *Yes. My name is Sebastian. I am here to help.*

"Sebastian?"

We are running out of time. He came forward and touched the tip of his nose on Dillan's forehead. A ripple of energy zinged through me, like the open current that sizzled from Dillan into me. It sent my skin tingling. I closed my eyes and sparks exploded behind my eyelids. The raw power a hundred times over, like what I imagined being struck by lightning would feel, knocked me out.

Chapter Thirty-Five

Dillan

Roll the Dice One Way

illan gulped a lungful of air, closely followed by coughing that sucked balls. He kept his eyes closed and groaned. His body hurt like a wrecking ball had just rammed through it. He rolled to his side and punched the ground several times, hoping to distract himself from some of the searing pain. No go. His breathing was ragged, sickening to his ears. It sounded like his lungs had holes in them. The burn on his shoulder pulsed and itched. He could still feel Bowen's wicked teeth puncturing his skin. The coughs that wracked his body turned into gut wrenching puke. Acid climbed his throat and spilled out his mouth. At this point, staying dead seemed like the better option.

Dillan?

Sebastian's concern rang in his head like a speaker at full volume. He covered his ears and flopped onto his back again. The pain ebbed and flowed with no sign of easing. Jesus H. Christ. Hellhounds had the ability to yank back a soul that had just left its body. As payment for the life returned, they ate a piece of the person's life force. The pain came from ripping the fabric of the soul. Not the most pleasant of experiences. Since he was clearly alive again, it meant Selena had managed to whistle.

"Selena!" He sat up. Huge mistake. The world spun like he'd just chugged down ten shots of tequila. "Dammit, Sebastian. Remind me never to die again."

The mutt laughed his barking laugh. *I live to serve.*

He shifted to his hands and knees and breathed in with his nose and out through his mouth. He had nothing left to puke out. He'd meant what he'd said about not dying again.

"Ah, shit!" Kyle gasped from somewhere. "Holy mother of hell."

He laughed. And it cost him. The jarring motion of the laugh made his brain feel like a pinball in his head. Still, a part of him took perverse pleasure in hearing the other guy suffer.

"What the hell happened?" Kyle asked in gasps.

From the length of his pause, Dillan guessed Sebastian filled him in.

"Kiss my ass, hellhound."

"My sentiments exactly," he replied. As much as it grated on him, he had to agree with Kyle. Sebastian bringing someone back was a bitch to go through.

When the pain finally receded, his mind cleared enough to think. Still on his hands and knees, he looked around. When he spotted Selena unconscious a yard away, his heart could have drilled a hole through his chest. Crawling to her, he gathered her into his arms and checked for a pulse. When she breathed on his wrist, he heaved a great sigh of relief.

"What happened to her, Sebastian?" he asked, watching Kyle attempt to sit up and fail.

Sebastian trotted to where he sat with Selena across his lap. He touched his snout on her forehead and huffed, disturbing her curls.

I might have shocked her system when I revived you.

"Human speak please." He gathered her closer.

She fainted. The hound turned toward Bowen's body. *I take it he was the Manticore in question.*

"Bring him to Rainer. Tell him this was all the Maestro's doing. He'll know what to do."

What about you and Kyle? Sebastian leveled his red eyes on him.

"Kyle? What? You two close now?"

You are still my favorite.

"Better be." He shared a grin with his partner then sobered. He looked down at Selena and brushed away a stray curl from her face. "I have to bring her home, and maybe get some answers. Go. I have my car. Hilliard and I will drive the rest of the way to the Fallon farmhouse."

Are you sure you are up to it?

He paused and checked. The previous nausea subsided. Only a dull ache remained in his muscles. When he was sure he could stand with Selena in his arms, he pushed up with one leg then balanced with the other. "I can drive," he said. To Kyle, "Hilliard, you better get up. I'm not carrying you to my car, princess."

• • •

Selena's grandfather charged out of the farmhouse when he saw Dillan pull her body out of the backseat. Her grandmother followed after the large man, a serious look on her face. He expected panic. But they were calm. They vaguely reminded him of his parents.

"We heard the battle even from here," Selena's grandmother said in an even tone. "You two look terrible."

"Thanks," he said. When she threw a steely gaze his way, he dialed down the sarcasm. "I know it looks bad, but we're fine."

"Selena?" Her grandfather took her from his arms. "Why is she unconscious?"

"She's fine," her grandmother said after putting a hand on Selena's forehead. "Bring her to her room. I'll come up and check on her after I deal with these two."

The big man grunted once and did what he was told. She studied Kyle—who'd been quiet the whole time—and then Dillan. She kept her hands on her hips.

"I've asked Rainer this question a dozen times," he drawled, "but maybe you'll give me a different answer. What exactly are you hiding here?"

"Sloan!"

He ignored Kyle's shocked gasp and stared the old woman down. It had shocked him when Rainer asked Selena to speak with them. He suspected they ran the show.

Her lips twitched. "Let's get you two cleaned up." She turned on her heel and gestured for them to follow her into the house. Shrugging, he glanced at Kyle, who scowled at him.

"Don't look at me like that, Hilliard. If it wasn't for Sebastian you'd be worm food right now, too. Remember that."

• • •

A shower, clean baggy clothes, and some food later, Kyle and Dillan sat at the kitchen table. Selena's grandfather took the third seat while her grandmother washed dishes. He kept his eyes on David, trying to figure out who he was in all this. The old man leaned back until the front legs of his chair lifted off the floor.

"Look, we appreciate your help with tracking the Manti—" He stopped himself and cleared his throat then began again. "We appreciate your help with Bowen, but this is really none of your business, pup," he said in a guttural voice.

"But what do you have to hide?" he pushed.

Caroline dropped a glass into the sink. "Why do you want to know?" she asked without facing them.

"Rainer asked Selena to speak with you about all this."

"That rat bastard." David cussed while Caroline massaged her forehead.

"Bowen was working with the Maestro," Dillan continued.

Caroline leaned her hands against the sink. "I can't believe he would harm a hair on that child's head. He'd been part of her protection since she arrived in Newcastle."

"A Maestro can be a persuasive bastard," David said. "Bowen was young. He hadn't come into his powers fully yet."

"Where's the body?" Caroline asked Dillan.

"My partner brought him to Rainer."

"Good." David shared a look with his wife when she turned around. "We will need to extend our condolences to his parents."

She nodded, on the verge of tears. Dillan's chest tightened. Selena was right. He had a weakness against the waterworks. He stifled the urge to comfort and stayed on topic. "Why does everything lead back to Selena?"

"That's not important anymore." David crossed his arms over his chest. "Right now we need to concentrate our efforts on finding the Maestro before the conjurer uses someone else to kidnap her."

Dillan leaned in, not letting the old man off that easily. "If I know what's going on then maybe I can help you. I want to protect Selena as much as everyone else in this room."

"Dillan," Caroline said in the gentlest of voices, "please trust us when we say it would be better for you not to know. Considering your connection with the Council—"

"What about my connection with the Council?"

"What my wife is trying to say is" —David glanced at his wife— "if we tell you, we have no guarantees the information will not make it back to your grandfather. You are the first son of the first son, in line to take your grandfather's seat in the Council. You two are irrevocably connected. We can't risk it."

Dillan had to pick his jaw off the floor. "What does Granddad have to do with this?"

"He will want Selena," David replied. "Trust me on this."

"But why? What's to stop Granddad from finding out anyway?" he challenged even if it seemed like a losing battle.

All three looked at each other before Caroline answered, "We have safeguards against your grandfather and the Council."

This conversation got Dillan nowhere, but still he fought on. "What about Selena? Doesn't she have the right to know?"

"It's not that simple. Despite what Rainer wants her to do." Caroline's tone was filled with worry.

"Bowen just threatened to kidnap her. He was behind all those dog killings. And the Maestro is still after her," he insisted. "What more do you need? Back me up here!"

"Don't drag me into this," Kyle answered.

"What of it, pup?" David grunted. "You were still in your mother's belly when we settled here. We reserve the right to keep our secrets."

"David, keep your voice down. You'll wake Selena," Caroline said.

Needing to move before he punched someone, he pushed his seat back and moved to the counter. He leaned against it and crossed his arms. "Does Granddad—"

"Dillan." Compassion entered in the way Caroline said his name. "Our life here is outside of the Council's control. And we would like to keep it that way."

"What she means is, I will personally break every bone in your—"

"David!" she gasped.

"I think we're moving off topic here." Kyle finally spoke up.

"You must understand." Caroline sighed heavily. "James and Lara didn't want this life for her."

"What life?" Selena asked.

Dillan's heart dropped when he saw her standing by the doorway.

CHAPTER THIRTY-SIX

Selena

TRUTH, SET ME FREE

They all turned to look at me like they couldn't believe I stood there. When their initial alarm wore off, a range of expressions formed on their faces. Gramps turned grim. Grams covered her mouth with both hands, tears brimmed her eyes. Kyle snorted and shook his head. And Dillan stared directly at me, his brow forming a brooding knot.

I didn't know how to react, so I stayed still in the clean pajamas someone—I assumed Grams—changed me into, waiting for an answer to my question. Four sets of eyes on me was no joke. The silence weighed on my shoulders, threatening to crush me. But I held my ground.

"Dillan, let's go." Kyle pushed away from the table and stood up. "We'll wait on the front lawn."

I moved out of Kyle's way. When Dillan crossed my path, I grabbed the sleeve of his shirt. He pulled me closer and planted a kiss on my lips.

"I'll be right outside." His breath ruffled the curls that fell across my forehead.

I gathered up my courage for what was to come. I looked into his blue eyes then nodded. He returned the nod and trailed Kyle out of the house. I blinked and focused on the two people I thought I could always trust. Now, I wasn't so sure.

"Come, my dear." Gramps pointed at the chair Kyle occupied before. "Let's have a talk."

My stomach twisted in nervous knots. When I thought I could move without falling over, I took a deep breath and crossed the room.

Kyle's chair still felt warm when I settled on it. I spread my hands on the table and waited. My heart beat a wild tempo in my chest. I was a little girl again, listening to my grandparents explain why my parents would never come back. My life crumbled in this kitchen many years ago. Now, maybe, it wouldn't be as bad. Maybe that day prepared me to hear whatever they had to say.

Or, maybe not.

For long minutes, we did nothing but stare at each other. No one wanted to break the tense stillness in the room. Annoyance crept up on me like an unexpected visitor. What were they waiting for?

"Are you going to tell me what you were all talking about or what?" I finally asked.

Grams sighed. "Rainer told us Dillan shared information about the Illumenari with you." At my nod, she continued, "Your parents were both Legacy."

My stomach flipped. "And you?"

I didn't hesitate to ask. If my parents were part of the Illumenari, and if the Sullivan family tree meant anything, my grandparents were, too. Gramps confirmed it without flinching.

"We were Council," he said.

"Were?"

"We left a long time ago."

The million dollar question: "Why am I getting the feeling they didn't die in a hurricane?"

The first stab of betrayal went through my chest like a rusty knife. I curled my hands into fists to keep them from shaking. I promised myself I'd listen, so I would.

"No, my dear, I'm sorry." Gramps shook his head.

The second stab of betrayal rattled my insides. "What part of my life *isn't* a lie?"

Grams let out a startled breath.

"Now, Selena, that's not fair." Gramps wrapped an arm around Grams. "We were only doing what your parents wanted. They didn't—"

"Want this life for me. I heard."

"Then you should understand that we thought keeping you in the dark about all this was for the best." Gramps slapped the table with his free hand.

I winced. I was more confused now than when this conversation started. Forget turning my life upside down. They placed everything I thought was true into a food processor and pressed the puree button. Mr. Sloan has been right.

"David, please." Grams lay her wrinkled hand over his scarred one. "This is too much for her to take in all at once."

"Why?" I asked through my teeth, moving my now trembling fists to my lap. "Why didn't they want me to know?"

"They risked everything so you could have a normal life," Gramps said.

"As if. I have visions of the future, and creatures I didn't know existed until now are after me. Well, one. Bowen's…" I choked on the word. "Did you know about him?"

Grams nodded sadly. "He was a good boy. We didn't expect him to—"

"Well, if you told me about him then maybe he wouldn't have had to…" I still couldn't say it. "I feel like Dillan's the only one on my side in all this."

Gramps scratched an eyebrow with his thumb. "That's not fair, Selena."

"Everything we've done, we did it because we love you."

My grandfather spoke again before I could speak the insult at the tip of my tongue. "Caroline, we've become complacent. We didn't even realize what Bowen was doing until it was too late." Gramps checked his rising tone. "And we still have the Maestro to deal with."

"Never mind that for now." I surprised myself at how calm the sentence came out. I wanted to move away from the topic of Bowen. So I asked, "What really happened the day my parents left me with you?"

Gramps's face turned grim again. "You have to know, Selena, they loved you very much. They put everything they had into keeping you safe."

The cold recounting from Gramps became the third stab of betrayal. "I don't understand. What are you really trying to say? What am I?"

"You're a very special girl, Selena. What we call a Seer." Grams smiled through the sheen of tears in her eyes.

The word pinged in my mind. It sounded familiar, yet not, at the same time. "A Seer," I repeated.

My grandfather nodded. "Your powers go beyond just having visions of the future. In the wrong hands—"

"We thought if we didn't train you that your powers wouldn't get strong enough to attract attention," Grams interrupted.

"Why do you think we chose one of the remotest towns within one of the widest states?"

"I think what your grandfather is trying to say is we specifically chose this town to protect you. Keep you safe. Your parents died putting up the shield that's kept us under the radar all these years."

The knot on my brow tightened. "Then why don't I feel safe? So much for their protection."

"Selena! I won't tolerate your rudeness," Gramps barked.

That did it. I stood up so fast that my chair crashed to the floor. "Well, I've had enough of the secrets and lies."

I ran out of the kitchen to the front door. I couldn't take it anymore. After yanking it open, I stumbled out until grass pricked the underside of my feet. The cold night air shocked my system. I panted for no reason other than to try and ease the pain and frustration gripping my insides. Strong arms wrapped around me, sending a sobering electric charge through my body.

"Step away from her, Sloan."

The command in Kyle's voice startled me.

"Just let me make sure she's okay, Hilliard," he said without any heat.

"If you don't move, I'll be forced to make you move."

"Kyle!" I looked over Dillan's shoulder at my best friend. He held a long staff in his left hand. "Put that thing away."

He didn't move. "Selena, we need to talk."

"Oh, yeah?" I stepped away from Dillan. "*Now* you want to talk? After all the lies?"

His gaze faltered. "I had to lie. Unlike some people, I know how to follow orders."

"Screw you, Hilliard!" He had his sword out in a flash of blue sparks.

"Dillan!" Panic punched my gut. I couldn't take a brawl right now. "Please, don't do this." I positioned myself between him and Kyle, staring up at him until those eyes, sapphires in the night, looked at me. "Please."

He inhaled, and on the exhale reverted his sword back to a

charm.

"Thank you," I mouthed before facing Kyle. "So, you're Illumenari too," I said to him. It sounded more like an accusation.

"Only by birth." He lowered his staff.

"And your parents?"

"Legacy."

"Riona and Garret?"

"Mercenaries."

I didn't care that Kyle wouldn't look at me when he answered all my questions. If he was feeling guilty, he should be. I was too pissed at him to care. This cold commanding person was a stranger to me.

"All the years you wanted us to be in the same group?" I forced myself to ask.

"To stay close to you," he said in a deadpan voice. "My mission was to keep an eye on you. Protect you."

His vulnerability softened me a little. "What about Mr. Sloan? You knew about him?"

"Yes."

"And Dillan?"

"Only by reputation." He looked up then, anger in his storm cloud eyes. "Why don't you ask him the real reason why he's here in Newcastle?"

I turned around to face Dillan just as he paled. Fear covered my chest like ivy. "What's he talking about?"

"It doesn't matter," he said, locking eyes with me. I saw a deep hurt there.

"I'm sure it mattered to Katarina," Kyle spat out.

Dillan stepped forward, slamming into me. "Hilliard, I swear—"

I held him back as best I could. "Kyle?"

"A disgrace, that's what you are, Sloan. The very first Guardian ever demoted. And all because you couldn't do your duty."

Guardian? What the voice told me in the Fall Festival clicked. *Find the Guardian.* It had meant Dillan. I looked up at him now. He froze at Kyle's words, his expression hardened. I didn't have the patience to stay and figure this crap out. I looked beyond his shoulder to the farmhouse. Tonight was the worst night of my life and I had to get away from all the crazy. I backed away from him.

"Selena, where are you going?" Kyle asked.

"I need time to think."

"It's not safe out there for you," he insisted, coming to my side.

"I don't care!" I pushed him.

A whistle kept the both of us where we stood. I glanced back at Dillan.

"If you really want to be stupid at least take Sebastian with you," he said without any emotion.

CHAPTER THIRTY-SEVEN

Dillan

No Rest for the Wicked

*D*illan paced the length of the farmhouse's porch like a caged animal. In his head he lectured himself about allowing Selena to walk away with Sebastian. It still wasn't safe. He should be there in case they needed help. Once he'd made his decision to follow, he'd get about ten steps away from the farmhouse just to turn around again and double back. Then the pacing resumed.

"Will you stop?" Kyle sat on the top step, his back against the railing. "You're making me dizzy."

He stopped and pointed at him. "If you just kept your pie-hole shut…" He snorted as he paced, trying his best to dissipate the frantic energy flowing in his blood. "She didn't have to know about my demotion, Hilliard."

"Doesn't feel so good when someone else spills your secrets, huh?"

Cracking his knuckles at the dig, he thought of the myriad of torture techniques he could use on Kyle and still keep him alive for days. The prick had gotten on his last nerve. Mentioning Katarina to

Selena ranked high on his list of low blows. He stared the guy down, imagining him strapped to an electric chair with him at the lever. Then he stopped the pleasurable yet morbid thought. Selena didn't need to mourn the death of another person in her life tonight. No matter how much he hated him.

By the time the nearly full moon had reached its peak, his feet had worn a path in front of the farmhouse. David and Caroline hadn't come out since Selena stormed off. What they told her, he had no idea. Out of respect, he didn't reach out toward the kitchen with his hearing no matter how much he wanted to. Kyle had filled him in on David's and Caroline's identities when they reached the front porch. Selena had one of the best Illumenari pedigrees, coming from the original ten families. Her grandparents hid their power well. They officially scared him. But they had to trust Selena more. Whatever came her way, she could take it.

"How did you know it was Bowen?" he steered the conversation toward more useful avenues as he took a seat several steps down and balanced his arms on his knees, staring out at his car parked yards away.

"Call it luck." Kyle shrugged. "I was driving here to apologize to Selena for being a monumental ass and spotted Bowen standing over a mutilated dog. It was easy to connect the dots after that."

His steely stares started losing their power. He hadn't seen battle the way Dillan had. He was still a kid, at the end of the day. Not a real Illumenari. Untested. He proved that when Bowen practically left him for dead. He stopped and faced him. "Look, I get you're mad that Selena is pissed at you."

"Why do you care what I'm feeling?"

"What were you going to say?" He did his best imitation of Kyle's deadpan voice. "'Hey, Selena, I want you to know that I'm an Illumenari son and I'm here because you need to be protected. I can't tell you how. I can't tell you why. But you have to trust me.'" He glanced at him over his shoulder. A pathetic expression crossed over Kyle's face. He rolled his eyes then faced forward again, scanning the prairies for a hint of Sebastian and Selena. The darkness consumed everything. A great place to hide a Maestro. He made up his mind to give them an hour. If they weren't back by then, he'd go after them no matter how Selena felt about the matter. To keep himself occupied until then, he went back to his conversation with Kyle. "I don't think she'd believe you."

"And you think that because?"

"Hilliard, you're her best friend. She'd think you were messing with her. But if someone she barely knew told her, she'd take it better. At least, based on experience, that's what happened."

"But she still feels betrayed."

"As much as I hate to admit this, you were just trying to protect her. But holding back information doesn't do anyone any good." He shrugged. "I get why you won't tell me what's really going on here. With my connection with my grandfather, I wouldn't trust me either."

"And you hate that."

"More than you know."

"Look, I'm sorry that I told her about your demotion and Katarina."

The familiar ache that came from hearing her name settled in his chest. He shook his head. "Believe me, if it wouldn't hurt Selena to lose another friend tonight, I'd strangle you for being a rat."

That made Kyle laugh.

"Ha, ha. Yeah, it's so funny."

When Kyle finished his little laughing jag, he patted Dillan on the shoulder. "You'll have your hands full with her, you know that right?"

A half grin formed on his lips. "Take it easy on her will you. She misses you. It's a prick move not to answer her text messages."

"I messed up, didn't I?"

"Like a royal pain in the ass."

Chapter Thirty-Eight

Selena

Mental Conversations While Walking the Dog

About ten minutes east of the house grew a solitary Ponderosa pine—an oasis in the miles and miles of grass. Its cool fragrance seeped into my pores. I found it years ago while taking a walk before dinner. When I needed to think, I sat under its branches. Tonight I was glad Sebastian was with me.

You sure you are all right? he asked for the fifth time since I convinced myself he wasn't going to eat me.

I flinched at the mental contact he made. His deep voice wasn't the one I kept hearing in my head since the attack at Valley View. Someone else helped me that night and kept warning me even if I refused to listen. I set aside that enigma and focused on the humungous dog lying on his belly while I used his side as a pillow, my fingers linked as if in prayer just below my chest. The warmth of his fur gave me endless comfort. And the soft undulation of his breathing calmed my nerves. Of course, I'd only just met him, but I went with my gut. Plus, Dillan would never allow me near him if he didn't completely trust the huge creature.

I pretended he was just any other dog. No matter how big he looked, he seemed so gentle. I didn't even remember what scared me about him anymore. But at the back of my mind I had a feeling that—like all dogs—he could be really dangerous if he wanted to. He reminded me of Dillan that way. Another reason why he didn't freak me out too much. I already had too many things to freak out over.

"I'm fine," I said sheepishly. "A little confused and hurt, but overall coping the best I can."

Then—

"Wait. Not yet." My hand landed on his side on its own.

Sebastian snorted then rested his massive head on his front paws.

A breeze swirled around us. I had no sense of time here in the clearing. I stared up at the stars through the gaps between the pine needles, wishing my life hadn't changed. Even if I didn't feel any different, I knew nothing would ever be the same. Okay, I had to admit, my life never felt normal because of my visions, but I did go through the motions of living it normally. I went to school. I made friends. I got a job. Normal, teenage stuff. Now, because of all the information swirling in my head, I had decisions to make. Hard ones.

I gathered my thoughts and organized them in my head according to priority.

First, no more secrets, and Sebastian could be practice.

"I have visions of the future," I said without warning.

I know, he replied.

I sat up to glare at him. "What do you mean 'you know'?"

He opened one red eye and watched me with a cool stare. His ear twitched. Realization bloomed like a flower in my chest. Right. I lay down on him again.

"You can read my mind." I still couldn't believe I said the words.

I should have been uncomfortable at having my mind read, but I wasn't. I spoke to a telepathic mythical creature for crying out loud. I'd pretty much maxed out on the bizarre.

Yes.

"And during the festival, that was you, too, but you looked smaller. Plus, you scared the shit out of me."

I can shift as needed to seem normal. And you needed a nudge to get out of there.

"Thanks," I said sarcastically. "Why were you there?"

Bowen.

My throat closed. I should have put the two together. How could I? Even after seeing him transform, I still couldn't a hundred percent think of him as a Manticore. So, I pushed forward. I searched the almost full moon for the courage to ask my next question. No point in stalling anymore.

"Am I really going to die?"

Yes.

No emotion. Just the facts. Could anyone really be ready for death? I let a shiver run its course. No tears for the inevitable I'd feared long enough.

I sighed and changed the topic. "What happened to Bowen's…" Still couldn't complete sentences involving him. We had our differences, and he did mess up when he cheated on me, but he wasn't always an idiot.

Rainer has informed his parents.

I said a silent prayer for Mr. and Mrs. Gage. The devastation of losing someone…

"I'm sick and tired of all the secrets."

Sebastian huffed.

A stab of uncertainty went through my heart. If my parents hadn't instructed Grams and Gramps to keep their world a secret from me… I breathed and let the thought and the anger that came with it slide. No point in getting riled up over something already done. I was thinking unusually clear right now. I reserved the right to be irrational another day.

"Why do you think my parents wanted me hidden away?" I asked without thinking. It felt less complicated that way.

Seers in the wrong hands can become powerful weapons.

"Is that why the Maestro wants me?"

It seems so.

I took the time to process that information. "My grandparents said my parents died putting up a shield that would protect me. How could they have known what I was when they died before I had my first vision?"

That explains the strange energy in the air. Sebastian licked his chops. *And what does it matter why they did what they did? You cannot change the past.*

He was right; no point in wasting what little time I had left. So I let my mind wander to thoughts of Dillan and smiled. "How did you and Dillan meet?"

A small yelp, like a puppy whining, escaped his throat before he said, *I had been cursed to live in a deep cave in Italy. Against his father's wishes, he broke the curse. For my freedom, I gave him my loyalty.*

I remembered Dillan saying something about being in Italy, but it had to do with his car. My brow furrowed. "What are you, Sebastian?"

A hellhound, he answered matter-of-factly.

The image of Cerberus came to mind. "But you don't have three heads."

A series of low coughs rumbled through him.

If I didn't know any better, I'd think he was laughing. Could hellhounds even laugh?

Of course we can. Another snort. *Just keep it to yourself. We have a reputation to maintain.*

What Kyle said about Dillan earlier nagged at me. "Okay, so tell me why Dillan's here. And don't give me the CliffsNotes version either," I warned. "Kyle said he used to be a Guardian."

I felt the hellhound's fur rise. I knew what I'd asked of him. Secrets, when long kept, had the habit of being difficult to share. A long silence passed between us, only broken by rustling grass and branches creaking high above us.

I waited. I needed to know.

Maybe Dillan should—

"I'm asking you."

Another pause. Then what seemed like a sigh escaped him.

Understand this, he began. *To be a part of the Illumenari is hardship personified. The responsibility of keeping the world as you know it safe is difficult to bear during the best of times. Hence, the life of an Illumenari can often be a short one.*

I thought about all those crossed out lines on the Sullivan family tree and my parents. Kyle's parents, too. So many deaths.

He continued, *Dillan's life has been harder than most. His family comes from a long line of Illumenari. He can even trace his lineage back all the way to the ten founding families. Being a member of his family comes with much expectation. He grew up living up to what his grandfather expects of him.*

"Where does Katarina fit into all of this?"

Without missing a beat, he said, *Katarina was…is someone like you. A Seer. A high level one.*

My heart faltered. "What's with the pause?"

He lifted his head and looked up at the dark sky thoughtfully. *Illumenari who can see the future are both valuable and vulnerable. They are powerful, which is why they are always targets.*

I shivered and remembered the Fall Festival. Dillan said I was a target without knowing what I could do. I had to hand it to him. The guy had good instincts.

The responsibility of a Guardian is not only to protect. If a threat comes, the Guardian must make a decision to end the life of the one he guards. Better to kill the asset than to have her fall into the hands of the enemy.

"So." My voice faltered. "Dillan…"

That is his failing.

My feelings of worry and relief warred with each other. I worried over what I was about to find out and how it would affect my relationship with Dillan. But, at the same time, I was relieved that he couldn't kill Katarina in cold blood.

Then everything clicked for me. The voice said, *Find the guardian.* Dillan was once a Guardian. He was demoted because he couldn't kill Katarina. Now I was the target. He said he would protect me. But how far would he go to keep me from the Maestro?

CHAPTER THIRTY-NINE

Dillan

NEXT STOP GATES OF HELL

*D*illan woke up the next morning with one thought: give Selena space. So, after a bowl of Coco Puffs, he ducked out and drove all day. He filled up the GT once then doubled back. Quickly, he realized no matter how far he drove, he kept returning to the bookstore. That invisible line that connected him to her tugged him back every time.

He parked in an alley across the street from the bookstore and got comfortable. She needed space. The detached look on her face last night proved that. She had a lot to process. He punched the dashboard anyway. The sting of the blow distracted him from his edginess. He wanted to be by her side, comfort her. No matter how much she seemed to have needed it last night, she still pushed him away. He thought they had an understanding. They kissed…several times. That had got to mean something, right? The confusion she made him feel was gonna kill him. He'd felt it the day they first met.

Selena arrived for work just as he'd made the decision to

drive away. He let go of the key in the ignition as she trudged with heavy feet toward the entrance. Why she felt the need to work a shift at Ormand's with everything going on baffled him. She should be home, laying low. For a second, the thought of kidnapping her until all this blew over crossed his mind. But where was safe? The Maestro would eventually find them. Still, he had to do something.

Not a minute later, he was out of the car, walking across the street. He ran through the reasons why he was at Ormand's. The best he could come up with? He needed a book. Smooth. He had a sinking feeling the longer he stayed in Newcastle the lamer his moves got. He was hella rusty. A book? Really?

And what did he have to be nervous about anyway? Yet when he reached the door and saw her face, he froze, hand on the handle. How could she look worse than she did last night? His heart lurched. She had bags under her eyes. Her curls hung limp around her tired face. And she hardly had any color on her cheeks. And there was nothing he could do about it. Dammit! Stomach twisting with worry, he kicked the wall by the door then turned on his heel. The last thing she needed was him making her feel worse. He crossed the street back to his car.

What are you doing?

Sebastian's question startled him. "Jesus, mutt, some warning would be nice," he said.

You look bad.

He didn't know where Sebastian was exactly, so he couldn't get a read on his expression. Yes, hellhounds had expressive faces. Speaking of faces…he frowned at the bookstore.

"You should see Selena."

I know. He paused then said, *I should not have told her about Katarina.*

"It would have come out eventually. I blame Hilliard." He leaned his head back on the leather seat and sighed. "Maybe better that she heard part of it from you. I would have lied my ass off."

Sometimes, for someone with your kind of power, you can be so weak.

A comeback formed in his throat but he wasn't feeling it. They had no time to joke around anymore. Worse? A part of him agreed with Sebastian. All his life, Dillan devoted himself to being the best at what he did. He trained hard. He learned all the text. All the blood, sweat, and tears, but the second it mattered most, he choked.

You did not choke.

"What did I say about getting out of my head?"

Sebastian huff-sneezed, which always told Dillan the hellhound was annoyed. *That* he could handle. Pity he couldn't. Then a thought hit him.

"Hey," he said in all seriousness, "where are you? The sun's still out. Shouldn't you be keeping a low profile?"

I believe I have found the Maestro's lair.

He sat up and leaned his hands on the steering wheel. Their first lead since finding out about Bowen. "So you're in Greenwood?"

Yes.

"I didn't think your range reached that far. Is this something we need to talk about?"

I have considerable talents. He bark-laughed. *Something to discuss another day.*

Dillan snorted. "So?"

From the powerful smell of decay and sulfur, I believe this is the place.

"Do you need back up?"

Stay where you are. Selena needs to be watched. I will call you when I have more information.

And like a line going dead, Dillan's head went all quiet. Sometimes he forgot just how powerful Sebastian was. Most of the time, he got the feeling the hound held back. He rolled his eyes to the ceiling of the GT and sat back. He crossed his arms and watched the bookstore. Sebastian was right. Now more than ever Selena needed to be watched. If the Maestro had another card to play, it would happen soon.

CHAPTER FORTY

Selena

GUILTY UNTIL PROVEN INNOCENT

*O*rmand's closed early. In fact, the second I came in to make up for the shift I blew off yesterday, he kicked me out. I didn't ask, not really feeling like working anyway. On my walk back to the diner, I worried over what to do next. The way I saw it, I had two choices: talk to Kyle or talk to Dillan—both important and impossible to avoid.

When Sebastian walked me home last night, I'd hoped they would have left. My heart dropped when I saw them sitting on the porch. Of course they had waited. No matter how much they pissed me off sometimes, they were still good guys. I told Kyle we'd talk, so I had to make good on that promise. But when I saw Dillan standing there, I couldn't speak. I finally knew what I was and the guilt of what I had to ask him to do overwhelmed me.

As I walked, random thoughts flowed through my mind, like the time I'd watched a butterfly leave its cocoon. Or the time Penny and I chased kittens in Hay Creek's barn. Or even the time I was so mad at Kyle that I punched him. I didn't even remember what the fight was about. How long until I didn't have these memories anymore? How long did I have to create new ones? I shook my head to clear it of all things morbid.

I detached myself from thoughts of Bowen. No amount of perspective changed the fact that he'd never freestyle across a pool again, and that I'd never get a chance to make things right between us.

I'd seen Dillan's car outside the bookstore. He was watching out for me. While I appreciated that he had to do it, I wasn't ready to talk. He didn't try to stop me from walking, so I called that a win.

A block from Maggie's, a car pulled up to the curb. I ignored it and quickened my steps. Getting kidnapped had no place in my bucket list of things to do today.

"Selena," a familiar upbeat voice called out.

My heart leapt to my throat and beat there for a few seconds before it found its way back to my chest again. Tripping from suddenly stopping, I straightened and walked over to the black Camaro. I bent over the open passenger side window to get a better look at the driver.

"When'd you get a car?" I asked, feeling a mix of worry and happiness.

Penny grinned mischievously and said, "It's my sister's. Come on, let's take a drive."

"I'm on my way to grab a bite. Wanna come with?"

"Not hungry," she whined. "I just wanna drive, Selena. Come with me. *Please.*"

I thought twice about getting in the car, but the opportunity to get some answers from her tempted me. After hesitating for one more second, I opened the door and hopped in. She waited until I buckled my seatbelt before pulling out into the road.

"So," I tried to sound calm over my racing heart, "where are we going?"

"Just driving. I wanna get out of here, you know?" she answered flippantly.

"Since when?"

She didn't answer.

We drove past Maggie's and the movie theater. The commercial buildings started thinning the farther away from town we got. Pretty soon wide open grasslands replaced buildings. The silence in the car got so heavy that, at any moment, I expected my ears to start ringing. Penny being this quiet disturbed me.

I tried to make conversation just to fill some of the void. "I texted you a couple nights ago."

"Really?" She sounded genuinely surprised. "I must not have gotten them. You know the reception at Hay Creek can be spotty, too."

She overcompensated. I caught the fake enthusiasm in her voice. She'd never been good at pretending. And when she did, it was obvious. Like now. But to be sure, I had to test it.

"Dillan kissed me," I said.

"Oh, that's nice," she replied without any excitement.

Penny ignoring a scoop? Impossible. I twisted around to face her and noticed the empty expression. It was like looking at a house with no one home. The girl sitting beside me looked like Penny and sounded like Penny, but I knew my best friend better than anybody. The girl driving hadn't been Penny for God knew how long.

"We're not supposed to be here," I blurted out when she parked the car in front of Greenwood's entrance. I hadn't noticed we were heading for the cemetery until we were already there. I was too focused on Penny.

"There's nothing to worry about," she assured me in a gentle voice. "I have something to show you. Trust me." She got out of the car and shrugged on a jacket.

My hand shook when I unbuckled the seatbelt. I stepped out of the car, fought the urge to run, and zipped up my own jacket. No matter what happened, I wouldn't leave her, normal or not.

"Here, take my hand." She reached out and just smiled at me. There was no warmth behind those lips. I took her hand and wanted to drag her out of there. "You'll like what I have to show you."

A light mist clung to the grass. Frogs croaked and crickets chirped. Sounds that should have reassured me, but they didn't. The clammy touch of Penny's hand sent chills up my arm and down my body. The sun had set and the light turned into a dark haze, causing everything around us to look gray. No breeze disturbed the pines and the tombstones looked uneven and unclean. The atmosphere felt like we'd walked into a distorted black and white picture.

"You scared?" she whispered.

I gripped her hand as if letting go meant losing her forever and asked back, "Aren't you?"

"Scaredy cat. I'm here."

"No, you're not," I said under my breath.

We passed the large, graying angel that marked Kyle's parents' grave. Acid rose up my throat from the anxiety twisting my stomach. The inside of my mouth tasted bitter. The nippy air around us seemed to whisper one word: *Run*. The voice in my head certainly said so.

Penny led me toward the mausoleum section.

No one really visited the older graves from the Civil War days. Everyone in town and the surrounding ranches and farms mostly came for the graves by the gate. The tombs belonged to the rich ranch owners from half a century ago or more. Today, all the mausoleums were musty, dusty, and locked up.

A lamp hung at the entrance of one crypt near the edge of the invisible divide between the hundred-year-old graves at the back and the younger plots by the entrance — a yellow beacon in the creeping darkness. It illuminated a large concrete box with lion statues on each side and a heavy copper door tarnished green with age. The crypt stood like an open-jawed beast ready to swallow anyone who crossed its path.

The copper door creaked, and as Penny pulled me nearer, a thin figure stepped out. The need to back away overwhelmed me. I tugged against her hand, but she kept moving forward, like something was calling to her.

I recognized the shaggy hair of the thin figure. The lamplight made the rich, wood brown seem sickly. No more glasses, opening up a face that had smiled at me when I'd come into the store that afternoon. The claws of fear clamped down on my lungs. I suddenly couldn't breathe. A part of me denied immediately what I was seeing. But another part of me erased my initial surprise. Recognition punched me in the gut so hard that I almost doubled over.

"Hello, Selena," the man said.

All the points added up in my head. The unease I felt at the store. The attack in the storeroom. If Kyle hadn't picked me up for Greenwood or if Dillan hadn't been waiting for me, he would have taken me already. I should have listened to the voice in my head when it told me I'd regret working at the bookstore. Quickly, I realized every time I didn't listen to the voice, I got into a shitload of trouble. Like right now.

"Selena, you remember Ormand." Penny's voice didn't sound like her own.

I glanced at her blank face, and then at Ormand's weirdly cheerful expression. "It's you. You're controlling her," I said. "Why couldn't you just grab me at the bookstore earlier? Why use Penny to do your dirty work?" With each question, I got angrier and angrier.

Ormand's thin frame, practically skeletal in the lamplight, bowed. "And what fun would that be?" he hissed. His flat, beady eyes stared at me from inside hollow sockets.

"I guess I shouldn't be surprised that it was you all along," I challenged, holding on to Penny like an anchor, masking my fear with fake courage as best I could.

His tsk sounded like ball-bearings colliding. "It pissed me off at first. Being sent here, to this god-awful place, to watch over you. Me, a Maestro, puppeteer of the living and the dead, sent to babysit. So imagine my surprise when this pretty puppet—" he pointed at Penny, "—told me you were a Seer. Everything started to make sense. So I decided to have some fun. Did you like what I did to that boyfriend of yours?"

My blood boiled at the mention of Bowen. "You sick son of a bitch! Who sent you?"

"It doesn't matter," he boomed like a thunderclap. The ground vibrated beneath our feet. "I've changed my mind. I'm keeping you all for myself. So come, let's leave this boring place. I've had my fun." He hooked his boney fingers at me.

I felt the power behind his last phrase. The double timbre of his voice drew me in. A haze slowly overrode my ability to think. My brain stopped working properly. Every step brought me closer to the edge of something I knew I needed to fight against.

Ormand reached out for me. A winner's smile contorted his face into a perverted imitation of the kindness he once showed me. His illusion of being alive vanished. He resembled a corpse then, pale and cold, calm and flat. His flesh smelled like sour tomatoes. I wanted to gag, but my mouth wouldn't move. My feet kept bringing me closer and closer.

When I stood just beyond his greedy grasp, something yanked me back by the scruff of my jacket. With a quick flick, I tumbled onto a rug of soft fur. Sebastian bounded away, taking me with him. Ormand hissed like a thousand disturbed rattlesnakes. I looked over my shoulder. He pulled Penny to him using an unseen force and put a hand with sharp nails against her neck. Thin trails of blood flowed to her jacket's collar.

"If you want her back alive, give yourself to me!" he yelled after me.

CHAPTER FORTY-ONE

Dillan

No Longer the One

The next time Dillan opened his eyes, he sat in that dark room again.

"Oh, shit," he said and it echoed. When had he fallen asleep?

He struggled to get out of the chair, but like the last time, an invisible force kept him pinned down. The last thing he needed was to stab himself just to wake up. He was too far from Rainer for healing. Gritting his teeth, he pulled up as hard as he could. The band of panic squeezing his lungs didn't help. He tried again. A slight budge happened on his third attempt, but the force still pulled him back down. The chair didn't even wobble.

You'll only hurt yourself more if you keep struggling.

He flicked his gaze to every corner of the darkness, searching for the source of the singsong voice. He didn't care that he breathed hard and sweat soaked his shirt from the effort to get away. Now wasn't the time to be stuck in a dream. So he braced himself again for another pull up. A pulse in his temple ticked and the muscles on his neck strained. He felt the same budge, but when he slumped back, it was harder this time. Apparently, the more force he put into gaining freedom the more whatever was holding him down rebelled.

Oh, Dillan. She stepped out of the darkness directly in front of him. *Always so stubborn. I like that about you.*

"What do you want from me, Katarina? Cut through the bullshit and get on with it."

She clucked her tongue at him, playing coy. He growled, blessed annoyance replacing his panic. Her hair rippled like she was underwater when she shook her head. Then she smiled that sinister smile of hers. He had only ever seen it in this dream state. She looked like Katarina, but was it really her?

Oh, I'm the real thing, Dillan.

"Get out of my head!"

Her blue lips formed a perfect O. *Oh, but we are in your head. So you see my little dilemma. How can I leave when all you do is think about me?*

Calling on his training, he exhaled all the tension in his body and closed his eyes. "That's not true," he said softly. "Not anymore." The truth in his words lent him strength. He'd make it out of this in one piece.

Then why are we still here?

He honestly didn't know. A voice he didn't expect pinged behind his closed eyelids.

Sloan, Sebastian said. *I can cut the bonds holding you back. But that is the most I can do. The rest is up to you.*

Katarina said this was all in his head. Did he really want her to disappear? She haunted him because he'd failed her. Maybe if he accepted it she would set him free. Fresh out of options, he thought it was worth a try. Sucking up his pride, he prepared himself for what he needed to do. The one face he'd been picturing more times than he really should appeared in his mind's eye. Her springy curls he wanted to run his fingers through. Those unique aquamarine eyes he could stare into all day. They reflected her heart and soul. And her blushes that stopped his heart every time. If there was someone who needed his help now, it wasn't Katarina.

"Okay, do it," he said to Sebastian.

Do what? Katarina asked.

He relaxed his muscles then pulled up. No resistance. With a smirk, he sprang out of the chair. Katarina's eyes widened as she stumbled backwards. She screamed when he reached her. Not allowing her to resist, he pulled her against him and wrapped his arms around her cold body. She stiffened. Seconds later, like she always did, she relaxed. Her sigh touched his collarbone.

The rightness of his actions surprised him. He bent down and whispered into her ear, "I'm sorry, Katarina. I should have done everything I could. I was weak and I let you down."

He felt her fingers hook onto his shoulders from behind, like she hung off a cliff. *Dillan.*

"You have the right to kill me," he continued. "It was my fault you were taken. But you have to understand…I can't let you. Not when someone else's life is in danger. I have to help her, Katarina. I have to save her."

The way you wouldn't save me, she said in a sob.

The reality of her words threated to buckle his knees. "I know. Please forgive me. I was a coward. The one thing I had to do and I couldn't. I'm sorry."

She started to dissolve in his arms, but he held on, crushing her to his chest. *This is not over.*

He jerked awake. Those were the same words she'd said the night he'd stabbed himself. It took him a second to figure out he was still sitting in the GT. Quickly, he checked himself for stab wounds. When he wasn't bleeding from anywhere, he breathed in relief. He ran shaking hands through ruffled hair and stared up at the ceiling.

The sun had gone down while he napped. Not good.

Realizing his mistake, he got out of the car and headed for the bookstore. He wasn't sure when Selena's shift ended. He just hoped she was still there. But about halfway across the road, Sebastian's voice rang inside his head.

Dillan!

"Whoa!" He froze in the middle of the street. A headache came to life, forcing him to rub at his pounding temples. "Take it easy. My head's about to explode."

A car honked and screeched to a halt. He jumped back then slapped the hood. Thank God for Illumenari reflexes. He gave the man driving the finger before backtracking to the GT.

Dillan, drive to Valley View, now!

"What's with the panic?" He got into the car and started the engine.

Ormand is the Maestro. He took the girl named Penny hostage.

His heart bounced around in his chest. "Selena?"

I got her out in time.

Enough said. He shifted the GT into gear and drove like the devil out of downtown.

CHAPTER FORTY-TWO

Selena

GUARDED INDECISIONS AND MOCKING CONCERNS

*L*ike a projector running out of film, the vision ended with nothing but white. The kind of white that felt hot behind the eyelids. I groaned, fluttering my eyes open. I lay below a large chandelier. Vision doubling, I rubbed my eyes with heavy hands. What the hell did Sebastian do to me? Everything about my body felt heavy, especially my stomach. Last thing I remembered was him rescuing me, then nothing.

Staring up at the impressive crown molding on the ceiling until my vision cleared, I took a couple of deep breaths. Then I closed my eyes and counted to ten. When I opened my eyes again, I turned to the right. Chocolate upholstery. Turning to my left, a low coffee table with several coffee-table books about flowers and a crystal vase with white lilies, orchids, and roses sat in silence. The hellhound brought me to Valley View and somehow I ended up in the living room. Then purring: a deep rumbling that could only come from one source.

I looked straight down my body. Constantinople lay curled up on my stomach. His tail flicked impatiently while he watched me with his lime-green eyes. That explained the heaviness.

"You're getting fat," I said groggily and reached for the cat, giving him a friendly scratch on the forehead. He closed his eyes in appreciation, like he allowed me to touch him and not the other way around. Arrogant cat. Very like a blue-eyed boy I knew. "Remind me to smack Sebastian with a rolled up newspaper for knocking me out. Bad, hellhound."

I sat up when I heard murmuring coming from the far side of the room. Constantinople gave me an annoyed meow for being moved off his perch. He leapt to the floor and slinked his way toward the voices. I followed the cat with my eyes and watched him rub against Dillan's jean-covered legs. He looked down at him, and then, moved his eyes to me. My lungs squeezed. I flicked my gaze to Kyle, who stood with him and turned to look at me, too. In my periphery, I saw Riona enter the living room. I turned my head and gawked at her.

"You're finally awake," she said.

"I think this is the first time I've ever seen you in leather pants and a T-shirt," I managed to say.

She handed me the glass of water she brought. "Just prepared for a fight, that's all."

I accepted it and drank deeply then put the half empty glass on the coffee table. "Riona?"

"Yes, sweet?" She took a seat on one of the armchairs adjacent to the couch I was on and crossed her legs. I had a hard time fully believing the gorgeous woman was a mercenary. Whatever that meant.

"Did you lie to me, too?" I traced the patterns on the upholstery, afraid of what I might see on her face if I stared at it too long.

Soft lips brushed my forehead. I looked up.

"I'm sorry." She touched my cheek before she sat back down.

The sincerity in her eyes almost broke me. I sighed and looked around the room for a clock. "How long was I out?"

Both Dillan and Kyle looked in our direction. They finished their conversation and joined us. About time.

"Only a few hours. It's about eleven now." Riona let Constantinople jump up on her lap. She waited for the cat to get settled before gliding her fingers over its silky gray fur.

"*Et tu Brutus? Et tu?*" Dillan said when he reached us.

"My sentiments exactly. That cat has no sense of loyalty," added Kyle as he sat beside me. I forced myself not to move away. He took my hand in both of his, a gentleness in his steely eyes. "Feeling okay?"

I wanted to pull away, but didn't. We still hadn't aired things out, and the contact felt awkward. So, instead of confronting Kyle, I jumped to what needed to be done.

"Penny," I said before I stood up and started pacing. "We need to get her back. Who knows what that *thing* is doing to her right now?"

Dillan came to my side and grabbed my arms before I walked into a side table. "No point in working yourself up. If you sit down—"

"How can all of you be okay with this?" I interrupted him.

He ran his hands up and down my arms before he continued with the patience of a monk, "As I was saying, if you sit down, Kyle will fill you in on the plan we've come up with to save her."

The honesty and something else—worry maybe—in his clear-blue eyes soothed some of my panic. Ugh! What I would have given for a snarky Dillan Sloan right now. When he nodded, I deflated and sank back down on the couch. I drank the rest of the water Riona had brought in one gulp.

"What's the plan?" I asked.

Kyle faced me. "We'll storm Greenwood."

"Who are *we*?"

"Garret, Dillan, Sebastian, and me," he said.

I looked at Riona. She smiled and said, "Oh, I'll be there."

"But Ormand is after *me*," I insisted. "I need to be there with you."

"No, you don't," Dillan commanded.

"Yes, I do." I stood up and moved toward him. "There's something you should know."

He waited, staring straight at me.

Kyle pushed off the couch. "Selena, don't do this!"

"I'm done lying." I shook my head at my best friend.

"Selena, please."

"I'm sorry, Kyle. He has to know."

My best friend turned his back on me, his hands in tight, trembling fists.

"Dillan, remember when we were trying to figure out why they were after me?" I paused, choosing my words carefully. "I didn't want to believe that I was a target because of what I can do."

"What *can* you do?" he asked in a voice so quiet it frightened me.

"I…" I gulped. "I have visions of the future."

At first, my words didn't seem to register. His face stayed expressionless until what I said finally sank in. First he covered his mouth then rubbed his hand up until it reached his hair, tangling his fingers there.

"You're like Katarina," he whispered. Pain and confusion entered his eyes. He stared at his hand. "A Seer. No wonder Ormand wants you."

I came forward, wanting to touch him. To soothe him. Something.

"Don't!" He jerked away. "Don't come near me."

I stopped. "I didn't mean to lie to you."

"Who else knows?"

"Does it matter?"

"Who!"

I flinched. "My grandparents, Kyle, Penny…Sebastian." I glared at Kyle. "And apparently Garret and Riona, too."

Kyle didn't even have the decency to look repentant. I would have hit him if Dillan hadn't distracted me.

"Sebastian knows, too?" he staggered, clutching his forehead. "Of course. Damn you, mutt." He barked a bleak laugh before his features hardened. The infamous Dillan mood shift. It still gave me whiplash. To Kyle, he said, "We'll stick to the plan."

"Ormand won't let Penny go if he doesn't see me there. An exchange has to be made. We can use Rainer as back up. Surely he can still fight."

Dillan opened his mouth as if to say something then closed it again. He took out his phone and tapped a quick message. "He'll be there. But I'm still not convinced you should go with us."

Eyes wide, I said, "The moment you leave you know I'll just follow."

"Not if we tie you up."

"Like that's going to stop me."

"Why can't you just do as I say?"

I grinned. "Because you'd probably do the same thing if you were in my shoes."

"Okay," he finally said, exasperation in his tone. He checked his phone for what I assumed was a reply from his uncle. "Rainer is on his way to Greenwood, but we're closer so we'll get there first. Kyle…you, Garret, Riona, and Sebastian go in and distract Ormand while Selena and I make a grab for Penny."

"That's insane!" Kyle ran his hands through his hair, disheveling the strands. "You have to hear yourself. We can't run interference while you hand Selena over to Ormand. I won't allow it."

"Kyle" —I touched his chest— "Dillan's plan makes more sense." It did sound crazy, but if it could give us a chance to get Penny back, I'd go with it.

"I'm not sacrificing you," he said through his teeth.

"You don't have a choice." I tried to smile, but failed. "I'm who he's after. Penny, Bowen, and whoever else, was used to get to me. If I don't go, then there's no guarantee Ormand will stop."

"And since it's a Hunter's Moon tonight we won't have to worry about being able to see in the dark," Dillan said.

My gaze darted to Kyle for an explanation.

"Brightest night of the year," he answered. "I still haven't agreed to this insane twist in the plan!"

"What about a weapon. I'll need one too," I said.

"No!" they both shouted at me.

"No fighting for you!" Kyle added.

"As much as I hate to do it, I agree with Hilliard," Dillan said. "You're untrained. Protecting you will be easier if we don't have to dodge your nonexistent weapon handling skills."

I resented his superior tone. This was the Mr. Rock Star National Geographic I knew how to handle. "But I don't want to be defenseless. Give me a bat at least," I argued. "I know how to swing a bat."

Kyle sighed. "I still don't want you with us."

"We don't have any other options," Riona finally said. "Think of what your parents would do in this situation."

"They wouldn't sacrifice anyone to get what they need!" He glared at his guardian. "I'm not willing to risk losing her."

"Who said anything about losing me?" I tried to put as much confidence into the lie as I could. "Dillan will be there to back me up."

"That's what I'm afraid of." He settled his glare at me.

Dillan wouldn't meet my eyes when I looked to him for reassurance. I had a hunch as to what he was thinking. "He'll know what to do."

My words snapped his eyes up to meet mine. "Selena—"

"What's everyone waiting for?" Garret asked as he walked into the living room with a grin, holding a mean looking sword. He wore jeans, a T-shirt, and a motorcycle jacket.

"What?" he asked when all eyes stared at him. "Did you expect me to come out in armor?" He kissed his sword's scabbard. "This baby's more than enough to keep me safe."

My eyes went to Kyle. "Promise me you'll be careful."

"Are you worried about me?" he mocked.

"I just don't want you to die before I get a chance to kill you for spilling my secrets to Riona and Garret." I crossed my arms and frowned.

He smiled and hugged me.

I didn't return the gesture, even if I appreciated the contact. "Please, just be careful."

"Always am," he said into my ear before letting go. "Are you sure I can't convince you not to go?"

I shook my head. "Short of tying me up like Dillan suggested, no."

"Don't tempt me."

"Let's get a move on," Garret boomed. Riona unfolded herself from the chair, carefully setting Constantinople down, and joined her husband.

Dillan made a move toward the foyer along with the rest of them.

I hurried to his side. "We need to talk."

He stopped and gave me a hard stare.

"You guys coming?" Kyle asked from the front door.

"Go on ahead. We'll be five minutes," Dillan answered him without breaking eye contact with me.

Chapter Forty-Three

Dillan

Tell Me *Your* Secret

The Fates really had it in for him. He cursed them as he led Selena through the terrace double doors. The cold night breeze barely registered when he took a deep, bracing breath of it. His feet kept going until he reached the banister. He couldn't have the conversation he was about to have in the car. Being in closed quarters would only make the feeling of his world closing in on him worse. His breathing already went from calm to hard and deep while he stared up at the Hunter's Moon. Ironic really. The night he'd be facing down hordes of puppets would be the brightest night of the year.

"I'm sorry," she said.

"For what?" he asked, not looking away from the moon. The night Katarina was taken was a full moon, too. He hated the similarities. When this all started, he aimed for repentance. To regain his status within the Illumenari. He wouldn't have believed anyone if they'd told him he'd find redemption in attempting the very act that got him banished in the first place. Oh the Fates were cruel bitches.

"For not telling you." Her words pulled him back to the present he currently didn't want to be in.

"Everybody has secrets, Selena. This town more than most, apparently." He would have laughed at the absurdity of it if not for the seriousness of their situation.

She turned to face him. "You're very calm about this."

"I'm not calm."

He felt her eyes rake down his body. By now she would have noticed his tight lips. The tension on his shoulders. His clenched fists. He'd punch the banister if he didn't have to conserve his strength. He knew they'd go balls to the wall at Greenwood and would need every ounce of energy he had. In the heat of battle he could lose himself. But right now he barely kept it together.

"I can't believe I didn't figure it out sooner," he spat out.

"How could you? Only my friends and family know. I've kept it that way since I had my first vision." She paused. "Sebastian told me Katarina can do the same thing. That you were her Guardian."

"You know, when I said I would protect you, I didn't think it would come to this." He hissed, reminding himself to gut the mangy mutt. Breathing out some of his anger, he made the decision to tell Selena everything. She had the right to know. If he died tonight at least someone else would know why. Why he'd failed.

"Katarina and I were stationed with my parents in Turkey." He concentrated on the sky, letting the vastness make him feel small. "She got a lead on a case we'd been following for some time. I won't bore you with the details. Long story short, she had a vision about Budapest." With each sentence that fell out of his lips, his fingernails dug deeper into his palms. "I told her we should wait for Sebastian for back up. The hellhound had been conducting surveillance for my dad. But Katarina insisted we go."

"Why?"

In his periphery, he saw her reach out. She stopped before her hand touched his arm and pulled back. He silently thanked her for that. He couldn't handle being touched right now and the shock that came with it.

"She would have gone by herself," he continued through his teeth. "She is…was reckless that way."

"Maybe she's still alive somewhere."

"She might as well be dead." He looked at her then. "I'm sure Sebastian told you what Guardians are supposed to do when all options of escape are exhausted."

She nodded.

He returned his gaze to the moon. "We ran into an alley across from Hero's Square. Katarina didn't let me check to see if everything was safe before she entered. It was a trap. We were surrounded in seconds. I fought hard to keep her safe." His throat closed when he swallowed down the bitter lump there.

"I'm sure you did everything you could."

Something in her words pushed him to step toward her. He grabbed her arms. Her eyes grew wider than the moon. She barely breathed. He leaned in and said, "The one thing I needed to do and I couldn't. I couldn't bring myself to stab her heart with my sword. I let her down, I let my family down." He let her go and turned away, ashamed of the welling in his eyes. He blinked the rising tide away. "The next thing I know, I'm waking up in that alley alone, badly wounded. They'd taken her. I know what you want from me, Selena. But I won't do it," he said grimly. "I don't want your blood on my hands."

"It might not come to that," she whispered. "Think of it as a last resort. We'll try saving Penny first."

"You say that like it's easy. We're walking into a battlefield against hundreds, if not thousands, of corpses and a really powerful

Maestro. It's a suicide mission."

"Dillan" —she touched his rigid forearm— "I'd rather die than be captured by Ormand. But I am not going to stand by while he still has Penny."

He whirled around to look at her. He didn't like the determination in her eyes, like she'd already made her peace with dying. "For what you're asking me? There isn't a prison sentence long enough to make up for it. You've got to know that."

"I already had a vision of my death. It's only a matter of time now," she said with more courage than he thought she was capable of having.

"Selena…"

"You're the only one who knows," she continued. "Well, Sebastian knows. He was in the vision. Long story." She raised a hand to stop him from commenting. "It's gonna happen. How exactly? I'm not sure. But it's better if you help out."

"Selena—"

"I know I'm asking you for a lot. It's not every day that someone puts her life in your hands, but I'm trusting you with mine. I have to trust that you can do for me what you couldn't do for Katarina." He saw her heart in her eyes. "You can do this. Just think of all the times I've annoyed you and focus on that."

"Selena, dammit, don't joke about this."

"I'm counting on you. If you care about me, even just a little, you won't let Ormand take me alive."

Unable to take the distance between them any longer, he hugged her. How could he not? The resulting shock became second nature now. And even if the voltage fried him, it wouldn't stop him from touching her. She reached up and closed her hands around his forearms. He stood still, letting her body heat comfort him. He ran through all the possible scenarios. When he finally let her go, he knew what he had to do.

CHAPTER FORTY-FOUR

Selena

STICKS AND STONES AND GRAVEYARD BONES

*J*ust outside the gates of Greenwood, Dillan put his game face on. He summoned his sword from his leather cuff and said, "Whatever happens, stay behind me. Look only at my back. Stop when I stop, run when I run."

I took a deep breath—the bat in my hands—and followed him without a word as he jogged toward the cemetery gates, sword gripped with both hands. The voice inside my head that usually warned me off was oddly silent. I pushed the thought away when we passed the arch. The gloom in the air settled heavily on my shoulders, like a weight pinned me in place. I suppressed any desire to backtrack and kept moving. Adrenaline zipped through my veins. If this was what entering a zombie shoot 'em up game in real life felt like, sign me up.

As if they heard my thoughts, a group of corpses hobbled toward us.

Or maybe not.

"Easy to kill, just way too many," commented Dillan as he hacked at the groaning, gurgling corpses in various stages of decay. Some looked as fresh as if their burial had been only yesterday, while the rest barely held their skeletons together. It felt like being in a scene from *The Walking Dead*—reality TV style. "Sure wish we could have done this during the day."

"I don't think Ormand would wait that long."

A head rolled to my side. I stopped a beat and kicked it away like a soccer ball before hurrying to catch up with Dillan. He never once looked back to check if I kept up with his pace. And disturbing him didn't enter my to-do list for the night. As long as he kept the puppets away from me, I'd keep going.

The ground felt slick and squishy under my feet, almost like stomping on wet sponges. I didn't want to know what caused the ground to feel that way. I just kept my eyes on a fixed point on Dillan's back. He picked a path toward the mausoleums and committed to it with single-minded determination. Worry mounted when we hadn't run into Kyle or the others. I sent a silent prayer up to the heavens for their continued safety. But if they were anything like Dillan, they'd be fine. No matter how many puppets got in his way, he hacked through them. Each slash met with rotting flesh. The ones he'd missed, I slammed my bat into. It was like a scary version of Whack-A-Mole.

One corpse managed to grab me by the shoulders from behind. My yelp died before it even left my lips. I didn't have time to swing my bat. Dillan had already severed the arms of the puppet, and with a quick upward slash, reduced it to goo. I gritted my teeth and stifled the urge to touch my shoulder when he positioned himself in front of me again.

"I'm definitely going to need a shower after this." I grimaced.

"Trust me. You better burn that jacket," he said above the chorus of moans around us.

"Just keep moving!"

In minutes, he managed to get us close to the mausoleum Ormand used for his lair. Green light reached out toward us. The closer we got, the thicker the gross smell got. Like inhaling rotten eggs and wet garbage mixed with the sickly sweet smell of burnt barbeque.

"Breathe through your mouth," Dillan said over his shoulder.

I opened my mouth, breathing in and out, but the stench still made my eyes water. Because of the constant groaning of the puppets, I hadn't heard the others until we actually caught up with them. Garret busily fought off another group of corpses. Riona held her ground by his side, drawing symbols in the air. A crackling flame burned the horde behind the one Garret just dispatched. A cool trick, but totally useless since they just kept on coming. Where were Kyle, Sebastian, and Mr. Sloan? They should be helping keep Ormand busy. My worry hit a painful peak in my chest. In a corner beyond the fighting, Penny stood, pale and motionless, drool dripping from her chin. It took all of my willpower not to run to her.

"What took you so long?" Garret pushed hard on a big corpse and slashed down.

"What happened to Sebastian? Wasn't he supposed to be with you?" I asked.

"The hellhound ran off somewhere," Garret grunted. "Stupid mutt."

"Tired, old man?" Dillan taunted while he decapitated a skeleton.

"Boys!" Riona said. "Not right now." She kicked a female corpse to the ground so hard it turned to goo in seconds.

I swung my bat at the head of an old woman hobbling toward me. At least I thought she was old. "Where's Kyle?"

A watery hiss came from behind the mausoleum. "He's right here."

I covered my mouth as Ormand turned the corner. Nothing

of my good-natured boss remained. His olive-toned skin stretched so tightly over his face that he looked like a mummy without its wrappings. His sneer uncovered pointy teeth and black gums. Obsidian eyes stared out of deep, almost hollow, sockets. Only clumps of hair remained on his head. He wore a black robe that brushed the dirt. In the hours since I first saw him at Greenwood, he'd rotted into something that was never human to begin with. His boney fingers curled around Kyle's throat, lifting him several inches off the ground.

Kyle struggled to get away, but stopped when he saw me.

"Good. You've brought her with you." Ormand licked his lips. "I was just explaining to this *boy*," he spat, "that I was looking forward to the reunion."

Kyle stared at me as if trying to say something with his eyes. I couldn't understand what he wanted me to know. My initial shivering fear turned into bone chilling dread. Planting my feet firmly didn't stop my knees from shaking. My skin crawled. I glanced at Dillan, but he no longer stood by my side. He leapt forward, sword raised. Ormand freed one hand from Kyle's neck and with an unseen force coming from his fingers, flicked Dillan to the side like a flimsy toy soldier.

Dillan hit another mausoleum a few yards away with a loud *thud*. The collision knocked him unconscious. While his body lay limp on the ground his sword turned back into a charm. Overwhelmed by too many corpses charging them at once, Garret and Riona couldn't help us. They barely managed to keep the foul smelling creatures away from me.

Kyle took advantage of Ormand's one-handed hold and pulled himself free from its grip. The action left deep gouges along his throat from his long fingernails. Dark crimson blood flowed freely from his wounds and the sides of his mouth as he coughed.

"I wish you hadn't done that," Ormand said. He kicked Kyle

firmly on his backside, sending him to the ground on all fours. "You filthy *boy*."

My best friend tried to crawl his way to me. The wounds on his neck sizzled, smoke coming out of them. His body convulsed.

"See, now the poison's spreading." Ormand frowned, which looked more like a happy pout. "Too bad. I was hoping to play with you more."

I felt sick to my stomach. Kyle's body twisted like a pretzel. The ground felt unsteady beneath my feet. I struggled to breathe. Of all of us there, I felt the most useless. Where was that voice encouraging me to fight when I needed it?

"I knew you would come. But a bat? Do you plan to kill me with a splinter?" He glided closer to Penny's unmoving form. He wrapped an arm around her waist while his other hand touched her cheek. "Beautifully obedient, isn't she?"

"Stop touching her!" I snarled like a feral cat, ready to swing. I might not be able to kill him, but I could hurt him.

"Oh." His brows lifted. "I like feisty. Let's make this a little more interesting, shall we?"

"I'm here, so let Penny go!"

Ormand waved his finger from left to right. "That's no fun," he said. "Come, this place has gotten too noisy for my taste." He lifted Penny and drifted back into the gloom behind him.

Without thinking twice, I ignored Garret's bellow for me to stay put and leapt forward. I followed the monster that held my other best friend hostage deeper into the cemetery with a group of corpses running after me. I forced myself not to pay attention to them. The light of the moon allowed me to see where I was going. I wasn't planning on tripping any time soon. Ormand kept a safe distance at all times, only giving me enough leeway to catch up.

The mausoleums created a long, dark alley. They were eerie representations of houses for the dead. A thick mist swirled around my knees, making it look like I waded through smoky water. The alley opened into a clearing where Ormand stood at the center with Penny in front of him like a shield. Before I could reach him, I was yanked back by boney fingers that grabbed my arms and legs. The sour breath of the corpses holding me wafted at my face. I grimaced and tried not to breath in the stink. One yanked away my bat. A lot good it did me anyway.

Ormand's triumphant laugh sounded like dying cats. He kept his hold secure on Penny, throwing his head back. When the echoes of his laughter faded, he returned his beady eyes to me. "Welcome to the old section," he said with a wave of a hand.

I called on my inner Dillan and said, "Could have fooled me."

"Sarcasm." He tilted his head toward Penny. "I like that. I enjoyed so very much playing with you and your little friends."

An involuntary shiver rushed through my body. "Is that why you waited this long instead of grabbing me earlier?" He turned to Penny as if he wanted to whisper something into her ear. I growled when he licked her cheek. "Stop touching her!"

He smacked his lips together. "Come to me and I'll let her go."

Before I could respond, a rustle came from my left.

"Let the girl go, Ormand," Mr. Sloan said as he stepped out of a group of pines with the hellhound by his side. He held a long sword in one hand and a dagger in the other.

"Rainer Sloan," Ormand cooed. "Aren't you retired?"

"Walking my dog and stumbled through here. Imagine that? You're having a party and I wasn't invited."

Sebastian growled, baring his long canines. His hackles stood.

"Don't come any closer, Legacy, or the girl dies." Ormand sank his nails deeper into Penny. "And keep your hound leashed."

"No! Let her go. I'll come with you."

"Selena, you don't know what you're saying." Mr. Sloan glared at me.

"Shut it, Rainer!" I scowled, and he raised an eyebrow at me. I ignored him and returned my attention to Ormand. "Just let Penny go."

Ormand waved away the puppets holding me in place. "Come then," he said like he'd won the race.

I gathered the last of my courage and took a step forward. "Give Penny to Mr. Sloan."

"Come closer."

Another step. "Give her to him, *now!*"

Just as Ormand shoved Penny into Mr. Sloan's arms, a hand grabbed my arm and yanked me back.

"Selena, do you trust me?" someone said.

I twisted to see Dillan standing by my side. I hadn't even heard him coming. Blood dripped down the side of his face from a head wound. The fear and resolve in his eyes told me what I needed to know. I nodded once. Then with a deft flick of his wrist, he upended his sword and plunged its blade into my chest.

Chapter Forty-Five

Dillan

Whoa! Hold On a Sec

Ormand screamed in deathly anguish. Rainer chose that moment to charge and they clashed in a screech of metal and claws. Dillan didn't focus on them. He couldn't. He had other things he needed to do.

Selena's body went limp in his arms. Her weight pulled him down, reminding him of what he'd done. The hilt of his sword stuck out of the middle of her chest. He didn't allow himself to think when the sharp blade went in. He barely felt resistance from skin and bone. She shouldn't have felt any pain. But, from the way his chest hurt, he might as well have been the one stabbed. He damned her for convincing him to take her life. He vowed never to listen to her ever again. Too much pain was involved.

Holy shit. He couldn't breathe. Each gulp didn't bring enough air into his tight lungs. His knees buckled, bringing Selena's lifeless body down with him. The hilt prevented him from applying pressure as blood seeped out of the wound.

"Sebastian!" he called into the chaos.

Too many things were happening all at once. Rainer grappled with Ormand. Garret and Riona barely kept the puppets at bay. Kyle still lay in a heap the last time he'd seen him. The slacker. He'd better heal himself fast or Dillan would have to kick his sorry ass from here to hell and back. His hands shook. He couldn't think beyond the tunnel vision.

"Sebastian!" He didn't recognize his voice because of the overwhelming panic. "Dammit, mutt! Get your ass over here."

A dark shadow loomed over him. He instinctively moved between Selena and the shadow, protecting her. But he couldn't do much without letting her go. Sebastian touched his snout to his chest, pushing him back gently.

Dillan. His voice stood out from the noise in Dillan's head. *I need you to focus.*

"I'm fucking focused," he growled.

Sebastian's skeptical head tilt met him the one second he lifted his gaze away from Selena. All he needed was to hear her voice again and everything would be okay. Her face was losing color fast and her skin already felt clammy to the touch.

"I'm focused," he repeated with a calmness he barely felt. "Tell me what I have to do."

There is no guarantee I can bring her back.

"Just tell me." It came out rough. Too rough. The walls of his throat closed.

The hellhound he pinned all this on nodded once. *You have to heal her as you pull out the sword. Channel your energy through the blade instead of the pommel.*

"You will not die on me," he ordered. He touched her ashen cheek with numb fingertips. One second she looked at him, the next she was gone. He shook out his badly trembling hand. Unable to stop the tremors, he moved it to the hilt. The second his fingers wrapped around the grip, Selena's eyes opened. He gasped, wide-eyed. Instead of the usual aquamarine, clear yellow stared back. Before he could call her name, she shoved him aside.

Everything seemed to stop at once.

All eyes stared at the girl who stood up with a sword sticking out of her back. Even Rainer and Ormand, locked in battle, stopped and stared. They all stared like idiots.

"Sebastian, what the hell's happening?" he asked from his seated position.

This is not me. I swear.

A transparent white aura enveloped Selena, fanning her curls—making them seem like a wild mane around her head. No one moved while she scanned the awed expressions of those present.

In the silence, she reached for the hilt of Dillan's sword and pulled it out of her chest. The blue light from the blade burned bright white the second she touched it. The flames danced from hilt to tip. He had never seen or felt such power. All the hair on his arms stood on end. Sebastian's hackles went up. A low growl came from deep within his chest. He closed a hand on the hellhound's fur.

"Don't. Move," he whispered.

Selena's yellow eyes flicked from him and Sebastian to Ormand and Rainer. A second later, she moved toward them. Without hesitation, she pushed Rainer aside. Then, with teeth bared, she stabbed the shocked Ormand in the chest. With Dillan's sword. To the hilt. The flames on the blade engulfed Ormand fast. The Maestro had no time to scream before he turned to ash. From the flames came a shockwave.

Holy shit! He shielded his eyes.

The puppets surrounding them melted into black goo. In one stroke the chaos ended. This wasn't the Selena he knew. Not by a long shot. What the hell did they just get themselves into?

"Da-yum! Did Selena just save us?" Garret asked from

somewhere.

Sebastian snorted.

Dillan was too shocked to speak.

"I don't think that's Selena," Rainer said cautiously.

Like lightning, she flashed from the ash mound that once was Ormand to Rainer. She brought the sword down so fast Rainer barely had time to block the blow. The power of her stroke brought the Boogeyman to his knees. A part of Dillan took perverse pleasure in seeing Selena kick his ass. She was scary beautiful. But something also told him they'd all be dead after she finished with Rainer. He swallowed.

Rainer kicked at Selena's feet. He sent her stumbling back. It gave him time to get on his feet. She charged again, sword over her head. She brought the blade down when a shadowed blur ran between her and Rainer. In seconds, the sword's blade was sandwiched between Selena's grandmother's palms.

"Caroline?" Rainer asked, just as shocked as everyone in the clearing.

"Not the right time." She grunted, barely holding on to the sword.

David ran into the clearing and delivered a perfect roundhouse kick against Selena's torso. She flew back, but didn't go down. He stood by Caroline. They both had their shoulders squared. Their Council powers pulsed around them.

"What the hell's going on?" he finally managed to ask.

"Shut up, Dillan," everyone except Sebastian said.

Selena, sword at the ready, didn't back down. She growled at David and Caroline like she didn't recognize them.

"Enough, Serena," David said.

Serena? Dillan's eyebrows came together.

"Selena's not in danger anymore, Serena," Caroline urged in that calm voice of hers. "Please return her to us."

"She's dead." A voice more mature than Selena's came from her lips. It sounded like two voices. Hers and this Serena's, who killed Ormand with one blow and brought Rainer to his knees. What did they say about Karma?

Heal her heart and I can return her soul into her body, Sebastian finally spoke up.

The lack of confidence in his voice didn't convince Dillan.

Selena—Serena—relaxed her stance. "What you propose will not work. For her to live, I must attach her energy to someone else's." She scanned all their faces. "The next time she is harmed, I will not hesitate to kill any of you. Am I making myself clear?"

The seriousness of her tone and the way she gripped the handle of the sword brought home her silent threat. Nods and grunts affirmed her words. Another new secret. Dillan hated it. But other than that, he had a feeling anyone in that clearing would have volunteered to save Selena by attaching their energy to hers. He opened his mouth to do just that. Unfortunately, she pointed at Sebastian.

"You'll do," she said.

CHAPTER FORTY-SIX

Selena

FOUR KISSES AND A FUNERAL

*D*eath—not all that it was cracked up to be. No matter what anyone said. No bright lights at the end of tunnels. No pearly gates. No burning pit. Depending on where you were supposed to go, of course. If you believe in that sort of stuff. Take it from me; death was just pitch black darkness. Quiet. A floaty kind of feeling. Peaceful.

Coming back to life however…hurts like a freakin' freight train running you over. Electric hooks pulled me out of that floating void. My body—the one I couldn't see, anyway—spasmed. Hot electric currents zinged through my veins. My blood sizzled beneath my skin. I screamed, maybe. Not too sure. Too much pain. I had to punch the jerk who thought bringing me back to life was a good idea.

Sparks from a warm hand on my cheek woke me. I opened my eyes, blinking slowly to clear my hazy vision of a dark figure sitting at my bedside. The corners of Dillan's cobalt-blue eyes crinkled. His lips parted slightly as he smiled. The warmth from his hand on my cheek quickly spread all over my body, pushing away my memory of the pain. He wore a sexy black suit with a crisp white shirt and a slim black tie. The guy cleaned up nice.

"We should really find out where the electric shocks are coming from," I said sleepily.

He chuckled. "We can do that."

I ran my fingers through his tousled hair. "No faux-hawk today?"

He brought my hand to his cheek then kissed the center of my palm. My lips pulled up into a slow smile.

"How are you?" he whispered. His voice was so gentle that I almost didn't recognize it. He was being extra nice today.

"I had a dream" was my answer to his question.

"What about?" He tilted his head to the side, not once losing his smile.

"That I died and I was brought back to life."

His expression turned thoughtful for a second. "I wish," he said, alternating kisses on each cheek, "you didn't have to suffer that pain."

I flushed. My proof of life. "Is it time?"

He dipped his chin once. "David and Caroline will meet us there."

"I guess the nap's over." I already wore a black silk blouse, a balloon skirt, and wedge boots before I shut my eyes for a second. "Do I look as tired as I feel?"

His eyes softened, and he twirled a curl that fell over my forehead. "We don't have to go. They'll understand."

Hard to believe that only a week ago I'd died. Like literally meeting my maker kind of died. Then I woke up in my room two days later with Grams sleeping on a chair by my bed. At first I thought it was a weird version of heaven.

I sat up and kissed Dillan. Just a quick peck. More time for Pop Rock kisses later. I had time now. No more death visions. And the best part, I wasn't a target anymore. It was back to a normal life for me.

"Let's go," I said.

• • •

My official story for missing a week of school was a nasty case of the flu. Lame, but believable. The day I woke up, Grams told me Dillan had come to sit with me every day since he brought me home unconscious from Greenwood. When he'd arrived for his visit, and he saw me up, Grams had to tap him on the shoulder just to get him out of his daze.

Since then we hadn't talked much. We still had to figure out what to call our relationship. Dillan did just kill me, so I decided I'd wait to have *the talk*. Last thing I needed was to freak him out any more than I already had. I eyed him in the car now. He looked calm, but he could be faking it for my sake.

Penny called several times during the week to check up on me. I still couldn't shake how bizarre she'd acted under Ormand's control. But I worried for nothing. The second we started talking on the phone, it was like nothing happened. She even came to visit me when I wasn't "contagious" anymore, bringing over my homework and filling me in on everything I'd missed.

The way Dillan and the others covered up Bowen's and Ormand's deaths was by burning down the bookstore. Official story was Bowen ran into the store to save Ormand but they never made it out alive.

"What's the real story?" I asked Dillan, smoothing over imaginary wrinkles on my skirt.

"Are you sure you want to know?" He gave me a sidelong glance. I didn't miss the knot his eyebrows coming together made. He was trying to be careful. I didn't need that shit.

"I want to know."

He sighed. "We cornered Ormand and he burned himself to death by casting a spell."

In the back of my mind something told me that wasn't what happened, but I was dead at the time so how should I know? I didn't worry about it. I was just glad the craziness was over. I reached over and squeezed his hand. He brought it up to his lips. A hot flush spread over my cheeks. A feeling, until recently, I thought I'd never experience again.

The GT eased into one of the only available slots left in Greenwood's parking lot. It seemed like everyone in town had turned up to pay their respects to the swimming star, now turned town hero. I smiled at that. Even after what happened, Bowen still deserved to be remembered in a positive light. He was as much a victim in all of this as we all were.

Dillan opened my door and reached in to help me slid out of the GT. I gathered my skirt close after a gust of wind threatened to give everyone in the lot a peepshow. The crisp autumn air touched my cheeks. The scent of pine and grass filled my lungs. And a secret smile, one that celebrated discreetly the life given back to me, played on my lips. Then the arms of the boy who had enough courage to overcome his fears embraced me.

"What's up?" I whispered.

Heat flashed in his eyes at the sound of my voice. It seemed he still couldn't believe I was alive. I had to fix that. I snaked my arms around him and pulled him closer. I waited until he spoke again.

"I thought—"

"I didn't." I cut him off. "I'm here."

He took my face in his hands and kissed me. A deep, life changing kiss. The slip of his tongue, the nibble of his teeth, all carried secret promises for later. I lost myself in him, letting go of the aching feeling that my life will forever be different.

Facebook status: It's Complicated.

"You're not seriously making out at a memorial, are you?" Kyle's sarcasm meant he was back to normal.

We separated then Dillan brought his lips back for one last electric touch. Just when he left me wanting more, he stepped away from my arms. Oh, he'll pay for that later. The jerk.

I sighed and faced my best friend. "Give me a break. I just *recovered*."

Kyle smiled from ear to ear. "It's good to have you back." He came closer. "Scared us for a bit there."

"Well, I didn't see you visiting the day I woke up."

His gaze fell. Just at the top of his scarf peeked out a scar. I pummeled the anger that came from seeing it back down before it overwhelmed me. That scar had brothers and sisters hidden beneath the black cashmere. Ormand left his mark on all of us—some more obvious than others.

"That's my cue." Dillan put a hand on the small of my back.

I glanced up at him. The newness of the compassion in his expression still surprised me. Something in him had changed, too. He leaned down and kissed my cheek before he left me alone with Kyle.

I watched him walk to the entrance of Greenwood, hands in the pockets of his coat. Then I looked at Kyle and said, "So."

"So," he echoed.

"What do you have to say for yourself?"

"First off, I'm sorry."

I grinned at his awkwardness. "Hold the sincerity, why don't you?"

He returned my grin. "I think you should ask me anything you want to know. That's the best apology I can make." He ran his fingers through his slicked back hair.

"No more lies?"

"I have none left. You're part of the fold now."

"Be ready when I take you up on that offer." I pocketed my hands and stared up at a sky that reminded me so much of Dillan's eyes. "Let's walk. The memorial's about to start." I linked my arm with his and we ambled to the massive wrought iron gates.

Before we reached the memorial site, I whispered, "Promise me, no matter what, even if it's for my own good, no more secrets." I stopped and looked into my best friend's stormy gray eyes. "I'd rather know the truth before someone else I care about gets hurt or worse." I squeezed his arm. "Promise me."

We stared into each other's eyes for the longest minute. Then he smiled his charming smile. He bent forward and gave me a kiss on the cheek. "I promise...even of it kills me."

"Is there something I should know about you two?" a cheery voice asked.

I whipped around. "Penny!" I drew my other best friend into the biggest, tightest hug I could manage without fusing our bodies together. I'd almost lost her. If it weren't for...I shook my head. She was safe now. Better yet, she was Penny again.

"Whoa! Hey!" She returned the hug. "What's with the sudden touchy feely? We just spoke on the phone last night. Epic conversation, by the way."

I blinked away sudden tears of joy. Penny, thank God, remembered nothing. Sebastian made sure of it. Or so I'd been told. I hadn't seen the hellhound since that night at Greenwood. Penny stayed good-old-gossipy Penny, and I loved her like I loved Kyle and Grams and Gramps and life. I overflowed with love today. Better than any drug.

"Can't a friend hug a friend?" I asked through the lump in my throat.

"So long as you're not in your experimenting with girls phase. You're pretty and all, but I don't dance on that floor."

I gave her a big smooch on the cheek.

Kyle coughed to get our attention. "We're being called over."

. . .

Whoever planned Bowen's memorial should do it for a living. If the whole resurrection thing didn't work out, I would have wanted the same kind. Okay, morbid, but I did just die. He would have loved his gravesite—on a hill, overlooking a stretch of pine. Stands of white roses flanked a blown up picture of him from when he won State. His parents sat at the front row of wooden folding chairs, holding hands. His mother wore a black veil, while his father remained politely attentive of the proceedings, his other hand on Bowen's sobbing younger sister.

After a few words from Pastor Tanner, the eleventh grade gathered around the hole where the casket had been lowered. Instead of flowers being thrown in, someone decided on water balloons. I grinned. He would have enjoyed the gesture. He practically lived in the pool. It was a fitting farewell to a swimming star and a one-time ex. A few tears escaped when I dropped my balloon and it popped on the coffin, causing a splash.

"Rest in peace," I said softly.

When I turned to walk away, Bowen's mother stepped in front of me.

"May I have a moment, my dear?" she asked in a voice just as smooth as Bowen's.

I bobbed my head once, only seeing her red lips below the veil. "I'm so sorry, Mrs. Gage."

She shook her head and gathered me into a hug. We stood in silence for a while, sharing the comfort being in each other's company brought.

"My son didn't know any better," she said after a while. "It is we who owe you an apology for not taking better precautions against threats like the Maestro."

"You couldn't have known. No one knew until the very end." I pulled back and looked straight at the other woman's veil. "I don't blame anyone."

A fragile smile played on her lips. "A gracious girl," she whispered. "Take care not to fall into the wrong hands."

Her warning stuck with me long after she had left. I stood alone near Bowen's grave, thinking of my future. Of what happens next.

"You okay?" Dillan came to my side and took my hand.

I linked my fingers with his, letting the warmth of his touch reassure me. "Just thinking."

"That's never good."

I punched his shoulder. "Well, live with it."

"Ready to go home?"

I gave Bowen's grave one last goodbye smile then nodded at Dillan.

We made our way to the entrance. At about fifty yards from the gate, he stopped—his spine stiff as a rod. His face paled, lips set.

"What is it?" I asked, my heart in my throat. Please don't tell me something was already up. We just survived *The Night of the Living Greenwood*. I wasn't ready for the sequel. I swallowed and followed his gaze.

At the cemetery entrance, Mr. Sloan bent over the half open window of a stretch limo. Some people gathered around to gawk at the expensive car. Not many of those rolled into a town like Newcastle.

Just as I faced Dillan again, his grip tightened around my hand. "What is it?"

"Holy shit." He paled even more.

Too worried to think straight, I followed his gaze back to the limo. Rainer opened the door and let out a girl wearing oversized sunglasses and a long black coat with a fur collar. Her wavy hair spilled down her shoulders. She turned to look straight at us and her lips twitched into a small smile. I squeezed Dillan's hand back, about to ask him what was wrong, but the next word out of his mouth froze my insides.

"Katarina," he said.

My gaze shifted from the girl to the black mass forming in the distance. It was as small as a puff of smoke, but it grew bigger the closer it got to us. It seemed to move fast. Like a tidal wave in the sky.

"What's that?" I asked, pointing toward the writhing dark cloud.

Curses so foul they made my skin crawl came from Dillan the second he followed my line of sight. His grip on my hand tightened to the point where I couldn't feel my fingers anymore. I tore my gaze from the cloud to look at him. He didn't meet my gaze, too focused on what was coming.

"Selena," he said, still not looking at me. "You're going to need to run."

I squeezed his hand as hard as he squeezed mine. "Why?" I barely got the question out. I knew enough of the world I lived in now not to dismiss anything as normal anymore. "What is that?"

Slowly, he turned his head to face me. Fear crossed his eyes. "Please, Selena. You need to find a safe place to hide."

From his clipped tone, I knew he was trying really hard to stay calm. I wasn't buying it. I could feel the sweat gathering between our palms. Something was up and I wasn't leaving until I found out what. No more secrets. No matter the threat, we'd face it together. We'd been through too much already.

"Not until you tell me what that cloud is." My voice hardened. He needed to know I meant business.

"That isn't a cloud." A muscle ticked along his jaw from clenching his teeth too hard. "That's a horde of banshees."

ACKNOWLEDGMENTS

I always begin this section of the novel by thanking the one constant in my life: family. Thank you for the unfailing love and belief. I cannot live my life to the fullest without you.

Dad, thank you for never giving up on my dream. For letting me run with my passion and never judging me. You were always there to drive me to my classes, waiting at McDo for hours until I got out, and accidentally mixing tea with coffee.

Mom, thank you for always having my back. You know more than anyone what's best for me. I didn't get that when I was younger, but I get it now. You are a force to be reckoned with. You never let anyone get you down. I want to be you when I grow up.

Bromonster, thank you for letting things slide. You've seen me at my worse, but you never let it affect you. Here's to many more years of hanging in there. I promise I will be better.

Liz, thank you for believing in the stories in my head and welcoming me into the Entangled family. I couldn't have asked for a better home for Til Death and the rest of the books to come in the series.

Stacy, thank you so much for the yummy last minute notes.

They helped put things into perspective for me. Thanks for making sure we get this one right. I owe you a beverage when we see each other again.

Heather, Morgan, and Katie, I couldn't have asked for a more amazing publicity team. You ladies kick ass. Your enthusiasm impresses me to the ends of the universe and back. Free chocolates for everyone!

Leia, Meann, and Ronald, thank you for asking all the right questions. Thank you for letting me into your world even just a little. And thank you for all the LoLs in and out of Twitter. You three crack me up. We have to meet for lunch again.

To Southville, for sharing with me such a proud moment. Thank you for letting me speak to your next generation of high school students. I forever hold the purple, pink, and green in my heart.

Angie, thank you for being the best Sis ever. You hold me up when I freak out. You get angry a hundred times more for me than I do. Your presence in my life, even a thousand miles away, means a lot to me. Your dream is just around the corner, Sis.

Sophie, thank you for the messages on Whatsapp and for squee-ing over White Collar. I forever love reading your thoughtful blog posts. I'm so flying to London. Better be ready.

To everyone in my mentions feed, especially Alyssa, Jaz, Andrew, Louisse, and Patricia, thank you for your continued support and for always making my day. Your messages even at 140 characters or less matter so much to me. Stay awesome!

To friends past, we may have parted ways for reasons beyond our control, but always know that you have a place in my heart. Our time together meant a lot to me. Thank you for filling my life with moments I can treasure.

To all the bloggers, thank you for being the life blood of a novel. Without you, half the people wouldn't have known. Keep on reviewing. Keep on recommending.

And last but never the least is you, dear reader. Thank you for entering the world of Selena and Dillan. You think Newcastle is a crazy place now, wait until you get to Book Two. It's about to get fifty shades of cray cray around here.